THE HOUSE ON
SEABREEZE SHORE

FIVE ISLAND COVE, BOOK 5

JESSIE NEWTON

COPYRIGHT

ISBN-13: 978-1953506368

CHAPTER ONE

Kelli Thompson looked at the house she'd owned for decades now, her heartbeat giving her an extra thump she didn't quite understand. She'd been coming here for a few months, and she'd brought Parker several times.

"Thanks, Rich," she said to the RideShare driver. "Could you help me with the boxes in the back?"

"Of course," Rich said, grinning at her over the console. "When are you gonna move in, Miss Kelli?" The older gentleman with rich, dark skin had a quick smile every time he saw Kelli. She'd gotten into his SUV many times for a ride from the ferry to this house, and they'd become friends over the past few months.

"Soon," Kelli said, reaching to unbuckle her seatbelt. Getting items for the house from Diamond to Bell Island wasn't easy, and she'd left Parker with Jean Shields today to get some things done.

The springtime ocean breeze met her as she got out of the car, and Kelli took a moment to breathe in the scent of flowers mixed with sea salt. She loved springtime in the cove, and it felt like it was coming early this year, as it wasn't even April yet.

The sky held a shade of blue rarely seen by the human eye, and Kelli looked up into it and felt the magnificence of life pressing down on her. Gratitude for the life she now lived streamed through her, because a year ago, she hadn't even known how unhappy she was.

She'd been through some trials in the past twelve months, that was for sure, and her mind flashed past Zach Watkins, Tiffany Mueller, her ex-husband Julian, hard work in a moldy, greasy kitchen at The Cliffside Inn, a tsunami, getting up at five-thirty to go to work every day, and losing everything she owned to water damage.

She'd also attended a court hearing to finalize her divorce, learned to let go of her tight grip on her son, and spent a lot of time with her mother and her boyfriend.

"Just in the garage, Miss Kelli?" Rich asked, and Kelli snapped out of her memories. She had plenty of others, and in fact, this house was stuffed full of them. She wanted to make even more here with her son, and she once again had the thought that she had more to do before she could move into this house.

And it wasn't moving in several small appliances, new

bedding, and a box of cleaning supplies. That all needed to be done too, of course, and she shivered as the breeze turned into a wind.

She stepped to the back of the SUV and picked up the new coffee maker, stacked a toaster on top of it, and then grabbed the basket where she'd put all the linens, as well as the new kitchen utensils. She was stocking the house one purchase at a time, using some money from every paycheck.

The house had hardly any furniture, but those were bigger purchases Kelli hadn't been able to afford yet. She'd been saving a little bit from every check as well, and she had four big items on her list before she and Parker could move into this house on Seabreeze Shore.

Two beds—one for her and Parker. A couch. A dining room table and chairs.

If she could somehow get those pieces, she could envision herself living in this house.

"Right there is fine," she said to Rich, and he set down the blender and the laundry basket filled with new sheets and pillows. "Thank you so much, Rich."

"You're welcome, Miss Kelli," he said. "You text me when you're ready to go back. I'll come get you."

"Yes, sir." She put down her boxed appliances too and stepped into him to give him a hug. "You say hello to Miss Everly for me, okay?"

"Oh, that reminds me." He stepped away and snapped his fingers. "She sent a buttermilk pie for you."

"She did?" Kelli turned as Rich hustled back to the SUV. "How did she know you'd see me today?'

"It's a weekend," he said as he opened the passenger door and bent inside the vehicle. "I've had the pie since yesterday, but it'll still be good." He lifted it from the glove box, and Kelli gaped at the personal-sized pie. He grinned as he handed it to her, and Kelli felt more love from him and his wife—a woman she had never met—than she had from anyone but her best friends.

"Thank you." Her voice choked slightly, and Rich held her tightly.

"She loves to bake," he said, stepping back. "So you're doin' something good for her."

"I hope she feels better quickly," Kelli said, as Everly seemed to have a multitude of health problems Rich had told Kelli about over the months.

"I'll tell her you said so," Rich said. "I best be going. Lots of people coming to Bell today."

"Yes, go." Kelli smiled at him as he got behind the wheel, and she stood in the carport until he left. She started hauling in the appliances and things she'd brought to the house that day, and nothing gave her greater joy than unpacking things she'd worked hard to afford. She put them in cabinets and closets that made sense to her, and Kelli enjoyed the progress she'd made over the weeks.

The kitchen sat clean and ready for her to use. She'd bought curtains and hung them on the windows, one over the sink and a huge one that overlooked the small back yard. The old table and chairs sat pushed into the corner, and Kelli needed to get rid of them.

She wasn't paying for any services here yet, though, so she couldn't just put it on the curb and have the garbage truck haul it away.

The pantry held bottled water, fruit snacks for Parker, the popcorn she and AJ shared when they came to the house for their private chats, and a box of protein shakes. Kelli needed to start thinking about stocking the house with more to eat, as well as all the home goods people needed to live.

Toilet paper, paper towels, towels, wash cloths, oven mitts. The list went on and on.

Kelli had lost everything in the tsunami that had hit Five Island Cove just before Christmas, and she'd been renting a fully furnished twinhome on Pearl Island since then. Everything she'd been able to replace, she'd brought here, like her own silverware, a few dishes, and now the linens and kitchen utensils.

All in all, she wanted to be ready to move into this house by summertime, but she still wasn't sure she'd make it. She worked as a teacher's assistant at the junior high on Diamond Island, and she managed to pay her bills with that income. There wasn't much leftover, and Julian had been sending her money for Parker before the divorce was final, and now that it was, she was receiving alimony too. The money she got from her ex-husband paid for all of Parker's school expenses, their groceries every month, and as she unboxed the toaster, she realized he'd paid for that too.

"You're getting closer," she said to herself.

After putting away all of the items she'd bought that weekend, she wandered from the back of the house to the front, where a large room spanned the width of the building. The front door sat squarely in the middle of the room, and a large staircase went up to the second floor directly across from the entrance.

The hall beside the stairs led to the kitchen and dining room, which took up the back of the house. Her father had kept an office in the space to the right of the front door, and the family had enjoyed their movie nights and family meetings in the room to the left.

All the bedrooms were upstairs, including the master suite, and Kelli turned to go that way. She'd shared a bedroom with her younger sister, Heather, while her older one, Sabrina, had always had her own room.

Once Sabrina had graduated and left the cove, Kelli and Heather had their own rooms. She'd always had to share a bathroom, and her parents were the type that didn't keep their bedroom door open.

Kelli still hesitated before going into the master suite, as she was never allowed in there as a child. She wasn't sure why. She'd started Parker's life with him in a bassinet right beside her in the master suite she and Julian had shared once upon a time.

When he couldn't sleep, she brought him into their bedroom. The door was hardly ever closed or locked, and Parker came into her bedroom at-will, even now.

Memories of the house flooded Kelli's mind as she stood in the large room that had once housed her mother and father's bed. She could see the hulking, dark-wood dresser that had sat next to the door, and the lacy, cream-colored curtains her mom had put over the bay window that looked over the back yard.

Kelli went to the window and looked out, the view of the yard, the cliffs, and the ocean beyond the most beautiful thing she'd ever seen. She did love the cove, though she'd always been afraid of the water. She wasn't as much anymore, but a hint of trepidation still stole through her from time to time when she thought about swimming in the ocean or getting on a boat.

She had to ride a ferry to work every weekday, and she'd had to do the same as a child and teenager growing up. Somehow, a ferry wasn't the same as any other boat, and especially if she stayed inside, she didn't worry about sinking.

Her parents had forced her to join the Seafaring Girls, and Kelli hadn't been happy about it. She was now, though, and she thought about the women she loved so dearly.

"You need to tell them all about this house," she said to her partial reflection in the glass. Only AJ knew she owned this house, and Kelli wasn't sure why she wanted to keep it a secret.

"You need to tell your mother."

She wasn't sure how her mom would take the news that Kelli had bought this house and had owned it all of these years. Her mother hadn't wanted it, not after everything that had happened here.

The walls started to whisper, little hisses of sound in Kelli's ears.

She turned quickly and left the master bedroom, skipped going into the one she'd once used, and hurried downstairs instead. She burst out the front door, as she'd done many times before, one instance of when she had fresh in her mind.

When her father had lost the Glassworks, it had felt like everything in Kelli's life stopped making sense. That was the beginning of the end for her family as she'd previously known it, and she remembered keenly listening to her parents argue in loud voices that only increased in volume. She remembered the feeling of unrest, the worry which writhed way down deep in her soul, and the fear that if her family fell apart, she'd crumble too.

She remembered jumping to her feet and leaving Heather and Sabrina huddled together in the hallway outside their parents' bedroom and racing down those steps. Two long strides, and she reached the door.

A twist, a pull, and she burst onto the front porch.

She stood there now, letting the fear and doubt and

worry wash through her. Accepting how she felt was the only way she'd been able to rid herself of it. If she didn't allow herself to feel the feelings, they built up to dangerous amounts, infecting her thoughts and influencing her actions.

She didn't want to live like that anymore. She wasn't afraid of what might happen anymore. She'd learned that she could take a situation and work through it. She could think, and she was smart enough to come up with solutions. She could help others, because she wasn't drowning the way she'd once been.

She drew in a deep breath and found her center. "You're okay," she said out loud. She had no idea how to start a conversation with her mom about this house, and she hoped all the progress they'd made over the past year wouldn't be undone when Kelli finally confessed she owned the house on Seabreeze Shore.

Her friends could help her, and she took out her phone to send a few texts. Number one, she needed to get this Wednesday off of work. Her friends met for lunch every Wednesday. Kelli could never go, and she tried not to let it bother her. In her quiet moments, though, it definitely bothered her that everyone had a job that allowed them the freedom and flexibility to lunch together every week.

Kelli didn't have that luxury, and her ideas of starting a yoga studio in the right part of the house where her father had once kept his office entered her mind again. That would have to wait though, as she needed money for furniture, food, and the necessities of life before she could even think about starting her own business.

A business that may fail.

Kelli was still mighty afraid of failing. Failing herself. Her son. Her friends.

Her principal said, *I'll call Miriam, and if she can come in on Wednesday, you can have it off.*

Thanks, Kelli typed out.

Before she got confirmation from her boss, Kelli sent a message to the group string that housed Alice, Robin, AJ, Eloise, Kristen, and Laurel.

I have something to tell everyone on Wednesday for lunch. Will everyone be there?

They'd talked about getting together for Sunday dinners, but it had only happened a couple of times. Alice and Robin loved to entertain, and without them, the dinners probably wouldn't have happened at all.

Messages started to pour in, and before another sixty seconds had passed, everyone had confirmed that they'd be there on Wednesday, even Laurel.

Kelli's lungs tightened, but she pushed through the pressure on her chest. This was okay. She could tell her friends about the house, and when she asked for their help with how to break the news to her mother, they'd all have solutions and suggestions she hadn't thought of.

That honestly wouldn't be that hard, because every time Kelli thought about telling her mother about this house, she pushed the idea away. She didn't even enter-tain it, and keeping the house on Seabreeze Shore a secret was second-nature to her now.

She took another breath and released the tight grip her fingers had on the railing. She looked down at her fingers as the tension released, a plan coming together. Kelli loved plans, and once she had one, she could execute it. Her friends would help her come up with a plan to tell her mother about this house.

"Kelli?"

She looked up from where she'd been staring at the porch railing, her pulse pounding at the familiar voice.

Her mother stood just on the other side of the white picket fence separating the front lawn from the street, pure confusion on her face. "What are you doing here?"

CHAPTER TWO

AJ Proctor finished her third freelance article for the week and sent it to her four biggest contacts. They all knew to check their emails on Sunday evenings, because AJ tended to work in spurts, and she liked taking the beginning of the week off from researching, interviewing, and writing as she negotiated contracts and sniffed out new stories.

She worked a lot from Wednesday to Sunday, and she put the finishing touches on her articles so they'd land in inboxes first thing on Monday morning. Some people over the months had learned to check their messages on Sunday evening, and she'd gotten exclusive contracts offered before the new week started from big papers out of New York and LA, Miami and Dallas, and she'd just submitted a story that would blow away the baseball world once it went to press.

"Done?" Matthew Hymas asked as he came into the little office they shared. He pressed a kiss to AJ's neck, and she grinned in his direction.

"Just finished," she said.

He moved away from her and sat at his desk with a groan. "Sounds good." He barely looked at her as he woke his laptop. "My dad wants me at the course by six, because Greg Sherman is going to be there for a press release at seven."

"Oh, right." AJ leaned back in her chair, grateful for her fiancé for making room for her in his life. He'd moved in the desk where she worked, and he'd been sharing his bed with her since a week or two before Christmas.

Matt shared his family with her, and he came along with her to spend time with her friends. She still hadn't met his children, as none of them had come to the cove in the past three months.

A blip of anxiety moved through her, but AJ had tactics to tame it before it grew into full-blown panic. She'd been seeing a counselor here in Five Island Cove every week since the new year had begun, because she couldn't be on her anti-depressants and anti-anxiety medication during her pregnancy.

She put her palm against her belly, trying to feel the life within her. She'd been told at her last doctor's appointment that she should start to feel the baby move at any point now, but she still hadn't felt anything except sharp disappointment.

In the beginning, Matt had asked her questions about her health every day. He doted on her constantly, and he was so good and so kind to her. He still was, but now that the morning sickness had ebbed away, all that was happening to AJ was an increasing midsection.

She definitely had a little baby bump now, but she didn't have to leave the house for anything she didn't want to, and she had covered up her pregnancy with sweaters and bulky winter jackets for the past few months.

Matt still hadn't told his parents about AJ's pregnancy, and she knew he hadn't told his kids. He hadn't been divorced for a year yet—that anniversary wouldn't happen until July. Their baby was due in August, and AJ had been trying to see things from his perspective.

She tried not to worry about what his silence might mean or not mean, but she wondered what his end-game was.

Their wedding was slated for May twenty-eighth, and AJ clicked to open the calendar on her laptop to see they were exactly sixty-eight days away.

"Are your children coming to the wedding?" AJ asked. The only time she ever brought up his kids first was when speaking about the wedding.

"Justin is," Matt said. "He'll be here in three weeks, remember?"

"Yes," AJ said. His youngest son was finishing his first year at NYU, and he'd asked if he could come live in Five Island Cove with Matt. He'd taken a job at the family golf course in order to save money for his sophomore year of studying civil engineering. "I'll have the room ready for him."

"It's ready already, sweets," Matt said, wearing a smile in his tone.

AJ turned her chair to look at him, and she found that handsome smile on his face. He kept his beard neat and trimmed, and when he'd asked her if he should dye his hair to keep the gray away, she'd steadfastly protested. She loved the silver in his beard and sideburns, and she got up to kiss him.

"Mm," he said, grinning to break the kiss.

"Have you told Derrick or Lisa?" AJ asked, settling herself on his lap, though he clearly had work to do for tomorrow's press conference at the golf course. Gregory Sherman was running for mayor of the cove this year, and AJ didn't doubt for a moment that he'd win.

His son was the Chief of Police, and everyone on all five islands loved Aaron Sherman. He was marrying one of AJ's best friends in only a few weeks, and the Cove Chronicles had called it the wedding of the year.

Robin had been thrilled, of course, as she'd been working on Eloise and Aaron's wedding for the past eight months. Eloise had finally embraced having the wedding of her dreams, and AJ couldn't wait to see it.

She and Matt had been planning something similar, and with Robin's help, AJ was sure she'd get the wedding she'd always wanted too.

"I'm going to tell them about it this week," Matt said.

AJ's eyebrows went up. He'd never committed to a timeframe before. He'd always said, *I'll tell them soon, AJ.* Or, *I'm just waiting for the right time, Ava.*

He'd never said, *Try to understand, AvaJane,* but that was the message she'd gotten.

She had been trying.

"This week?" she asked.

"Yes." He finally looked away from his computer and wrapped his arms around her. She directed one of his hands to her belly, and he grinned as he put his palm against their baby.

He hadn't wanted another baby; he'd told her that in precise words. They'd used protection when they'd been intimate, even though AJ believed herself to be past the age when she could successfully carry a baby.

Yet AJ had missed her period, taken a test, and found herself pregnant, all within four months of reconnecting with Matt. She knew it was fast, and unexpected. She had no idea how she'd feel if her ex-husband got himself a new wife and a new baby only a year after his divorce was final, and she had no idea how she'd have reacted if her father had met and married another woman at the same time she'd moved out to go to college.

"Lisa wants to come to the cove for her summer vacation before she starts medical school, and she needs to know what she's going to find here."

AJ bit back the question that popped into her mind.

Would he tell his daughter if she wasn't planning to come to the cove this summer?

She hated the poisonous thoughts, but she didn't want to be naïve either. She'd spent plenty of years with men unwilling to commit to her, and she couldn't stand the thought of Matt being one of them.

Perhaps it was time to say something. *Be brave*, she told herself. She didn't want to raise a baby alone, not at her age. At the same time, she absolutely would not marry a man who didn't want to marry her, who was embarrassed to be with her, or who couldn't tell his family about her and his life with her.

"Matty," she said, covering his hand on her belly with both of hers. "Be honest with me. Just be honest. I feel like you're hiding me and our baby from your family." She'd told him several times since Christmas that she wanted to talk to his parents, and he'd put her off.

"I want to talk to your parents about us and our baby. I want them to know they're going to be grandparents again. I want your children to know they're going to have a half-brother or sister." She stopped, because her heartbeat reverberated in her own ears and made her chest vibrate in a strange way.

"I don't care if you tell Melanie or not, because she doesn't really have to be part of our lives. But your kids do, and your parents are."

Matt didn't say anything for a few seconds. "I might have been hiding you and the baby from my family," he finally admitted. "I'm sorry, AvaJane. I'm not embarrassed about it."

"They're going to know," she said. "The baby is due August eleventh, Matt. They can do math. They'll know we've been sleeping together since November." Sooner than that, but that was one thing they didn't have to disclose.

"I know," he said. "You're right. I know you're right. I have this...mental block I can't seem to get past."

"Do you really think Justin hasn't told his siblings?"

"I asked him not to," Matt said practically under his breath. "I shouldn't have done that."

AJ cinched her bravery tight, because she didn't want any secrets between her and Matt. "If you don't want to be with me, it's really okay."

"Don't even say that," he said instantly. "It's not true, AvaJane. I've wanted to be with you since I met you way back in high school." He'd told her that several times, but she needed his actions to start to match up with his words.

"I need you to tell your family," she said.

"I know you do." He shifted, and AJ stood up. "Let's call my parents right now."

"Really?"

"Yes." Matt stood too and took her into his arms. "I love you, AvaJane. Please do not doubt that for even a moment."

"You didn't want another baby," she whispered, watching him for his reaction.

"A baby is a blessing," he said, his dark eyes serious and genuine. "Especially for you, and I'm thrilled you get to have the things you've wanted for so long. I'm just worried about raising another child. I'm *old*, AJ." He grinned at her, and AJ couldn't help smiling back up at him.

"So am I," she said. "We can do it. Together, Matty. We can do anything together."

"We sure can." He kissed her temple and reached for his phone. "Let's get them both on the speaker." He tapped and a moment later, the line started to ring.

"Matthew," his father said, as he always used Matt's full name.

"Can you get Mom?" Matt asked. "I need to tell you both something."

"Sure," Yancey Hymas said. "Give me a minute. She went into the storage room to find some chocolate chips."

Barbie Hymas made cookies as easily as breathing, and AJ wasn't surprised to hear she'd gone to find an ingredient to satisfy her husband's sweet tooth. The time passed between her and Matt in silence, and then his dad said, "We're both here, Matthew."

"We're both here too," Matt said. "AvaJane and I. Mom. Dad. We're going to have a baby."

"Oh, my goodness," Barbie said, her voice mostly made of shock.

Matt cleared his throat, his gaze seeking and finding AJ's. She reached out and cradled his face, a physical reminder that they could do anything together. "The baby is due in August, and we're getting married at the end of May. We want you there for all of it."

"Of course we'll be there for all of it," Barbie said. "Congratulations, you two."

His father said nothing, AJ noted, but his mother carried the conversation with her excitement and the call ended when Matt promised his father he'd be at the golf course on time in the morning.

AJ released the breath she hadn't realized she'd been holding in the bottom half of her lungs. "Thank you, Matt."

"We're not done yet," he said, still tapping on his phone. "Let's call Derrick first. Once Lisa knows, she'll want to call the boys and talk it all through." He smiled at AJ, and she marveled that he didn't harbor any apprehension in his expression. She only knew he was nervous about telling his kids about his new relationship and the new baby because he'd told her he was.

They made the call to Derrick, who said he suspected something, because Matt had been posting pictures of him and AJ on social media. He didn't seem terribly upset, and he said he'd come to the cove for the wedding in May.

"One left," Matt said with a sigh. AJ gave him a smile, because she knew this wasn't easy for him. It wasn't easy for her either and meeting his children would be worse. She'd only meet Justin before the actual wedding as things stood right now, and she wondered if she should suggest she and Matt go visit his other children where they lived so she could at least meet them once before she married their dad.

"Hey, Dad," Lisa said, and AJ hadn't even realized he'd dialed. "What's up?"

"Lisa," Matt said. "I have AvaJane Proctor on speaker with me."

"AvaJane Proctor?" Lisa asked.

"She's my girlfriend," Matt said as he sat down in his desk chair. "Wow, there's so much to tell. She's not just my girlfriend, Lise. She's my fiancée, and we're going to be married at the end of May. I'm not sure what your schedule is like, but we'd love to have you there."

He looked up at AJ, who nodded.

"Hello, Lisa," AJ said. "It's AJ. I'd love to include you in whatever you're comfortable doing for the wedding. Bridesmaid or...something."

His daughter said nothing, and she must've gotten that trait from her grandfather.

Matt just held up his palm, and AJ remembered that he'd told her once that Lisa needed a few minutes to absorb information. AJ's pulse ricocheted through her body, because he hadn't even mentioned the baby yet.

By the end of May, she wouldn't be able to hide the pregnancy, and she didn't want to. If she'd wanted to marry Matt in a skinny dress, she'd have done it months ago.

"Wow, Dad," Lisa finally said. "Okay, yeah. When? What day in May?"

"The twenty-eighth," AJ said. "It's a Sunday."

"Just a sec," Lisa said. "Yes, I can be there by then." She cleared her throat. "I'd like to be in the wedding, AJ. Thank you for offering."

Warmth filled AJ, and she beamed at Matt's phone. "Of course," she said. "I'm glad you want to participate. I can start to send you details, if you'd like."

"Sure." They exchanged numbers and email addresses, and AJ climbed back into Matt's lap while he chatted with his daughter about her upcoming finals, and her plans for moving to Colorado for veterinary school.

He then surprised AJ with the words, "AJ and I will be in Maryland for your graduation, Lise. Love you, baby."

"I love you too, Dad," his daughter said, and the call ended.

He sighed and pressed his face to AJ's chest. "You'll go to Maryland with me, right, AvaJane?"

"Of course," she said, still somewhat surprised. "I didn't realize you were going."

"I'm going," he said. "She's my oldest, and my only daughter. She's been at Johns Hopkins for four years on a scholarship." He wore the pride right in his eyes. "Of course I'm going."

"Then I'll go too," she said. Her stomach clenched, and AJ winced slightly. She was used to having different aches and pains in her abdomen since she'd learned she was pregnant, but this felt different.

She let out a cry and put her hand on her stomach.

"Hey, what's wrong?" Matt asked, covering her hand with his. "Are you okay?" Concern filled his voice and face, and AJ wanted to tell him she was fine.

But pain ripped through her core, moving from front to back, and all she could do was suck in a breath and then let out a scream. The piercing pain sliced through her with white-hot precision she didn't understand, and all AJ could think was, *Please don't let me lose the baby now.*

Not after Matt had just called his parents and told them. Not after he'd called his children and told them about her and the wedding. He hadn't mentioned the baby, but now that his parents knew, the word would spread quickly.

"Matt," she whimpered as the pain subsided. "There's something wrong."

"Let's go to the ER," he said, moving so that AJ had to stand up from his lap. She couldn't quite feel her legs though, and she leaned heavily against the desk in front of her.

"I can't move," she said, fear taking over in such a way that AJ couldn't name where she was or what was happening.

"Then I'll carry you." Matt scooped her into his arms, and AJ wrapped her hands around his neck as she started to cry.

"Hurry, Matty," she said as he hustled toward the front door. He set her delicately in the front seat of his SUV, and AJ's fingers trembled as she pulled her phone from her pocket. She needed all the help she could get, and she put her sister and Robin in a text together before sending a message to both of them.

On my way to the hospital. Having pain in my abdomen. Tell everyone to pray.

Tears streamed down her face as Matt got behind the wheel. She tapped to send the text, and then she dropped her phone as another wave of agony threatened to rip her apart cell by individual cell.

CHAPTER THREE

Kelli nearly stumbled down the front steps, her heartbeat rebounding through her whole body. "Mom," she said, noting the little dog on a leash she hadn't seen before. "When did you get a dog?"

"Are you moving in here?" Paula Watkins, her mother, wasn't going to let this go. Kelli needed to simply come clean. It was time—for everyone.

Kelli reached the waist-high fence as the clouds overhead shifted. She felt like the world around her was as easily pushed this way and that as the clouds by the atmospheric winds. The sunlight appeared, bathing both women and the little dog in warmth and golden rays.

She took a deep breath and glanced down at the dog. The brown and black creature sat and waited, as if Kelli's mom had spent long hours training it. "Yes," Kelli said, finally looking up into her mother's face.

She saw her own eyes looking back at her. Dark hazel that could look green with the right blouse or browner when wearing taupes, whites, and blacks. Kelli's mother's eyebrows dragged down in the middle, clear confusion coming from those eyes. Her face held a hearty sprinkle of freckles, as did Kelli's. Hers ran over her shoulders and down her back too, especially if she laid out in the sun for longer than fifteen minutes.

"I don't understand," her mother said.

"I bought the house when it came up for sale," Kelli said. "Years ago."

Her mother's eyes widened with each word. "Why?"

"I wanted it," Kelli said, turning back to the house. Since the collapse of her life in the past twelve months, one of the only things that had comforted her was the fact that she owned this house. She'd lost so many worldly things in the tsunami that had drowned the island over Christmas, but she still had the house. She could sell it and have a good start on a new life.

"I'm fixing it up," Kelli went on. "A little bit here and a little bit there. I come on the weekends and bring the things I've managed to buy. Parker and I are going to move in here before school starts in the fall."

Kelli had never spoken those words out loud before, but as she did, her determination to make them true bloomed. Five months. She could save up enough to get the basics if she counted every penny—and she would do exactly that.

"I can't believe it," her mother said. "It wasn't on the market long, and I assumed a corporation or something had bought it. But nothing was ever done with it."

Kelli swallowed, because she didn't know what to say. "Did you...did you ever want to buy it back?"

"No." Her mom shook her head decidedly. "No, I don't want to live here again." She peered up to the front door. "I don't even know if I could step inside."

"You don't have to," Kelli said. "I'm fine bringing Parker to you at your house. With Devon."

"Where's Parker?" her mom asked.

"Jean's got him today," Kelli said with a smile. "She loves him, and I think he helps her feel less lonely."

Her mom smiled and looked down at the puppy. "I'm glad he has her." She looked up again. "You know you can always ask me or Devon to help."

"I do, Mom." Kelli crouched down and patted the dog. "What breed is she?"

"She's a yorkie," Mom said. "I just got her a few days ago from Marjorie Carol. You remember her? She used to live up the road here, but she moved in with her daughter a couple of years ago."

"My goodness," Kelli said, straightening. "Marjorie Carol? She was old when I was a teenager." She grinned at her mother. "So she was rehoming the dog?"

"Yeah," Mom said. "I visit her every so often, as Regina lives near the house. Last time I went, Marjie asked if I might know anyone who would take little Tina.

I said I would, and Regina brought her over earlier this week."

She smiled down at the dog. "She's making a good transition."

"How old is she?"

"She's almost four," her mom said. "I like having her. She's good company."

"I bet she is," Kelli said. "What does Devon think?" The conversation was going fairly well, considering Kelli rarely knew what to say to her mother. So much had changed in the past year, and she wanted her relationship with her mother to continue to improve.

"Devon likes her," Mom said with another smile. "Will you be on the island tonight? You should come to dinner at the house." Her eyes flitted toward the front of the house where Kelli had grown up. "The stained glass windows are still in good shape."

"They cleaned right up," Kelli said. "I'm hoping to perhaps open a yoga studio in the half of the house where Dad used to have his office." She nearly choked on the word *dad*, but it still pushed out of her mouth.

She watched her mother for any reaction, but she gave none but a nod. The breeze picked up, and Kelli realized she'd left her jacket inside. "I can't come to dinner tonight," she said. "Jean has a library board meeting, and I promised I'd be back by six." She pulled her phone out of her pocket. "I should finish up here and get on the five-ten ferry."

Her mother nodded. "Tomorrow, then. I'd love to know more about the house."

"It's really okay if you don't," Kelli said. "I understand. To me, Mom, this house meant something. I couldn't imagine someone else living here. I... My memories of this place were good, right up until the day we left."

They hadn't left willingly, either. Kelli knew that. She knew Mom hadn't been able to pay the mortgage and the bank had evicted them. Life had not been good after that, though Kelli knew now that her mother had done her very best to protect Kelli and her sisters from the hard things of the world.

"Mom," Kelli said. "I know you did everything you could, and I appreciate it."

Mom looked away, but Kelli saw the tremble in her chin. She said nothing, and that was because if she did, she'd give away the emotions storming through her.

"I love you," Kelli said. "I don't want this to hurt you."

"I want you to be happy," her mother said, her voice very tight. "I know you loved this house, and I'm glad you bought it. You'll make it the perfect place to raise Parker." She smiled, her eyes flitting past Kelli and back to the stained glass windows.

Kelli didn't know what else to say, so she simply took another couple of steps and embraced her mother.

"I love you, Kel," her mom said, and Kelli returned the sentiment. She watched her mom continue down the road, the little yorkie trotting along beside her, feeling like she'd just conquered the world.

A COUPLE OF HOURS LATER, KELLI BOARDED THE FERRY. The sun had started its final descent into the western ocean that separated Five Island Cove from the mainland US. It was really only about fifty miles, but it felt like the chain of five tiny islands sat out in the middle of only water.

Water in every direction. Water, and water, and more water.

Kelli disliked water. She wasn't a fan of boats, and she always sat inside on the ferry if she could. Tonight, she could, and she took a seat on the end of a row where a gentleman had sat right in the middle. He had his head turned toward the windows, and when Kelli sat, he didn't look at her.

Kelli was used to men paying her little attention. She wasn't like AJ in any way, and she'd been overlooked so often that she'd jumped at the chance to get married from the first man who'd paid her any iota of attention.

Julian's face ran through her mind, and she let it. She had loved him unconditionally, and the marriage to her was everything she'd wanted. She would've liked more children, but it had taken her a long time to conceive Parker. They'd only gotten the one son, and Kelli had barely let him leave her sight for much of the first eight years of his life.

That was one good thing that had come from her visit to Five Island Cove. She was only supposed to come for a couple of days for Joel Shields's funeral, but everything had changed so much as they'd cleaned out the man's office and found so many secrets.

Kelli smiled as she thought of her friends, and she looked at her phone again, seeing all of them agree to lunch on Wednesday.

"Kelli?"

She turned to her right, toward the man sitting two seats over from her.

"My goodness," she said, smiling. "Shad."

Shad Webb lived right next door to her on Pearl Island. They shared a wall in the twinhome, and she'd often run into him as he left for work at the same time she did. She'd spent most of their brief morning exchanges apologizing for any noise Parker may have made playing his video games, the recorder his teacher required, or for setting off the smoke alarm when she'd tried to teach Parker how to make pancakes.

"You're heading to Diamond?" he asked.

"Yes," she said, folding her hands over her purse in her lap. She carried the buttermilk pie with her, as Jean would love it. "My son is staying with someone there. I'm going to get him and head back to Pearl."

Shad nodded, his dark eyes sparkling with plenty of

secrets. Kelli would almost call it mischief, if the man had been in his thirties. He wasn't; Shad was probably a decade older than her, but he still had a full head of hair, and it looked like someone had taken a white crayon, a black one, and a gray one and held them in one hand while they colored in his hair.

He was clean-shaven, with a square jaw and white teeth. He did something with finances for the town of Five Island Cove, and he'd been a lifelong resident of the cove. He had no children, though he'd been married before.

Not for a while, he'd told her when they'd talked about their significant others. That had been a quick conversation, as most of theirs had been.

"Do you have time for dinner?" Shad asked, and Kelli's gaze jerked to his. He was tall, tan, and trim, and she could only imagine what he'd look like on the beach in a pair of swim trunks. Or at dinner, for that matter.

She looked down at his shirt, which was a polo in a mixture of red and blue stripes. He wore black jeans with it, and somehow Kelli had never seen a sexier pair of pants.

"Dinner?" she asked. "Me, you, and Parker?"

Shad got up and moved over a chair so that he sat right next to her. "I was thinking just me and you, actually." He gave her one of those blinding white smiles. "I've been trying to come up with a way to ask you out for three months now."

Kelli's eyebrows went up. The only thing her mind could comprehend was, "Three months?"

Shad kept the grin on his face. He nodded, a slight chuckle coming from his mouth. He lifted one shoulder in a shrug, as if to say, *What can I say? You're the most beautiful creature I've ever met, and I want to take you to the nicest restaurant in Five Island Cove.*

He probably wasn't saying all of those things, but Kelli hadn't had a man's interest in a very long time, and she had a very good imagination.

She checked her phone, and she'd made it onto the four-forty ferry. They'd arrive on Diamond by five-fifteen.

"Okay," she said. "But I have to pick up Parker at the lighthouse by six."

He looked at his wristwatch, which also gave away his age. "I think we can make that work."

CHAPTER FOUR

R obin Grover approached the lifeguard station on her favorite stretch of beach, her breath burning through her chest. She'd taken up her running regimen again in the past week, and while she'd acclimated to getting up earlier, her physical body was still trying to figure out how to breathe and move so fast without dying.

Her steps slowed and she went up off the harder packed sand and around the wooden structure, her feet squishing through the softer sand up here. It wasn't beach weather yet, but soon enough, this west-facing island beach would be covered with tourists. Robin would run in the early morning hours, just as she was now, so she wouldn't have to worry about dodging the crowds.

Robin jogged at a slower pace back to where she'd parked, and she took several long minutes to stretch through her calves and back. She was getting closer to fifty, and she couldn't afford to pull a hamstring or over-extend a knee.

She finally got behind the wheel of her minivan and made the drive back to her house, which sat nearly in the middle of Diamond Island. Duke's truck wasn't in the garage, which meant he'd already left for the dock.

She thought of the new fishing boat he'd been using for the past few months since the tsunami. It felt like years since December, while at the same time, the memories were so strong, Robin would've sworn she'd just survived the storm yesterday.

Their new boat had been delivered by mid-January, and Duke had been out on the water every day since. He and his friend Bryan were going to Alaska again this summer, and as Robin now had a pretty substantial boat payment to make each month, she couldn't argue with the money.

She sighed as she got out of her nearly broken-down van, the constant thought of money on her mind. She hated that, as she felt like a couple of her and Duke's age should be buying Buicks or Cadillacs as their children became adults and they had more money to spend.

If anything, Robin had less, and she reminded herself that Mandie still had two and a half years of high school left. She didn't have any children out of the house yet, and activities and teenage years cost a lot of money.

Life happened, and Robin didn't want to deal with it alone. She paused on the front sidewalk and sent her husband a text, noting that she had four or five others she hadn't looked at yet.

She often put her phone on silent early on Sundays, as she and Duke lounged in bed starting about dusk. She'd gotten up, dressed, and shoved her phone in her pocket before leaving the house, only to have it just in case she encountered a problem. Robin knew if she looked at her phone before her run, she wouldn't go.

She'd just "check that email real quick," or "hurry and respond to a client. It'll only take a sec."

Before she knew it, the morning would be half over, and she wouldn't even know if or when Mandie and Jamie had left for school.

Love you, babe. Be safe and hurry home tonight. I'm going to make that sausage pizza.

She sent the message to Duke and navigated back to her home screen. A couple of texts from clients sat at the top, and she quickly answered their questions, both of which had come in last night.

Robin cursed herself for not checking her device before going to bed. She shouldn't have to be on-call twenty-four hours a day, but in the world in which they lived, almost everyone was. People expected their messages to be answered in a timely manner too, especially if they were paying her a lot of money to plan their weddings.

Robin had picked up as many jobs this spring and summer as she could. She could still have her Wednesday lunches with her friends and plan anniversary parties, high school graduations, and as many weddings as she could handle.

She currently had more clients than slots, something that had never happened before. Of course, she'd never been the wedding planner for the wedding of the year, and Eloise had really helped Robin's business by allowing her to plan her nuptials with the Chief of Police, Aaron Sherman.

The article in the Cove Chronicles had certainly helped too.

Robin smiled at the message from Eloise, who'd said, *Twenty-seven days, Robin! What can I help you with today?*

Robin would meet Eloise at one-thirty for a final fitting on her wedding dress. That would give the seamstress enough time to make any last alterations and give Eloise one more chance to try on the dress before the big day.

As Robin started to remind Eloise of the dress-fitting at the bridal shop that afternoon, her friend sent another text. *Aaron wants you and Duke and the girls to come for dinner this weekend. Friday? Or Saturday?*

Robin's grin widened, because she loved having other couples to go out with. She and Duke hadn't had a friend-couple like that in a while, and Robin sure did like Eloise and Aaron. Not only were they fine people by themselves, but they were adorable as a couple. He paid *real* attention to her, and Eloise deserved nothing less.

Not only that, but Billie and Grace absolutely adored Eloise, and she them. They'd been riding the ferry from Diamond to Sanctuary after school since January, where Eloise would pick them up and take them up to The Cliffside Inn with her.

She ran the inn full-time and lived in a tiny house she'd parked at her mother's, just down the hill from the inn. Her full-time chef lived in the small, one-bedroom apartment attached to the inn, and Rhonda also acted as the emergency manager whenever Eloise wasn't on-site.

She worked hard to leave the inn by six p.m., and she spent most evenings with Aaron and the girls at his house on Diamond. She'd move in there with them once she and Aaron tied the knot, but their routine likely wouldn't change.

Robin sent the message about the bridal shop, and then added, *Yes to dinner. Let me talk to Duke and see what his weekend is like.*

He went fishing every day, because just like Robin had picked up every available job she could squeeze into her working hours, he knew keenly about the boat payment that came due on the fifth of every month.

His income had gone up about twenty percent, but he was paying for it with punishing hours. She rarely saw him when it wasn't dark, though now that spring was almost upon Five Island Cove, the sun showed its face for far longer than it did in the winter.

The last text Robin hadn't read yet had come from AJ, and it was another one from last night Robin hadn't seen.

On my way to the hospital. Having pain in my abdomen. Tell everyone to pray.

Robin's chest tightened to the point where she couldn't breathe, and her fingers fumbled as she started sucking at the air. She dropped her phone, and the resulting *crack!* of plastic against cement made tears spring to her eyes.

She dove after the phone and grabbed it. A hairline crack spread across the screen, but she ignored it as she quickly tapped to call AJ.

"Come on," she said. "Pick up, AvaJane. Pick up."

CHAPTER FIVE

"Right here is fine," Alice Kelton said, and the RideShare driver pulled over. She'd have to walk a block to the high school, but she should've known she couldn't come at this time in the morning.

She'd left ten minutes after her twins and called the RideShare so she wouldn't have to figure out where to park. She hadn't said anything to Charlie or Ginny about why she was going to the high school that morning, and she hitched her purse higher on her arm after paying for her ride from her new home right here on Diamond Island to the high school.

Memories filled her mind as she finished the walk to the school, and the bell had already rung by the time she stepped foot on campus. She still knew exactly where her locker had been in each of the four years she'd attended school here, and she braced herself for the familiar scent of floor wax, sweat, and fruity air freshener that said she'd arrived at Five Island Cove High.

The main office sat immediately to her right, and her heels clicked against the worn tile as she went in that direction. She'd only taken one step through the doorway when her phone rang.

Since phones rang all the time in the office, none of the secretaries bothered to look up. Alice fished her phone from her purse and saw Robin's name on the screen. Alice hesitated, but in the end, she swiped her best friend's call to the left and silenced her phone.

Drawing in a cleansing breath, she lifted her eyes to the first desk. A blonde woman sat there, very busy with something very important on the desk in front of her. Alice approached the desk, gripping the straps on her purse looped over her forearm.

She hesitated for a moment, expecting the woman to look up at her and ask what she needed. When she didn't, Alice said, "Good morning."

That got the blonde to look up. "How can I help you?"

"I have an appointment with Arthur Rice," she said without looking at her phone to check the name.

"Oh, you want to be in the counseling office," the blonde said.

"Okay," Alice said, not quite sure where that was. Sure, she'd gone to this school, but she hadn't spent any time hanging out with counselors. "And that is...?" she prompted when the woman went back to her work.

Frustration ran through her, because she had plenty of work she needed to finish today too. Since the tsunami, Alice had signed several more clients, and after about nine months of running her own little law office out of her home, she was finally starting to see some good profit.

She made enough to pay the mortgage on the three-bedroom home she'd bought for her new life here in the cove. She could pay all the bills with Frank's alimony, and she put all of his child support into an account for the twins.

"Oh, across the hall," the blonde said. "Several yards down."

"Thank you." Alice turned and left the main office, automatically searching for the counseling office across the hall. She saw the sign sticking out from the brick wall, and since first period had already begun, Alice only had to dodge a handful of students.

This office wasn't nearly as large or airy, and only one woman kept the gate here. She at least looked up, her straight-cut bangs dyed an unnaturally dark black. Alice had never understood the gothic look, and it sure did feel strange coming from the woman in the counseling office at the high school.

"How can I help you?" she asked.

"I have an appointment with Arthur Rice," she said again.

"Sure, his office is down the left hall here." She pointed with a Barbie-doll hand, her fingers close together and her thumb practically glued to her palm. "Last one at the end."

"I can just go back?'

"Sure," she said. "I know he's in there. He just came out for coffee." The woman gave Alice a wide, warm smile and went back to her computer.

Alice faced the hall on the left-hand side of the office and stepped that way. Offices branched off both sides of the hallway, and Arthur Rice's had his name outside of it, just like the others.

She went to the doorway and slowed, peering inside. Her movement caught the attention of the man at the desk, and he looked up.

Alice's breath caught in her throat, but her hand had already started its upward movement to knock on the doorframe. She did that as the man rose to his feet.

He was likely several years older than Alice, if the salty gray hair in his sideburns and creeping up into his dark hair was any indication. He had wise, dark brown eyes and a full beard.

"Good morning," he said, his voice rumbling through Alice's chest. "You must be Alice Kelton."

"Yes," she blurted out, swallowing immediately afterward. She couldn't believe she'd let a handsome man render her mute. She'd met plenty of good-looking men in her life, and she certainly wasn't going to start dating this one.

She'd seen William Bridge for a couple of months, but

her children really hadn't approved of the relationship. His daughter had not been popular with the twins, despite the fact that she'd gone to live with her mother in Hawaii. That hadn't lasted long, and the teen had returned to the cove a week after Valentine's Day. While Alice really liked Will, and the childhood romance they'd once had as teens had been growing and exciting to Alice as an adult, she'd ended things with Will only a week later.

The past five weeks alone had taught her that she was indeed lonely, but she hadn't tried to find someone new to date. She'd been reading a lot of self-help books for single mothers, and she'd very nearly determined to devote her life to her children until they graduated from high school and left her home to make their own way in the world.

However, Arthur Rice had just swung her in the completely opposite direction.

"Come in," he said with a smile. With a sweeping gesture, he indicated the two chairs in front of his desk.

Alice gave him a smile too, and she stepped into the small space and took the outside chair. She settled her purse on the floor next to her feet and looked up as Arthur settled into his seat.

"Nice to meet you," he said, extending his hand across the desk.

"And you," she said.

"I really enjoy meeting the parents of my students," he said with a genuine smile. "We've exchanged a lot of emails, and this way, you see me as a real person, and I see you as a real person." He folded his hands and kept his smile in place.

"I see," Alice said. "Your last email said something about Charlie's grade in chemistry?"

"Right." Arthur seemed to startle a little, and then he bent to pull open a drawer. He took out a folder and opened it on the desk in front of him. He studied something inside and then looked up. "Are you aware that Charlie got a perfect score on his organic chemistry test?"

He plucked something from the folder and slid it toward Alice. Her defenses nearly touched the upper atmosphere, and Alice didn't even look at the paper. "We've had a lot going on in our family," she said. "We moved from..."

Her voice trailed off as her brain caught up with what the counselor had said. "Wait. What?" She reached for the paper at the same time Arthur started to chuckle.

"You thought Charlie was in trouble."

Alice peered at the paper, which bore a scrawled *100* at the top in blue pen. "Your email was very foreboding," she said, trying to read the first sentence and getting confused instantly.

"Charlie is a great student," Arthur said. "I want him to join the Academic Olympiad."

Alice's eyes flew to Arthur's, hers much wider than they'd been previously. Her pulse thumped haphazardly against her breastbone as she struggled to understand. "Academic... Olympiad."

The very idea sounded ridiculous inside her head, and Alice actually bit back a laugh.

"Our AP English teacher oversees the team, and we're particularly weak on science students this year," he said, not a smile in sight. He took another paper from the folder. "So we started looking through our honors chemistry classes, and when I spoke with Mister James, he immediately nominated Charlie, pulled a few samples of his work, and I emailed you."

"Why you?" Alice asked. "And what is Academic Olympiad?"

"It's a school team that does academic competitions over the summer."

Alice scoffed then, the last half of it definitely a laugh. "I don't think so." She shook her head. "There is no way you'll get Charlie to do this." She picked up the chemistry test and looked at it again. "He told me he'd done 'fine' on this test."

"He's the only one in the whole school who got every question right," Arthur said. "We find that for students like Charlie, it really helps to have parental support at home once we approach him here at school."

Alice's eyebrows went up. Her phone rang again, and once again, she found Robin's name on the screen. She hesitated once more, but in the end, she swept the call away like she had last time. Alice hadn't told anyone about her meeting with the school counselor that morning, because she had assumed the meeting would be bad news concerning Charlie and the classes he was failing.

Guilt pulled through her that her first thoughts had been negative. If Arthur had emailed about Ginny, Alice would've assumed something different. She swallowed, but the motion was somewhat difficult, and she really needed something to drink.

"Does it require time after school?" Alice asked.

"Yes," Arthur said. "Mondays and Wednesdays for an hour. Does Charlie have a job?"

"Yes," Alice said. "He works at the elementary school as a janitor every day after school."

"Oh, great," Arthur said with a smile. "Those are such flexible jobs. He can easily go in an hour later." He passed her another paper. "I'm going to give you this. It's the parental permission form we need for him to be on the team, and I'm going to have Sariah talk to him today."

"Oh, uh, okay," Alice said. Her phone rang again, and Robin really wanted to get in touch with her. "I'm sorry." She lifted her device. "My friend had called three times in ten minutes."

"Go ahead," he said. "I just wanted to talk with you face-to-face about your son."

Alice had made the mistake of looking into Arthur's eyes, and the call from Robin once again went to voicemail, this time without her having to swipe at all.

They both stood up in unison, and Alice noticed that he hadn't looked away from her either.

"I'll email you to let you know when Sariah had spoken to him."

"Who's Sariah?" Alice asked, trying to get in control of her hormones. She was only acting crazed because she was so lonely, and she missed Will. None of her self-help books had helped her know how to deal with handsome, kind, employed men.

"She's the Olympiad student captain," he said. "Great girl, and she was excited by the idea of adding Charlie to the team."

Alice nodded, not sure what else to say. The moment turned awkward, and she realized she was staring at the man. Clearing her throat, she turned to leave the office.

"Alice?" Arthur asked behind her.

She went out into the hall, because his office was far too intimate. After turning back, she asked, "Yes?"

"I hope this isn't inappropriate, but I'm wondering what you're doing for dinner tonight." He settled onto the side of his desk and folded his arms. In the white shirt and tie, along with the dark brown slacks, he looked every bit the working professional that Alice liked.

Her eyebrows couldn't get any higher, and she honestly had no response for the man. "Dinner?" came out of her mouth.

"Maybe you're seeing someone," he said, utterly at ease in his own office.

Alice thought of Will. She'd been thinking of him a lot lately, and she didn't know what it meant. "No," she said. "I'm not."

Before he could say anything else, her phone rang again.

Robin, again.

"I'm sorry," she said. "I have to get this." She gave him a final nod, not sure if she was telling him yes to dinner or simply saying goodbye. Striding away, Alice had never felt more foolish.

"Robin," she said, avoiding the secretary's eyes as she practically flew from the counseling office. "What's going on?"

"It's about time you answered your phone," Robin sniped at her. "What in the world are you doing this morning?"

Getting asked out by Charlie's counselor, Alice thought. "Nothing," she said. "Why have you called me so many times?"

"It's AJ," Robin said. "She's in the hospital after some abdominal pain and light spotting. I'm heading over there right now, and I'm just letting everyone know."

Alice's heart dropped to the soles of her shoes, and she couldn't remember how to walk anymore. She stopped right there in the middle of the hallway in the high school. "Is she okay?"

"I was only able to talk to her for a few minutes," Robin said. "Matt wasn't there, as he had the big press release for Aaron's father at the golf course this morning. I'm ten minutes out, and then I'll know more."

"I'm on my way," Alice said, realizing she wasn't living out on Rocky Ridge anymore, and she was as close to the hospital as Robin. "Have you called everyone?"

"Yes," Robin said. "You're the last."

"I'll be there in a few minutes," Alice said, realizing she hadn't driven herself to the school, and she needed her phone to call for a ride.

CHAPTER SIX

Kristen Shields saw Alice exiting the room Robin had said AJ would be in, and as the other woman looked left and right, their eyes met.

"Kristen." Alice sounded relieved to see her, and she looked like she hadn't been sleeping enough.

Kristen certainly wasn't, as the anniversary of the death of her husband loomed on the calendar only two weeks in the future. She'd been contemplating taking another step to move past Joel, but she hadn't told anyone about her idea to leave the house up the sidewalk from the lighthouse and find somewhere else to live.

She wouldn't go far, and of course she'd still go out to the lighthouse. Her son and daughter-in-law lived there, and Kristen needed the soothing influence of the ocean as she viewed it from the top balcony of the lighthouse.

Now was not the time to bring it up either, but Kristen

had been planning to tell everyone on Wednesday at their lunch. Kelli would be there, and that almost never happened as she had a day job that didn't allow her to lunch with her friends whenever she wanted.

Kristen reached Alice and drew her into a hug. "How is she?"

"She seems upbeat," Alice said, gripping Kristen tightly. "How are you? What are you doing to stay busy this month?" Alice stepped back, her dark eyes searching Kristen's. "You can come to my house any time. I'll put you to work filing." She grinned, and Kristen returned the smile.

"I might actually take you up on that," Kristen said. She'd helped Alice organize her home office, where she ran her law practice. Now that she'd moved to Diamond Island, she had more clients than she could handle. People always said that location mattered for a business, and in Alice's case, that had never been truer.

She handled divorces, custody cases, protective orders, and anything else under the umbrella of family law, and she was very good at her job. She was sympathetic and kind, as she'd definitely had some blows dealt to her in the past.

"I'm just heading out to get coffee," Alice said. "Do you want any?"

"Is everyone here?" Kristen asked. She'd been in bed when Robin had called, and everything seemed to take her longer these days. Just putting on her shoes made her fingers tremble, and Kristen put her hands in her pockets to hide the slight tremor from Alice.

"No, thank you," Kristen said. The caffeine only increased the trembling, and she didn't need the extra stimulant.

"I'll be back in a sec." Alice left, and Kristen faced the closed hospital room door. She wanted to go inside, because she loved her girls with a power like no other. A mother's love, though she had not given birth to any of the women behind the door.

In some ways, she had seen them become reborn. She'd watched Alice crawl her way out of the ashes after her mother's death. She'd been at Kelli's side when her parents had divorced, when her father had lost the Glassworks, when he'd died. She'd done the best she could with AJ as the girl slept around and then grew to realize how much more she was worth. She'd watched with a huge smile on her face as Eloise had embraced her academic side and earned scholarships all over the Eastern Seaboard. She'd been the first to know about Robin's engagement to Duke, and the way she'd become a new person without the pressure from her mother's thumb.

Kristen took a deep breath and walked toward the door. She knocked on it and opened the door a moment later. "Hello?" She scanned the room, finding AJ sitting up in bed, Robin standing at the bedside, Eloise sitting in the recliner with Grace on her lap, and Kelli looking out the window. She turned toward Kristen as they all did, and Kristen smiled at them.

"My girls," she said, entering the room and closing the door behind her.

"I told you we'd need the room big enough for four visitors," Robin said, grinning as she stepped forward to greet Kristen with a hug. "The nurse just left. They're getting the doctor to come check AJ. They might let her go home."

Kristen watched the fear roll across AJ's face when no one else did. Eloise had bumped Grace to her feet, and when Kristen released Robin, she took the blonde girl into her arms. "Is your daddy letting you miss school today?" she asked Grace.

"She's my shadow today," Eloise said, smiling down at Grace, who was in fourth grade this year. "Aaron's going to come get her after he's done at the golf course."

Kristen stepped over to Eloise, and they hugged too.

"You need to come up to the inn," Eloise said. "I've got an on-site masseuse now, and you'd love her."

"Oh, twist my arm," Kristen joked, and they laughed together,

Kelli had left the window, and Kristen hugged her, sensing something had shifted within the woman. She'd texted yesterday afternoon about having something to tell everyone this week, and Kristen wished she could take the strawberry blonde out into the hall and ask her what the trouble was.

Perhaps it wasn't a trouble at all, but Kristen had raised two children and worked with hundreds of girls through the Seafaring Girls program Five Island Cove had run for decades. She knew unrest when she felt it inside a person, and Kelli had something eating away at her.

Kelli offered her a timid smile as she stepped back, folding her arms as she then looked at AJ.

The gorgeous woman looked up at Kristen from the bed, and all Kristen could see was the scared fourteen-year-old who'd shown up on the doorstep one night long after the last ferry had left Diamond Island.

"My dear," Kristen said kindly, just as she had then. She bent down and hugged AJ, the woman's long limbs winding around Kristen's neck and holding her tight. Her chest heaved, and a couple of sobs shook through her, and Kristen knew she was teetering on the edge of a breakdown.

She couldn't take her anti-depressants during her pregnancy, and her fiancé and the father of her baby wasn't here.

"What am I going to do if they send me home?" she whispered.

"That's easy, AvaJane," Kristen whispered back. "I'll go with you and take care of you." She'd once told AJ that she was welcome at the lighthouse anytime. Any day. Any hour. She'd assured her over and over that though her own mother had left, AJ could always count on Kristen to take care of her.

This would be no different. Nothing had changed, at least for Kristen.

"Could you?" AJ asked.

"Of course dear," Kristen said, pulling back and smiling. She looked around at everyone. "What did the doctors say? I haven't gotten a very good update."

"She said AJ needs to be on bedrest for at least the next three weeks," Robin said, her eyes turning sharp as a bird's.

"They think I just had a little bleeding as the baby shifted. It was nothing," AJ said.

"It was not nothing," Robin argued back.

"It was probably stress-related," Eloise said. "That's what Doctor East said."

"And you're stressing me out," AJ said to Robin, glaring at her.

Kristen was used to her girls bickering amongst one another. Robin and Alice were the worst offenders, but they loved each other so fiercely. They'd been right beside each other over the past year since Joel's death, and right there when Kristen needed them too.

"This is more than stress," Robin said. "You have to be careful, AJ. If a woman who's been to medical school for nine years says you should be on bedrest for three weeks, you do it."

"You're not Doctor Proctor," Kelli said from her position by the window. "Please, AJ."

"I have work to do," AJ said. "Matt's kids are coming.

His parents..."

Robin met Kristen's eye as AJ's voice trailed off. "I have nothing else to do," Kristen said. "I can take you to my house, or I can come to yours. You and Matt are right here on Diamond."

"Things keep," Eloise said gently as she came to stand beside Kristen. "You can work if Kristen brings you your laptop. You can entertain from the couch." She exchanged a glance with Robin and then Kristen. "Right?"

"Yes," Robin said firmly. "I had to do a couple of weeks of bedrest with Mandie, and it's boring. But you'll have Kristen to talk to, and I'm sure there's so much you haven't binged on the streaming services. There's so many of them now, it wouldn't even be possible to keep up."

Kristen simply nodded, though every time she sat down in front of the TV, she couldn't find anything to watch she hadn't already seen.

So it was definitely possible to keep up with the streaming services. She didn't say so though, because she was very good at keeping things to herself that didn't need to be said. She'd learned that from Joel. There was no harm in letting him think he was right. She could simply get the remote control out from the under his chair when he went into the bathroom. It never worked when she said she'd seen it on his armrest and it had probably fallen.

The door opened and Alice entered with a precariously balanced cup holder for four cups of coffee. She had six stuck in it, and Robin darted over to help her. "All right," Alice said, half a sigh in her voice. "Here we go."

She passed out the coffee to everyone, but kept one cup back, and Kristen felt a bit awkward without something to hold and sip. She tucked her hands away so they couldn't be seen and pressed them into her thighs to get them to quiet.

At seventy-seven, Kristen didn't want to think about conditions like Parkinson's or neurological issues. She knew she was closing in on eighty, but she felt like she had plenty of life still to live. She'd read that shaky hands could come from panic, depression, anxiety, or post-traumatic stress syndrome.

With Joel's death date approaching, Kristen swung from panic to depression in the space between seconds. She could see him plainly in bed, not moving, his eyes closed. She pressed her eyes closed, hoping to erase the images as Kelli started to say something.

Thankfully, her sweet voice chased away the memories that seemed so fresh on Kristen's soul, and her eyes popped open when Kelli said, "We went to dinner last night."

"Yes," AJ said as if she'd suddenly become a cheerleader. "Way to go, Kel."

Kristen scanned the room to find shock on Robin's face, surprise resting in Alice's eyes, and wonder in the O-shape of Eloise's mouth.

"What's his name?" Kristen asked, because she'd

heard enough to know Kelli had gone to dinner with a man last night.

"Shad Webb," Kelli said, her face growing pinker by the moment. "He lives right next door to me and Parker. He's the other half of the twinhome." She smiled at her hands and then up at everyone. "He said he's wanted to ask me out since I moved in."

"Kelli." Alice rushed at her and hugged her. "Tell us everything." She stepped back and took the recliner. Grace climbed right up onto her lap like she was Eloise, and Kristen loved that the little girl felt so comfortable with all of them.

"We only had a few minutes," she said. "We couldn't go to a sit-down restaurant, but we went to that fast-casual shrimp taco stand, and we ate as we walked along the pier. They've got it mostly cleaned up now, and it was...nice."

"Sounds casual," Robin said. "Easy."

"It was casual and easy," Kelli said, nodding at Robin. "I had a good time. He asked if he could see me again, and I said yes. My mother and Devon are taking Parker tonight." She cut a glance at AJ. "If we're done here, that is. I can reschedule."

"You will absolutely not reschedule," AJ said, gesturing for Kelli to come closer. "I have Kristen to mother me. I'm the one who mothers you, Kel, and you will be going out with this Shad Webb man."

"Shad Webb, the financial director for Five Island Cove?" Alice looked up from her phone.

"Oh, I know Shad Webb," Eloise said. "He attends some of the same meetings as Aaron." She pressed in close to Alice and looked over her shoulder. "Yep, that's him."

"He's gorgeous," Alice said, her eyes still a bit too wide not to look stunned. "You didn't mention how good-looking he was."

"Let me see," AJ said, reaching for the phone. But Robin was mobile, and she beat AJ over to Alice's left side. She pressed in close too, and Kristen could only smile at the trio as they peered at the phone.

"Mm hm," Robin said, glancing at Kelli. "He is handsome. Looks a little older than you."

"He's nine years older," Kelli said, her hands twisting around each other. "Is that too old? I mean, he's fifty-four. Parker is only nine. If we got married or anything, he'll be—"

"Wait, wait." Robin held up both hands. "Married?"

"We're not going to get married," Kelli said.

"You might," AJ said.

"Right," Alice said. "We're not dead just because we're forty-five."

That brought the conversation to a halt again, but this time, everyone focused on Alice. "What?" she asked.

"Who did you meet?" AJ demanded. "And bring me that phone so I can see this gorgeous financial director."

Alice took the two steps and handed AJ the phone.

She whistled and looked at Kelli. "I'm surprised you've never mentioned him."

"It's been a rough few months," Kelli said, swallowing.

"This can't be your thing for Wednesday's lunch," Eloise said. "You sent that text way before you got on the ferry last night."

Kelli shook her head, her lips pressed together. "That's something else."

"I have something for Wednesday too," Alice said.

"So do I," Kristen said, bringing all of her girls' attention to her. The silence stretched for several long moments.

"Perhaps Shad has an older brother," Robin said, a playful smile on her face. Everyone started laughing, and the tension in the room broke.

"What did I miss?" Laurel asked as she entered the room. "You would not believe the traffic out there. They've got a one-lane road on the busiest street downtown." She accepted the sixth cup of coffee from Alice and looked around.

She hitched her police belt higher and took a sip from her to-go cup. "I have a gun if someone needs me to prompt them to start talking."

CHAPTER SEVEN

L aurel Baker grinned as the other women in the hospital room laughed. She did have a gun on her hip, but she wouldn't use it against these people. She'd let them into her life, and all of them were like sisters to her. She had a better relationship with some over others, something she was well-aware of as her eyes skipped past Eloise.

She did love Eloise, because Aaron did. Eloise was very good at keeping things from delving into awkward, but there wasn't the same closeness between them that Laurel felt with Alice or Robin.

AJ had been fairly engrossed in her own life and relationship, and Kelli lived on Pearl Island, which Laurel literally had no reason to visit, ever. She saw Kelli around town here and there, but nothing major. She worked at the junior high, so she couldn't attend the weekly lunches.

Laurel herself barely attended those, though she had been to several over the past three months.

She and her partner worked Sanctuary almost exclusively, and Laurel suspected that Aaron kept her there so she could check up on his girls when they got off the ferry in the afternoons and be nearby Eloise and her mother should either of them need help. The Chief had never said as much, but Laurel knew he trusted her.

Her phone buzzed, and her radio chirped as Robin started detailing the "very handsome older gentleman" that Kelli had gone out with last night.

Laurel looked at the picture, nodding. "I know Shad. I had to escort him home because there was this guy who didn't like how the town was managing the money for the Founder's Day Festival one year. He'd been sending him threats and whatnot."

Shad Webb was a well-known and well-respected man around the cove. He'd worked for the town for twenty-nine years, and Laurel had heard whisperings of retirement for a few of the positions in the city recently.

"Maybe I shouldn't go out with him," Kelli said.

"Nah," Laurel said. "It was years and years ago. My first year on the force." She sipped her coffee, and Alice had managed to get them to put the exact right amount of caramel in it. She didn't know how she did that, though Laurel had asked her how she ordered it and done it exactly the same. Whenever she ordered, the coffee was still far too sweet.

This still had notes of bitterness and Laurel drank greedily again. She hadn't eaten breakfast, but that was nothing new. Paul teased her that she shouldn't skip the most important meal of the day, but Laurel couldn't eat the toast and eggs her boyfriend did in the morning.

He'd started to hint that if she'd stay over at his place, he'd make breakfast for her every morning, but Laurel never did. She wasn't sure she was ready for that, though she and Paul had been intimate.

Every step Laurel took seemed to take a year where most women didn't need so much time to heal. She simply didn't want to rush into anything, and it had taken her six months to take the step of doing anything more than kissing.

She wasn't embarrassed about it, and she told Paul all of the things she was thinking and feeling. He was kind and attentive, and Laurel had started to fall in love with him. Even now, just thinking about him serving her breakfast, her stomach fluttered.

"No, I meant maybe I shouldn't go out with him if he's so well-known," Kelli said. "What do you know about him? Why has he been single for so long?"

Laurel lowered her nearly empty coffee cup and blinked at Kelli. "I'm not sure," she said haltingly. Even if she did, she wouldn't say. Kelli should get to know Shad, and he should get to tell her private details like that.

"You'll go out with him," Robin said, stepping over to Kelli and putting her arm around her. "And you'll ask him all of those things." She smiled at Kelli as if she were Kelli's mother, and they weren't the same age. "Right, girls?"

"Right," they chorused together, and in moments like that, Laurel was reminded that she was the odd man out. Odd woman out. She hadn't grown up with these women, and she hadn't been in the same Seafaring Girls troop they'd all been in.

She knew Robin Grover, because the woman was practically an icon for the quintessential resident of Five Island Cove. She ran in the morning; she did volunteer work around town; she threw great events for her clients. She'd been nothing but kind and inclusive to Laurel, and they'd actually run together a couple of times.

But Laurel's schedule was sporadic and hard to predict, and she hadn't been down to the beach in her running shoes for a while.

Laurel remembered her phone had chimed, and she checked it to find Paul had messaged. She knew Alice was sidling up to her, but it was okay, because Alice knew all about the misgivings Laurel had about her relationship with Paul.

Alice and Laurel had grabbed coffee several times over the past few months, and Laurel sure did like the woman. She was articulate and smart, and she didn't take crap from anyone, male or female.

"What does Paul need?" Alice asked, her voice almost a murmur. The conversation carried on around them, and

Kristen took the recliner Alice had vacated when Laurel had arrived.

"He's off tomorrow," Laurel said. "He wants to take his sailboat out."

"That sounds fun," Alice said.

Laurel snorted and started tapping on her phone. "I think it's more like a death wish. Look at this thing." She swiped open her gallery and tapped on the picture of Paul's sailboat.

Alice looked at the picture, a gasp going in on her next breath. "Does that float?"

"He claims it does. Says she has character." Laurel looked at *Daisy May*, the name of Paul's beloved sailboat. She hadn't even known he owned a sailboat until last week. "Every seven weeks, our schedules line up and we have the same day off. I'm supposed to pick up whatever food I want for the day, and I'm trying to think of what I want for my last meal."

Alice laughed with her, and Laurel quickly navigated back to Paul's text. He'd asked her if she'd heard anything about AJ yet, and then he'd asked if she could please bring some grape soda on their outing tomorrow.

She gave her report of AJ, confirmed on the grape soda, and had barely finished sending her text when the door opened again. She didn't think there'd be room for another body, and she prepared to step out when she actually got stopped short.

"All right," the man said, looking up from his tablet. "AvaJane, you're cleared for—"

"Doctor Carmen?" Laurel blurted out, though she knew it was him. She'd know that blue-eyed face and that lilting walk anywhere. She started to laugh as he turned toward her, surprise in his eyes.

"Laurel," he said, grinning.

She threw herself into his arms, forgetting for a moment about the audience they had. "You look great," she said, stepping back as quickly as she'd embraced him. "I can see you've been working out."

"That I have," he said, still smiling. "You must be friends with AvaJane here."

Laurel nodded, her eyes flickering to AJ. Because she was a cop, Laurel could take in a lot of details at once. She felt and saw all the curious looks from the other women in the room, right down to ten-year-old Grace Sherman.

Dr. Carmen started to tell AJ that her doctor had cleared her for release, and that he'd go start the paperwork. "About an hour," he said, patting AJ's leg. "Just enough time to order ice cream from the cafeteria." He flashed a blinding smile around the room, his eyes landing on Laurel's. "Can I talk to you outside for a minute?"

"Sure," she said, glad for a reason to step out. Robin particularly would pounce the moment the doctor left, and by following him, Laurel bought herself a few seconds of peace.

"Hurry back now," Alice said, plenty of meaning in her voice. "We need to make a few plans for keeping AJ sane over the next three weeks."

Laurel nodded and caught the door as it started to swing closed behind Dr. Carmen.

CHAPTER EIGHT

Eloise Hall darted up the steps ahead of Kristen and AJ. She wasn't sure which woman needed more help, in all honesty. Kristen seemed a bit on the pale side, and Eloise's stomach growled as she gripped the knob and twisted it.

Perhaps Kristen was just hungry. AJ had said she was on the drive home from the hospital. Eloise had plenty of work to do at The Cliffside Inn, and she glanced at the huge clock above the couch in Matt Hymas's living room as she turned back to receive AJ and Kristen.

"Right to the couch, AJ," she said. AJ still had over four months left in her pregnancy, but her belly was notice-able. With only half of it over, Eloise wanted to make sure AJ didn't lose her baby.

"Yes, ma'am," AJ said as she went by. She wore a smile instead of a glare, which she'd been shooting at Robin for at least two hours. Robin could be overbearing, but she was the nicest person in the cove. She cared about people —really cared—and she only wanted what was best for AJ.

AJ groaned as she sat on the couch. Kristen bustled about, getting a blanket for her from the back of the loveseat and finding a few more pillows to help prop up AJ.

"I'm going to make a quick lunch," Eloise said, hurrying into the kitchen. She had her final dress fitting in an hour, and she couldn't be late for it. She couldn't miss it, or she'd be wearing a billowing, white tent to get married in.

Her first wedding hadn't been anything spectacular, and the marriage had been one of the biggest regrets and mistakes of her life. She so wanted this wedding to be what everyone was saying it was—the wedding of the year.

She could do without all the press and publicity, but Aaron was the Chief of Police. Eyes followed him and everything he touched everywhere he went. That included Billie and Grace, his daughters, and Eloise, his fiancée.

"Grace, you call your dad and tell him where we are," Eloise said as the little girl came into the house last. "Then come help me with lunch."

"Okay," Grace said, skipping over to the dining room table and picking up Eloise's phone.

She started to poke through the fridge and cupboards, looking for something easy to make for the four of them. "When will Matt be back?" she called into the living room. Kristen had sat on the edge of the loveseat, and she had one hand on AJ's knee.

"He didn't say," AJ said. "Don't worry about him."

"Daddy, we're at AJ's house," Grace said, and Eloise glanced past her as she pulled out a package of ground beef. She could make taco salad in the time it took to brown the beef, and she set a pan on the stovetop.

AJ had lettuce, tomatoes, and cheese, but not much else in the way of toppings. No canned corn or black beans. No olives.

Eloise told herself it didn't matter, and she started breaking up the beef. She kept her hands moving, and after only fifteen minutes, she had salad ready to eat. She put some of everything in a bowl and took it into the living room.

AJ looked up at her with such appreciation, and while Eloise had often felt a bit removed from AJ, right now, she didn't. "Thank you, El." AJ's eyes shone with unshed tears, and Eloise's throat tightened.

She swallowed and glanced toward the kitchen as noise met her ears. "Grace, wait for me," she said, hurrying back that way. "Kristen, stay there. I'll bring you some too."

"Not much cheese for me, dear," Kristen said as Eloise arrived on the scene only a moment before Grace would've dumped the whole bowl of chopped lettuce on the floor.

"Okay," Eloise yelled, her grip on the bowl firm. "Gracie. You should get some help before you throw everything on the floor." She gave the girl a smile, but her patience was nearly gone. "Let me hold it for you."

She kept the bowl steady while Grace pinched the tongs together and added the lettuce to her plate. Eloise stayed nearby and let the girl finish putting together her salad. "Go eat at the table," she said. "I'll be right there."

Eloise quickly put together two salads, one with a lot of cheese and one with hardly any, and took the latter to Kristen. She smiled at Eloise, her warmth so real and so infectious. At the same time, she looked utterly exhausted.

So much passed between them that Eloise decided against taking up the other half of the loveseat and asking Kristen what was wrong.

She knew what was wrong. Kristen was tired, because she hadn't been sleeping. She hadn't been sleeping, because it had almost been a year since Joel had died. Kristen didn't like talking about her husband, and Eloise could admit to still having mixed feelings about the man.

A quick glance at AJ told her that the pregnant woman wasn't going anywhere, and Eloise returned to Grace and her salad at the table. She ate quickly, ignoring Robin's texts for the time being. Eloise knew where she needed to be and at what time.

As she started putting away the leftovers, she noticed

how quiet the living room had become. She paused when she found both AJ and Kristen asleep, a smile filling her face. She did love the two of them, and while they didn't seem like a likely pair, Kristen was the perfect person to take care of AJ for a few days.

AJ's sister and father lived on Pearl Island, and AJ had said she'd call them to let them know what had happened. Eloise suspected those phone calls hadn't been made yet, because if they had, AJ's family would be here.

"Come on, Gracie," she said. "I have to meet Robin to try on my dress."

"Dad said he'd be here at one," Grace said.

"It's past that," Eloise said, pushing against her irritation. The press conference for Aaron's father's should've ended hours ago. What could be keeping him?

Any number of things, Eloise thought. The man was the Chief of Police, and the island was still in various stages of clean-up from the tsunami. They held a huge spring bazaar every year too, and Aaron had been hiring temporary cops for weeks now.

She paused in the living room, wondering if she should wake Kristen to tell her she had to leave. She decided against it, and quietly led Grace out onto the porch. Two cars pulled into the driveway, one right after the other, staying over on the right so she could get out on the left.

"Dad," Grace called as she let go of Eloise's hand and ran down the steps. The girls missed their father when he worked, and the man worked a lot. He'd done the best he could, just like most people did, and Eloise smiled as he scooped Grace up into his arms, both of them laughing.

The girl certainly wasn't sick enough to stay home from school, but she'd done something that morning to convince Aaron she was. "Hey, sweetheart," Aaron said easily, setting Grace on her feet. "Sorry I'm a minute late."

"It's okay," Eloise said. "I was just headed out." She put one hand against his chest to steady herself as she kissed him.

"Is AJ inside?" Matt asked, interrupting them.

"Yep," Eloise said. "She's asleep, and there's taco salad for lunch. Kristen Shields is here with her, so you can still go to work and stuff." She gave him a smile, and she could see why a woman like AJ would like a man like Matt. He was tall too, athletic, with plenty of bulk in his shoulders and chest. He looked his age, much the way Aaron did, and the concern radiating from him was obvious.

"Thank you, Eloise," he said, turning immediately toward the house. He took the steps two at a time but opened the door gently.

"You're coming with me, little miss," Aaron said, and Eloise turned her attention back to the pair of them. Their eyes met, and Aaron swept his arm around her waist, his smile wide. "Are you going out to the inn after the fitting?"

"I don't think so," she said. "I'm tired after this morning." Eloise leaned into his strength. "I think AJ will be okay, but she's not one to sit around on the couch."

"Come to my place when you're done," he said, sobering. "I'll take care of you this afternoon."

Eloise smiled at him and leaned forward to press her forehead to his, letting her eyes drift closed. "You will, huh? The Chief doesn't have to work this afternoon?" Her voice barely came out in a whisper, making the moment private and intimate.

"The Chief has plenty to do this afternoon, but he's not going to do it," he whispered back.

"Mm." Eloise kept her eyes closed.

"Twenty-seven days," Aaron said, touching his lips to her cheek. "You sure we have to keep waiting?"

"Mm, yes," Eloise said, pressing into his next kiss that landed almost on her neck. "It's the wedding of the year, Aaron. We can't just move it up because you're getting impatient."

When he matched his mouth to hers, she felt the smile. He kissed her like he couldn't wait to make her his wife, and Eloise had always felt that level of care from him. She hoped such a thing wouldn't fade once they said I do, and she hoped she could kiss him back with as much tenderness and love as he gave her.

"I love you, Aaron," she said, breaking the kiss when she remembered they stood in Matt's front driveway, with Grace standing nearby. "Be safe this afternoon."

"Have fun at the fitting," he said. "Send me pictures."

"Nope." Eloise grinned at him as he stepped back.

"Love you, El." He reached for Grace and took her

hand, leading her over to his cruiser. Eloise waved to the girl and then got behind the wheel of her car. She'd ferried over in it this morning, and that had taken a few extra minutes, so she'd been one of the last to arrive at the hospital.

She made the quick drive to the bridal shop, and she got out of the car when she saw Robin walking inside, her phone pressed to her ear. Eloise paused and watched her best friend, the sound of her intense voice floating back to Eloise's ears.

Poor Robin had taken on so much in the past few months. If Eloise ever needed an example of what hard work and determination looked like, she never needed to look farther than Robin Grover.

She drew in a deep breath, hoping the dress would fit well today. She wanted to spend a few hours with Aaron, and she wanted Robin to be able to get to her next task, with another bride who needed the attention.

She pulled open the door and went inside, still praying for her dress fitting miracle.

"THE DRESS FIT AMAZING," ELOISE SAID, REACHING FOR THE butter. Alice nudged it a little closer to her, and Eloise took what she wanted for her bread. She loved the brown bread here at Casper's, and she was thrilled they'd taken their lunch a little farther away from the downtown area of Five Island Cove.

It wasn't quite summer yet, but the tourists had already started to arrive. The downtown area was so crowded already, and Eloise felt like she'd aged a decade in the past year. She simply had little tolerance for long lines and overpriced food that was served cold after a wait.

Casper's had been in the cove for about a decade, and they sat on the northern side of Diamond Island, a bit removed from the area flooded with hotels, resorts, and shops. People had to take a car to get there, and therefore, more locals ate there than tourists.

"Really amazing," Robin said, lifting her drink to her lips. "Like a glove."

"Well, there was that bit that pooched out a little," Eloise said. She took a bite of her bread.

"They're going to fix that zipper," Robin said. "Other than that, she's nearly ready."

Eloise didn't feel super ready for the wedding, but she trusted Robin, and she knew all the details would be taken care of. She had the dress. Aaron had his tux. They had a venue on the waterfront, and all of the invitations had been sent.

Laurel set down her menu. "I can't believe I haven't been here before."

"I'm glad we came here then," Alice said, reaching for Robin's phone. She'd pulled up a picture of Eloise in her dress, and the phone was making its way around the table.

She gave Laurel a smile, and Eloise watched the other woman bask in the warmth of it.

Eloise liked Laurel Baker just fine, though she suspected that the cop thought she didn't. She needed to do something about that, and the thought that she should ask Laurel to do something just the two of them entered her mind again.

She had Laurel's number, and perhaps they could go to a movie together or grab coffee or just get a couple of frozen drinks and sit on the beach for a few minutes. Eloise didn't know what she needed to say to Laurel to get things where they should be, but she knew if she put forth the effort, the words would come.

She'd seen the progress with her mother, and Eloise had gotten past some of her silence. The chatter continued around her, but Eloise pulled out her phone and sent a quick text to Laurel. The other woman sat only a few feet away, on the other side of the table.

"Sorry I'm late," Kelli said, rushing into the chair next to Eloise.

"We're just eating bread," Eloise said, smiling at her and tucking her phone away again. She refused to look down the table to Laurel to see her reaction to the message. "Did you get your issue sorted at the school?"

"Yes," Kelli said, smiling. She put one arm around Eloise's shoulder. "How was the dress?"

"Robin's got a photo," Eloise said as Alice handed over the phone.

"Is it just us?" Robin asked.

"I'm going to call AJ," Kelli said, peering down at the phone. "She and Kristen still want to participate."

"Let's get our orders in then," Alice said. "And then we'll call them."

"This dress is *stunning*," Kelli said, looking up at Eloise. "Are you excited?"

"You know what? I think I'm finally excited."

"Oh, you've been excited the whole time," Robin said, scoffing. "It's just getting closer, that's all. I see this in brides *all* the time."

Alice met Eloise's eyes, and that was a big mistake. They both started laughing at the same time, with Kelli and Laurel only a moment behind.

"She sees this is in brides *all* the time," Alice said, nudging Robin with her elbow.

"What?" Robin asked. "I do."

"Okay, let's order," Eloise said, because she could see this conversation devolving quickly.

"I'll call AJ," Kelli said. "Then we can get to the news."

CHAPTER NINE

Kelli propped her phone against the salt and pepper shakers and said, "That's as good as it's going to get, AJ."

"It's fine," AJ said. "I can hear. Kristen's right here with me."

"I'll bring you the shrimp ravioli," Eloise said, and Kelli's patience started to stretch thin. She wasn't sure why she was so irritated already. She hardly ever got to lunch with her friends, and she'd been fighting jealousy for months because of it.

Now that she was here, she felt harried and like she had so many other things she needed to get done today.

"All right," Alice said, her eyes landing on Kelli. "Who wants to go first?"

"I'm claiming last," Kelli said. She wasn't sure if that was a good idea or a huge mistake. If she went first, everything would just be out. If she went last, she could judge if her news was big or not.

"I was going to go last," Alice said. "I should've led with that I'd like to go last."

"Kelli called it," Robin said, giving Alice a slight glare. "I'll go first, because my news isn't that surprising. Duke is for sure going to Alaska again this summer. I hope I don't go insane with the amount of weddings I have."

She gave an exaggerated sigh, and Eloise assured her she could always come to the inn to work.

Robin looked at Alice, as if she'd go next. Alice nearly choked on her sip of water, and she coughed as she cleared her throat. "Okay, I'm next. I, oh wow, I don't even know if I can say it."

"That bad?" Laurel asked.

"Not bad," Alice said. "I'm just nervous about it."

"Spit it out," AJ said, her voice tinny through the phone.

"A man asked me to dinner, and I walked away because Robin was calling about AJ." She took a deep breath. "I called him back and said I'd like to go."

"Who is it?" Eloise asked, reaching for another bite of bread.

"Arthur Rice," Alice said.

Robin yelped, then shrieked, but Kelli had no idea who Arthur Rice was. "You have got to be kidding," Robin said, reaching for her napkin. "What are your kids going to say?"

"Who's Arthur Rice?" Eloise asked.

"He's a counselor at the high school," Laurel said.

Kelli's eyes flew back to Alice, who gave a single nod. "He's fifty, and he's handsome, and yes, he's Charlie and Ginny's counselor. He asked me out right there in his office, after calling me in to tell me Charlie was the smartest kid in the school in chemistry."

Kelli had no idea what to say. Alice looked uncomfortable, and that was saying something for Alice. She usually led out with supreme confidence in everything she did. There was no hemming and hawing for Alice Kelton. She had goals and agendas, and she always knew the right step to take.

"Charlie?" Robin asked. "That's great, Alice. Good for him." She smiled and reached over to give her a side-hug.

"And you got a date," Eloise said. "When are you going out with him?"

"Friday." Alice nodded like that was that, and that was more the persona Kelly expected from her.

"All right, Laurel," Alice said with a sigh. "Time for you to take the spotlight off me."

Laurel set her soda glass down. "Mine's sort of a question. You don't have to answer today or anything." She cleared her throat, and Kelli shot a glance at Eloise. There was something between the two of them, but Kelli didn't know what it was. She often felt like the one on the outside of things, and she'd had to come to terms with that. Sometimes it was easier than others.

"How do you know when you're in love?"

Silence descended on the table, and that was something very few people could do. Kelli had no answer for that, because she didn't know either.

"My goodness," Robin said, always the one to cover over awkward silences. "Do I need to clear a spot on my schedule for you and Paul?" She wore a look of delight, and Laurel smiled as she shrugged.

She was a beautiful woman, with lots of dark hair and a curvy figure that looked good even in her police officer uniform. She had some trauma in her past, and Kelli knew some of what Laurel had been through. She herself often felt so desperate for someone to love her, and she felt like she had the same question as Laurel.

She'd enjoyed spending time with Shad, and he'd brought pizza to her house last night. Parker's favorite kind had kept him happy, and when he'd gone outside to ride his bike with a couple of boys who lived in the twin-home down the street, Kelli had stood on the shared front patio with Shad.

He'd slipped his hand into hers, and Kelli's fingers still tingled with the anticipation and heat of a male touch. A male touch that possessed energy and hope. A male touch that wasn't just for the man, but for her too.

"I just feel like we're moving really slow," Laurel said. "I think maybe I'm in love with him, and I just don't know it."

"You should come have coffee with me and AJ,"

Kristen said over the phone. "We were just talking about this today."

"Yep," AJ said. "Come over next time you're off in the morning, Laurel. Kristen has lots of good insight."

Kelli would like to hear it, but she could stop by the lighthouse any time she wanted. Jean would take Parker down to the sea lion beach, and Kelli could go get Kristen's insight then.

"All right, Eloise," Alice said. "Don't worry, Laurel. I'll be thinking about your question."

"Yeah, you'll probably text me in the middle of the night when you can't sleep." Laurel grinned at Alice, who returned the gesture. They certainly seemed like they got along well, and Kelli wasn't sure why her annoyance and jealousy reared. Alice was allowed to have other friends, and Laurel was such a nice person.

"I don't really have anything," Eloise said. "Can I pass?" She looked at Kelli, but she picked up the phone instead.

"All right, AJ," Kelli said. "Or Kristen."

"I'll go," AJ said, and Kelli faced her toward the rest of the women at the table. The air conditioning blew in here, which really wasn't needed. Kelli suppressed her shiver, knowing it wasn't all to do with the air temperature.

"Matt called his parents and told them I'm pregnant. He told his children about us, and they're all coming to the wedding."

"That's great news," Alice said.

"Good for him," Laurel added, only reminding Kelli of how nice she was. Kelli honestly didn't know how AJ had lived with being a secret, but there were a lot of things about AJ which Kelli didn't understand.

She was her best friend in the whole wide world, and Kelli was glad Matt had finally come to his senses and brought her out of the shadows. AJ didn't survive very long there, and Kelli had seen her withering these past couple of months.

"Kristen's up," AJ said once the congratulations finished.

"I'm thinking about moving," Kristen said, and another wave of silence engulfed the table. Kelli couldn't believe it either, and her idea of showing up at the lighthouse with Parker and entering Kristen's little cottage up on the bluff vanished into thin air.

"Where are you going to go?" Robin demanded, actually taking the phone from Kelli. "You're not leaving the cove, are you?"

"Relax, Robin," Kristen said kindly. "Just right here on Diamond somewhere. Somewhere where I have more grass and less rock. Less wind. Less...Joel." She whispered the last word, and Kelli's heart immediately squished into a smaller box.

"Wow, Kristen," Alice said. "That's a big move."

"She said just right here on Diamond," Eloise said, but Kelli knew it was way more than just the physical move.

"I'm just thinking about it," Kristen said. "I'm looking

at some fifty-five-plus communities. There are a couple of them that haven't started being built yet, and I put my name and email address on the information list. That's all."

When Kristen said *that's all*, that really was all she was going to say.

Kelli realized in that moment that it was her turn to share. Her mouth felt like she'd stuffed it full of paper towels and then tried to speak.

"You're up, Kel," AJ said, and Robin still held the phone, this time facing Kelli.

AJ knew this news already, and Kelli seized onto that fact. She drew in a deep breath and blew it out. "I own my childhood home on Bell Island," she said. "I bought the house on Seabreeze Shore."

Robin looked like she'd been struck by a brick. Alice gaped at her. Laurel didn't seem all that confused, but Eloise blinked rapidly. "The one with the stained glass windows?"

"Yes," Kelli said. "My father made those windows."

"You don't even like your father," Robin said.

"I've owned it for a while," Kelli said, ignoring her. "I own the Glassworks too. I own it all." She didn't need to explain how she'd gotten the Glassworks, as they all knew that story. She couldn't what the house and her father's old glass-blowing shop meant to her. The nostalgia and the thought of someone else using them just couldn't be adequately put into words. She felt the same way about the house and the Glassworks as she did about love—she couldn't define them, but she knew she wanted them.

"Wow, Kelli," Eloise said. "I knew about the Glassworks obviously, but the house too."

"I think it's great," Alice said, smiling at Kelli. "Good for you, Kelli. Are you and Parker going to live in the house?"

"Yes, eventually," Kelli said, scanning the table again. "I'd love some help, if anyone has a few spare hours on the weekends. That's when I go."

"I can help," Eloise said instantly. "Just tell me what you need me to do, and I'll do my best to figure it out."

"Yes," Robin said. "Duke has some tools."

"Aaron has a lot of power tools too," Eloise said.

"I can come on Saturday," Alice said.

"Yes," Kelli said, smiling at her. "Then I can hear all about the hot date."

Alice laughed, and Kelli did too. That broke the shock and silence at the table, and thankfully, their meals arrived a moment later. A few minutes passed while everyone got situated, and Kelli disconnected the video call with Kristen and AJ.

She then met Eloise's eyes, and a quiet understanding passed between them. Kelli put her hand on Eloise's knee under the table, a silent thank you for volunteering to come help with the house on Seabreeze Shore.

CHAPTER TEN

"I'm sure you want to know about Doctor Carmen," Laurel said, watching Alice place a plate of peanut butter chocolate chip cookies on the edge of the desk. Laurel's favorite—and Alice knew that. "I mean, I know you don't bake for just any reason."

Alice trilled out a laugh that made Laurel smile. She leaned forward and picked up two cookies, as she'd run four miles with Robin that morning. Laurel found that if she wanted to be friends with people, she had to make an effort to spend time with them. Eloise's text flashed through her mind, and Laurel still didn't know what to do about it.

"Actually," Alice said, forgoing the cookies and reaching for a sugarless mint instead. "I want to hear about you and Paul."

There was him too, but Laurel didn't know what to say about him.

"Doctor Carmen was the doctor who took care of me when I came into the hospital when I finally got brave enough to leave my abusive ex." The words flowed from Laurel easily, and she wondered if that meant she'd taken another step forward in her healing. "He was kind. He listened. He got all the right people there to help." Laurel took a bite of her first cookie and cocked her head to the side, the rest of the explanation unspoken.

"I didn't think anything of you and Doctor Carmen," Alice said.

"Sure you did," Laurel said around her mouthful of cookie. She finished chewing and swallowed. "I have eyes, Alice. Everyone did, especially Eloise."

Alice's lawyer eyes sharpened, and she placed both hands on the desk in front her, her elbows also touching the tabletop. "What does that mean?"

Laurel took another bite of her cookie. She didn't know what to say. Alice and Eloise were very close; Laurel knew that. Out of all of them, Alice seemed to be the one they all came to. Perhaps Robin.

No, they flock to Eloise.

Or Kristen.

As Laurel warred with herself, she realized that the six of them were so intertwined, it was impossible to find a crack or weakness among them.

THE HOUSE ON SEABREEZE SHORE 97

She took her phone out of her pocket, jostling her police tools to do it. Her waist sometimes ached in the evenings after a long day of carrying radios, handcuffs, weapons, and more. She needed a massage something terrible, and a brand-new idea burst into her head.

"Tell me what Eloise means," she said, sliding the phone across Alice's desk. The other woman caught the phone, then cocked one eyebrow at Laurel.

"Eloise?"

"Just read it."

Alice picked up the device and tapped a few times.

Laurel finished her cookie, Eloise's message burned into her retinas.

I would love to get to know you better. Perhaps we could go to a movie or get lunch, just the two of us.

She'd added a smiley face to the end of the message, but Laurel had been confused from the very first word.

"She wants to get to know you better," Alice said. "I've noticed you two aren't as chatty and friendly as you are with the rest of us." She handed the phone back, and Laurel frowned at it.

"She thinks Aaron was cheating on her with me," Laurel said.

Alice opened her mouth, stopped, and shut it.

"She didn't tell you."

"She hasn't mentioned that."

"It's not true," Laurel said. "Everything blew up

months ago. She's nice enough that she lets me come around with you guys." Misery streamed through Laurel. She really liked these women, and she didn't want any fences between them. "I was thinking I should suggest a massage," she said, watching Alice for a reaction. "Heaven knows I need one desperately, and Eloise said she has a new masseuse at the inn. Would she like that?"

She could've asked Aaron too, but Laurel had kept everything strait-laced and professional between them since the blow-up in the grocery store parking lot. That night, she'd taken a huge leap forward in her relationship with Paul, and she supposed she should thank Aaron and Eloise for that.

"I think she'd love that," Alice said. "That's a great idea."

Laurel nodded and started tapping. "She's probably going nuts that I've not answered for over a day." She quickly sent the message and looked at Alice again. "I just don't want to mess anything up with her."

"You won't," Alice said. "Laurel, you're a great person. I hate that someone did something to tell you otherwise." She reached for a cookie and they both took a bite of theirs. "Also, here's a tip with Eloise." Alice smiled and brushed crumbs from her fingers. "Give her the space to talk. She has something to say, but she won't say it if there's too much other chatter."

"Okay," Laurel said. She was a master of awkward silences, and she could give Eloise the space she needed.

Her phone buzzed, and she smiled at the text. "A massage is perfect!" she read from the phone. "Let me check the schedule here at the inn, and we'll see if we can make something work with everything else we have going on."

"That's going to be the tricky part," Alice said. "She's getting married in three weeks."

"It's almost the summer season," Laurel said. "The first one for Cliffside."

"And you work the weirdest hours." Alice smiled at Laurel, and she was so glad she'd dropped by. "How was the sailing earlier this week?"

"I didn't die," Laurel said with a grin. "Boat didn't sink." Surprisingly. She'd had a great time with Paul, because Laurel loved being with Paul. She loved his laugh and the way he took care of her. He loved the shape of his mouth against hers and the way he looked in a pair of swimming trunks. She loved the way his mind worked and the way he took time to get his thoughts lined up before he spoke.

"I think I'm in love with him," she whispered, but before Alice could say anything, the front door burst open.

"Mom!" Charlie yelled, and he didn't sound happy.

As Alice's office sat right off the front of the house, the angry teenager appeared in the doorway only a moment later. He wore fury on his face and it came storming off of him in such a way that Laurel stood automatically, tensed and ready for a fight.

"What in the world were you thinking?" he demanded. "Academic Olympiad? I'm not doing that. It's for losers and geeks." His chest heaved, and he waved a paper. "She said all I have to do is have you sign this, and I'm good. All ready to meet with them after school on Mondays and Wednesdays."

Laurel had never heard the level of sarcasm Charlie used in his voice. Alice came to stand next to her, and she glanced at her friend. "I was going to talk to you about it," Alice said.

"Don't worry, Mom," Ginny said as she entered the house too. She closed the door behind her, disappearing for a moment to do it. "Sariah Page talked to him, and you should've seen him turn red." She giggled like this was something funny, but Laurel still had her hand on her weapon.

"Shut up," Charlie growled, glaring with the force of gravity as his twin walked down the hall and into the kitchen.

"I should go," Laurel said when Charlie looked back at Alice. "You're okay here?"

"I'm the one who's not okay," Charlie said, deflating right before their eyes. He tossed the paper to the ground, but it just floated lazily for a few seconds, finally hitting the floor. "Academic Olympiad?" He sounded like he couldn't believe his mother would sell his soul to the devil or that she'd done something equally as horrible.

"Take the cookies," Alice murmured. "Wait. I might

need them for Charlie." She picked up the plate, gave Laurel a quick hug, and walked her to the door.

"You've got this," Laurel said to her as she left, and as she walked away from Alice's house, she sent up a silent prayer for her.

CHAPTER ELEVEN

"He said you scored the highest out of the whole school," Alice said, standing very still in the kitchen. The cookies hadn't worked. Charlie had just said she'd made them for Laurel, which was true. Alice could make about five things, and cookies was probably the top item she could do.

"They need you," she tried next.

Charlie just glared at her on his next turn. He paced in the small space between the kitchen and the living room, where Alice had put a small dining room table. She'd seen Frank pace like this many times. Her ex-husband manifested himself in Charlie from time to time, and since Charlie had grown out his hair slightly, he looked less like his father.

As time went on though, and he became more of a man with every passing day, the more he reminded Alice of Frank. He was extremely good-looking, and Alice knew about all the girls that called, texted, and put notes in his locker. Ginny had said they'd even found a package of Oreos—Charlie's favorite cookie—and a note in the car one day after school.

Charlie had been loyal to Mandie Grover, Robin's daughter, and Alice had talked herself blue in the face about sexting, sending and getting nude pictures, and other things she'd never thought she'd need to discuss.

Thankfully, she'd included Ginny in the conversation, because life for teens wasn't the same as when Alice had grown up. Ginny was a beautiful girl, and she'd been asked on several dates recently. Prom sat right around the corner, and Ginny had had a date for a month now. They were going to pick up the dress tomorrow.

She thought of Arthur, and she swallowed. Today's conversation wasn't anywhere near over.

"I'm not doing it," Charlie growled. "I don't care if they need me. I don't owe them anything."

"Sariah is cute," Ginny said, reentering the conversation at the worst time possible.

"Why aren't you at work?" Alice asked the pair of them.

"He was spitting mad, Mom," Ginny said. "You should've seen him. It was like he was a volcano about to explode. Poor Sariah." She shook her head.

"Poor Sariah?" Charlie asked, finally pausing long

enough to look at his sister. He pushed his dark hair off his forehead. "What does that mean? I was nice to her."

"You were not," Ginny said, looking at him with wide eyes. "She stopped you in the hall, and you were sort of short with her. Said you had to get to work."

"I did," he said. "*We* did."

"So she mentioned the Academic Olympiad thing, and you were like, 'this is why you stopped me?'" Ginny looked from Charlie to Alice and back to her brother. "You legit rolled your eyes. She looked at me, concerned, and I said something like, 'don't worry. He's usually pretty nice.' Then she said something about the Sadie's beach party, and if you wanted to go with her. You got all red in the face, growled something about 'never doing the stupid Academic Olympiad because it's for losers,' and stomped away. I had to apologize for you and run to catch up with you."

Ginny looked at Alice, who didn't know what to think. Of course Charlie would think other girls were pretty. He'd like other girls. Still, her heart beat strangely in her chest, because she did not want him to hurt Robin's daughter.

"He would've left me, Mom. He wasn't even thinking clearly."

"And you drove home in this angry state?" Alice demanded, folding her arms.

"He let me drive," Ginny said quickly, swallowing as she looked at her brother.

"You're lying," Alice said. She used to let such things slide, but no more. "Charlie drove home, and you're covering for him, because we've talked about making sure you're safe to drive."

"Fine," Ginny bit out. "He drove home. He was beyond reason, just like he is now." She jumped to her feet. "And he made me miss my shift at the ice cream shop. You owe me fifty bucks, *Einstein*." She swatted his chest, and he had the decency to flinch away from her, an apologetic look on his face. She stormed out of the main rooms of the house, leaving Alice with Charlie.

Alice's mind screamed at her to get Ginny back in there. She needed to tell the twins about her date with their school counselor, and she wasn't going to do it twice.

Instead, she looked at Charlie, all of her maternal instincts firing. "Do *you* want to tell me what happened?"

"Do you want to tell me why you're going out with my counselor and haven't told me?" Charlie's shoulders raised, and all that furious fire returned to his eyes.

Alice swallowed, because no, she didn't want to detail that. She studied the plate of peanut butter cookies. "Mister Rice called me in to his office this week."

"That doesn't mean you leave with a date, Mom."

"I went to see him," Alice said, ignoring the ice in her son's tone. "Because he said he had something to discuss with me about you. It was your perfect score on the organic chemistry test. He was quite proud of you, and he gave me the same permission form you left on the floor in my office." She sighed and rounded the counter. She pulled out the chair at the head of the table and sank into it.

Pushing both hands through her hair, she said, "I didn't know how to bring it up with you. I didn't think you'd be interested, but he said he'd have the captain talk to you. Then he asked me to dinner." Alice looked up at Charlie. "Robin was calling, so I ran away without answering him, but I did like him Charlie, okay?"

She tapped the table at the seat next to her. "Come sit down."

He'd stopped pacing, and Charlie was far more mature than Alice had given him credit for. "Did he tell you?"

Charlie took the seat, looking more and more miserable by the moment. "He pulled me out of fifth period. I thought I was in trouble."

Alice smiled at him, and she'd take her assumptions about the same thing to the grave. "What did he say?"

"He asked if I'd given any thought to the Academic Olympiad. I told him I didn't know what he was talking about. He seemed confused, and he said he'd talk to Sariah and then you, tonight, on your date." He switched his eyes from the table to hers, glaring at her. "The bell rang, and off he went, leaving me there like a fish with my mouth open. So then I was late, trying to go the wrong way back into the classroom to get my crap, and then stupid Sariah Page stopped me in the hall."

"She's not stupid," Alice said automatically. "Charlie, Ginny made it sound like she asked you to the beach party."

Charlie sighed and reached up and pushed his hand through his hair again. "I think she did? She said something about it, and then asked if I wanted to go with her."

"Do you?"

Charlie's face grew pink again, turning red right up by his eyes. "I mean, she's really pretty. She's super smart... Oh, my *God*. I called her a loser."

Alice didn't smile or placate him. His eyes rounded, and he fumbled for his phone. "What should I do?"

"Do you have her number?"

"No," he said. "Maybe I can get it from someone."

"Charlie," Alice said slowly. "What about Mandie?"

All of the franticness in his fingers and face evaporated. He met Alice's eyes, his searching hers for an answer.

"You like her too, right?"

He nodded, still silent.

"You can't turn into your father here," Alice said quietly. "You talk to me. Tell me what you're thinking, so I can help you treat these girls the right way."

Charlie looked so lost for a moment, and Alice just wanted to gather him into her arms and tell him everything would be okay. She'd done that when he was a little boy and had skinned his knees. A warm washcloth, a

Band-Aid, and chocolate pudding fixed him. Now, Alice had no idea what to do to help him.

"Are you upset about me going out with Arthur?"

"I mean, I guess not," he said. "He's just some guy."

"He doesn't have a daughter at the school you dislike?" Alice's eyebrows went up, and Charlie opened his mouth to speak.

He promptly closed it again as understanding washed across his face. "Mom," he said. "Did you break up with Will because we don't like Tori?" He sounded stunned, aghast even.

Alice couldn't vocalize the truth, so she just shrugged.

"Mom," Charlie said again. "You're kidding."

"You two are more important to me than a man," she said quietly.

"Ginny," Charlie called, getting to his feet. "Get back in here." He walked to the opening of the hallway and yelled her name again before turning back to Alice. "Family meeting. I'm calling it."

"What?" Ginny demanded from down the hall.

"Family meeting," Charlie said, returning to his seat. He sat back down as Ginny appeared in the kitchen.

"Family meeting? Why?" She headed for the chair on the opposite end of the table, as there were just the three of them. The fourth chair Alice had stored in the carport, because it stuck out too far in the walkway, and they didn't need it.

"Charlie called it," Alice said, keeping her eyes down.

She hated that she was here alone, doing this. At the same time, she'd been so much happier since leaving Frank. She'd been alone in the Hamptons too. Here, now, at least she got to make her own decisions and she didn't have to bend to anyone's will.

"Mom's got a date with a new man tonight," Charlie said. "It's Mister Rice, our guidance counselor."

Ginny's eyes landed on Alice, the weight of them boring into the top of her forehead. "Mom?"

"It's true," Alice said. She repeated the story of how she'd met him and why, finally looking back to Charlie. "So Charlie needs to decide a couple of things. First, how to apologize to Sariah Page. Second, if he's going to do the Academic Olympiad or not. Third, how he feels about Mandie."

"What?" Ginny asked. "You love Mandie. Like, *love* her. Isn't that what you said the other day?"

"Shut *up*, Ginny," Charlie growled.

Alice's heart thumped painfully in her chest. "You're a junior in high school," she said calmly. "Do you think you're in love with her?"

"I don't know," Charlie mumbled.

"Have you slept with her?"

"Mom," Charlie said.

"Have you?"

Charlie turned a shade of red Alice couldn't even identify. She had nothing to say either, because she could not fathom a conversation with Robin about this.

"We've talked about it," he admitted. "We haven't done it."

"Dear Lord," Alice said, pressing one hand to her heart. She knew teenagers had sex; she simply didn't want to think about *her* teenagers doing that. "Have you told her you love her?"

He shook his head, his teeth pressing together to make his jaw jut out.

"You have a lot of other girls interested in you," Alice said, glancing at Ginny. "Maybe, I don't know. Maybe you should take some time to see if you like one of them more than Mandie."

"You think she was just convenient for me," Charlie said. "Because she was around when we first moved here."

"I didn't say anything like that," Alice said. "Nor do I think that." The thought had occurred to her, but Charlie and Mandie got along so well. If they hadn't, he wouldn't have perpetuated the relationship past the beginning of the school year, months ago.

"Arthur Rice," Ginny said, looking at her phone. "He is handsome, Mom."

"She broke up with Will because of us," Charlie said.

"What?" Ginny asked, gasping. "Mom, that can't be true. You said he wasn't what you wanted." She looked frantically at Charlie. "That's what she said."

"Mom's a liar sometimes too," Charlie said with a smile.

Alice couldn't help the grin that popped onto her face.

She even laughed lightly. "You two didn't like Tori. How am I supposed to make a family out of that?" She shook her head, because there was more than just how the twins felt about another student. "Will's a great guy. I liked kissing him, about like I did in high school."

"He's really rich," Ginny said.

"There was that too," Alice said. "But honey, I married a rich man once, and it was a horrible thing." She shook her head. "I didn't like how Tori dictated everything. She wants to move to Hawaii. Okay, great. She doesn't like it there. Sure, come home." She shook her head again. "I want a man who's more of a man than that. So no, he wasn't what I wanted."

"We still had something to do with it," Charlie said.

"A little," Alice said. "But that's life, guys. Everyone has a little bit of influence on you and what you decide to do. I hope I'm right there next time Charlie thinks about sleeping with his girlfriend, especially when another girl has just asked him to a Sadie's beach party, and he actually thinks he might want to go with her."

"I never said I wanted to go with her."

"But you do," Alice and Ginny said at the same time.

Charlie rolled his eyes. "I'm so glad I have you two to tell me how I feel and what I think." He got to his feet. "The family meeting is over."

"Wait," Alice said. "Are you two okay with me going out with Arthur? He's coming to pick me up at six-thirty. You can meet him."

"I met him in the hallway today," Charlie said over his shoulder. "I'm good. I also have to go to work. I said I'd be late, not that I wasn't coming at all."

"Okay," Alice said, hastening to follow him. She caught him right at the front door, pressing her palm against it so he couldn't walk out yet. "Will you hug me, please?"

He turned into her and hugged her, and Alice gripped him with as much strength as she could muster "I love you, Charlie," she whispered. "You are such a beautiful boy. You're becoming an amazing man, and I'm doing my best to help you get there."

"I know that, Mom," he whispered back. "I love you too." He squeezed her extra-tight, released her, and opened the front door. "Be home by six-thirty."

Alice watched him walk down the few steps to the front sidewalk and head to the car he and Ginny shared. Sighing, she closed the door and turned to find Ginny standing on the cusp of the great room at the back of the house, watching her.

"Your dress will be ready Saturday at eleven," Alice said, smiling at her. She approached her and drew her into a hug too. "I love you, Ginny. Thank you for being my friend and my daughter. Thanks for helping with Charlie." She pulled away and brushed Ginny's hair off her forehead. "He wants to apologize to Sariah for calling her a loser. Could you get her number for him?"

"Okay," Ginny said. "Why was he so gruff at school?"

"He'd just found out I was going out with Arthur tonight," Alice said, retracing her steps to the office, where she bent to pick up the permission form for the Academic Olympiad. "Sariah stopped him only a few minutes later, and he was in a rush and already upset."

Ginny nodded, her eyes round. "He's scary like Dad when he's mad."

"I know." Alice gave her a small smile. "Next time, try to get him to let you drive. I'll tell him again that he can't drive when he's upset like that."

"I didn't mean to lie."

"You love him," Alice said, passing her. "You two are very protective of each other."

"He really does have a lot of girls who like him," Ginny said, taking a seat at the counter and reaching for a cookie. "I have a few talk to me about him every single week."

Alice didn't know what to do with that information. She hung the permission form on the fridge with a magnet and sighed as she faced Ginny.

"Sariah is super pretty," Ginny said, munching away happily now. "They'd look so good together, and I know he likes her."

"How do they know each other?" Alice asked, picking up a cookie she hoped she could finish.

"She's in his history class," Ginny said. "They've been in the same one all year."

"She must know he's dating Mandie."

"I guess." Ginny shrugged and finished her afternoon snack. "I'm still going to make him pay me for my shift."

"I got it," Alice said, pulling open the silverware drawer. She lifted out the utensil organizer and plucked three twenties from the assorted bills there. "There you go, sweetie."

"How long has there been money in that drawer?" Ginny demanded, and Alice could only laugh.

WHEN THE DOORBELL RANG AT SIX-THIRTY, ALICE STOOD IN the kitchen, fully dressed, make-upped, and ready to go. Both Ginny and Charlie scrambled to their feet, and they dang near knocked one another down in their attempt to be the first one down the hall toward the front door.

"Ginny," Charlie protested when she beat him. "You said I could open the door."

"You can," Ginny said.

Alice stayed right where she was, marveling at how much she loved her children. She walked to the corner of the wall, staying out of sight of the front door.

"Good evening," Arthur said, his deep voice sending rumbles through Alice's chest from twenty feet away. "How are you two tonight?"

"Good," Charlie said. "Where are you taking my mom tonight?"

"It better be somewhere nice," Ginny said.

"Yeah, because she can't cook," Charlie added. "And we just eat a lot of fast food."

Arthur started to chuckle, and Alice grinned, because she'd had the same reaction. "Thanks a lot, Charlie," she muttered under her breath. "Selling me out for not being able to cook."

A lot of men wanted a woman who could, and Alice's pulse picked up the pace. She straightened her shoulders and flipped her hair over her ear. Ginny said, "She likes expensive things," and Alice nearly tripped over her own feet in her haste to interrupt this conversation. Letting them get the door for her was a huge mistake. Huge.

"Hello, Arthur," she said, interjecting herself right over the top of Charlie's statement. "Thanks, you two." She joined the twins on the threshold of the house. "We need to have a little chat about how to answer a door, don't we?" She laughed, and thankfully Arthur did too. He offered her his arm, and Alice plucked her purse from the hook right beside the door.

"I'll be home by ten," she said. "Wait up, and I'll tell you all about it." She grinned at the twins. "Pizza money is on the counter." She hooked her hand through Arthur's and stepped onto the front porch with him. It was a tiny space, so she continued down to the sidewalk alone, taking his arm again when he joined her.

"They'll watch until they can't see your car," she said in a quiet voice. "And clearly, we don't get fast food every night. Fridays are pizza. I do like expensive things, but I've sold most of them to be here with my twins and free from my ex-husband."

They arrived at his SUV, where Alice finally dared to look into Arthur's dark eyes. She wanted to trace her hand down the side of his face and feel that beard. "If any of this is a deal-breaker for you, you can simply drive me to a friend's house, and I'll hang out there until ten."

"Absolutely not," he said, his smile instant and his eyes twinkling with mischief and desire. "I want every minute with you from now until ten, and then I want to see you again tomorrow."

Alice ducked her head and smiled, let him open the door for her, and waved to the twins after he'd gotten behind the wheel and started to back out.

Here we go, she thought. *Another first date.*

CHAPTER TWELVE

E loise sat at the tiny table in her tiny house, the morning light barely peeking through the windows all along the top of the wall. She loved her tiny house, and she was planning to leave it here on her mom's property once she and Aaron got married.

That way, she could have somewhere to come rest during the day if she needed to. Billie and Grace liked to come here in the afternoons and raid Eloise's cupboards for snacks. She had a television mounted to the wall, and she let them watch cooking shows and the Disney channel if she had a lot of work to do at the inn.

Grace liked to come with her and help in guest rooms or check people off the list as they arrived. Billie would, but it wasn't her favorite thing to do. Eloise had been tempting her with the promise of the swimming pool, which Eloise would be opening in a couple of months.

Billie said she'd come help with that, handing out towels or picking them up. Eloise suspected the teen would likely lay in the sun and try to improve her tan, and Eloise likely wouldn't say anything about it.

This afternoon, though, the girls weren't riding the ferry to Sanctuary Island, where the tiny house and the inn was. Eloise already had a package of sandpaper, Aaron's sander, and his electric drill in her car. She had an appointment for a car spot on the ferry in a couple of hours, and she was meeting Kelli at the house on Seabreeze Shore on Bell Island at ten.

She picked up her phone as it brightened again. Laurel had texted: *I don't work Thursdays very often, and I have the next two off. I'm almost always off on Sunday, and every other Tuesday.*

She'd suggested a massage as something she and Eloise could do together. Eloise had finally been able to breathe when she'd texted yesterday afternoon, and they'd been trying to align their schedules since.

I had this Tuesday off, Laurel said. *So earliest would be Sunday, then next Thursday.*

Got it, Eloise said, and she tapped to get over to her calendar for the inn. She had just hired a woman named Linda Melrose to be the on-site masseuse at The Cliffside Inn. She could really only do four or five people per day, and Eloise could bring in a second masseuse for couples' sessions.

"Let me check with her," she muttered to herself.

She did want to spend some time with Laurel, and if they scheduled something for Sunday, Eloise wouldn't have to move too many clients. A lot of people left on Sundays and the inn was fairly quiet, especially in the off-season. She had no idea what the summer would look like, as the inn had only been open for three months now.

They'd been good months, though, and Eloise could pay the two full-time people she'd hired. With herself, the three of them ran the inn from check-out to check-in, housekeeping, and getting the food out every morning and evening.

Rhonda Wilkinson lived on-site and acted as the chef and manager whenever Eloise wasn't around. Eloise ran check-out in the mornings, checked on guests staying through the day, made sure their Five Island Cove activities board was updated, and did various administrative tasks in a small office off the kitchen.

She'd hired a woman on an hourly basis to come in and clean the rooms in the inn, and she arrived at ten o'clock. Eloise and Rhonda helped with the housekeeping, and then Fiona stayed to do check-in until five.

Eloise stayed another hour, and by six, Rhonda helped any other guests when they arrived, served dinner, and managed things until the next morning. Eloise had put her on a salary, and it was the best money she'd spent so far.

Could you and Marc do a couples' massage on Sunday? she

sent to Linda, and the woman answered instantly with, *Yes.*

Eloise started negotiating the time, then texting Laurel to work it all out. Before she knew it, her alarm went off, and she looked up in surprise. The whole reason she set alarms was to make sure she stopped whatever she was doing and moved on to the next thing. Right now, that was getting ready and getting down to the ferry for her scheduled appointment that would take her to Bell Island.

Eloise sent one final text to Laurel—*can't wait*—and got up to get dressed. She really couldn't wait until their afternoon together in a couple of days, because Eloise needed to make sure everything was perfect before the wedding, and that included her friendship with Laurel.

———

"OH, WOW," KELLI SAID WHEN SHE CAME DOWN THE STEPS. Eloise had texted when she'd pulled into the driveway of the house, and Kelli had said she could park all the way in the carport. She'd parked, gotten out, and set the tools on the hood before Kelli appeared.

"I'm not even sure I can use one of these."

"Aaron showed me a video," Eloise said with a smile. "He says they're really easy, like running a vacuum cleaner, especially for what you're doing." She'd shown Aaron all of Kelli's texts, and he'd said all they needed was a sander, a specific type of sandpaper, and some stain.

Kelli had picked out the color she wanted to redo the floors in the house, and she and Eloise were going to see if they could knock out the entire bottom floor. She'd already called a disposal company to come get the stain-soaked rags, as they could apparently combust if left in a trash can. Kelli didn't have services at the house right now anyway.

Eloise gazed at the house, and it seemed to have weathered the years pretty well. Kelli had told her that there had been no major structural damage she needed to address, and she wasn't terribly worried about the house cosmetically either. She did want to provide a nice place for herself and Parker, and she'd been saving for the bigger furniture pieces.

"Come in," Kelli said, reaching for the sander and hefting it into her arms. Eloise grabbed the box of sandpaper from the backseat and followed her. "I know you guys didn't come here very often."

She closed the door behind Eloise. "I'm not doing much with the kitchen. If there's leftover stain, I might do the cabinets in here."

Eloise took in the charming space. Kelli was right; they hadn't spent hardly any of their teenage years here. Kelli had been the shyest of the girls in the group, and her parents had gone through a divorce—and much more—just as they'd all started high school. Since AJ lived on Pearl, the two of them rode the ferry together, and AJ came here more than anyone else.

"You could paint them," Eloise said. "They're in great shape, and Aaron says they have sprayers now to make the job easy." There weren't very many cabinets either, so the job wouldn't take long.

"We'll see," Kelli said, and Eloise reminded herself that Kelli didn't have a lot of money. She wasn't sure what the alimony or child support situation was, but she knew Kelli didn't work full-time at the junior high for no reason. "I put all the stain in the supply closet there." She indicated a door on Eloise's right, and she opened it. Sure enough, a vacuum cleaner stood there, along with a broom, dustpan, mop, and several containers of stain.

"Oh, I like this color," Eloise said, turning to smile at Kelli. "Let's go see what the floor looks like." She had some experience fixing up an old building, as she'd taken The Cliffside Inn from disaster area to functional, and she followed Kelli past the empty dining room, the stairs that led to the second floor, and into the wide open area that took up the front of the house.

"I'm going to put the living room over there," Kelli said, indicating the space to the right. "This is my father's old office." She spoke of the space with reverence, and Eloise marveled at that.

To her knowledge, it had been Guy Watkins who'd ruined everything in Kelli's young life. He'd cheated constantly on her mother, trusted the wrong business partners and lost his livelihood, the Glassworks. With that gone, he couldn't support his family, and things had degenerated from there.

Paula Watkins had divorced him; they'd lost their house; Kelli had retreated ever further into herself. Even so, by their senior year, she was getting asked to attend parties and dances, while Eloise wasn't.

That was so long ago, she told herself. High school didn't matter. She wasn't the same person she'd been back then, and she had the entire world in front of her now. Feeling blessed and incredibly lucky, Eloise set the sandpaper on the wide windowsill and turned to take in the office.

"The stained glass in here is stunning," she said, watching the sunlight glint in different shades of pink, gold, blue, and sea foam green. She turned and looked up at the beautiful windows causing all the colors, and the last name WATKINS sat among the flowers and birds that had been pieced together by small pieces of colored glass.

"It's why I wanted the house," Kelli said. "My dad's windows are in every room here." She plugged in the sander and faced the room too. "Okay, so the tutorial I watched said you just need to check the boards. Sand them down, and apply the stain."

"Sounds easy enough," Eloise said, focusing on the project at hand.

"I did buy a few planks in case there's one that needs to be replaced."

"Smart." Eloise and Kelli had been brainstorming for a couple of days about where Eloise would be put to the best use, and Kelli had decided on this floor. She also wanted all the walls down here painted, and she wanted to hang window treatments over all the windows on the second floor.

"Did you decide on the type of blinds you want?" Eloise asked.

"I'm going to do the cheaper ones," Kelli said. "I don't need real wood slat blinds."

Eloise nodded and opened the box of sandpaper. She scanned the floor as she started toward Kelli and the sander. "The wood looks really good, Kel. You probably didn't need to buy any replacement planks."

"Yeah, there's one over there where you were just standing," she said. "My dad's desk used to be in front of that window, and you can tell where he stood, paced, or slid his chair all the time." She took the sandpaper from Eloise, but she then stepped back in the direction Eloise had just come from.

"AJ said to tell you thanks for the soup last night."

"I didn't take her soup," Eloise said, her throat narrowing.

"She knows you sent it from Monroe's." Kelli tossed her a smile and toed the ground. "Right here. Come see."

Eloise moved over to stand next to Kelli. "How are they doing? Really? Every time I text her or Kristen, I get some fake message back about how great everything is."

"You can't text AJ for news," Kelli said. "Not if you

want the truth. If you call, she can't hide her emotions." Kelli smiled at Eloise. "They're doing okay. I think Kristen is grateful she can help, and AJ hates being alone. So for right now, it's a win-win."

"Any other complications?" Eloise couldn't even imagine having a baby or being pregnant at her age, though she had been watching AJ's pregnancy with interest.

"Nope," Kelli said. "So of course, AJ thinks she doesn't need the full three weeks of bedrest." Kelli rolled her eyes and shook her head. "Jean is taking Parker for me on Sunday so I can go to brunch with Shad. I'm going to stop by the house after and see—really see—how they're doing."

"Good idea," Eloise said. "I can stop by other times too. I'm on Diamond almost every evening."

"I'm thrilled for you and Aaron," Kelli said, her voice quiet. "You two seem genuinely happy together."

"I've loved him for a long time," Eloise admitted, her voice equally as reverent. After drawing in a deep breath, she asked, "How are things with Shad? Does he treat you right?"

Kelli emitted a lovely sigh. "He's so wonderful," she said. "I keep looking for flaws, but I can't really find them."

Eloise grinned at her. "Good. You deserve a man who will take good care of you."

"Everything is just...harder than I thought it would be," Kelli said. "Even simple things like changing the light bulbs. I don't have anyone to hand me the new lightbulb, so I'm climbing up and down the ladder, doing it all myself. I have to do everything, and I mean, I sort of did with Julian too, but I don't know. This feels different. If I don't do something, there is literally no one who will."

"I know," Eloise said, as she'd lived that life for many years. "For me, it was a new door handle on my brownstone that broke me." She smiled a sad smile and kept looking out the window. "I couldn't screw on the left side of it, because the handle had to be pushed down at the same time you had to screw in. Well, there's just one of me. Two hands. I can't hold a screw, operate a screwdriver, and hold down the handle. I felt keenly in that moment that I was so alone, and wouldn't it be so nice to have a partner there to help me."

Kelli put her arm around Eloise's waist and leaned her head against Eloise's bicep. "That when I'm going to call you guys."

Eloise leaned her head against Kelli's. "Yes, you should. Or your new, handsome boyfriend."

"I'm not sure he's my boyfriend," Kelli said. "We haven't kissed or anything."

"Held hands?"

Kelli straightened and nodded. "Yes, a couple of times."

"Oh, you're smiling," Eloise teased. "I know that look." It had a feeling that accompanied, and the best way to describe it was *magic*.

Kelli inched away and toed the floor some more. "I think this board is a little loose."

Eloise copied her, pressing her foot against the floor. She kept testing it, not finding any boards that needed to be replaced until she came to the far corner of the room. It was the front corner, and it looked like there had been some water damage.

"Kel," she said. "Does the roof leak over here?" She peered up at the ceiling, but she couldn't she any obvious signs of water damage.

"I don't think so," Kelli said.

Eloise stomped on the floor again, and this time her foot went right through it. "Oof," she said, a cry following the grunt. She went all the way to her knee, fearing she'd stomp right through the whole foundation of the house.

Such a thing was silly, of course, but in the moment it took her to find solid footing, her mind panicked. So many scenarios ran through her mind, and none of them were good.

"Oops," she said. "I broke this. I didn't mean to."

"You didn't break it," Kelli said, approaching from behind Eloise. "It's an old house, and that plank just rotted. We'll pull it out and replace it." She put her hand in Eloise's and helped her stand. Eloise pulled her foot out of the hole she'd created, having to shimmy and shake it to get the sole of her shoe free.

As she did, she heard a distinct, metallic sound. She paused; Kelli had too. "Did you hear that?" Eloise asked.

"I heard it." Kelli dropped to her knees and began pulling at the soft wood. It came off easily, and she piled it against the wall on her side. "Oh, my goodness." She breathed, bending down.

"What?" Eloise asked, squatting to get a closer look.

Kelli had both hands down beneath the floor, and she'd widened the hole enough to bring up a silver, metal lockbox.

Flashbacks to the inn, when Eloise had found papers and folders hidden inside the walls, assaulted her. Panic filled her system, and her first thought was to get out of there. Grab the lockbox and run. She was heavier than Kelli, and she likely wouldn't make it far, but perhaps she could get to the back yard and toss the box off the cliff. It would go soaring out into the ocean, and Kelli wouldn't be able to examine what was inside.

Because, in Eloise's opinion and experience, nothing good could come from a hidden, metal box stored beneath the floor of a house for decades.

Nothing.

CHAPTER THIRTEEN

K elli stared at the box, her mind whirring. "There's no keys here," she said, pacing away from it. Eloise had taken the box from her and gone into the kitchen. It now sat on the counter where Eloise had left it, and they'd been through everything they could think of to get it open.

"I'm telling you, you don't want to see what's inside," Eloise said. She stood at the back window, staring outside, nearly lost inside her own head.

She had found papers at The Cliffside Inn, and they'd revealed her father to be a gambler and to be running a gentleman's club at the inn. Her brother likewise had been revealed to be a dangerous man, and they'd all had something to lose at his hand.

Kelli reasoned that her father's secrets had all come out already. What else could there possibly be?

An image of Zach Watkins's face flashed through her mind. *There could be other children*, she thought. Her half-siblings, technically, as her father had slept around constantly despite being married to her mother and having three daughters with her.

She didn't want to repeat the experience of finding out she had more people in her family than she'd known about. She didn't want to talk to her mom about that. She didn't want to open wounds that had been stitched shut.

Perhaps Eloise was right. Perhaps this box should stay shut.

The wind rattled the glass in the windows, breaking Eloise's concentration. She sighed and turned toward Kelli. "Let's just leave it here and get to work on the floors. You can deal with it later."

"Okay," Kelli agreed. She wouldn't have access to Eloise's help forever, and her heart stung as she remembered that only Eloise had volunteered to come help her with the house. When Eloise had needed help with the inn, everyone had dropped everything and shown up. Kelli herself had hauled out enough moldy insulation to last a lifetime.

Bitterness and jealousy accompanied her back to the office, where the hole in the corner mocked her. "I'm just going to call a locksmith real quick," she said, pausing to pull out her phone.

"Kelli," Eloise said.

"I know," she said, tapping to complete the search.

"You go ahead and get started with the sander in the opposite corner. I'll get that patched up over there and come help." She turned away from Eloise, because she didn't need any more free advice. It was her house, her life, and her desire to know what was in the lockbox.

"Yes, hello," she said when a woman answered. "I found my father's old lockbox, and I don't have a key. Is that something you could help me with?"

Five minutes later, she had an appointment with Ezra, who'd be there that afternoon to open the lockbox.

"Fifty bucks," she said to Eloise, a smile coming with the words. "Let's see what we can get done before he arrives."

KELLI WIPED HER HAIR BACK OFF HER FOREHEAD, THE sunlight, weak as it was, pouring through the front windows making the space stifling and hot. "He's here," she said, turning her head toward the sound of knocking on the front door.

Her heart started knocking against her ribcage. Her back twinged with pain as she twisted and then turned to go answer the door. She could put the fifty-dollar locksmith charge on her credit card and worry about it later.

"Hello," she said as she looked at the man on the stoop. The wind rushed into the house, and the clouds shifted to conceal the sun. "You must be Ezra."

"I am." The man carried about seventy extra pounds, sported a scraggly goatee, and had yellow teeth when he smiled.

Kelli was glad she wasn't there alone, but she smiled and stepped back to let him in. "It's back here in the kitchen. I can bring it out."

"Whatever's easiest," Ezra said. He wore a shirt with his name on it, all the letters inside the shape of a house key. Kelli turned and walked past the beautiful staircase that led up to the bedrooms. In the kitchen, she picked up the lockbox, feeling the weight of it. Her father had definitely put something in here, and then hidden it under the floorboards.

The only question in Kelli's mind was *why?*

Not only that, but why hadn't he told her mother about it?

"Right here." She handed the box to Ezra, who took it and looked at it with knowledge in his eyes that Kelli didn't have.

"This is no problem," he said, and he set the box back on the counter. He shifted his bag around to the front of his body and started pulling out tools. Only two minutes later, the box popped open.

Relief streamed through Kelli, followed immediately by anxiety. What would she find inside the box? Eloise had warned her not to open it, and perhaps she was right.

"Fifty dollars?" Kelli asked.

"Let's say twenty," he said. "That took two minutes, and you weren't very far out of my way."

Kelli nodded and dug into her pocket for a bill. She didn't need to put twenty dollars on her credit card. "Thank you," she said.

He wrote her a quick receipt, and she walked him to the front door. Eloise sat on the steps, her fingers flying across the screen as she texted, and Kelli said, "Thank you," again, closed the door, and leaned her back against it.

Eloise looked up as a sigh hissed from Kelli's mouth, and a small smile appeared on her mouth. "Ready?"

"Will you come open it with me?"

"Of course." Eloise stood, but neither of them stepped toward the kitchen.

Finally, Kelli took the first step, and she reached for Eloise's hand as she passed. "I'm scared," she said. "What if I find something terrible?"

"Then we'll deal with it," Eloise said. "We've dealt with so much this year. What could possibly be in that lockbox that we can't deal with?" She gave Kelli another smile, and Kelli took some strength from it.

They stopped in front of the box and Kelli reached for it with a slightly shaking hand. She lifted the lid, her eyes searching for understanding right away. She took in the two stacks of money, and the breath left her body.

"Oh, my word." She exhaled as she reached for the money. It was bundled with bands signaling how much was in each wrapped stack, and the top one was two thousand dollars' worth of twenty-dollar bills.

Beneath that sat another one. Then one of fifties, which was labeled with a five-thousand-dollar band. Her breath caught in her throat as she pulled out three of them. Her mind couldn't do the math after that, because the bottom two bundles of money were hundreds, bundled into ten-thousand-dollar stacks.

Tears filled her eyes, and she started to sob. "Has this been in the floor all these years?" She turned to Eloise, searching her face for the answer. "My mom could've kept the house with this. We wouldn't have had to move. My life could've been normal."

"Oh, honey." Eloise took the money from her and dropped it back into the lockbox. She took Kelli into a hug and held her while she cried.

Thankfully, Kelli had been crying a lot lately, and she could get it out quickly. She took a deep breath and released Eloise. "Thanks for being here."

"Of course." Eloise picked out all the money. She laid it all on the counter, from the largest denominations to the smallest, which was a stack of five-dollar bills totaling five hundred dollars. "Let's add it up."

She got out her phone and started typing. After a minute or two, she said, "Kelli, look." She tilted her phone toward Kelli, who looked at the screen, not comprehending the number sitting there.

77,500.

"Seventy-seven thousand dollars," Kelli said. She counted the bundles on the counter. Fourteen. She could tuck them into her oversized purse and walk away from the house as if nothing had changed.

So much had changed.

She could buy beds for the house. A couch and loveseat set. A dining room table. She wouldn't have to save every dollar she made, and she wouldn't have to wait until fall to move into the house.

"Is that all that's in here?" Kelli started to lean forward to see what else sat in the lockbox when the lights flickered. They went out completely in the next moment, and Kelli hadn't realized there was a storm coming that was strong enough to knock out the electricity.

She fumbled to get her phone out of her pocket. She flipped on the flashlight and shone it down into the box. The light glinted blindingly off the silver metal, and Kelli squinted against it.

"There's a folder here." She reached for it as she held the flashlight above the box, and she pulled it out. The bottom of the box reflected the light back to her, and she quickly moved it so she didn't go blind.

She set the folder on the countertop next to the bundle of fives. "There's not much in it." A thin folder with only a few pages couldn't be that damaging, could it?

Eloise put her arm around Kelli's waist and said, "Open it."

Kelli drew in a deep breath and flipped open the

folder. Once again, she found herself trying to absorb everything at once, but she was stopped short by the very top line.

THE LAST WILL AND TESTAMENT OF GUY DENNIS WATKINS.

"It's my father's will," she said. "It was never found."

"Well," Eloise said in a hushed voice. "It's been found."

CHAPTER FOURTEEN

Robin listened to Laurel and Alice chatter like chickens as the ferry cut through the water separating Diamond Island from Bell. She had a dozen emails to respond to, and just as many texts that needed answering.

The pressure she felt bearing down on her brought tears to her eyes. But Robin didn't have time for tears. She could respond to her brides, her suppliers, and the managers at venues, restaurants, and floral shops.

Once that was finished, Robin would be able to focus on her friends. Kelli needed help with the house, and while she hadn't texted anyone about coming to help, Robin had seen her face at lunch on Wednesday.

So Robin had texted around, and she'd managed to get everyone except AJ and Kristen on their way to Bell

Island that morning. Eloise had stayed the night with Kelli on Pearl Island, and Aaron would bring the girls to the house on Seabreeze Shore that evening.

Gratitude filled Robin for her friends and relationships. Duke had gone out fishing that morning, the same as always, and she missed him. She was tired of passing in the night, and she wondered if she should sail up to Alaska with him and then fly home.

You can't afford that, she thought. But she needed to do something to solidify her relationship with Duke. She needed to make sure her girls knew she had time for them, despite the events that dominated her life.

She wanted to be there for her friends, something that had always been extremely important to Robin.

"AJ says Matt is on his way to Rocky Ridge," Alice said, and Robin looked up from her emails. "He's gone with his father to look at the course there."

"I thought it was closed," Robin said. "Years ago."

"Only two or three," Alice said. "They're thinking of buying it."

"Kristen is there with her, right?" Robin asked.

"Yep, and Kristen says they're doing good."

"I haven't had time to go visit her," Robin said. "I feel bad."

"You've been busy," Laurel said. "Don't feel bad. I stopped by yesterday, because I was in the neighborhood. AJ looked good, and Kristen was in good spirits. Jean had brought over some iced banana bread, and they had their cards out on the table." She smiled, and Robin nodded.

She was planning to make orange rolls tomorrow morning. Her mother loved them, and she was coming to dinner at Robin's house. It wouldn't take much more time to make an extra pan and drop them by for AJ and Kristen. She missed hearing their voices and seeing their faces, and something squeezed in her chest that she knew wouldn't go away until she showed up with something delicious in her hands and could alleviate the pressure.

The ferry started to slow, and Robin returned her focus to her phone. A couple of more emails got answered before the boat docked and she tucked away her device. She was going to scrub, sand, and saw anything Kelli needed her to, and she wasn't going to think about work.

It was Saturday, for crying out loud, and Robin didn't have to work seven days a week.

The wind kicked up as she followed Alice off the ferry. The first drops of rain splattered the sidewalk as they left the station, and Laurel said, "Good thing Eloise is picking us up."

But Eloise's car wasn't waiting at the curb, and the three of them retreated to the RideShare line, because it was covered.

"I'll call her," Alice said after five minutes of standing in the wind and rain.

"She said she'd be here," Robin said. "She knew which ferry we were coming in on."

"El," Alice said. "We're here. Are you close?" She cocked her head and listened, and then said, "We can get a ride. Don't leave."

"She forgot," Laurel said, and Alice nodded.

She finished the call and said, "She and Kelli got busy looking at something online and they lost track of time."

"It's fine," Robin said, though the plan had been disrupted. She told herself this wasn't a wedding. It didn't matter if they didn't start on time. It didn't matter if the limousine wasn't waiting at the curb the moment they arrived.

She shivered and looked up at the weepy sky. "How long is this supposed to last?" Robin had lived in Five Island Cove for her entire life. She was used to rainy Aprils and stormy Septembers. The skies always cleared, and there was nowhere she'd rather be in June, July, and August than on the beach with the full sun overhead.

"I don't know," Alice said.

"Looks like a few days," Laurel said, lifting her phone a couple of inches. "It's supposed to get worse before it gets better."

"It's not a thunderstorm, right?" Robin asked. She'd had quite enough of severe storms to last the rest of her life.

"Doesn't seem to be," Laurel said. "But there's talk of a squall."

"That's just wind," Alice said.

"No," Robin argued. "It's more than wind. It's wind for a long time, and we always lose power in a squall."

"They're microbursts," Alice said. "They might be intense for a few minutes, but then they're over."

As if trying to prove a point, the wind gusted again, causing a couple of people to murmur as their umbrellas got tugged on and they had to steady themselves.

By the time Robin got in a car with Alice and Laurel, she was soaked to the bone and shivering. "I hope this house is warm," she said.

"It's not going to be," Laurel said. "Eloise said there's no services, and that means no heat."

"They had electricity yesterday," Robin said. "How is that possible if there's no heat? And if there's electricity, why can't she turn on the furnace?"

"I don't know," Laurel said. "That's all Eloise said."

"It'll be warmer than standing outside in the storm," Alice said, and she looked like a drowned rat too. Robin hadn't been able to get a word out of her regarding her date with Arthur, as Alice said she'd rather tell everyone at once than have to repeat it six times.

The short ride gave Robin very little rest, though she did close her eyes and let her body simply move with the car. She needed moments like that to find her center and remind herself that it was okay to stop and breathe.

The car slowed, and she opened her eyes. The house sat on her side of the car, and she easily peered through the water-spattered window at it.

It was just as she remembered, though she hadn't come here often as a youth. It rose for two formidable stories, the exterior a bright and airy white that could use some refreshment. The front porch held pillars that looked like they'd come from an expensive colosseum, and she remembered Kelli detailing how her father had made them.

He mostly worked with glass—and he'd been very talented in that regard—but he did other types of sculpture too.

The house had shiny, stained glass windows in the couple she could just make out under the eaves, as well as in one of the bedroom windows upstairs. All of the glass looked wavy, like it had been hand-poured by someone who wanted their touch in every aspect of the house.

She got out of the car while Alice paid the driver, and she looked at the carport where Eloise's SUV sat. Two vehicles could be parked there, but Kelli didn't have one. A lot of people in the cove didn't own cars, as the spots to ferry them from island to island were rare and expensive. There were large lots at the ferry station, and an extensive RideShare system that was almost as inexpensive as riding the bus.

"Come on," Alice said. "We can't stand here in the rain." She hurried toward the carport, with Laurel in pursuit.

Robin moved a little slower, though she hated the feel of rain on her skin. She was already wet, and it wasn't going to matter if she stayed outside for a few more seconds.

Alice beat her up the steps to open the door, and the scent of warm peaches mixed with something slightly chemical met Robin's nose. She ran her hands through her hair, slicking it back, before she followed Laurel into the house.

General exclamations of welcome met her ears as Robin peeled off her coat and hung it from the doorknob. Kelli had no coat rack or hooks by the back door, and as Robin took in the kitchen, she realized such a detail would definitely come later.

The kitchen held no furniture as it expanded from one side of the house to the other, leaving space for a dining room table and perhaps even a portable island. Robin's organizational and interior design mind started firing, and she had to rein it back so she wouldn't say something insensitive to Kelli.

For Robin knew exactly why the house felt empty and bare. It was. Kelli had no money to furnish it. She hadn't the means to buy bookshelves she'd fill with pictures of Parker and baseball trophies and little knickknacks that testified of her personality. She didn't have extra dollars to spend to put art on the walls, or even homey touches like a welcome sign or all the home décor Robin saw in the high-end homes.

She didn't live here either, and that also added to the somewhat abandoned feel the house gave off.

"What are you doing here?" Kelli asked, stepping into Robin. "You're all soaking wet."

"Eloise forgot to come get us."

"I did," she said, and she didn't sound too apologetic about it. She gave Robin a smile too. "I kept the secret. Surprise, Kelli. They all came to help."

Kelli's green eyes welled with tears, and she turned away from Robin as if she could hide her emotions from anyone. Her hands trembled in tandem with her chin as she said, "Thank you for coming. There's not a ton to do, actually. Eloise and I have been working on the floors in the main area out front. Other than that, it just needs to be cleaned from top to bottom and then furnished."

She reached for a lockbox Robin hadn't noticed. Her breath stuck in her lungs. Everything spun for a few moments.

"We found this under the floorboards," Kelli said, turning to face the group with the metal box in her hands. "I've been pinching pennies for months, trying to put together enough money to get things situated here so Parker and I can move in before school starts again in the fall."

"That's months from now," Alice said.

"Do you see any furniture here?" Kelli asked, her bright eyes turning sharp for a moment. "It was going to take that long to have the money I needed."

"Was?" Laurel asked, because she always heard the nuances in conversation that other people missed.

"This box had seventy-seven thousand dollars in it." She surveyed the group while the rest of them simply stood there and looked at her.

Finally, Alice asked, "Does it belong to you, though?"

"That's a good question," Eloise said, stepping to Kelli's side and linking her arm with Kelli's. "We don't know. Her father's lost, never-been-read will was at the bottom of the box."

"My goodness." Robin covered her mouth with one hand and stared at the pair of them. "What did it say?"

"We didn't read it," Eloise said. "Robin, you texted me just after we found it, and I managed to convince Kelli to wait until today, because I knew you'd be here."

"We should call AJ and Kristen," Kelli said. "They'll want to hear the news too."

"It probably all goes to your mom, right?" Laurel asked.

"I don't know," Kelli said. "They were divorced when my dad died. He'd left the house years before. Mom too. I'm not sure why he left this here."

"Perhaps he forgot about it," Alice said.

"When's the last time you forgot about seventy-seven thousand dollars?" Robin asked. She practically salivated for that kind of money, and she peered into the box as Kelli opened it. Stacks and stacks of bills sat there, along with a manila folder that couldn't be holding more than a few sheets of paper.

"My goodness," she said again.

Behind her the door flew open as the wind rushed in. All of the women standing in the kitchen cried out. A loud clap of thunder drowned out their voices, and the light in the room dimmed even more.

"Help me close this," Eloise yelled, the wind singing as it soared through the narrow doorway. She left Kelli's side to wrestle with the door, and Robin took a couple of quick steps to help her.

Her adrenaline pumping, she managed to help Eloise get the door closed. They locked it, tugging on the door-knob to make sure it was latched properly and wouldn't be opening again, and turned back to the group.

Tension rode in the air, and Kelli said, "Let's go into the living room."

Robin thought she might have some chairs there, but she was wrong. This room was just as bare and just as life-less as the one on the other side of the wall from it. The floor was a mixture of light and dark brown, and in her opinion, yes, it could be refinished.

"We've been working over here." Kelli set the box on the steps and moved into the other half of the house. It wasn't quite half, as the foyer bled into the living room on the right-hand side of the front door, and the wide, immaculate staircase went up. A bathroom sat behind and opposite the staircase, and Robin suspected that would be the safest place for them in this storm.

"Oh, this is beautiful, Kel." Alice stood in the wide

entrance to the room, and Robin joined her to take in the space.

The floor here had been refinished with a dark, beautiful stain that brought out the grain in the wood. It looked brand-new and perfect, like somewhere anyone would want to lay down a rug and put in a cozy chair so they could sit and read for a while. If the sun had been shining, the large stained glass window with Kelli's childhood surname in colored blocks would send blitzes of light everywhere.

"I only watched about six online videos," Kelli said, the pride in her voice not hard to find. "This is what we've been working on. It's almost done."

"Where did you find the box?" Laurel asked.

"Over in that corner." Kelli pointed to the front, far corner of the room, and Robin could admit she wanted to tiptoe over there and see if anything else had been left behind in the recesses of the house.

She didn't, because the stain here was obviously wet. The scent of it filled Robin's nose and throat to the point that she coughed.

"Let's maybe go upstairs," Kelli said. "There's an old bed in my room. Or we can go in the room underneath the stairs here. There's a bean bag there."

An old bed and a bean bag sounded like adequate furniture for fifteen-year-olds, but not five women in their mid-forties. Laurel was a decade younger than the rest of them, but Robin was sure she didn't lounge around on a bright pink bean bag in the evenings.

Kelli picked up the box and bypassed the stairs, opting for the small room under the stairs, just across from the bathroom. "AJ and I would sit in here and eat popcorn," she said, the nostalgia thick in her voice. "I have a few bags in the kitchen if anyone wants some."

Robin waited for everyone to file into the room, and then she squeezed herself in too. "I'll leave the door open," she said, noting that Alice and Eloise had taken up the spots on the bean bag. Laurel slid to the ground and sat with her knees up in front of her, her back pressed into the wall behind her. Kelli stood, and Robin decided she could probably get off the floor if she went down.

She sat with her back against the open door, letting some of the cooler air into this room. The hum of air blowing filled the house, and Robin asked, "Is the furnace on, Kel?"

"Yeah," she said. "We can adjust it if it gets too hot."

"So you must have electricity," she said, glancing toward Alice and then Laurel.

"I hooked up a construction-only line earlier this week," Kelli said. "So there was no connection fee, and it's a lower rate. It only comes on when I call them and tell them I'll be here."

"Oh, that's smart," Robin said, glad this place had heat. She wasn't sure how cold it could get inside an abandoned house, but she suspected pretty cold.

The roof overhead rattled with the wind, and Kelli bent to set the box on the floor. "Let's see what it says, should we?"

"Are you nervous?" Alice asked.

"A little," Kelli admitted.

"Wills have no expiration date," she said, adopting her lawyer voice. "Whatever that will says, it's a legal document."

Kelli hesitated. "So if it says he left the Glassworks and house to Zach...?"

Alice swallowed and shrugged. "I don't know, Kelli."

"Joel owned the Glassworks," she said. "Kristen signed the title over to me last year. How can someone else get it just because there's now a will?"

Alice glanced around the group. "That would be something we'd take to the probate judge," she said. "Your dad's lawyer didn't have a copy of the will?"

"My mother said he didn't have a will at all. There was no lawyer."

Alice frowned. "But the lawyer would know that wasn't true."

"Do you keep copies of wills for your clients?" Eloise asked.

"Yes," Alice said simply. "It's just a copy, but it's fully executed if signed by the person. I have them in my client files in my office."

"Do you know when each of your clients passes away?" Laurel asked, and Robin loved her keen mind.

"No," Alice admitted. "But in Five Island Cove? I would, yes." She looked at Kelli again. "I honestly don't know, Kelli. If there never was a will, and the house and the Glassworks passed back to the bank, that was likely done by a probate judge as well. They can't change that, but I don't know what they'll do with the emergence of a will."

Kelli nodded and swallowed. She bent again to open the box, and Robin suddenly didn't want her to. "Wait," she practically yelled.

Kelli flinched and pulled her hand away from the box. "What?"

"We should call AJ and Kristen," Robin said, standing up. Her heart beat furiously in her chest, and she simply needed another minute to get her head on straight and be ready for whatever that folder contained.

"I'll call them," she said, tapping on her phone. She dialed AJ, because she'd have better service and more minutes. The line rang. And rang. And rang.

Then it dropped.

"That's weird," Robin said. She dialed again, and this time, her phone struggled to even connect the call.

"I'll try Kristen," Alice said, and she got the line going and on speaker. It rang and rang, and then finally Kristen said, "Hello, dear."

Alice smiled and said, "Kelli found her father's will, and we're going to read it together. Can you get near to AJ so she can hear?"

"Give me a minute," Kristen said, and it sounded like scraping and then labored breathing over the line. "My goodness. His will? How is Kelli?"

"She's on speaker," Alice said, glancing at Kelli. "We're all on speaker—me, Eloise, Robin, Kelli, and Laurel."

"Just a minute," Kristen said. "Let me see if AJ is awake. The poor thing had a terrible night..."

CHAPTER FIFTEEN

AJ heard the bedroom door squeak open, but she didn't turn toward the sound. Perhaps Kristen would leave if AJ held very still. She gripped her phone in her hand, letting the edges of the plastic case lean into her skin.

She didn't care about the slight pain. She also didn't care about some defunct golf course out on Rocky Ridge. Matt and his father had gone out there this morning to look at it, as apparently the owner had finally listed it for sale.

Yancey Hymas, Matt's dad, had tried to buy it when it had first closed a little over three years ago now. The owner hadn't been interested.

AJ wasn't interested in her husband working out on the farthest north island. It was a long ferry ride. She didn't want to live out on the outer islands for the same reason. To top all of that, they'd gone today—the worst day this year to go.

The storm raged outside the window AJ could look out without moving a muscle. Rain had been pounding the glass for an hour, and she'd lost contact with Matt that long ago too.

"AJ, dear," Kristen said, coming round the end fo the bed.

She didn't have time to close her eyes and feign sleep, so she lifted her head. "Yeah?"

"It's Alice and the girls. They've found Kelli's father's will, and they thought we might like to hear it."

AJ pushed herself up, the struggle mighty. "Yes," she said, some measure of blood moving through her again. Excitement was what it was. Finally, something to care about and listen to that wasn't a television show, Kristen reading a fantasy novel to her, or worrying about Matt.

Kristen smiled and perched on the edge of the recliner that faced the bed on a diagonal. "We're here," she said, and she then peered at her phone and tapped a button.

"...in this box," Kelli said, and AJ hated missing out on things. Robin had texted to say they were all going to Bell that morning to help Kelli, and AJ had wanted nothing more than to go too. She'd wanted to attend lunch on Wednesday as well, but she hadn't been able to.

She told herself her baby was worth missing out on a few lunches. She told herself Kelli would understand that AJ couldn't be there, but that if she could, she would.

"It's just a few sheets," Kelli said. "It lists my mother as the beneficiary, as the financial power of attorney, and the healthcare power of attorney."

"So it's a pour over will," Alice said, her voice very authoritative. "Those are the best kind, because all the assets just pour from one spouse to the other. So your mother owns all of this."

AJ frowned, but she didn't say anything. Kelli had bought the house from the bank, not from her mom. What would Paula Watkins do if she learned she owned the house and the Glassworks again? Could the bank really take anything back from Kelli without reimbursing her?

"Are the titles there?" Kristen asked.

"I have the titles," Kelli said. "From when I bought the house and when you signed over the Glassworks."

No one said anything, and since AJ dealt with professional athletes and their personal drama, she had no idea what Kelli could expect.

"Sabrina, Heather, and I are listed," she said. "Equal shares—one-third each."

"So that's one-third of the seventy-seven thousand," Robin said. "Or maybe one-fourth?"

"That money probably will go to your mom, Kelli," Alice said.

"Money?" AJ blurted out.

"She found seventy-seven thousand dollars in the box too," Laurel said.

"Holy sharks," AJ said.

"I already know my mom doesn't want the house," Kelli said. She might be able to hide her distress from the others, but AJ could hear it even over the phone. "Surely Sabrina and Heather don't either."

Again, silence draped the conversation until AJ wanted to yell at someone to say something, preferably Alice. Shouldn't a lawyer know what to do in this situation?

AJ reminded herself that her patience was very thin right now, and she didn't need to say anything. She leaned back against her pillows and took a long, deep breath. The stress wasn't good for the baby either, and the only reason AJ had made it through the past five days of lying around, watching TV, and pecking out a single article was because of the life inside her.

She would do anything to protect it, and that included only walking from the couch to the bathroom, or the couch to her bed, or the bed to the shower.

"I think," Alice finally said. "You'll need to show them this will. Explain how you purchased the house and Glassworks, when you did that, and for how much. See what everyone says."

AJ waited for Kelli to say something, but she suspected she wouldn't. AJ knew, though, that Kelli's sisters had wanted to leave the cove as much as or more than Kelli had. Neither of them had returned to the cove for longer than absolutely necessary, and Kelli didn't speak to either of them very often.

"I don't really talk to my sisters," Kelli said.

"It might be time," Eloise said. "Just like it was time for all of us to reunite. To come home. Look at us now." She spoke in a kind voice, which made it impossible to be annoyed with her. Yet, AJ still very nearly rolled her eyes. Boy, she was in a bad mood today.

Just another reason to keep your mouth shut, she said. *Let Kelli reason it out. She doesn't need you to rescue her.*

So much of AJ's life had been dedicated to rescuing people. There had always been Kelli, who'd always been less sure of herself than AJ was. Always fading into the background while AJ enjoyed stepping forward into the spotlight. Always clamming up when AJ would speak out.

AJ had also protected her younger sister, Amelia. After their mother had left, AJ had felt the weight of being that protector keenly, and she'd done everything she could to make life easier for Amy.

They'd just started to rekindle their friendship, relationship, and sisterhood after the tsunami, and AJ looked at her own phone. Amy had texted ten minutes ago to say she couldn't get off Pearl Island that day due to the storms, and she'd bring AJ the freezer meals she'd made just as soon as she could.

She'd been looking forward to her sister's visit, and having it canceled had definitely added to her sour mood.

"That's all," Kelli said. "No big surprises. I guess I just have to figure out what to do with it now."

"I can help," Alice promised.

"I can't pay you, Alice." Kelli's regret laced through every letter.

"No need," Alice said. "You're like a sister to me, Kel. Let me help if I can."

AJ smiled at Kristen, who had likewise been mostly silent.

"There's something else here," Kelli said. "It looks like...a list of names?" Silence came through the line again, and AJ hated with the power of the sun that she wasn't there to see what was happening.

Crinkling paper came through the line before Alice started to read.

"Ellen Holt," she said, clear confusion in her voice. "Betsy Dinerstein. Sidney Tyler."

AJ sucked in a breath, and so did Alice, almost in tandem.

"Sidney Tyler?" Robin said. "Wasn't that Zach's mother?"

AJ started nodding, though she wasn't in the same room as anyone.

"Sidney Tyler was Guy's secretary," Kristen said, as if they all didn't know. A snowball effect had been happening since last summer when Zach Watkins, claiming to be Guy's son, had followed Kelli to the cove.

The man had turned out to be a fraud, not related to

Kelli in any way. He thought she'd have money from
Guy's estate, and he'd asked after everything in the
family, from the house to the art pieces to the
Glassworks.

"Minerva Thacker," Alice read. "Jill Bunton." She kept
reading, but none of the names tickled anything in
anyone's mind.

"Oh no," Alice moaned.

"What?" AJ demanded at the same time as several
other voices. No one said anything, and AJ found herself
straining toward Kristen's phone. She held it out, her arm
almost straight, her head bowed.

"AJ's name is on this list," Alice said, her voice nothing
but a haunted whisper.

"What?" AJ demanded. "My name? Why?"

"AvaJane Proctor," Alice read. "It's the third one from
the bottom."

"Why?" AJ asked. "What is that list?" Her heart
pounded in the back of her throat, and she searched every
memory she had for any with Guy Watkins in them.

Kelli's dad had always scared her a little bit, and that
was saying something. AJ hadn't been intimidated by
anyone.

"Why is your name on this list?" Kelli asked. "These
are women my dad had affairs with, AJ." She sounded
hysterical and near tears. In fact, in the next moment,
Kelli burst into tears. AJ let the horrible, gut-wrenching
sobs flow over her and through her and around her.

"Why is your name on this list?" Kelli asked, her voice louder.

"Kelli," Eloise said. "She didn't, I'm sure of it."

"Right," Robin said. "Come sit down."

"Why, AJ?" Kelli yelled, and AJ pressed her eyes closed. She'd slept with a lot of boys as a teenager. Some were college boys. As far as she knew, none of them had been married, and she'd never slept with anyone over the age of twenty-seven.

"I didn't," she said, her voice feeble and weak. No one would believe her if she spoke like that. She cleared her throat, and said, "I didn't, Kelli. I didn't sleep with your dad," as strongly as she could.

But the emergency siren drowned out her voice, cutting through the storm and the silence as effectively as it had been designed to do.

In the next moment, the call disconnected and the power went out.

AJ sat there in the black silence, gray light coming in weakly through the window behind Kristen. Somehow in the dim light, their eyes met.

"I didn't," AJ said again, but she couldn't even hear herself above the siren that told everyone to seek shelter and seek it quickly.

Kristen's phone buzzed with an earsplitting sound, and AJ's joined it half a second later. She startled and scrambled to find her phone so she could silence the emergency broadcast.

Squalls coming. Seek shelter on high ground as soon as possible. All ferries are grounded, but stations are open for sheltering.

She tapped okay so the message would stop screaming at her and so it wouldn't get sent again. The warning siren continued on and on, the wail of it like a slow, shrill banshee whose voice had started to lose its ability to strike fear in the hearts of all who heard it.

Not AJ's though. She was still plenty afraid of the warning siren, especially because Matt was now stuck out on Rocky Ridge without somewhere safe to stay.

CHAPTER SIXTEEN

"Don't cry, dear," Kristen said, stroking AJ's hair. She'd climbed into bed with the other woman a few minutes ago when AJ had burst into sobs. She leaned her back against Kristen's chest now, her crying subsiding for a moment before returning in earnest.

"Matt's out on Rocky Ridge," she said again, and it seemed to be the only thing AJ was capable of speaking right now.

"I know, shh." Kristen soothed her the best way she knew how. She wasn't used to hunkering down during a storm. After running the lighthouse for so many decades, Kristen was used to standing up in the control room on the top level, sending out messages and conveying information to the mayor, other major organizations like hospitals, the police station, and the National Weather Service.

She'd likely have seen the squalls before anyone else, and she'd have been the one to trigger the emergency siren in the first place.

Rueben had called, but Kristen had swiped the call away because she'd been on an important phone call with Alice. Finding Guy Watkins's will was a huge thing, and Kristen could only imagine what Kelli was going through.

She was probably sobbing much the same way AJ was, but for an entirely different reason. Kelli didn't deal well with the unknown. It scared her—heck, it scared most people—because she'd had to handle so much of it in her life.

Kristen peered over AJ's shoulder and body to her phone on the bed. It lay next to AJ's, and they were both dark. They had no service right now, and Kristen knew the electric company shut down power to the islands whenever there was the threat of heavy wind and rain— which was exactly what a squall was.

They usually only lasted for a few minutes, and Kristen whispered this to AJ as they waited.

The power didn't come back on after a few minutes, and ten more passed before Kristen admitted it. "Maybe it's a squall line," she said, really wishing she'd picked up Rueben's call. He'd know what was going on out there, and he'd have told her where to go to stay the safest.

AJ didn't respond, and Kristen began to pray silently that the squall line would be short. They could be hundreds of miles long, spanning fifteen or twenty miles, and they almost always formed out in the ocean. They could bring tornado-speed winds with them, and sometimes a squall transformed into a hurricane if the conditions were just right.

She'd lived through several squalls in her nearly eight decades in Five Island Cove. Once, Joel had been stranded out on the Claw, and he'd survived a line of squalls that had gone on for seventy-five minutes.

The battering of the rain against the large picture window in AJ's bedroom increased until Kristen's brain told her it wasn't just water anymore. "Hail," she said. "It's a real cold front coming in."

"There has to be a way to get in touch with Matt," AJ said, sitting up. "I'm not going to just sit here and do nothing." She started to scoot down the bed.

"You're not getting out of bed," Kristen said firmly. "You can do everything you need to do right there." She put her legs over the edge of the bed and stood. The light had faded to almost nothing, but Kristen had a flashlight on her phone. "Do you want your computer?"

"Yes," AJ said. "Perhaps I can get an email to him, or an IM."

"Okay, stay here. I'll be right back." Using the light on her phone, Kristen maneuvered around the shoes left on the bedroom floor and out into the living room. AJ spent all of her time in bed or on the couch, and Kristen brought her food, water, her computer, and anything else she needed.

They'd watched movies, played games, and sat for hours talking. The past few days had been a wonderful distraction for Kristen, and as she padded over to the desk where AJ normally researched and wrote her articles, she said, "Protect us, Lord. And protect all those women in the house on Seabreeze Shore."

CHAPTER SEVENTEEN

"The house sits up high enough to avoid any storm surging," Kelli said, reassuring herself as much as the others. "It's the hail that we need to watch out for."

"The lightning," Laurel murmured, her face eerily lit up from the cellphone flashlights. She had her head tipped back as she looked up at the ceiling, as if she could see the thunder and lightning through all the wood and plaster protecting them.

"Let's take stock," Robin said, sounding very much like one of Kelli's high school English teachers. Mrs. Robinson was forever telling her students to "check everything." Or to "make sure you have all the pieces. It's okay to double- and triple-check."

Robin was definitely a double- and triple-checker, which was what made her such a great mother, a fantastic wedding and event planner, and a great friend.

"Let's start with the obvious," she continued. "It's not going to stay warm in here forever." She surveyed the group, and she too looked other-worldly with all the blue and white light being thrown around the tiny room under the stairs.

Kelli's panic reared, but at least she'd stopped crying. She'd taken the single sheet of paper from Alice to see AJ's name for herself, and it had been blurry through the tears. She'd sobered up and calmed down, but she could still see her father's handwriting. All those names printed neatly in pencil...

What were they? Could they really be the women he'd had relationships with?

No, she told herself as Eloise said she had a blanket in her SUV. She never left home without it, in fact. As she got up to go retrieve the blanket, Kelli thought they could probably stay decently warm in this small room if they shut the door.

"There's blankets on the bed upstairs too," she said. "I'll go get them. If we stay in here, and close the door, and bundle up together with a couple of blankets we should be fine." She started to leave the closet too.

Alice groaned behind her, and Kelli turned back. "I'll check the food and water situation," she said. "Laurel? Want to come with me?"

"Sure." Laurel got to her feet easily, something Kelli would've been able to do a decade ago too. Now, though, she hadn't even dared to sit down on the floor. She'd taught classes back in Jersey, but that had stopped months ago. She had a mostly sedentary job now that somehow left her physically exhausted at the end of every day. She could barely feed herself and Parker before she parked herself in front of the TV or computer and stared at something mindlessly.

As she went upstairs, her lone phone the only thing providing any light, she thought about how she made lists and crossed things off too. An image of those fourteen stacks of money flowed through her head. The grayish-black letters on ivory paper, spelling out the will of her father from decades ago.

She needed to talk to her mother. She should call Sabrina and Heather too. They all needed to get on one call and start talking to one another again. Kelli was done not talking, and her frustration only inched up with every step she took toward the second floor.

The cellular network had gone out, and Robin had said they did it purposefully. Then they could turn it back on without any issues, after they'd inspected their equipment and made repairs. The electric and gas companies did the same thing on Five Island Cove, and Kelli had just forgotten.

She sighed as she reached the top of the stairs, her calves burning and her lungs working hard to get the oxygen they needed. She kept her cool as she collected the blanket and two pillows from the bed in her old bedroom.

She'd slept here once recently, when she'd run away from her friends. AJ had followed her, because AJ alone knew Kelli better, almost, than Kelli knew herself. She'd said, "I know the places you hide," and that was a true statement.

"Did I miss something?" Kelli asked, her unrest and doubts churning as they grew and grew. She loved AJ with her whole heart, and she could not imagine her very best friend in the whole world sleeping with her father.

But Sidney Tyler's name had been on the list. So had Ellen Holt's, and she used to live next door to Kelli's family, right there in the house Kelli would've been able to see had the squall not covered the cove in a black thunderstorm.

The rain changed to hail, and Kelli jumped away from the windows. Her father had poured them all, adding a blue tint to the ones on the second floor to make the light cooler. He'd done some stained glass windows, something he'd perfected over the course of his career. The windows in the kitchen sported a yellow-tinted glass to make everything bright and sunny.

The windows were one of the main reasons Kelli had wanted the house so badly. Her mind flashed to the memory from earlier this week of her mom standing at the fence, her new dog on a leash at her side.

She'd said she didn't want the house. Any profit she might have gotten from it would've gone to her, and she hadn't died yet. Sabrina and Heather shouldn't have any claim to it.

It was the cash that haunted Kelli. Her mother could use it as much as Kelli could. No, she hadn't lost almost everything she owned in the tsunami, but she didn't have much. She worked at a grocery store and managed to pay for the little two-bedroom house on the west side of Bell Island.

Truth be told, Kelli had no idea what seventy-seven thousand dollars would mean to her. She quickly split that money four ways—enough for her, her sisters, and her mother—and arrived at almost twenty grand. She could buy a couple of beds, a couch, and a dining set with that much. With much less than that.

Her hopes returning, Kelli left the room and pulled the door closed. The more protected she could keep the interior of the house, the better off they'd be. If the windows got smashed in, for example, with the door closed, the chill and the water would be contained in the bedroom.

"I can't afford new windows and to clean up water damage," she muttered as she headed for the steps. Worry consumed her again, and she nearly tripped over her own feet. She flung her hand out and grabbed onto the railing, feeling it give beneath her grip.

She cried out, stumbling down a couple of steps as she desperately tried to catch herself without breaking anything. Her tailbone hit the wood. Pain shot up her back and down her legs.

She came to a stop finally, breathing hard and holding onto a railing that swayed. It had stayed connected to the wall at the bottom of the steps but not the top.

She sat about halfway down, and Alice called, "Kelli?" Her footsteps approached, and she shone her light up the steps.

"I'm okay," Kelli said. "I just tripped over my own stupid feet." Her mind wouldn't stop circling, and that was the real problem.

"You sure?" Laurel went around Alice, as she seemed to have night vision too, and came up the steps. She put her hand on Kelli's knee from a few stairs down.

"Yes," Kelli said, accepting the other woman's helping hand to get back to her feet. She rubbed her lower back and tailbone. "I probably won't be able to walk in an hour, but right now, I'm fine." She put a smile on her face, though she didn't have a happy bone in her body right now.

One of her only condolences was that Parker was with her mother, and she knew no one would take better care of him than her.

She thought of Shad, who'd stopped by last night and met Eloise.

The squall wouldn't reach Jersey, and she wondered if Julian would worry about her or his son.

She pushed him out of her mind, because he didn't get

to take up space there anymore. He'd let her go so easily, and Kelli wanted people in her life who wouldn't. People like Alice, Robin, Eloise, and Laurel.

People like Kristen and AJ.

"What do you think about that list?" she asked Alice as she reached the foyer.

"I don't know," Alice said, almost under her breath. "What I do know is we have microwave popcorn we can't eat without a microwave. A box of six packages of fruit snacks. Eight protein shakes. Ten bottles of water, and we can probably get water out of the faucets too. And half a box of pizza."

"That's from last night," Kelli said. "Eloise suggested we bring it for lunch today."

"I think we'll survive for a while," Alice said. "Maybe."

Kelli had witnessed Alice practically waste away in front of her last summer. She hadn't been healthy, but she'd been alive.

"The squalls shouldn't last long," Kelli said.

"Right," Alice agreed.

"But what kind of damage will they do?" Laurel asked. "And how long will it take to restore services?" She blew out her breath, sounding plenty frustrated. "I wish I had my police radio. Those work no matter what."

Kelli wished that too. So many wishes ran through her mind that they tangled and knotted. She wished she'd never opened that lockbox. She wished she'd told her friends about the house sooner. She wished she had a better education, so she could provide a better life for her son.

She wished she hadn't let months go by without talking to her sisters or her mother.

She wished, she wished, she wished.

Dreams were made with wishes, but reality was built with action. Kelli knew this better than most, as she'd watched Julian dream big and then work harder than anyone else to achieve what he wanted.

She simply needed to do the same.

"All right," she said when she entered the room. Laurel came in behind her and closed the door. "We should be safe here, even if the windows blow in." She tossed the blanket on the bean bag, embarrassed by the dirty quality of all of it. She pushed away the inadequacy. No one could expect her to have guest beds made up and the cupboards full of food in a house she didn't live in.

"Let's do a Tell-All," Eloise said, eliciting several groans from the others. "What? I'll go first. I'm afraid my wedding dress makes me look like a great white elephant that's gone extinct."

A beat of silence followed, and then Kelli burst out laughing at the same time Robin did.

"Stop it," Eloise said. "I'm being serious."

"There's no such thing as white elephants," Laurel said with a grin. Alice chuckled too, and Robin still laughed full-out.

"Yes, there are," Eloise said. "I've seen myself in the mirror."

"Stop it," Alice said, but she still giggled. "I think there are white elephants. They're the albino breed, right?" She looked around the room for confirmation, but Kelli was still trying to get control of herself. She didn't know anyway.

Robin stepped over to Eloise and put her arm around her. "Eloise, I've seen you in that dress too, and you look *nothing* like a white elephant." She grinned at her and then around at everyone else. "Alice has stuff to tell us about her date with Arthur Rice."

"Ooh, yes," Laurel said, picking up the blanket and fluffing up the bean bag. She sat on one end of it, and added, "Sit right here, Eloise."

Eloise did, and Kelli noticed something pass between the two women. Laurel tucked a blanket around her right side and tossed the other half of it over Eloise.

Alice gave a happy little sigh and used the support of the wall to sit down on the ground. "You guys come sit here," she said. "I think this blanket is big enough for all of us."

Kelli wasn't particularly cold, but if the storm persisted for very long, she would be. She sat on Alice's right while Robin took the spot on her left. Eloise's blanket was bigger than the one Kelli had, and it did cover all three of them.

"Okay," Alice said. "Arthur Rice." Another soft sigh,

and Alice studied her hands in her lap. "We've actually been out twice now..."

"Twice?" Robin demanded. "Oh, you better start talking."

"And there better be a kiss," Eloise added.

"Eloise," Alice said in a shocked voice. "After two dates?"

"Start talking," Robin insisted. "Because yes, Alice, you've been known to kiss on the very *first* date before. Many times."

Kelli had never kissed on the first date, and she hadn't had many of those at all. She pictured Shad in her mind, and she tried to once again push against the feelings of inadequacy. If Alice had kissed Arthur already, then Kelli would be behind in her relationship.

She hated these feelings, and she managed to get some of them to submerge. *It's not a contest*, she told herself. *There's no race to win. You're not behind.*

She'd told herself those things before—when she'd been trying to get pregnant for the first time.

This time, she convinced herself of it, and she overcame the horrible urge to compare herself, her life, and her relationships with other women's.

It felt like her first major victory in a long time, and Kelli settled in to hear the story of Alice's *two* dates with Arthur Rice.

CHAPTER EIGHTEEN

A lice's mouth wouldn't stop. It matched her mind, which revolved around a couple of her elderly clients, AJ, Matt, Kristen, Arthur, and then the twins. Charlie and Ginny seemed to pop into her head every other second, but she kept babbling about her date with Arthur.

"He took me to Renegades," Alice said. "It's that brand-new place out on Pearl? Anyway, the ferry ride was lovely. It was a beautiful night. Seems strange that was only two nights ago." She could practically feel the breeze pushing against her face, playing with her eyelashes.

"He told me about his first wife. I'd already mentioned something about Frank, because the twins—my word, the twins." She gave a light laugh that very nearly turned into a sob. Robin reached over and took Alice's hand, and the silence stretched as she squeezed it.

"Charlie and Ginny answered the door, see. I figured Arthur is their counselor at school, and they should get to meet him."

"Wow," Eloise said. "Leading with two teenagers out of the gate. Risky."

"Or smart," Laurel said. "It's not like he didn't know you had kids."

"With teens, it's always risky," Alice said, smiling at Laurel. "Charlie told him I'm a terrible cook; Ginny led with how I like expensive things, and he better be taking me somewhere nice." She shook her head. "I swear, the conversation can go downhill in a matter of breaths."

"Was Renegades nice?" Robin asked. "Duke and I have talked about going."

"It was nice," Alice said. "But not expensive. They're up in that castle. You know, the one that's had about a dozen different owners, and no one ever has enough money to finish it?"

"The Blackburn Castle?" Kelli asked, drawing all eyes to her. Alice forced herself to slow down, though images of AJ and Kelli as teenagers flashed through her mind. The two of them had been inseparable, and she couldn't fathom AJ ever doing something to hurt Kelli. It had always been the opposite—AJ *protected* Kelli.

"Yes," Alice said. "I haven't heard it called that in a while."

"My sister dated the Blackburn boy," Kelli said quietly. "At least until they left the cove."

"It's nice enough now," Alice said. "They've got the restaurant open, at least. The grounds are still under construction, but I saw signs for their gardens, and they're going to have a dedicated wedding center."

"Wow," Robin said. "That's good to know. I might need to go out there and check them out. Add them to my list of venues."

"It's right up on top of that cliff," Alice said. "The views for a wedding would be stunning."

"Maybe you and Arthur will get married there."

Alice whipped her attention to Laurel, who wore a smile as she tilted her head back against the wall behind her. Her eyes were closed, and she didn't even crack them when Alice scoffed. "I don't think so."

"You don't think you'll ever get married again?" Kelli asked, throwing Alice's attention back across the small room.

"I... I've been on two dates with the man."

"So what?" Robin asked. "Some people fall in love at first sight."

"Just you and Duke," Alice threw back at her.

"No," Robin argued, though she had fallen for Duke in about as much time as it took for lightning to strike. She'd admitted it before, but Robin sometimes had a hard time sticking to her stories. She was as genuine as they came, and Alice did love her.

She squeezed her hand and gently said, "Yes. And look at the two of you now. Out of all of us, you're the couple that's endured. Blissfully in love and working hard to support each other."

Robin's eyes filled with tears, and Alice wished they could spend the afternoon beside the pool at her expansive beach house, the way they had last summer. Robin needed it, and so did Alice.

The problem was, neither of them truly had the money for such luxuries this year.

Robin looked away, and Alice took the opportunity to continue her story. "Arthur was kind and attentive. He's smart without being overbearing. He didn't lecture me the way Frank did sometimes." She shrugged. "We had a great dinner, and a nice walk along the beach. I showed him where Dad and Della live, and we came back on the last ferry leaving the Ridge."

"You summed up three hours in three sentences," Eloise said. "You're hiding something."

"No," Alice said. "We held hands on the beach, but every couple does that."

"The first time I met Aaron on the beach, his dog knocked me down." Eloise said, folding her arms. "Try again."

The group twittered at her comment, and Eloise's dark eyes sparkled with happiness. No, joy, which was so much higher than happiness.

"There were no dogs, thankfully," Alice said. "It was a nice night. They had some tiki torches lit, and it was fiery and romantic..."

"Is that where you kissed him?" Laurel asked.

"No," Alice said, nudging her with her elbow. "I didn't kiss him on the first date."

"Fast forward to date number two..." Robin prompted.

"We went out again last night," Alice said, the whole night playing right in front of her. "I may or may not have led with a kiss, so it was *almost* the first date."

"How do you lead a date with a kiss?" Kelli asked.

"My question too," Laurel said. "You fascinate me, Alice. I've never done what you're doing."

"No one does what Alice does," Robin said. "Don't even try."

Alice simply smiled at her friends, and while she didn't normally kiss and tell, they needed something to pass the time, and she didn't mind sharing the surface details. As long as they didn't ask how she was *feeling* about Arthur, or if he'd said anything to her about how he felt.

They'd only been out twice. She *wasn't* going to marry him any time soon.

"Weren't the twins there?" Eloise asked.

"Ginny was at work last night," Alice said. "She should be there right now too. Or she was probably on her way." She fell silent for a moment, and she actually picked up her phone to see if she had a signal. Nothing. "I'm worried about them."

"Charlie was on his way to my house," Robin said. "Jamie went out with Duke this morning."

"So they're alone." Alice met Robin's eye, so much teeming beneath her tongue. She hadn't told anyone about the conversation with Charlie and Ginny about the Academic Olympiad or Sariah Page.

"If they're together," Robin said, her eyes searching Alice's.

Did you know they've talked about having sex? The question poised on the end of her tongue, but she couldn't quite get it out. Alice should've called Robin first thing after Charlie had left for work on Thursday afternoon, and every moment that passed made telling her that much harder.

She was going to find out eventually, and then she'd be upset that Alice never said anything. At the same time, Alice felt like she owed it to Charlie to keep some things in confidence. She didn't have to call her BFF every time she heard some juicy piece of gossip. He was her son, and she wanted him to trust her.

Robin's fingers in Alice's grew tighter and tighter until Alice winced. "Sorry," Robin murmured. "Go on."

"Charlie had a date of his own," Alice said, the words grinding through her throat. "The academic team at school asked him to join them for this summer season, and he went to meet with a few of them, get to know them, that kind of thing."

Ginny had come through for her brother, and she'd gotten Sariah Page's phone number. Charlie had snatched it from her and hurried into his bedroom, despite Alice's protests that he not call girls in private.

He'd come out ten minutes later, proclaiming that he was going over to Sariah's that night, where she'd be hanging out with "a few people" from the Academic Olympiad, and he was going to learn more about the team and them.

"Did you apologize to her?" Ginny had asked.

"Yes," Charlie said. "Thanks for helping me with that." He'd grinned at his sister, and she'd grinned back at him, nodded, and that was that. Alice loved the close relationship they had, and she wished they could be together right now. They'd be so worried about each other.

"Arthur arrived to pick me up, and I invited him in. I showed him the house, which I'd actually taken an hour or two to clean up. He told me where he lives. And then, you know how the situation just opens up and the opportunity presents itself?" She glanced around, but Kelli and Laurel both looked so perplexed.

"We were leaving, and he reached past me to open the door, and we were so close, and our eyes met, and I just... kissed him." She'd actually grabbed onto his collar with both hands and drew his face toward hers. She'd paused then, because she wanted the man to take control in that situation.

Arthur had, no questions asked. No hesitation. He'd cradled Alice's face in one palm while sliding the other hand along her waist, bringing her closer. Her heart had felt close to bursting by the time he touched his lips to hers, and Alice hadn't been kissed that well in a long time.

"Is he a better kisser than Will?" Eloise asked.

"I'm not answering that," Alice said, a touch of sadness moving through her. "I do still miss Will."

"You do?" Robin asked, surprise in both words. "Why?"

"Memories," Alice said, shrugging. "Anyway, it was a nice kiss, and then we went to a cooking class at the all-inclusive."

"I didn't know you could do that if you weren't staying there," Kelli said.

"You can in the off-season," Alice said. "There's a locals special through Memorial Day. Half-price for local couples. The food was great, mostly because Arthur made most of it." She laughed again, chasing away some of her worries. They didn't go very far though, and the sound died in her throat quickly.

"Someone else tell me about their last date," Alice said. "Kelli? Let's hear about Shad."

Kelli's face grew warm, and she shook her head. "Pass."

"You can't pass," Alice said, glancing at Robin for corroboration.

"Yes, I can," Kelli said, lifting her chin. "We've been out a couple of times too. I haven't kissed him. I like him. He's nice. The end."

Awkwardness rode in the air, and Alice swallowed. She knew why. Kelli had just been thrown back in time three decades to when dating was a competition.

"I'm glad he's nice," Alice said with the warmest smile she could muster.

"I think I'm in love with Paul," Laurel said, and that elicited a gasp from Eloise and a squeal from Robin. Laurel herself grinned like a fool, and she opened her eyes to meet Alice's. "I haven't told him yet or anything."

"Do you think he'll say it back?" Alice asked.

Fear crossed Laurel's face, and she blinked rapidly. "I hadn't even thought of that." She switched her gaze to Robin, then Eloise. "What if he doesn't say it back?"

"Alice is always asking nonsensical questions," Eloise said, pinning Alice with a glare. "Of course he's going to say it back, Laurel. I've seen the way he looks at you, and he's been in love with you for a while."

Laurel nodded and swallowed. "Then what?"

"Then," Robin said gently. "You ask him what he's thinking about marriage, the future, a family. You see if you two are on the same page for all of those things. If you are, then maybe you'll start talking more about marriage." She smiled pleasantly, and Alice wished she had that much charm.

She had asked a harsh question, and she regretted it. Sometimes the lawyer inside her jumped the gun, and her mouth got ahead of her mind.

In the silence that ensued, they breathed together, and it was nice to not be alone.

Someone's phone chimed, and they all held very still for a moment. Then the chaos started.

CHAPTER NINETEEN

Eloise was the winner—she'd gotten the text. It was from Aaron, and he'd said he'd used the emergency network to get a message out to her.

"He says he and the girls are safe at the station. They're in the basement in the jail down there." She smiled just envisioning Billie and Grace at their father's side, behind bars. "He says nothing can touch them down there. All of his cops are in and safe. He wants to know if Laurel is here, because he's with Paul, and Paul would like to know."

Eloise looked up to Laurel, who gave her the thumbs-up.

"He says he can only use the emergency system for a brief time, but he wanted to update us. As far as he knows, AJ and Kristen are safe. He managed to radio out to Duke, who said he was on the way back in and that he should be back by now. He said he and Jamie would shelter in the docking building, which does have a cement foundation."

"Praise the Lord," Robin said, the air rushing out of her lungs afterward. "I'm so tired of weather causing problems."

"We've been hit hard this year," Kelli said, her voice low.

"It's only been three months since the tsunami," Robin said, wiping her eyes. "I can't afford another boat. I can't even afford the one we have now." She clapped her hand over her mouth and shook her head.

"It's okay, Robin," Alice said softly, and Robin turned into her and let Alice put her arm around her shoulders as she wept.

Eloise's heart bled for Robin and Duke. They were hit especially hard with the tsunami, with house damage as well as completely losing *The Lady Hawk*. As Duke's fishing boat paid their bills, it had been a devastating loss.

Still, Robin was not a quitter, and she and Duke had clawed their way back from the brink of bankruptcy. She'd taken on dozens of new clients, and they'd gotten a loan for a brand new boat, which they'd named *Soaring Eagle*.

He'd been back out on the waters within a couple of weeks, and they'd been scraping by the best they could every day since. Eloise knew the feeling; most days, she felt one breath away from closing The Cliffside Inn. It took a lot of work to keep running, and she didn't have the experience with financial documents, taxes, and payroll. She'd been taking an online business class, and she'd been talking to Earl Gilroy, the manager at a bed and breakfast on Diamond Island that was about the same size as Cliffside.

"I'll tell him Laurel is here with us and safe." She started typing, hoping she could get the message through in time. "Should I ask him about the kids? Mandie? Ginny? Charlie? Maybe he can find out where they are and if they're okay." She glanced at Robin and Alice, both of whom nodded.

Eloise added that to the text, and then added that she loved him and would he please keep those pretty girls safe until she could get to them all. She smiled as she sent the message, glad when it appeared to go through.

Aaron didn't answer right away, and no one spoke. She didn't want to miss a text if it came in, so she kept her phone out and in her lap. The air around her face had started to cool, and her stomach grumbled for something to eat.

She said nothing, though. Four pieces of pizza and a handful of protein shakes wouldn't take them very long to consume, and she wasn't going to be the first one to eat. She'd looked through the pictures of her dress fitting again that morning, and it was like she had new eyes to see with.

Suddenly, the dress wasn't right. She carried too much weight. The buttons on the back didn't lay flat.

Her anxiety over marrying such a perfect man had hit a new high, and the only reason Eloise hadn't called the whole wedding off was because she'd been with Kelli. She'd been near panic when she'd looked up and out Kelli's front window to find her standing with Shad Webb on their front porch patio area.

He'd grazed his hand along hers, and Kelli had bloomed to life. Eloise suspected that her ex-husband hadn't paid her much attention at all, and Shad was quite the opposite. Kelli was opposite of Alice too, in that she didn't want to spill all the details of the relationship.

Eloise had witnessed Shad giving Kelli a pretty bouquet of flowers, leaning in to whisper something in her ear, and sweeping a kiss along her temple. Then they'd separated, and he'd gone down the steps to a waiting car.

Kelli had watched him go, and when she'd returned to the house, she'd hummed as she put the flowers in a vase.

Where did you get those? Eloise had asked.

They grow around here, she'd said, her smile as warm as the summer sun.

Eloise hadn't called her on the little fib. Parker had come running downstairs, and they'd had to bustle out the door too, so they could drop him off at her mother's before coming here.

"Let's play a game," Robin said, and while Eloise groaned inwardly, she didn't have a better idea.

THE NEXT MORNING, ELOISE'S STOMACH DEMANDED FOOD. Now. Something. Anything. She came to full consciousness but kept her eyes closed. The others in the room breathed in and out steadily, as if still sleeping.

They'd exhausted their water bottles last night. The pizza was gone, as were the granola bars. Her mouth felt sticky and dry, and Eloise somehow needed to use the bathroom.

She managed to get up from the bean bag in the pitch blackness, and since her phone had long since died, she couldn't use the flashlight to navigate to the door. Thankfully, a sliver of light peeked out from underneath it, and her eyes had adjusted enough to the darkness to be able to avoid stepping on Laurel.

Laurel. They were supposed to get massages at The Cliffside Inn this afternoon, but Eloise didn't think that was going to happen. Yesterday had not gone according to anyone's plans, that was for sure.

Eloise opened the door, relieved at the rush of cooler air as it hit her in the face. She drew in a deep breath and steadied herself by holding onto the door with both hands. Her head swam, and she wasn't sure if that was from lack of food or lack of sleep or both.

Probably both.

"Leave that open, would you?" someone asked from behind her, and Eloise did what they said. She went across the hall to take care of her business, but they couldn't flush the toilet. They'd been moving water from the one upstairs to down here to do that over the course of the last eighteen hours, but Eloise didn't want to make the trek upstairs to see if there was more water in the tank in the master bedroom.

As she stood and studied herself in the mirror, a wisp of air started to blow across her feet. It took her sluggish mind a moment to figure out what that was, but then she said, "The furnace is on."

She watched her eyes widen in the mirror, realizing the nightlight in the bathroom was also illuminated. She yanked open the door and called, "The furnace is on. The power is on."

That got everyone moving, and Eloise wasn't the only one groaning and complaining about aches and pains. They were far too old to sleep on the floor or a bean bag, and Eloise counted herself lucky that she had a power cord for her phone in her car.

She grabbed her device and headed out to the carport. The sun had barely started to come up, and there were still plenty of clouds for it to fight through. "The squalls are gone," she called over her shoulder. "The sun is coming up."

After starting the car and plugging in her phone, Eloise waited the painful sixty seconds for it to restart. She had three messages from Aaron, and her heart warmed with every single one.

I love you too, baby. I can't wait to see you again. The girls are good, and they wish you were here with us too.

I'll see what I can find out about the teens. Might be hard, because I don't have their numbers. Can you send them to me?

"I didn't get that message," she murmured, and she wished she would have. Helplessness filled her, because she couldn't even imagine not knowing where her children were, and as the hours had run on, Robin and Alice had become more and more restless.

Robin had left the room for a little while, and Eloise had heard her pacing upstairs. She'd wanted to go check on her, but Alice had simply shook her head. Worry ate at Eloise even now, because she knew and loved her friends' children.

You must not be getting these, Aaron had said. *When you do, let Alice and Robin know that I went and got their kids. They're here at the station with me. It was hairy out there, but I found out Charlie was home alone, and Ginny had been driving to work when the sirens went off. She went to the nearest shelter, which was a bank. Mandie was home, and I rounded them all up and I've got them.*

"Thank you, Aaron," Eloise whispered, her love for him doubling and then tripling. In the next moment, she jumped from the car and raced inside. "Aaron has the kids," she said. "All of them. He went out into the storm and got them."

Alice met her in the kitchen. "My kids?" She had her phone in her hand, but the screen was still dark.

"Your kids," Eloise said. "He went to a bank and got Ginny, and your house and got Charlie. They're with him at the station."

Alice began to cry, and she grabbed Eloise in a tight hug. "Thank goodness," she said.

"Where's Robin?"

"She went upstairs again. I think she thinks she's going to get solar power or a blessing from heaven if she uses her phone up there."

Eloise smiled and dashed down the hall. "Robin, Mandie is safe with Aaron. He went to your house and got her."

Robin's footsteps ran toward the top of the stairs, where she stopped. "He did?"

"Yes. He sent the message last night, but I didn't get it until just now."

Robin thundered down the steps. "Can we call them?"

"Let's go out to my car," Eloise said. "My phone is charging out there."

All five of them piled into the car, and Eloise made the call to her fiancée.

"My love," Aaron said, plenty of relief in his voice. "There you are. I think the network stopped sending my messages."

"I got them this morning," Eloise said. "Everyone's in the car with me. The power's back, but I think we'll try to get back to Diamond as soon as we can."

"I'm going to my mother's," Kelli said.

"Right," Eloise said, flipping the car into reverse and backing out. She slammed on the brakes. "Oh, there's debris."

"Baby, be careful," Aaron said. "All five island were hit with hail, some as big as eggs."

"Eggs?" Alice repeated. "That's insane."

"Lots of reports of car damage," he said. "Downed trees. Power lines. If you have power, you're ahead of a lot of people."

"Maybe I should call my mother," Kelli said. "If we have power and she doesn't..."

"The kids are safe?" Robin asked. "Can we talk to them?"

"I put them to work," Aaron said. "I put everyone to work that I could." He chuckled. "But they're safe, Robin, yes. You should be proud of your daughter. She helped a little boy in the middle of the night who couldn't stop crying. She pulled him right onto her lap and sang to him until he fell asleep. He won't leave her side."

Robin wept again, and Eloise simply watched her. "Was he alone, Aaron?"

"He'd been riding his bike home when the storm hit," he said. "I don't know what it was like for you guys, but it came out of nowhere here. It had already started to become a lightning storm by the time the sirens went off."

"Did you call his mother?" Alice asked.

"Yep," Aaron said. "But he was stuck here. He's only seven. Mandie was real good with him."

"I'm glad," Robin said. "When you see her, tell her I'm on my way home."

"Be careful," Aaron said again. "It's nasty in places out there."

"I love you," Eloise said, and Aaron repeated it back to her before the call ended. "Okay, Kel," she said. "Let's call your mom."

LATER THAT DAY, ELOISE FINALLY PULLED UP TO AARON'S house. Ten hours had elapsed since she'd phoned him from the driveway of the house on Seabreeze Shore. It had taken that long to get down to Kelli's mother's house, where they picked up Paula, her boyfriend, Devon, and Parker.

Eloise had driven them all back to the house on Seabreeze Shore, only to have Paula refuse to go inside. In the end, the woman had no other choice, and Kelli had been in tears when Eloise and the others had piled into her car to go to the ferry station.

They'd waited for a ferry for five hours, as it seemed the entire population of Diamond Island had come to Bell the day before.

Eloise had never known such frustration and boredom at the same time. She didn't dare use her phone, and she'd had it on power-saving mode all day so she could message Aaron if necessary.

The man came out onto the front porch, and a sob worked its way up from Eloise's stomach. She hurried toward him at the same time he flew toward her, catching her in his arms and holding her against his strong chest.

"You made it," he whispered. "Shh, it's okay."

She cried for a moment, not even really sure why. She'd been separated from him during the tsunami, and she hadn't felt like this. They'd had radio contact though, and she'd had his girls with her.

"I love you," she murmured, tilting her head back so he'd kiss her. He did, and Eloise had never felt so safe and so loved.

"You okay?" he asked, lighting his lips down her neck. "Why are you crying?" He lifted his head and looked at her. Eloise should've felt foolish, but she didn't. It was perfectly okay for her to feel the way she did, and she didn't need to hide anything from Aaron.

"I'm just so relieved to be here," she said. "It's been such a long day."

"Come tell us about it," he said, taking her by the hand and leading her inside. "Move, Prince." The dog wouldn't move, and Aaron had to bully his way past the big, black animal. "He was left here alone, and he wasn't happy about it. Made a big mess too."

"Oh, you poor thing." Eloise stopped to pat Prince and give him some love. "Were you alone? Did you run out of food?"

"He pooped in the kitchen," Aaron said over his shoulder, and none too kindly. "The big brute."

"At least it was on the hard floor," Billie said, appearing at the end of the hallway.

Eloise grinned and flew toward her. "Hello, sweetie," she said, taking the teen into her arms. "Are you okay? Where did you sleep? What did your dad make you do today?"

"Oh, come on," Aaron said from the kitchen, his voice half full of teasing. "She got off easy. Her job was inside."

"He made me organize everyone and make sure anyone under the age of eighteen had a parent with ID check them out."

"That's the perfect job for you," Eloise said, stroking Billie's hair.

"That's what I said," Aaron called from the kitchen.

"I'm glad you're okay," Billie said, her eyes big and round. She hugged Eloise again, and Eloise held the girl tight. She tried to act brave and be brave, and she was. She did hard things. She watched out for Grace, and she was alert and attentive on the ferry when she rode alone. But she was still just a child, and all children needed love, safety, and security, and there simply hadn't been enough of that lately.

"I'm so glad you were with your father," Eloise said. "Can you imagine being in the bank like Ginny? Or riding your bike home like that little boy?"

"He was so scared," Billie whispered. "I was too, El. We

were down in the basement, and it was dark and stinky down there. There were all these bars and emergency lights, and it was creepy."

"Remember that next time your friends want to do something that could bust them," Aaron said, and Eloise turned toward him.

"Aaron," she said, chastising him. "Now's not the time."

He looked from her to Billie, and said, "Sorry, Bills. Come give me a hug." His daughter did what he asked, and he stroked her hair too, murmuring something about he was sorry she was scared. That taken care of, he looked at Eloise. "How are things on Bell?"

"We found Guy Watkins's will." She moved forward and took a seat at the table, where Aaron had been putting plates. "Where's Grace?"

"Napping," Aaron said. "Bills, go wake her, would you? It's getting late."

Billie went to do that, and Eloise stood up again. She interrupted Aaron on his way back into the kitchen, snaking her hand along his chest.

"What's that look for?" he asked, grinning at her. He put both hands on her waist and brought her body flush against his. "You're staying the night, right?" he whispered.

She nodded, because she couldn't even fathom trying to get from Diamond to Sanctuary tonight. "I called my mother. She's okay."

"Good," Aaron said, his eyes dancing with desire. "Guy Watkins's will?"

"It was hidden in the floorboards," Eloise said, quickly recounting how she'd found it and what was inside. "So there's a list of names, and we need to figure out how they're connected."

"Oh, and you want Detective Sherman on the job."

Eloise ran her fingers down the side of his face, then over his shoulder. "You are the best at digging into places no one knows about," she said.

"You didn't like it when I dug last time."

"No, I didn't like you meeting Laurel in the parking lot at the grocery store in the middle of the night." She let her hand trail down his side, getting closer and closer to his waist.

He seemed to know it, and he tensed. "I guess you two didn't get your massages today."

"We rescheduled for next week," she said. "So she needs next Sunday off too."

"You're really putting a kink in my scheduling," he whispered.

"Let's save the kink for somewhere else," she whispered back. "If I got you the names, could you see if someone can figure out how they're related?"

He pressed his mouth to hers, his demanding and promising her a good time later.

"She won't wake up, Dad," Billie said, and Aaron pulled away as quickly as the squalls had hit.

"Aaron," Eloise said as he walked toward the hallway.

"Yes," he said over his shoulder. "Get me the info, and I'll see what I can do."

Eloise smiled, met Billie's eye, and said, "Did you sleep at all last night?"

"A little," she said. "Grace cried quite a bit. Ginny finally got her to calm down enough to go to sleep, but she's real tired."

"All right," Aaron said a moment later, a sleepy Grace clinging to him and draped over his shoulder. "El's here, Gracie Lou. Don't you want to say hello?"

That got the little girl to perk up, and Aaron transferred the nine-year-old from his arms to Eloise's. She took Grace to the table and sat down, cradling the girl in her lap. "Tell me where you were when the sirens went off," she said.

"Dad had just brought us home from getting groceries," Grace said. "We hurried and put the stuff in the fridge and freezer, and then we ran to the station."

Eloise watched Aaron smile at his daughter. "Mm hm," she said. "Were you afraid?"

"A little," Grace said, looking up at Eloise. "Were you?"

"Yes," Eloise said truthfully, a smile quickly following. "But I was with my friends, and that made it better."

CHAPTER TWENTY

K elli stepped backward up the stairs, dragging the bean bag with her. Devon was on the other side, pushing. Together, they managed to get it into her old bedroom, where Devon had replaced the twin mattress too.

Her mother had remade the bed and pushed it against the wall. "It's like a couch," she said, and she and Parker climbed onto it. Devon sank onto the end, panting, and Kelli knew exactly how he felt.

She thought of the money in the lockbox under the kitchen sink and how she could buy a real couch with it. She didn't want to tell her mom about the box in front of Parker or Devon, and a naughty part of her mind wondered if she had to tell anyone at all.

Of course you do, she told herself as she surveyed the three of them.

Her mother had almost had a nervous breakdown walking into the house. She'd put up a fuss, nearly bursting into tears. In the end, Devon had been the one to get her to come inside, and Kelli had taken her through each of the rooms, showing her there was nothing left here.

She sat down in the bean bag. "Hopefully, the power won't be out for too much longer at your place," she said.

"Can we get something to eat?" Parker asked.

"I'll call for some of those breakfast burritos," she said, smiling at her son. "Does that sound good?"

"Yeah," he said, his smile wide and beautiful. He had her reddish hair, and she loved the way it haloed his head in light.

"Mom?" She lifted her phone, which had charged a little bit in the hour since the power had returned to the house here on Seabreeze Shore.

"I like the sausage gravy ones," she said, her eyes trained out the window. Kelli wasn't sure if she was looking at it or through it. A haunted quality rode her expression, and Kelli wished she could erase it.

None of them had much to talk about, and once Kelli had ordered four burritos, she looked at the three people on the bed. "I started seeing someone," she said.

Her mother tore her eyes from the window, her eyebrows high. "Who is it?"

"His name is Shad Webb," Kelli said, sliding her eyes

to Parker's. He should know who Shad was. "He lives next door to us in the twinhome."

"I've met him then," her mother said.

Kelly nodded. "When we moved in, yes. He's a little older than me, and we've been out a couple of times now."

Devon grinned at her, nodding. "That's great, Kelli."

Her mother didn't say so, and Parker said nothing.

Kelli looked at him, willing him to look at her. When he finally did, she asked, "Do you know what that means, bud? Seeing someone? Going out with them?"

"It means he's your boyfriend," Parker said.

Kelli smiled and gave a little shrug. "Kind of. I'm not sure if we're to that status yet. We're getting to know each other. See if we like each other."

"What about Dad?" Parker asked.

"Dad and I aren't together anymore," Kelli said, and it wasn't the first time she'd used those words. Her mother put her arm around Parker's shoulders and kissed the top of his head.

"He'll always be your dad," she told him. "But he doesn't live with your mom and you anymore, and he might be seeing someone else too. Your mom isn't doing anything wrong." Her mother's eyes told a different story, and Kelli wasn't sure how long she could last in this bedroom. It was bigger than the room under the stairs where she'd spent the night with her friends, but only marginally. Her mother's persona seemed to fill all the empty spaces, and Kelli could practically taste the displeasure on the air.

The doorbell rang, and she jumped to her feet. "I'll get the burritos."

"I'll come help." Her mother followed her downstairs, and Kelli already had the front door open to collect the food by the time she arrived. She turned and brushed by her, her heartbeat scampering through her veins.

"I have some paper plates," she said, heading for the kitchen. She set the white paper bag of food on the counter and bent to open the cupboard under the sink. She didn't keep the paper plates down there but pulled out the lockbox.

"Mom," she said, turning as her mother entered the room. "I found this under the floorboards."

Her mother stilled; her face went white in a single breath. "What is that?" She pressed one hand to her pulse as if preparing to recite the Pledge of Allegiance.

"It's a lockbox," Kelli said, watching her for every tiny movement. "You don't recognize it?"

"It's your dad's," she said. "He kept money in it when he'd travel for shows. We always had to have the highest security at the hotels. A safe in the room if he could get it." She sucked at the air, her eyes growing wider. "I haven't seen it in years and years."

"It has money in it," Kelli said. "And his will. He left everything to you. The house, all the assets, the—"

"I don't want it," her mom said before Kelli could even

finish her sentence. "You keep it. You found it in the house you legally bought. Keep it." She turned away, her movement sure and strong. Her stride told Kelli the conversation was over, but Kelli needed to know more.

"Mom," she said, putting the box down and following her. "Wait a second. Wait." She jogged after her and barely caught her before she started up the steps again. "Don't you even want to know how much there is? We could split it four ways. Me, you, Sabrina, and Heather. It's a lot of money."

Her mom brushed tears from her eyes. "No, dear, I don't want it." She drew in a breath and straightened her shoulders. "You have no idea what I've done to recover from what happened. I cannot take even one step backward. I won't. Taking your father's money would be a leap backward, and I can't do it."

"Is that why you couldn't come in the house?"

"The house is yours," she said quietly.

"It just has too many memories," Kelli said.

Her mom nodded. "Some good, but a lot of bad. I tried to protect you girls from so much. I really did. Lord knows I did." Tears slipped down her face, and Kelli grabbed onto her and hugged her.

"You did, Mom. I didn't even know things were bad until Dad lost the Glassworks."

"Good," her mom said, sobbing into her shoulder. "But they were bad long before that."

Kelli thought of the eleven names on the list in the folder. "What made them bad? Other women?"

"A lot of other women," her mother said. "My own inability to provide for three girls. My permissiveness. So much of my own weakness exists here. I hated who I was when I lived here, and I've worked and worked to become someone else."

"I'm sorry," Kelli said. "We can go. Let's just take our burritos to your house. It can't be that cold." The sunshine had arrived, albeit weakly. "I'll call a RideShare right now."

"What's your twinhome like?" her mom asked. "Maybe we could get a ferry there."

"Robin says the ferry station is jam-packed," Kelli said. "But I could call Shad and find out what things are like at the twinhome. I know that's where he was yesterday when everything went black."

Her mom nodded and turned back toward the kitchen. "I'll take up the food while you call." She stepped away and then turned back, her eyes searching and scared. "You don't think it's too soon to be dating, do you?"

Kelli didn't know what to say. A seed of doubt planted itself in her mind, but she uprooted it and threw it away. "He's so good to me already, Mom," she said quietly. "I'm not even sure I knew how that felt."

Her mom pressed her lips together and nodded. "Okay. I just worry about you."

"You don't need to worry about me," Kelli said. "I'm becoming someone different than I used to be too."

Her mom reached out and cradled her face in one hand. "You sure are, baby. You're so much stronger than me." With that, she dropped her hand and returned to the kitchen. Kelli watched from the doorway while she found the paper plates and picked up the bag of food. She didn't even look at the lockbox, but she did pause next to Kelli before she left the kitchen.

"Maybe ask your sisters if they want some of that money. You can split it between the three of you."

Kelli nodded. "You said it was from the sale of his pieces?"

"That's where he used to keep the money, yes," her mom said. "Until he'd put it in the bank. Your father was somewhat paranoid. He liked having cash in the house in case he needed it."

"Why would he need it?"

"If he saw something he wanted to buy, or he needed to purchase art supplies. That sort of thing."

"You didn't pay bills with cash though, right?"

"No." Mom frowned. "Nothing like that."

Kelli nodded, feeling so out of the loop when it came to what life had really been like for her mother when she'd been married to Kelli's father. She waited until her mom was all the way upstairs before she pulled out her phone and texted Sabrina and Heather on the same thread.

I bought the house on Seabreeze Shore years ago. I'm fixing it up for Parker and myself, and I found Dad's lockbox. It has money in it. Mom said we could split it three ways. Are you interested in that? She wasn't, and she indicated that I should ask you if you are. Let me know.

Before either of her sisters could respond, Kelli dialed Shad.

"Kelli," he said, his voice rich and pleasant. He sounded happy to hear from her, and warmth came through the line. "I was just going to call you."

"You were?" She sagged into the wall behind her, her smile stretching across her face. "Why?"

"I've got power here, and you do too. I can see your porch light burning. I had some stuff thawed from being out of the freezer for a while, so I started to put together a homemade spaghetti meat sauce. I was hoping I could feed you and Parker today."

"That sounds amazing," she said with a sigh. "Can I bring my mother and her boyfriend? They don't have power yet, and the house here has no food or furniture."

"I would love to meet your mother and her boyfriend."

"You met them when I moved in," Kelli reminded him.

A beat of silence passed. "I'm sure I don't remember because I was struck with your beauty."

Kelli burst out laughing. Shad chuckled too. "I've heard the ferries are a bit of a mess," he said. "Maybe coming from Bell to Pearl won't be bad."

"I guess we'll find out," Kelli said. "Plan on dinner for us though. I don't think we'll be there by lunchtime."

"The sauce needs hours of time anyway," he said, and Kelli smiled into her sparsely furnished kitchen. "See you then, sweetheart."

"Yeah," she said with a sigh. "See you then." The call ended, and she clutched the phone to her chest the way she had when Henry Myers had called and asked her to the prom. She hadn't been asked out much as a teenager, and he'd called because he lived on Sanctuary and his parents wouldn't let him come all the way to Bell to ask a girl on a date.

She pushed away from the wall as her phone chimed. After tucking the lockbox back underneath the sink, she checked her phone.

Both Heather and Sabrina had texted to say they'd be happy to split the money Kelli had found. They'd both expressed shock that she'd bought the house where they'd grown up. Kelli didn't know how to respond. She wasn't sure if the bridges between them were completely charred or not.

I did buy it, she said. *I'm refinishing the floors and I hope to have some furniture soon. Parker and I will live here, and I'm hoping to make better memories for ourselves. You should both come. Bring the kids. I'd love to see you, and Parker would love to know he has cousins. Or we'll come to you.*

With the money in the lockbox, she could afford an airplane ticket.

She sent the text and then quickly typed out another one. *I love you guys.*

She and her sisters didn't talk about serious things very often. Tears pressed behind her eyes when Heather's message came in. *I'd love to have you and Parker here whenever you can come.*

Kelli noted that Heather did not say she'd like to return to the cove. Her sister had disliked Five Island Cove more than Kelli, and she'd suffered more heartache here.

I'd love to come help you move in when you do, Sabrina said. *And mom says you're seeing someone new already?*

Kelli shook her head, though a smile touched her lips. *I'll tell you about him later. We were hit with squalls, and I've got a lot going on right now.*

She needed to go eat, and then they needed to get to the ferry station.

I love you both too, Heather said.

I love both of you, Sabrina said.

Kelli looked up, marveling at how healing those words could be. She tucked her phone away and headed for the stairs. "Guys," she called when she got to the top of them. "Let's hurry and eat. Shad has power and he's making us dinner."

"THIS LOOKS AMAZING, SHAD," PAULA WATKINS SAID, AND Kelli did her best to keep her smile to herself.

"Thank you," Shad said, his smile nothing but genuine. The introduction had gone well enough, and Shad had managed to squeeze five chairs around a table meant for two. He'd not only made the spaghetti meat sauce from scratch, but he'd put together a Caesar salad and garlic bread too.

"This reminds me of my mother's cooking," Devon said, grinning. "I feel like a little boy again."

Shad took Kelli's plate, his eyes lingering on hers for a moment. "Lots or a little?" he asked. He hadn't served anyone else except for Parker, and Kelli basked in the glow of his attention.

"A little," she said. "I ate that burrito this morning."

"Give her a lot," Kelli's mother said her face practically shining. She wasn't saying anything about how it was too soon for Kelli to be dating again now, she noticed. "She hasn't eaten since the burrito."

"I've had two pieces of garlic bread," she said, reaching for a third. She wasn't even sure who she was anymore. Going out with a handsome man. Bringing her family to his place to meet them. Not for the first time in the past year, she felt like she'd entered someone else's life, but this time, it was a paradise and not a wasteland.

Shad dished her a full plate of spaghetti and assured her she didn't have to eat it all. They all settled down to eat, and Kelli's mother asked, "What do you do for a living, Shad?"

"I work in the finance department for Five Island Cove," he said pleasantly.

"Shad is the financial director for the cove," Kelli said. "He's been doing that for a while now."

"Twenty-nine years," he said. "I'm actually toying with the idea of retirement."

"Oh really?" Kelli's mother's eyebrows shot toward the ceiling. "That's interesting."

Kelli twisted her fork in her spaghetti, watching her mother. By "interesting," she meant "how old are you?"

"Retirement is fantastic," Devon said, covering one of Paula's hands with one of his. They exchanged a glance. "I'm semi-retired."

"What does that mean?" Shad asked kindly. "Do you consult?"

"Actually, yes," Devon said. "I sold my business, but I still go in from time to time to help out, do trainings, that kind of thing."

"I see." Shad took a bite of his bread, his dark eyes harboring those secrets again. "I don't have anything official in the works. The ride from here to Diamond gets a little tiring is all."

"Do you guys ride the ferry together in the morning?" Paula asked, and Kelli felt like she was watching a ping-pong tournament. Her mother would fire a question across the net, and Shad would lob the answer back.

"Not usually," he said, locking eyes with Kelli. "But we should."

"How did you ask her out?"

"Mom," Kelli said. "You said this wouldn't be Twenty Questions, and newsflash, I'm forty-five years old." Almost forty-six.

"That reminds me," her mother said, and Kelli had literally never heard her talk this much before. "What kind of cake do you want for your birthday? I can put the order in at the grocery store, and we'll have a little family party at my house."

Kelli glanced at Parker. "What kind of cake should I get, bud?"

"Can they do that one with chocolate on the top and bottom?" Parker asked. "With that raspberry jelly in the middle."

Kelli grinned at him, though she didn't particularly like the gelled layer in between two chocolate sponges. "Sure," she said. "With the cream cheese frosting."

"I can order that," her mom said.

"When is your birthday?" Shad asked, and he tried to be oh-so-casual about it.

Kelli heard the interest, and she supposed she'd like him to know. The man brought her flowers just because; she couldn't wait to see what he'd do for her birthday. "It's the first week of May," she said. "May fourth."

"May the fourth be with you," he said, chuckling.

Kelli simply blinked at him, but Parker started laughing. "That's right, Mom. You have a Star Wars birthday."

"What?" Kelli asked.

"It's a saying from the movies," Shad explained. "You know, the Jedi all say, 'may the *force* be with you.' Well, the fans of the movies have deemed May fourth as Star Wars day. May the *fourth*."

"I see," Kelli said, smiling as she looked between Parker and Shad. "I didn't think you'd be a Star Wars fan."

"Oh, yeah," Shad said. "Grew up with that. We wanted the Millennial Falcon so bad. My brother was sure we were going to get it for Christmas."

She'd heard about his brother too, a man who lived on Sanctuary now, with his wife. They'd had three kids, but they were all grown and off on their own. Theodore was younger than Shad by a few years, and he'd had a sister who'd died when she was only six, due to complications from multiple sclerosis.

"I take it you didn't get it," Kelli said.

"No, ma'am," he said, laughing again. "My father was a fisherman, and we didn't have enough money. I didn't know it at the time though. My mother told me later, after my dad had passed away."

Kelli reached over and ran her fingertips up his arm. "I didn't know your dad had passed."

"Yes," he said, looking down at his plate for a moment. "About four years ago now. Mom's still doing great though."

"She's on Diamond?" Kelli asked, and she realized she'd taken the ping-pong paddle from her mother.

"Yes," Shad said.

Kelli fell silent, because she didn't want to throw another question at him. "Parker," he said. "Is your mother going to make you go to school tomorrow?"

Parker looked at her with hope in his eyes, but Kelli simply cocked one eyebrow. The boy's face fell, and Kelli laughed as she reached over and tousled his hair. "Yes," she said. "We have to go to school tomorrow. I took two days off last week."

"Yes, tell me about the house," Shad said, giving her an encouraging smile.

Kelli glanced at her mother, noting that she'd shut down completely. "Maybe later," she said. "Mom, why don't you tell Shad about the succulents you grow? He's got some in his garden he keeps killing."

Her face lit up, and that got her talking for the rest of the meal. Mom loved gardening, and she loved spending time tinkering in her yard. Shad had a bit of a green thumb to go with his skills in the kitchen. By the time her mom said they better get going so Parker could get to bed, Kelli was exhausted from all the talk of hedges and fertilizer, starts and potting soil.

"Take your time," Mom said. "We won't go back to Bell until morning." She closed the front door behind her, leaving Kelli alone with Shad—finally.

"They're nice people," he said, picking up the bowl with the leftover Caesar salad.

"They are," Kelli agreed. She picked up her plate and stacked it on top of Parker's. "Thanks for entertaining us and feeding us." She gathered all the plates and followed him the few steps into the kitchen.

His house was exactly like hers, just flipped. Her kitchen sink was on the right side of the house, and his on the left. They seemed to be directly across from one another, with only the wall in between them. Kelli supposed that made sense, because all of the plumbing and electrical could be run right down the middle, and both houses fed from it.

"I love spending time with you," he said as she joined him at the sink. "If you have to bring your family along, so be it." He gave her a glorious smile, and Kelli ducked her head as she thought about kissing him.

Alice had said the opportunity just presented itself, and she'd seized it. Kelli didn't even know what that opportunity looked like. Foolishness ran through her, because she should. She wasn't a sixteen-year-old flirting with her first boyfriend. She'd been out with other boys, and men, and she'd been married before.

"I'm going to go to the lighthouse after work tomorrow," she said. "Just to see Jean and see how they fared in the squall."

"Sounds like a good idea," he said, swirling a blue sponge around in the pot that had once held the spaghetti sauce. She worked in the other sink, rinsing the dishes and setting them in the dishwasher.

It was a perfectly suburban life, one she'd thought she'd had. But Julian never touched a dish, and he didn't even know how to make boxed macaroni and cheese for his own son. She'd never dreamed that a man would cook her dinner and then clean up afterward too. She felt like Belle from Beauty and the Beast, except she was no beauty, and Shad was anything but beastly.

"If I can get her to take Parker," Kelli said. "Would you want to go to dinner?"

"Absolutely." He abandoned the pot for a moment. "What happened at the house, Kel?

"What do you mean?"

"I mean you shut down really fast when I asked about it, and your mom looked like I'd carved out her heart."

"That house doesn't have fond memories for her," Kelli said, focusing on the way the water went round and round on the plate, taking the deep red sauce with it. "She didn't know I'd bought it either, until a couple of days ago. Last week. I've owned it for years, and I never told her."

"I see," he said.

"I'm sure you don't," she said with a sigh. "My family life is very complex, Shad. It would take hours to explain it all."

"Good things we have hours," he said.

"Not tonight," she said.

"I'll give you that," he said, returning to his chore. "But you can start."

Kelli wanted to wall off her heart. Shut her mouth and go about her business. That was what Kelli always did, because then she didn't get hurt.

She pushed against that idea. She needed to let someone in, and she liked this man. He'd been gentle with her and kind to her son. "My dad cheated on my mom a lot," she said. "In fact, I found a lockbox concealed under the floorboards, and it had a list of women's names on it. I think they might be women he cheated with."

She shook her head. "I'm not sure." AJ's name was on that list, and Kelli refused to believe her best friend would do something so hurtful to her.

"Wow, a lockbox under the floorboards," he said. "Sounds very Nancy Drew."

They laughed together, and as the dishes got done and the leftovers put away, Kelli told him about the lockbox. About the Glassworks. About her father and her mother and her sisters.

Somehow, Shad had poured her a glass of wine and taken her out onto his back terrace. They sat in a swing which he kept moving with his toe, and Kelli said, "I'll have to show you the list. You've lived here a long time. Maybe you'll know some of the women. Maybe there's a connection between them I'm missing."

"I can do that," he said. "My mom might know too. She's been here forever."

Kelly finally fell silent as she looked up into the stars. The swing squeaked in the night air, and while it wasn't exactly warm, sitting next to Shad kept her toasty with nerves and anticipation, especially when he set his wine glass down and took her hand in his.

"I used to wish on stars when I was a little girl," she said, enjoying the feel of his fingers between hers.

"I bet you did," he said. "What did you wish for?"

"Ponies and bicycles," Kelli said with a giggle. "As I got older, the magic in the sky seemed to bleed away." She sobered, remembering when she and AJ had gone up onto the roof at Friendship Inn, a building that Kelli hadn't seen in decades. "It sort of died when I realized I couldn't fix everything with a wish and a prayer."

"It feels alive tonight," Shad said, gazing up into the darkness with her. He'd turned off the lights on the porch and inside, and it felt like the two of them were the only humans left in the universe.

Kelli felt it throb and expand, and she nodded. "It does."

Shad slipped his fingers out of hers and lifted his arm so she could cuddle into his side. If she did that though, she wouldn't be able to kiss him.

She turned toward him, and his hand came to the side of her face instead of across her shoulders. "I don't tell very many people about my dysfunctional family."

"Thank you for sharing them with me." He gave her the perfect smile, and Kelli leaned toward him.

That was all the hint he needed, because he closed the distance between them and kissed her. Suddenly, the whole world felt alive with magic, and power, and a buzzing energy Kelli hadn't even known existed until Shad's lips had touched hers.

CHAPTER TWENTY-ONE

A lice narrowed her eyes at the pretty blonde girl who'd walked through the door behind Charlie. Ginny came after her, the three of them practically talking over one another. They went right by her office without even looking inside, and Alice wondered if the reuniting her friends were doing with their families was as anti-climactic as hers.

Charlie and Ginny had been excited to see her when she'd finally walked through the door. Their first question had been about food, with the second if Sariah Page could come over so they could study for a chemistry test.

Alice's suspicious nature had kicked into gear then. Hadn't Arthur called her into his office less than a week ago because Charlie had scored perfectly on his organic unit in chemistry? Would there be another test so soon?

Charlie's laughter filtered back to her from the

kitchen, and it only annoyed Alice. If he was going to be spending time with another girl—a very pretty, very smart girl—he should tell Mandie.

"What's to say he hasn't?" Alice muttered to herself, shifting some papers around on her desk. She wasn't going to get any work done in here, and she might as well go meet this girl that could cause a lot of drama in her life.

She couldn't even imagine telling Robin that Charlie was spending more and more time with another girl. *It's not your business*, she told herself as she planted both palms against the desk. *Let Charlie and Mandie work out their relationship themselves.*

She didn't have to tell Robin anything. At the same time, Alice already felt in trouble and like she'd done something wrong for not mentioning Sariah to Robin while they'd been stuck in that tiny room underneath the stairs.

She'd taken a picture of the will with her scanner app, and Alice thumbed around on her phone to get to it. She emailed it to herself, then turned to her computer. The email popped up, and she marveled at the technology she had at her fingertips these days. Law school would've been so different with laptops and apps, instant messaging and the Internet. That had just barely been coming into mainstream life, and she could remember when Della had gotten the dial-up service. If Alice called home twice and got a busy signal, she knew her father or Della was on the Internet.

She smiled at the memories, because they seemed so sweet now. She needed to get out and see her father, as she hadn't been to Rocky Ridge for a few weeks. Besides her date with Arthur, that was, and she wasn't going to pop in for a visit to her dad and step-mom while on a first date.

She downloaded the PDFs and printed them, clipping them together in order though there were only four pages.

Kelli had texted several minutes ago, which had prompted Alice to leave her mocktail on the kitchen counter and come into the office. The twins had already left to go pick up Sariah, who didn't have a car, and Alice had thought about working before they'd walked in.

My mom said she doesn't want the money or the house. I talked to my sisters, and we're going to split the money. Does that fulfill the will, do you think? Or do I need to show it to my mom? Do we need to go to court?

Alice honestly didn't know. If no one was contesting the existence of a will, or no one had asked for the owner of it to come forth, what did it matter? Kelli didn't want to drag her mother through the murky memories of the past. They all just wanted to keep facing forward, putting one foot in front of the other, like they'd been doing for the past thirty years.

Alice thought of AJ and how she'd come face-to-face with her mother only a few months ago. She'd said something similar—that seeing her had pushed AJ backward into a place she didn't want to go.

They'd gone to dinner and tried to start a relationship again, but AJ's mom barely responded now. As far as Alice knew, AJ was going to invite her to the wedding, but she'd told them at one of their Wednesday lunches that she didn't expect the great and powerful Diane Proctor to come.

In truth, AJ didn't want her mother at her wedding. Alice knew keenly the dichotomy of those feelings, because she'd lived them daily with Frank. She wanted him to come to Ginny's dance concert, but at the same time, having him at the dance concert was torture. His presence stressed her out, and she'd later realized, stressed the kids out too.

They were all so much happier now that he couldn't walk into their lives at any moment and demand they be the type of people he wanted them to be. Life was much messier, as was the house, and Alice was blissfully happy with it.

Alice read over the will again, trying to find anything out of the ordinary. She couldn't; the document was a standard, run-of-the-mill pour over will. The section on the power of attorney and power of healthcare was a paragraph long. Nothing frilly or fancy about it.

The signature looked real, and Kelli had said it was her dad's handwriting. There was nothing to do with the will, but Alice carefully created a file for it, putting Kelli's name on the tab.

She then tapped to open her phone's note-taking app,

where she'd typed in all the names from the fourth sheet of paper. She could still feel the paper in her hands, and see the letters in her mind's eye.

Her heart jumped when her eyes landed on the third one from the bottom.

AvaJane Proctor.

Poor Kelli had gone slightly crazy when Alice had read that name. AJ had vehemently denied having anything to do with Guy Watkins, and Alice couldn't believe it herself.

She wouldn't believe it.

The fact remained that AJ's name was on the list. Alice dealt with the law and facts, not feelings.

She just needed to figure out who all of these women were, and why Guy had written their names down on this list and then kept it with his will and a box full of cash. Presumably, the few sheets of paper in that box were the most important items Guy wanted to keep safe.

So why that list?

"Mom?" Charlie said, and Alice looked up from her monitor and over the screen to the doorway of the office.

"Hmm?"

"Can we have some of this drink out here? It doesn't have alcohol, right?"

"Yes," Alice said, abandoning the list and the will for now. "Or rather, no. It doesn't have alcohol. You can have some."

"Great." He knocked twice on the doorframe and disappeared, taking his wide smile with him. Alice sighed, but she followed him anyway. She watched as he got down three glasses and poured the bright pink liquid from the blender. He laughed. He ran his hands through his hair. He grinned at Ginny, but he really turned on the charm when he looked at Sariah.

Alice realized with horror that she was watching her son flirt, and that he was very, very good at it. No wonder all the girls liked him. Alice herself was drawn into the room by his charisma, and he said, "There's a little more, Mom."

"I'm okay," she said, looking at Ginny and then Sariah.

"Oh, this is my mom," Charlie said quickly. His eyes danced with anxiety for a moment. "Alice. Mom, this is Sariah Page. She's the captain of the Academic Olympiad."

"Nice to meet you, ma'am," Sariah said, and Alice smiled at her.

"You too." She meant it, but there was something a little too...good about Sariah. She was *too* nice. *Too* pretty. *Too* perfect.

"Thanks for letting Charlie do the Olympiad," she said next. "With someone like him on the science side, we're going to be really strong this year."

"Oh, are we doing the *Olympiad?*" Alice asked, her gaze switching to her son.

Charlie's face grew redder with each passing second. "I thought I might try it," he said.

"It's not a pair of jeans," Alice said. "You don't try them on and then discard them later if they don't fit."

"I know that, Mom," he said.

"If you join, you're committing to the whole season." Alice folded her arms and cocked her hip.

"I read the paper," Charlie said.

Ginny looked back and forth between them, as did Sariah. Alice didn't need to make a scene or embarrass her son. "Okay," she said. "Tell me where to sign. I assume you two are going to be able to work out the car situation? The practices are after school, right?"

"Yes," Charlie said. "Ginny's going to take it to work on Mondays and Wednesdays if she's got a shift. I'll use Ride-Share those days to get home, and just walk over to the elementary school from the high school when I'm done with practice."

"Mm."

"If Ginny doesn't have to work, she'll RideShare home, and I'll have the car to take to work and then home."

"You've got it figured out, sounds like." Pride swelled inside Alice. "That's great, Charlie. Ginny, you're okay with all of that?"

"Yep," she said. "Mom, when can we go get my dress? We never did on Saturday, because of the squall."

"Right." Alice sighed as she picked up her mocktail from earlier. She'd been sitting at the counter, but the teens had taken it over. She took a seat at the table and then a sip of her drink. "Tomorrow? After school? When are you working?"

"Tuesday, Wednesday, Friday, Saturday," she recited. "We can go tomorrow."

"I think I have a client call at two," Alice said. "We can go when you get home, if I'm done. If I'm not, we'll go when I am."

"Okay."

Silence fell over the four of them, and Alice knew exactly what it was saying. *Get out of here, Mom.*

"Okay," she said, groaning as she stood. "I slept on a twin-sized mattress with Robin last night. I'm going to go take a hot bath and go to bed."

"Love you, Mom," the twins chorused.

She grinned at them both, bent down to kiss Ginny's head, and then paused in the kitchen to hug Charlie. "Common areas of the house, please," she whispered. "No bedrooms."

"All right," Charlie said, though Alice didn't really believe he'd take Sariah into his bedroom. "Can I drive her home alone?"

Alice released her son and looked right into his eyes. He was such a good boy, and he wanted to do what was right. Still, he had the hormones all sixteen-year-old boys do, and that was what worried Alice the most.

"You do what you feel is right," she said, smiling as she stroked her fingers down the side of his face. "Be safe, no matter what."

"Okay, Mom."

She left them in the kitchen, and she turned on a small fan on her dresser for white noise, then lit her lemon-pink grapefruit candle and set her phone to play classical music. She filled the tub with hot, steaming water and put in lilac- and rosemary-scented bath salts.

As she sank into the luxury of the tub, with all of her favorite scents and the soft music, Alice believed she could chase away the aches, pains, and hardships of the past couple of days.

When she got out of the tub, she'd call Arthur and set up another date. Then, she'd study that list and make some notes to go over with Kelli when they talked at two o'clock the next afternoon.

CHAPTER TWENTY-TWO

Through the darkness, Laurel scanned the parking lot at the station, looking for Paul's car. He'd often said it was pretty ridiculous that he had a car at all, because he could take a police vehicle home with him any time he wanted.

There were simply too many cars to find his. People streamed toward the police station and away from it in steady lines. Cars jammed the lot as well as the street in both directions. Apparently, the station had been one of the bigger shelters on Diamond, and there'd been over sixty minors here without their parents.

Aaron Sherman, of course, had put a system in place to make sure the right kids got reunited with the right parents. Laurel's guilt kicked in when she joined the stream of anxious people, and she couldn't believe so much was still going on here.

She'd waited at the ferry station on Bell for hours before she'd been able to get back here. She could've swam the few miles between the islands faster, and she'd seriously considered it. But with the increased number of ferries and the still-churning waters, and Laurel had settled for pacing the station every so often.

"Hey, Rhonda," she said breathlessly as she entered the station. People talked, phones rang, and the general buzz in the air testified that something major had happened. The lights burned white overhead, almost making Laurel flinch back. "Have you seen Paul?"

"Yeah, he took over for the Chief." She nodded toward Chief Sherman's office. "He's in there."

"Thanks." Laurel took a deep breath and started weaving past the extra tables that had been set up. The main room was already so crowded, and having extra bodies didn't help the somewhat sweaty smell that always seemed to permeate the police station.

She arrived at the office door, which stood open. Paul wore his uniform, and he had his back turned toward the entrance. Laurel took a moment to admire his broad shoulders and trim waist, something springing up inside her she couldn't deny.

Love. She was definitely in love with him.

"That's what I'm saying, ma'am," Paul said to the windows. "If you've lost an animal, you need to come down here to file the report. Our online system is far too overwhelmed. We don't have people checking those submissions, and we won't for a while."

Laurel entered the office, which was blissfully free of other people besides Paul. She closed the door behind her, meeting Paul's eyes when he swung around in surprise. An instant smile formed on his face, and he said, "Yes, ma'am," as he lifted one arm to gesture her forward.

She waited though, because she didn't want him to rush through his call. She held up one hand as if to say, *Take your time*, and she forced herself to stay back.

"Thank you for calling," he said. "I apologize for the inconvenience." He set the phone in the cradle on the Chief's desk and immediately started moving around it. "Laurel."

"Paul." She hurried toward him then, and she'd never thought the Chief's office was very big. It seemed to take a few steps to get to Paul, though he was moving toward her too.

"You're okay." He took her face in his hands and looked at her. Into her eyes. Down her body. "You made it back."

"Took a while," she said, smiling at him. "You playing the part of Chief sure is sexy."

He laughed and slid his hands along her shoulders to her waist. He held her against his chest, wrapping her in a tight hug. "I was worried about you. We had no contact, and I hated that. You should've seen the Chief. He wasn't happy he couldn't be in constant communication with Eloise."

"I bet," Laurel said. She held him tightly too, her heartbeat starting to thump too fast. Could she tell him now? Was it even the right time? "How much longer do you have to be here?"

"I told Aaron I'd stay until eight," he said. "I'm just overseeing everything out there, and we've got big signs that say we're closing up at eight. He'll be back in the morning at six a.m."

"Nothing is online?"

"The server still isn't even up," Paul said, running his hand through her hair. "We've got power and phone lines. We've got men and women. So we went old school. People have to come here to get their kids, report missing animals, missing property, or anything else that might require police attention."

"Who would be out stealing things in a squall?" Laurel asked, stepping back. "People never cease to amaze me."

Paul gave her a smile that sure felt full of love. He reached for her again, this time cradling her face in one hand as he lowered his head to kiss her. Laurel sure did like kissing Paul. He was gentle with her while being hungry at the same time. He moved slow with one stroke and accelerated things in the next.

She kissed him back, hoping the way she felt would come through in the action.

The phone rang, and he pulled away. "Hold that

thought," he said, his voice throaty and gruff. He reached for the phone and said, "Acting Chief, Paul Leyhe. How can I help you?"

Laurel pressed her lips together and then smiled, the taste of him still in her mouth. She wanted to spend the night with him, and she wanted to tell him she loved him. She wanted to talk about their future, a family, and everything else they needed to in order to advance their relationship again.

Her phone chimed, and she quickly took it from her back pocket. Relief cascaded through her at her mother's text. *No squall here*, she'd said. *Bad thunderstorms. They rang our alarm too, but we didn't lose power. So glad you're safe, sweetie. Call me when you can.*

Her parents lived on Nantucket now, and that island sat a bit northwest of Five Island Cove, about ten miles away. Squalls could be that wide, and one of Laurel's first texts had been to her mother.

"Thank you," Paul said, and he hung up again. "Eight o'clock can't come fast enough."

"No, it can't," Laurel said. It was barely four now, but the lasting storm had kept the sky dark for an hour now. She stepped into Paul again, sliding her hands up his chest to the back of his neck.

"Paul," she said, her nerves firing on all cylinders. "I'm in love with you." The words left her mouth easily, and Laurel liked saying them. A giggle escaped her mouth when his eyes rounded. "I've been feeling it for a while, and being away for the past couple of days without being able to talk to you? I just...I love you."

"I love you too," he whispered. "I have for months."

Laurel tipped up and pressed her mouth to his, kissing him with more passion and drive than before. She wanted him right now, and she hated that this job was going to keep him from her.

He kept kissing her as he walked her backward until they reached the couch. He laid down on it, then brought her into his chest again. "So what do we do now?" he asked, laughing a little. He stroked her hair, and Laurel pressed her cheek to his chest. His heartbeat was strong and booming too, his adrenaline likely as high as hers.

"What do you want to do?" she asked. "Get married? Have a family? Wait a while? There's time for things."

"I don't want to wait," he murmured. "I want you with me all the time. In the morning. At night. Whenever we can see each other."

Their schedules didn't always line up, but Laurel spoke with him every day. She made it a point to find him and see him in person every day. He did the same for her.

"Do you want children?" he asked. "I sort of got the impression you didn't."

Laurel took a breath and contemplated what she wanted her future to look like. She'd had plenty of time to do that in the house on Seabreeze Shore too. "I think I have a lot of fears," she said. "But as I overcome each one, things change." She tilted her head back. "Just like with you. I couldn't imagine ever wanting to be with a man. But with you... I love being with you like this. I love holding your hand and going to dinner. I love being in your bed."

"Mm." He watched her for a moment, and he wore his detective eyes.

"What?" she asked.

He closed his eyes and tightened his hold on her. "You never stay overnight," he said. "We make love, and you leave."

"It's..."

"When we go to your place, you make me leave."

"I know." She sighed, not sure how to explain. "I think it's one of those defense mechanisms I need to overcome."

"Maybe you can try tonight," he whispered, pressing his lips to her forehead. "I can come to your place when I'm done here. I can see if I can find food, and we can eat. We can make love. We can shower together." He grinned, and Laurel laughed with him.

"That's your fantasy?" she asked. "Showering together?"

"Mm, yeah," he said. "Very romantic. Then, maybe I can stay the night."

Laurel liked all of his suggestions. "Maybe," she said anyway. She shifted so she could kiss him, quickly saying, "Definitely," between kisses.

The phone rang, and she stilled. "You better get that."

"One more kiss," he said, moaning when she gave it to

him. The line stopped ringing, but Paul didn't stop kissing her.

Finally, Laurel pulled away when someone rapped on the closed door. She got to her feet quickly, as did Paul. She still wore yesterday's clothes, and she sat back on the couch as Paul straightened his uniform and opened the door.

"You are in here," a woman said. "I've got your sister out here."

Paul peered out the doorway. "My sister? My sister doesn't live in the cove."

"She says she's your sister."

He looked at Laurel. "Would Julie be here?"

"No way," Laurel said. "Why fly into the belly of the beast?" She stood and joined him in the doorway. The crowd had started to thin, it seemed, and she definitely didn't see Julie.

"I can make dinner tonight," she said, slipping her hand into his. "I've got time. Then you can just come over when you're finished here."

"You sure?"

"Yes."

"Okay," he said. He kissed her one more time, this one quick and without the passion and promise of more later. He slipped away from her, stepping out of the office and walking toward the fray of people.

A woman who certainly wasn't his sister stood at the end of the row of tables. She looked nervous as she handed him an envelope—just a regular, white envelope, the kind Laurel had once used to pay her bills before everything moved online.

She had dark brown hair that fell to her shoulders. It looked wavy, with straight-cut bangs across her forehead. She glanced toward the office, and for some reason, Laurel wanted to shrink out of the doorway.

The woman's dark eyes caught hers before she could, and Laurel studied her. No freckles. Definitely some Botox treatments in her lips. Small chin. Standing next to Paul, the top of her head barely hit his shoulder, so she was a similar height to Laurel.

She carried no extra weight on her frame, and she nodded to Laurel as if they knew one another. Laurel frowned and stepped out of the office, because she didn't know this woman. She couldn't see Paul's face fully, but he lifted the envelope and the woman turned to leave.

"What was that about?" Laurel asked as he approached the office again.

"She said her name was Betsy Dinerstein, and she had some information for the Chief. Some case he's been working on."

"What case?" Laurel asked, though it really wasn't any of her business what the Chief did. *Betsy Dinerstein* tickled her mind. She knew that name. Where did she know that name from?

"I don't know," Paul tossed the envelope on Aaron's desk as the phone rang again. He sighed as he sat in the desk chair. He looked regal and commanding there, and Laurel sure did enjoy the sight. "I'm sorry, Laurel. Things are crazy."

"It's fine," she said. "I knew they would be."

He reached for the phone, giving the same spiel as he had before. He explained that they weren't taking property damage complaints at the police station, but that those items should go to an insurance company.

"It's highly unlikely that someone was out in the hailstorm, hitting your car with a baseball bat," he said, rolling his eyes. "You need to call your insurance company, sir."

Laurel smiled encouragingly at him, and the call ended a moment later. "I'll make dinner," she said. "You come when you can."

"Yes, ma'am," he said, giving her a tired smile. "Sorry, Laurel. I should've told the Chief I couldn't do this."

"Not at all," she said. "You're his second. There's nowhere you should be but here." She gave him another smile, and he walked her to the door. He kissed her again, and Laurel could get lost in his touch.

"Paul," someone called, and he pulled away.

"Yep." He strode out of the office, leaving Laurel in the doorway. She turned back to Aaron's desk, that white envelope standing out to her.

"Betsy Dinerstein," she muttered to herself, retracing her steps to the desk. Like a flash of lightning to the brain, she realized where she'd heard the name.

It had been on the list Kelli had found with her father's will. The one with AJ's name on it too. Could there be a connection between all these women? If so, what was it?

Without thinking or hesitating, Laurel snatched up the envelope. She shoved it down the front of her jeans and turned to leave the office.

CHAPTER TWENTY-THREE

AJ watched the front of the house, aware that Kristen had been busy in the kitchen for thirty or forty minutes. Sharp guilt almost felt the same as the labor pains she'd experienced last week, but she didn't say anything.

The labor pains had been false, and the doctor had stressed that AJ needed to take things easy.

Having someone around constantly wasn't as easy for AJ as she'd thought it would be. She adored Kristen, and she'd enjoyed talking to her this week.

AJ just needed a break from it all. She needed Matt to pull into the driveway, and she needed him to hold her and tell her he'd been fine, and she was fine, and they were fine.

Finally, a swath of headlights cut through the deepening darkness outside, and her first inclination was to jump to her feet. She reminded herself in time that she couldn't do that, and she stayed in the recliner Kristen had positioned to face the window.

A minute later, the front door opened, and Matt entered the house, a ragged look on his face and plenty of wind accompanying him. He didn't see her, and AJ's heart bled for the man.

He'd always been so *good*. Good to her and good for her. Tears came to AJ's eyes, and she lifted her hand as Matt let his backpack slide to the floor.

He caught sight of her then, and the instant brightness that filled his face told AJ how he felt. "AvaJane," he said, her name conveying the great love and relief he felt too. He hurried toward her, and AJ pushed herself to her feet slowly and carefully.

Matt took her into his arms and held her tight, their baby a five-month-old bump between them.

"I'm so sorry," he said. "I missed you so much."

They'd been separated for a lot longer than two days before, and slight foolishness ran through AJ as she wept into his shoulder.

"I was okay," he said. "We were taken in by some really kind people who, of course, knew Dad."

"The Ringwolds," AJ said, because he'd told her all of this on the phone when service had been restored earlier that day.

"Mm." Matt swayed with her, the scent of him more

like fish and sweat than his normal musky cologne and fresh cotton. "I need to shower."

"I do too," she whispered.

"Mm," he said again, his grip on her nowhere near softening.

"I think I'm going to go check on Jean and Rueben," Kristen said, and that got Matt to step away.

"Thank you so much, Kristen," he said, turned and crossing the room to her. He engulfed her in a hug too, and she patted him on his broad shoulders. He said something else AJ didn't catch, but she didn't need to.

Kristen's smile said a lot, and she nodded. "Rueben is almost here," she said. "I won't be driving."

"You'll come back, though, right?" AJ asked.

Kristen looked at her. "I was thinking you'd like a day or two alone." Her eyes held questions that AJ didn't know how to answer.

"She would," Matt said. "I'm going to be working from home tomorrow." He watched AJ, and she wasn't sure what he was trying to convey. "She'll be okay Tuesday, but maybe you could come get her for the weekly lunch you ladies do on Wednesday and come stay with us again for a few days after that."

"I can do whatever you'd like," Kristen said. "I don't have much going on right now."

She also didn't want to be alone. AJ had picked that up, and Kristen hadn't been too terribly subtle about it.

"Maybe we can start looking at some of those places online," AJ said. "When you come back."

Kristen smiled and nodded, moving to embrace AJ as another pair of headlights flashed in the window.

"You don't have to go," AJ whispered, her chest suddenly tight.

"I know," Kristen said and nothing more.

Rueben came to the door and helped her with her bag, nodding to AJ and shaking Matt's hand. Sixty seconds later, they were gone.

"You were okay here, right?" Matt asked, returning to her. He put his hand on the back of her elbow and guided her through the living room and into the family room. Past the office where they worked, and the kitchen Kristen had cleaned from top to bottom.

"I was fine," AJ said. "It was just like when we were up at The Cliffside Inn, waiting for the tsunami to hit. It's the fear of the unknown."

"You hate being out of contact, too," he said.

"Yes, I do." AJ felt somewhat crazy for her near-break-down, and she knew some of that was because she wasn't taking her medication right now.

"Do you want to shower with me?" Matt asked, releasing her and reaching back to take off his shirt.

"Mm," she answered, as that seemed to mean *yes* in Matt Hymas's vocabulary.

AJ BLINKED AT HER PHONE, MATT'S STEADY BREATHING IN the bed next to her soothing and something she'd missed last night. She found it strange how worry could amplify things so much.

It could also cover up other things, and AJ remembered walking along the beach once in Miami. She should've been enjoying the heat of the sun, the rush of the waves as they tried to cover the shore, the call of birds, the sound of children laughing, and memories being made.

All she remembered was the strength of the breeze and how cold it made her skin. It had seeped right into her soul, because AJ had been so worried about her college education, where she should be headed, and how to make sure her sister got out of the cove.

Now, she wasn't cold, and she'd only been separated from Matt for one night. The worry had definitely made it feel much longer and much worse than that.

This new text she'd just gotten from Kelli felt the same way. It sent ice down into her lungs, the hooks of it tugging against AJ's ability to breathe.

I'd like to come over in the morning, Kelli had said. *When is too early for you? I have a meeting at 2, so let me know.*

She could come any time. AJ hadn't done any articles this week, unable to focus and seek out new leads. She and Matt hadn't combined their resources yet, but he'd told her she didn't need to worry about money. She was living with him, and he was fine to pay all the utilities, for groceries, for anything she needed.

Since AJ was trying to eliminate as much stress from her life as possible, she'd taken him at his word. She hadn't worked, and she'd tried to nap, rest, and relax as much as possible.

Any time is fine, AJ typed out. *Matt's working from home tomorrow, and Kristen's gone back to the lighthouse.* That might influence Kelli's decisions, as perhaps she'd want to see Kristen too.

I'll drop Parker off at school and come over then, okay? Probably close to 9.

Can't wait, AJ said, though she definitely could wait to see Kelli face-to-face. She'd already texted her half a dozen times, telling her she had no idea why her name would be on any list of Guy Watkins's, and that she absolutely did not sleep with him. Or even get close to sleeping with him.

Kelli hadn't responded until that text about coming over tomorrow.

AJ exhaled and set her phone face-down on her nightstand. She needed to relax, and stressing about what Kelli might or might not say in the morning wasn't the way to do it.

CHAPTER TWENTY-FOUR

"I'm home," Robin called, pure exhaustion flowing over her.

"Mom," Mandie yelled. She and Jamie came tearing down the hall from the living room at the back of the house. They bulldozed into Robin, both of them hugging her tightly. She put her arms around them too, her tears fresh as she embraced them.

"Oh, you guys," she said. "I'm so glad you're all okay." She stroked Mandie's hair and leaned back. "You're okay? You were here alone. I'm so sorry."

"It's okay," Mandie said. "Only for a couple of hours. Chief Sherman showed up in the middle of lightning storm, demanding I go with him." She gave Robin a tearful smile. "Now that was a scary drive."

"I'll bet it was." Robin saw Duke appear down the hall as he stepped out of the kitchen. Her heart squeezed, because he was still the sexiest man on the planet. Her life partner. Her husband. Her lover.

"At least you didn't have to stay in the house alone all night," Robin said. Every time she thought about such a thing, she shivered. She turned her attention to Jamie. "You were with Dad. How was it?"

"I'll never get the smell of fish off me," Jamie said soberly. "But we were safe. There were a lot of us piled into the underground, where they normally store fish."

"Gross," Robin said with a smile. Yes, fish could stink, but fish were her and Duke's livelihood. Without fish, they wouldn't be in the cove, and they wouldn't have what they did.

"Come on," she said. "I heard Dad found frozen pizza and that it would be ready when I got home." The three of them walked down the hall, and Mandie and Jamie peeled off as Robin stepped into Duke's arms.

She didn't have to say anything. He didn't either. He simply held her as another squall raged through Robin's whole body. She tried to hold back her tears, but she failed. She shook in his arms, and he simply let her.

"You're all right," he whispered after a few moments. "I'm all right. The girls are all right."

She nodded against his shoulder, glad and grateful for his steadiness and strength. "What about the boat?" she asked.

"She took some damage," Duke admitted, clearing his throat. "But I've already got her patched up. After I got

Mandie from the station this morning, we went back to the dock to work on her. It's fine, love."

Fine was not what Robin wanted to hear. Not for a brand-new fishing boat that had cost them forty-five thousand dollars.

"When are you going to go out again?"

"Tomorrow, if the storms clear a bit more."

She nodded, but she didn't want him to go fishing tomorrow. She didn't want to work, scrambling around her office and moving sticky notes. She had a million phone calls to make to her beachside venues to find out what damage they'd sustained. She had an anniversary party on Wednesday that was supposed to be catered by The Seafood Source, and she wondered if they'd even have the food.

Her task list stretched for a mile in her mind, and she worked to shut it off.

"Maybe you could take a day off," she said, meeting her husband's eyes. She wanted him to see how very tired she was. She wanted someone to acknowledge it. She wanted someone to give her permission to take a day off.

Duke, who'd always been so good at seeing what Robin needed, nodded. "I will if you will."

Robin put her palm against his chest. "We can stay in bed all day."

"Mm, I like the sound of that." He put his hands on her hips and they swayed together, as if dancing. He leaned down and kissed her, and Robin didn't care about pizza or planning. She just wanted to lay in this man's arms and listen to the sound of his breathing as he slept.

"The pizza is ready," Mandie said in a sharp tone, and Robin broke the kiss with her husband. She looked over to the girls, catching the look of disgust on Mandie's face. She actually smiled at it, because she wouldn't think it was disgusting to be kissing Charlie.

"I heard you got to spend the night in jail," Robin said. "And that you helped a little boy."

"Yeah," Mandie picked up a plate and handed it to Robin as she stepped over to the island. "I really like kids. I'm thinking about being a teacher. Or opening a daycare or something."

Surprise darted through Robin. "Oh?" Mandie had never said anything about what she wanted to do when she finished high school. "Where would you go to college?'

"I don't know." Mandie put a piece of pizza on her plate and turned toward the table. "Dad got one of those bundt cakes."

"I picked it out," Jamie said. "I got the strawberry fields one, Mom. I know you like that one." She beamed at Robin, who put her arm around the thirteen-year-old's shoulders and smiled at her.

"I do," she said. "Thanks, bug."

Since Mandie had moved on to dessert so rapidly, Robin didn't think she wanted to talk about her future, college, or classes. Robin didn't want to discuss them either. She wanted to eat and go to bed, and thankfully, because she and Duke had a Sunday night routine where they did retire to their bedroom early and let the girls have the run of the house, she got her wish.

DUKE WOKE HER IN THE MORNING, HIS FOUR A.M. ALARM singing through the darkness. "Sorry," he mumbled, rolling over to silence it. He turned back to her, retaking her into his arms. "Are we really staying home today?"

"Can we?" she asked.

"You have an office here," he murmured, pressing his lips to her earlobe a moment later. "You'll work no matter what."

He was probably right, but Robin didn't admit it. She pressed into his touch and slid her hand south along his body, hoping he'd get the hint to keep kissing her. Duke had always been able to pick up on her subtle hints, and she enjoyed making love to her husband.

She dozed afterward, as did he, and it wasn't until Mandie knocked lightly on the door and called, "We're going to school," that Robin opened her eyes again. Light poured in the bedroom window, and she sat up.

"Okay," she called. "Have a good day." Slight guilt cut through her that she hadn't gotten up to see the girls out the door. Duke usually drove them, and she wondered who'd taken them today.

"They're fine," Duke said. "Lay back down."

"I'm awake now," Robin said, twisting to look at him over her shoulder. He had his phone held up above his face, a frown forming between his eyebrows. "What?"

"Guess we better shower," he said, handing her the phone. "Your mother is on her way over."

Robin's plans for a peaceful, relaxing day went up in smoke. She read her mom's messages—*wanted to come see you for a few minutes. I'll be there in about an hour if that works?*—her heart sinking to the floor.

"When did you get this?" she asked, but she could see the timestamp right above it. Ten minutes ago. "I don't want to entertain my mother today."

Jennifer Golden was impossible to entertain anyway. Robin had been working on her relationship with her mom for months now, after a long drought of not trying very hard at all.

Duke got out of bed and padded into the bathroom. "Maybe she'll only stay for a few minutes."

"Maybe," Robin said, frowning just the way Duke had. "Why did she text you?" She switched Duke's phone for hers and saw that she had three missed calls from her mother.

A great sigh filled her lungs, and she blew all the air out as Duke started the shower behind her. She hadn't bothered to clean up the kitchen last night, and she had no idea what the girls had done for breakfast or lunch this morning.

She skipped showering and left Duke in the bedroom to go get the house tidied up. Her mother owned the house, and Duke and Robin paid a nominal amount in rent. The least she could do was make sure her mother knew how much she appreciated the gesture by keeping the place in good repair.

"Hello," her mom called only several minutes after Robin had started doing the dishes. Not an hour. Not even close.

"In the kitchen, Mom," Robin called, making her voice as jovial as possible.

Her footsteps came closer, and Robin put the last two plates in the dishwasher. "You're alive," her mom said.

Robin bent to close the appliance and then she turned toward her mom. She wore a pantsuit in navy blue, with a white top with plenty of ruffles along the neckline. "Wow, you're wearing heels," Robin said. "What's going on?"

"I'm meeting with Jonas today," she said. "This morning, in a little bit. And then I have a lunch date."

"Ooh, fancy," Robin said. "A date with your lawyer, and then a date with your friends." She gave her mom a smile and crossed the distance between them to hug her. "What are you meeting with Jonas about?"

"My estate," she said, stepping back and clearing her throat. She lifted her chin slightly, and Robin stepped back, surprise already filling her. "The lunch date isn't with my friends. It's with a man named Tony Rudd."

Robin opened her mouth to speak, but nothing came out.

"We met on the cruise over Christmas," her mom said, that defensive look in her eyes blazing hot now. "You'd know about him if you didn't work so much."

Irritation coated Robin's mouth. All of her walls shot right back into place too. Of course it was her fault she didn't know every intimate detail of her mother's life. She should be calling and texting daily to find out if she had oatmeal for breakfast or raisin bran.

"You could've sent me a text," Robin said, folding her arms. "We have a very expensive boat to pay for now, and I need to work more."

"Your poor girls had to call me for a ride this morning," her mom said, shaking her head. "I asked Jamie what she had for breakfast, and she said she didn't eat breakfast."

"She's not a big breakfast eater," Robin shot back. Her mom didn't know that, because her mom preferred to dote on Robin's siblings and their children. None of them lived in the cove anymore, and they sent cards and emails, gifts and surprises. Robin lived here, and she saw her mother more than any of them. She spent time with her and made sure she knew when the girls' activities were.

But she didn't send cards or continually play to her mother's ego.

Her mother ignored the comment about Jamie's eating

habits and said, "I noticed the van is still in the garage. Is Duke not going to work today?"

"Morning, Jennifer," he said, right on cue. He glanced at Robin, noting the stiffness in her stature in less time than it took to blink. He turned back to her mother and gave her a big hug.

She laughed, because Duke was a big man, with a big personality, and Robin's mother had always liked him.

"We're taking today off," he said, setting her down and stepping over to the coffee maker, which had no coffee. He started filling the pot. "We had a rough weekend, as I'm sure you did."

"She was at home," Robin said through her teeth. Her mother had a built-in generator too, so she hadn't even lost power for very long. She'd had her bed, her clothes, plenty of food, and all the comforts she normally did.

"Tony would like to meet you," she said, moving from one topic of conversation to another so rapidly. "I was wondering when you might be available."

"I don't know," Robin said. "I have an anniversary party on Wednesday evening, and a wedding on Saturday, and one on Sunday."

"Friday evening?" her mom asked, as if Robin just waved a magic wand and weddings planned themselves. She never made plans the night before a wedding, and this Friday was the night before a double-wedding weekend.

"I can't Friday," Robin said. "Perhaps a day during the

week next week? I won't have another wedding until Eloise's after Sunday." That gave her two weeks to fit in her mother and her new boyfriend.

She almost always met with clients and venues and businesses during the day, so her evenings were free. Weekends were tough for her, because she did some consulting on the weekends, along with fittings, last-minute prep, email answering, and the returning of messages.

A vein of tiredness ran through her, and she lifted her hand to rub her forehead.

"I'll see if Monday or Tuesday would work," her mom said.

"That should be fine," Robin said.

"You look tired, dear. You shouldn't work so much."

Robin let her hand fall back to her side. "Mom, I'm doing the best I can." She immediately regretted the sharp tone in her voice. "I'm sorry. It was just a really long week-end, and I didn't get anything done I needed to."

"Jennifer, we're doing what we can to get back on our feet," Duke said, coming to stand beside Robin. "I'm going to Alaska again this summer, and that should get us back in the clear. Robin won't work like this forever." He put his hand on her waist and drew her closer to him. She loved being his, and she leaned into his warmth and strength before facing her mom again.

Her mom studied her, barely looking at Duke. "You remind me of a woman I knew once," she said. "She was so dedicated to her family. Worked her fingers to the bone to make ends meet. I really admired her."

"Great," Robin said. "Then you admire me too."

Her mom hugged her, and Robin was as surprised by that as much as anything else. Maybe not the boyfriend, but close. Clearing her throat, her mother stepped back. "I wonder what happened to Jill. They up and left the cove so fast."

"Jill who?" Robin asked just to be nice.

"You remember Jill," her mom said, but Robin clearly didn't, or she wouldn't have asked. "Jill and Howard Bunton? They lived around the corner from us for a few years. You were, oh, let's see. Fifteen, maybe? Her husband worked for Guy Watkins for a while. Then, one day, they were gone."

"Jill Bunton," Robin said, the letters written in Guy's handwriting leaping into her mind's eye. "I do remember her." Her eyes widened. "Howard worked for Guy?"

"He did all the shipping for his pieces," her mom said. "Jill started working as a cleaning lady. Oh, how she cleaned. Day and night it seemed, so they could have what they needed."

"The cleaning lady," Robin said, a fuzzy memory coming to her mind. "I do remember her."

"All right," her mom said in a falsely cheery voice. "I have to go. I'll talk to you later."

"Thanks for driving the girls," Duke said. "Robin and I were busy."

"Duke," Robin said, horrified at what he'd just insinuated. But her mother just laughed as Duke walked her toward the front door.

"Jill Bunton," Robin said, quickly grabbing her phone and typing the name into it. "The cleaning lady." If she could sneak away from Duke today, she'd do a little Internet research to see what she could find out about the Buntons and what they'd done for Guy Watkins.

CHAPTER TWENTY-FIVE

Kelli stared at the list of names by the light of her bedside lamp. The sun would rise in less than an hour, but she'd been up for at least thirty minutes.

She'd taken another day off of work, and since she had some leeway now in her finances, she'd decided she better get some answers before she went insane.

She'd scheduled to meet with Alice at two o'clock that day, simply to find out any legalities about the will she'd found, and to find out if she needed to have Heather and Sabrina sign something saying the three of them were going to split the money evenly, and then it was all done. Executed. Finished.

Kelli didn't want to take more than her share, but she was willing to take the money. Heather and Sabrina seemed to be as well.

Her alarm went off, and Kelli closed the folder,

looking at the front cover of it. Her dad had not written anything on the front of it or the tab. The four-page will sat inside, with this extra sheet of paper with a list of eleven names. No explanations for anything.

Kelli sighed as she got out of bed and got in the shower. Her morning was just as hectic as always, because she hadn't told Parker she wouldn't be working that day.

As they pulled up to the elementary school in the RideShare, she said, "Okay, remember Jean is going to pick you up this afternoon. I'm going shopping for beds and a couch."

She grinned at Parker, who smiled back. "Okay. In the circle drive?"

"Right here in the circle drive," Kelli confirmed. She needed to call the bakery and have them deliver a gift basket to Jean too. The woman had saved Kelli by taking Parker so many times, and Kelli wanted her to know how much she appreciated it.

"Okay, 'bye, Mom."

"'Bye, baby." Kelli watched her son get out of the car, and then she said, "I need to go to 391 Lakeshore Drive, please."

"You got it," the woman said, putting the car in gear. The ride from school to AJ's didn't take very long, and Kelli's stomach played nicely until the cute, almost-beach house came into view.

"Thank you," she said, swiping her RideShare pass and stepping from the car. The wind played with her hair, a reminder that it could do almost anything it wanted, and Kelli turned her face into the breeze.

She walked toward the house and up the steps to the covered porch. She wasn't sure, but she thought Matt Hymas had lived near here growing up.

She rang the doorbell, and not three seconds later, AJ stood there.

"You're supposed to be in bed," Kelli said, everything softening at the sight of her best friend. Everything AJ had told her was of course true, and all of Kelli's fears and doubts dried right up.

"Come on," Kelli said, stepping into the house. "Where are you? The couch?"

AJ closed the door and the moment she turned toward Kelli, she took her into a hug.

Neither of them said anything, which was a little surprising for AJ. Kelli was used to letting actions say more than words, and when AJ finally released her, she wiped at her tears.

"Let's sit down," Kelli said, realizing AJ had not said anything yet. "You're not supposed to be up. Where's Matt? I would've just come in if I thought he wasn't going to answer."

She looked into the formal living room, but he wasn't there.

"He's working," AJ said. "Has his headphones in. I told him you were coming."

Kelli nodded and went into the family room. A

blanket and pillow lay on the couch, and that was obviously where AJ had been lying. "Lay down, sweetie," Kelli said, her maternal instincts kicking in. "Have you eaten? Do you need something to drink?"

"Matt got me all set up before he went into the office," she said with a smile. She did ease herself onto the couch, and Kelli took the spot next to her.

She set her oversized purse on the floor and withdrew the folder. "I found this under the floorboards in my dad's office." She handed the documents to AJ. "It's his will and that list."

AJ's eyes held plenty of apprehension, but she took the folder and opened it. She scanned the will quickly, saying nothing, and then turned to the last sheet of paper.

The dark beige, nearly brown, color of it testified of its age, as did the nearly-smudged pencil her father had written in.

"Betsy Dinerstein, Sidney Tyler, Ellen Holt," AJ read. "Jill Bunton, Minerva Thacker, Annalise Green..." Her voice faded. After several long seconds, she said, "I know Annalise Green. She's barely older than us, Kel. Remember? She was the goalkeeper on the soccer team my freshman year. She was a senior."

Lightbulbs lit up in her head. "I do remember her. You didn't like her much, because she thought you'd slept your way onto the team."

AJ nodded, and Kelli was glad there wasn't any animosity between them. She reminded herself that AJ knew who she was and what she'd done in high school. She'd never been embarrassed about it until recently.

Kelli marveled that she'd overcome that hurdle so fast. Everything she regretted seemed to stretch on and on and on. It took her years to overcome the things she regretted, and she often felt like she needed to seek out the person she'd behaved poorly in front of, apologize, and assure them she'd grown, changed, and hadn't ever done something so regretful since.

Such a thing was hardly ever doable though, so Kelli stewed over the things she'd done until she finally let them go.

"There's no way on this planet Annalise Green would've slept with your dad," AJ said.

"I don't think that's what this list is anymore," Kelli said. "I think it's something else."

"What?" AJ's eyes lingered at the bottom of the list for a moment, where her name sat. "The two girls below me also played sports at the high school," she said. "Brittany Larsen and Camila Cho."

AJ looked up, a faraway look on her face. "Brittany was a year older than us. She played basketball. Camila was a year younger. She played tennis." By the time she finished talking, AJ's voice was almost a whisper.

"I don't understand it," Kelli said.

AJ shook her head. "I don't either, Kel. Here's the real question." She closed the folder and placed her hands over it. "Does it matter? Does it matter if you know who these people are to your father? He's been dead for a long time."

Kelli didn't know how to answer that. "It feels like I need to know right now." She'd felt the same way about Zach Watkins, and that whole situation had turned out terribly. "Maybe I'm searching for something I'll never find."

"Maybe," AJ said instead of contradicting her. She sighed and looked down at the folder. In the next moment, she pulled in a breath. "Kelli—have you seen this?"

AJ gripped the edge of the folder.

"What?" Kelli leaned forward, but she didn't have to look far. AJ had closed the folder so the back was facing up, not the front.

"There's writing here." She tilted the folder, as it looked like it had been erased or had faded so much, the letters were barely legible.

AJ lifted the folder closer to her face. "It says, 'Tell Joel? Get Glassworks back.'"

Kelli sucked in a breath and reached for the folder. She didn't mean to pluck it from AJ's grip in a somewhat violent manner, but she was afraid she had.

She too peered at the letters, the imprints of them right there at the top of the folder, nearly impossible to see. She tilted the folder, and the light caught the graphite, making them much easier for her eye to make out.

"Tell Joel?" she repeated, her voice going up as her dad had written it as a question. "Get Glassworks back."

That last sentence was not a question, and Kelli didn't know what to make of it.

"This folder could've been used for anything," she said, lowering it to her lap. "It wasn't marked at all."

"What did he tell Joel to try to get the Glassworks back?" AJ asked. "We know Joel bought it out from under him..."

Kelli's mind spun, because yes, she did know that now. That news had come out almost a year ago, after Joel Shields had died and left all of his papers behind.

Kristen had signed the Glassworks back over to Kelli, but she'd done nothing with the land or building yet. She honestly didn't know what to do with them; she wasn't a glassblower or artist. She'd simply wanted them to keep them in her family. Her father had been so talented, and she had so many good memories at the building where he'd completed so many great art pieces.

"Let me call Alice," Kelli said. "Maybe she can come here for our meeting at two."

"Oh, you're meeting with Alice?" AJ asked.

Kelli nodded, her focus on her phone. "Yes, she's looking at some of the legal aspects of the will for me. I also need to call my sister again. Do you care if I hang out here with you?"

She looked up at AJ, whose bottom lip started to tremble. "I'd love that, Kel," AJ whispered. "Thank you for believing me."

"Of course I believe you," Kelli said, abandoning her phone and leaning over to give AJ a hug. "I know I'm crazy. It might hurt to know what this list is, but I feel like right now, I need to know."

"Then I'll help you any way I can." AJ had always been a fiercely loyal friend, and Kelli appreciated that now more than ever.

She sent her text to Alice, who responded instantly with, *Of course. I'll be there at two*, and she sighed as she leaned back into the couch.

"I haven't heard a word about Shad Webb," AJ said. "Do you feel like talking about him?"

Kelli grinned and she glanced at her best friend. "Sure, I can talk about him."

CHAPTER TWENTY-SIX

A lice looked up as her doorbell rang. It took a moment for her mind to leave the document she'd been studying, and then a few more for her to wonder who could possibly be stopping by in the middle of the day.

Her stomach growled as she got to her feet, and she glanced at the top of her monitor, where the clock sat.

Just after noon; no wonder she was hungry. Alice wasn't a big breakfast eater, though she did enjoy coffee. Sometimes she had a fruit cup with it, but more often than not, she counted the cream and sugar as her treat for the day.

Someone knocked, and Alice got out of her desk chair. "Coming," she called. Maybe she had a package she had to sign for. She stepped out of the office, rounded the corner, and reached for the doorknob.

She pulled open the door, expecting to see a delivery man and falling back a step when she found Arthur standing there.

A grin formed on his face as his eyes traveled up the height of her body to her face. "Do you have time for lunch?" He held up a plastic bag that had a suspicious-looking lobster on it.

Alice grinned back at him, her heartbeat cartwheeling through her chest. "Is that a lobster roll from Tradewinds?"

"Perhaps," he said, stepping forward and into the house.

Alice didn't move an inch, which meant he now stood in her personal space. He leaned toward her, inhaled, and said, "It's good to see you."

She tilted her head slightly, and that was all the encouragement Arthur needed. He kissed her, his mouth aligning perfectly with hers.

The man had some experience with women, because he could kiss Alice and make her weak in the knees on the first stroke. She reached up and threaded her fingers through his hair and stood right there in her open doorway to return his kiss.

He pulled away with a chuckle. "I have to be back in thirty minutes."

"Maybe you could come back tonight for dinner too," she said. "You never did answer my text." She closed the door as he walked further into her house.

"I had a meeting," he said. "Office? Or kitchen?"

"Let's go in the kitchen," she said, following him as he started that way. "I don't like eating where I work. Then I feel like I never get a break."

"Smart," he said.

"How long do you get for lunch over there?" she asked.

"Forty minutes."

"And you have thirty left?"

"I called in the order." He put the bag on the table and started unpacking it. With two clear plastic containers on the table, and Alice grabbing a couple of forks from her utensil drawer, they sat down to eat.

Alice thought of when she'd snuck off campus as a teenager. It never had been to eat with her boyfriend, but to make out with him.

She looked away from Arthur and at her lobster roll, something she'd mentioned to him on their first date.

"I didn't know Tradewinds delivered," she said.

"Everywhere delivers now, Alice. If the restaurant doesn't, FoodShare will."

"Oh, do you like FoodShare? I haven't tried it."

"I pretty much eat exclusively food that someone else brings me." He laughed and opened his plastic container too. He'd ordered the fish tacos and krab salad, and he forked up a bite of the latter.

"It's just a RideShare driver picking up and delivering food," he said. "You can order from almost anywhere now."

"Interesting," Alice said. "I'll have to try it." The twins' eating habits would change dramatically if she started letting them use FoodShare. Charlie had asked about it a while ago, but Alice had said no and ordered pizza.

"Ginny cooks sometimes," Alice says. "Some nights are cold cereal or pancakes." She didn't want to admit that she couldn't afford to feed herself and her kids at a restaurant, fast-casual or not, seven days a week. But she couldn't. She didn't think most people could.

Her first bite of the lobster roll reminder her why she loved Tradewinds, and she groaned with the creamy lobster meat and the tart, mustardy sauce that set their rolls above the others.

Arthur smiled at her and picked up one of his tacos. "I hope I didn't interrupt."

"You can always interrupt if you're bringing me lunch," she said with a smile. "Or even if you're not." She was comfortable with him, and Alice sure did like that. She liked that they talked about grown-up things—situations and experiences they were having right now—and didn't have any past to reminisce about. She'd liked that with Will too, but when it came time to be forty-five instead of fifteen, there'd been very little there.

"Anything exciting going on at the high school?" she asked him.

"Actually," he said. "I'm getting an award."

Alice's eyes widened at the same rate her joy did. "Arthur, that's fantastic," she said. She got to her feet and stepped over to him to give him a hug. The angle was awkward, and Arthur reached up to put his arm around her. He sort of patted, and foolishness filled Alice, causing her to step away quickly.

"Oh, okay," he said, chuckling as she retook her seat. "I should get an award every day."

She laughed too, hoping to cover the awkwardness with the sound of her voice.

"What was the award for?" she asked.

"I'm getting counselor of the year," he said, his smile twinged with pride.

"Arthur, that's amazing. Really."

"Thank you." He ducked his head and focused on his food. Alice finished her roll too, and then stood to put their containers in the recycling bin.

She turned to find Arthur standing right behind her. He took her into his arms and kissed her again, this time with more passion than when they'd stood out in the open for anyone to see. His fingers tangled in her hair, and he broke the kiss only to move his mouth to her earlobe.

"Arthur," she gasped as he pressed her into the kitchen cabinets next to the garbage can. Her foot caught against it, causing it to slide. Arthur didn't seem to care, and Alice didn't either.

Everything inside her fired now, his hands sliding down the sides of her neck to her shoulders. He stood right in front of her, giving her no room to move, but Alice didn't mind at all. She didn't want to move even an inch.

She reached up and ran her hand through her hair, leaning her head back to give him better access to her neck.

"The twins won't be home for a while, right?" he asked.

"No," Alice gasped, but she wanted to know why he'd asked. "Don't you have to get back to work?"

"I can stay," he said, reclaiming her mouth. Alice lost herself in his touch, and it had been such a long time since Alice had felt this strongly about a man. Even Will didn't ignite her the way Arthur did.

"I want you," he said, circling her nipples with his thumbs. "Do you have time?"

He was really asking if she'd sleep with him, and while Alice wasn't sure how much time had passed since he'd shown up on the front stoop with lunch, it couldn't have been more than twenty minutes.

"I have time," she said, pushing against his chest gently. She met his eye, the desire and hope in his plain to see. "Is it too early?"

"You tell me," he said, placing one hand flat against the cupboard next to her head.

"Who's the last woman you went out with?" she asked.

"Sarena Fletcher," he said. "She's a few years younger than me, and I met her at a singles' karaoke night."

"Wow," Alice said, sliding her hand down the front of his dress shirt. Her fingers paused when they touched the top of his belt. He put his other hand against the cabinet on the other side of her head, as if bracing himself to stand there, Alice contained in the space between his arms.

"How long ago was that?" she whispered.

"A year or so ago," he said, pulling in a breath.

"Did you sleep with her?" Alice asked, arching her back and pressing her chest against his in the small amount of space they had.

"No," he said. "She was interesting, and I liked her. We were more like friends. In fact, we're still friends."

"You don't want to be my friend?" Alice asked.

"I want to be your friend," he said. "I want to be your lover. You turn me on in a way no woman has in a long time. You're beautiful and interesting. I love spending time with you, and I love talking to you."

"Did you bring me a lobster roll from Tradewinds so you could sleep with me?"

He looked like she'd slapped him across the face, and that was all the answer Alice needed.

She matched her mouth to his and pressed on his chest to get him to back up. Then she tugged on his tie and led him to her bedroom.

ALICE COLLECTED HER PAPERS AND GRABBED HER PURSE. SHE reminded herself that she could be a few minutes late to meet with AJ and Kelli, because it was, well, AJ and Kelli.

Neither of them were paying her, and she'd so been enjoying her conversation with Arthur, and she hated to cut things short with him.

He'd left only ten minutes ago, when she should've been in a car on her way to AJ's. She'd still been in bed, and she'd watched him get re-dressed in the dim light, blissfully happy. Happier than she'd been in a long, long time.

"Game face," she muttered to herself. "Channel your inner Kelli." She didn't want to tell anyone that she'd slept with Arthur only a week after meeting him. After two dates.

Great dates, sure. Lots of texting, yes. A few phone conversations, of course. She supposed the lunch they'd just shared could be considered date number three, but Alice still felt like she'd accelerated things in her love life too fast.

As she tapped to request a RideShare, a flush of heat overcame her, very much the way it had when they'd made love.

Alice smiled to herself, because Arthur was a far better lover than Frank. She'd laid in Arthur's arms, and they'd talked about her love of the law. How much she wanted her children to be happy and healthy and free from harm. He'd told her about his first wife, and why they'd broken up.

He'd told her what had brought him to Five Island Cove, and why he'd stayed. Only when her alarm went off, reminding her of her meeting with Kelli, did she realize how much time had passed.

She strode down the sidewalk toward the RideShare, thinking of Arthur's final kiss goodbye. "Pick you up at six?" he'd asked. "I can come at five too."

"Let's do five," she'd said.

Charlie had to work until six, and Ginny would be scooping ice cream until ten. Her mind whirred, and she thought perhaps they could make love in her bed again the moment he arrived, then go to dinner, and have another romp at his house before the night ended.

She shook her head in disbelief. She wasn't sure if she wanted to set that precedent, but then she remembered the way he'd—

"Ma'am?" the driver asked, and Alice looked up. Heat filled her face, as if the twenty-something would know what she'd been thinking about. "Where to?"

"Sorry," she said, quickly rattling off AJ's address.

Game face, she told herself again. She couldn't be thinking about Arthur's body and how hers had reacted to his while with a client. She shouldn't for her best friends either.

At least not if she wanted to keep their private activities private, which she did.

She sent a group text to Charlie and Ginny, telling them about her date and that she'd be home before eleven.

They both responded before she arrived at AJ's, and

Alice paid the driver and got out of the car just as a text from Arthur came in.

Your place or mine tonight?

A grin exploded across her face, especially at the next text.

I'm erasing all of these texts as soon as I send them. Well, at least this one. That was the best afternoon I've had in my life. I hope you enjoyed it too.

She giggled, her thumbs flying across her screen. *You better erase that. What if one of your students sees it?*

You erase them too, he said.

Deal, she sent to him. *And the answer to your question is both.*

She hoped that would be enough to let him know that she'd had an amazing afternoon with him, and that she could scarcely wait three more hours to be with him again.

The front door opened, and Kelli came to the top of the steps.

Gotta go, she said. *No more texts. I'm with my friends.*

Deal, Arthur said. *To everything you said.*

Alice deleted the entire thread, though she wished she could read the part about how that afternoon with her had been the best one of his life time and time again.

Alice had never felt very desired by Frank. If she was so fantastic, why did he chase other women? Why did he sleep with them? Why didn't he come home during the week?

For a long time, Alice had believed he simply had a sexual appetite she couldn't satisfy. When he did come home on the weekends, they'd make love three and four times, and it was never enough.

After a while, Alice simply felt used, and when she'd told Frank that, he'd said he needed the release. At that point, she knew he'd been sleeping around on her, probably extensively, in the city, and she hadn't let him touch her again.

It had felt so nice to be touched again, and touched by a man that obviously adored her and craved only her.

"Are you coming in?" Kelli called, and Alice once again pulled herself out of her thoughts.

"Yes," she said, tucking her phone into her purse and striding down the driveway.

CHAPTER TWENTY-SEVEN

Kelli listened to Alice detail that since her mother was the primary beneficiary of the will, anything she'd have done when her father had died could still be applied.

"She would've taken his name off bank accounts," Alice said. "Her car insurance, home owners insurance, all of that. She'd have gotten any life insurance, as well as any death benefits, social security or pension payments."

Kelli just kept shaking her head. "Dad didn't have life insurance," she said. "That's why his death was so hard. He literally left my mom penniless." She thought of the seventy-seven thousand dollars. Why had her father never mentioned it?

"All of that's been done," Alice said. "And she refused the money, so." She shrugged one shoulder. "I did draw up a one-time agreement between you and your sisters that spells out where the money is coming from, that your mother doesn't want it, and that the three of you are agreeing to split it, and we'll list exactly how much each of you will get."

"Okay," Kelli said.

"Everyone will sign it, including your mom, and then the money will be distributed." Alice looked up from her clipboard. "Do you have the money?"

"Not here," Kelli said. "It's still in the house on Seabreeze Shore."

"I'll need it," Alice said. "I'll deposit it into an escrow account, and we'll pay from there. That way, everything is done legally, for everyone involved. Not that I think you'll have any problems with Sabrina or Heather, but I personally think it's better to be safe in this situation."

"Okay," Kelli said again, starting to get overwhelmed. She swallowed and shook her head. She wasn't going to get overwhelmed by this. Alice was going to take care of it.

"I can send everything electronically," Alice said. "I use a program for that, and it's a few taps and done. No one has to come here."

Kelli nodded, a trickle of relief filtering through her.

"I do that all the time for my freelance contracts," AJ said, squeezing Kelli's hand.

Alice noticed the moment and paused in her speech. "What do you think about that list of names?" she asked, her eyes locked on AJ.

Kelli wanted to jump to AJ's defense, but she bit back

the words. They exchanged a glance, because they'd been talking for hours about this very thing.

"I don't know, honestly," AJ said. "I think Guy made it for something...or someone."

"Someone?" Alice asked.

"There's writing on the back of the folder," Kelli said, bending to retrieve it from the coffee table where she'd put it. "We're not sure what it means."

She handed the folder to Alice, who examined the back of it, her eyebrows shooting up. They immediately folded into a frown, and Kelli watched her tilt the folder to catch the light too.

"Keep the Glassworks," she said. "Could he have known Joel was the one who bought it out from under him?"

"So what?" Kelli asked. "He was going to give Joel a list of names?"

"Maybe." Alice put the folder down, still eyeing it. She cleared her throat and folded her hands on the clipboard resting on her knees. "We know, uh, that Joel." She cleared her throat again. "Hit on Amelia. What if Guy was providing him a list of girls and women who might be open to that?"

"Why would I be open to that?" AJ demanded, her eyes hard as rocks. Her grip was too, and Kelli tried to let go of her hand.

"She's not saying you are," Kelli said. "But maybe my

dad *thought* you would be. It wasn't exactly secret that you slept with a lot of boys."

AJ glared at Kelli next, and she almost shrank away from her. Almost. She held her head high, because she didn't have to back down from the truth. Not anymore.

"And Joel didn't hit on you," Kelli said. "He chose your sister. Maybe...I don't know, AJ." She rubbed her hand across her eyes and up into her hair. "We've been talking about this for a while," she told Alice. "We could all sit here and hypothesize forever, but the truth is, the two men who know aren't here anymore."

"No," Alice said. "But some of the women are." She spoke the sentence slowly, as if she knew that Kelli needed time to absorb the idea.

"We could ask them," Kelli said. "The ones we can find, at least."

"I know Robin said her mom knew one of them," Alice said. "She's been texting me about it."

"Eloise asked Aaron to look into all the names," Kelli said. "She said she'd let me know when or if he found anything."

"So we're all working this." Alice sat back and smile. "I guess we should've known that we would."

"It's what we do," AJ said quietly. She did release Kelli's hand then and got slowly to her feet.

"Where are you going?" Alice asked, rising to her feet too. Kelli was glad she wasn't the only overprotective one.

"I'm allowed to walk into the bathroom," AJ said,

smiling at Alice. "Be right back." She lumbered away, and Kelli wanted to tell her she was going to get twice, maybe three times as big as she was now, but she didn't have the heart.

"How do you think she's doing?" Alice asked, also watching her.

"She's fine if she thinks we believe her." Kelli bore the weight of Alice's eyes as she swung them toward her.

"You don't believe her?"

"I do," Kelli said. "It's important that we *all* tell her we believe her."

"I will," Alice said. "AJ had some problems as a teen, but she would've never done that."

"I know." Kelli switched her gaze to the folder, wishing something so small and so mundane didn't hold such great power over her. "Real quick—how's Arthur? Just between you and me. When are you seeing him again?"

"Dinner tonight," Alice said, a new light coming into her dark gaze. "You? How's Shad?"

"Good," Kelli said, warmth flowing through her. "He's picking me up here when he gets off this afternoon. Dinner tonight for us too."

"Good for you, Kel." Alice grinned at her and looked down at her list. "I think I covered everything dealing with the will."

"Okay," Kelli said. "Thank you, Alice. I'll bring the money tomorrow when I come to work. I'll pay you from it for your time and trouble."

"Don't be silly." Alice waved her hand. "We're best friends."

Kelli watched her, and a year ago, she would've kept her money. This year, Kelli knew Alice wasn't much better off financially than she was.

"You'll have to set up the bank account. Deal with the paperwork. Distribute the money. I'll pay you."

"Let's say three hundred dollars," Alice said. "Is that fair?"

"Yes," Kelli agreed instantly. "You can keep it from the cash, like I said. Okay?"

Alice nodded and glanced at her phone as a message popped up. "It's Robin."

"Maybe we could go shopping this afternoon," Kelli said. "If we're done here, I think AJ needs a nap, and I have money to spend on beds and couches."

Alice's face lit up again, because the woman loved shopping. "Let's see what Kristen and Robin are doing," she said. "Eloise will be at the inn, and I know Laurel is on Sanctuary too."

"We can put out the invite on the group text," Kelli said. "Even though it's last-minute." She liked getting invited even though she couldn't attend ninety percent of what her friends did. She simply wanted to know they'd like her to be there if she could.

She started typing. "I'll do it."

"Okay," Alice said, obviously distracted by Robin's text that had come in.

Kelli sent the message and looked up. "Done."

Alice's frown had deepened, and when she looked up, her eyes held trouble. "You guys will have to go without me." She got to her feet. "I just remembered I have a call at three I forgot about."

Kelli heard the lie, but Alice left so fast Kelli couldn't even think of a question to ask. She looked toward the front door and then the hallway AJ had gone down to use the restroom. She hadn't come back yet, and it had been several minutes.

Worry needled Kelli, but the group text on her phone went off several times.

Working, Laurel said. *Have fun!*

Me too, Eloise had said. *Send pictures.*

I can come, Kristen had said, and Kelli did want to see her. Her smile filled her face as Robin said, *I would love some retail therapy. I just need about thirty minutes to finish up with something. I can meet you there?*

Yep, Kelli said and she looked back down the hall. AJ still hadn't returned, and Kelli didn't want to leave without saying good-bye.

She picked up the folder and slipped it into her purse. She walked over to the office and knocked on the open door. "Matt?" she asked.

He turned from his computer and pulled out one of his headphones.

"Hey, Kelli." He got to his feet and stretched, his T-shirt lifting up above the waistband on his gym shorts. "Where's AJ?"

"She went to the bathroom several minutes ago," Kelli said. "I have to go, but I thought you'd want to know."

He looked in the direction the hall led, but of course he couldn't see through the wall. "Okay," he said. "I'll check on her and tell her you're leaving."

"All right." Kelli waited while he went down the hall and into a bedroom. He didn't come right back, and Kelli's nerves began fraying along the edges.

She texted AJ. *Are you okay?*

She didn't respond.

Finally, Matt came out into the hall. He wore a guarded look and said, "She's not feeling well, Kelli. She said she'll call you later."

Kelli nodded, wondering what she'd said or done to upset AJ after being there practically all day. Perhaps it had been something Alice had said or done.

"Thanks, Matt," she said, and she stepped out onto the porch. She tapped to call a RideShare, and then she tapped to call Kristen.

"I'm coming to you," she said. "I can give Parker a squeeze, and then we can go, okay?"

"Okay," Kristen said. "What about Robin?"

Kelli went down the front steps, her intuition so much better than it had once been. "I don't think she's coming either," she said. "It's probably just going to be me and you."

"Sounds good to me," Kristen said, and Kelli had to agree. She did want to know what was going on with Robin and Alice, but she could be patient. After all, nothing stayed secret for very long between their group of women.

CHAPTER TWENTY-EIGHT

R obin didn't know what to do besides what she'd already done. She'd calmed Mandie and got out the chocolate ice cream, hot fudge, and canned whipped cream. The only reason they had those particular pick-me-ups was because Robin had gone grocery shopping that morning.

She'd splurged with the ice cream and whipped cream, and she'd used her homemade hot fudge to help get the story out of Mandie.

"I just don't believe it," she said again, though the drama had unfolded already and Mandie was safely tucked away on the couch, a movie on and a blanket over her feet. Jamie had said she'd watch out for her, and Robin had come back into the office to get some more work done.

Nothing more had been accomplished though. She'd

texted Alice several times, and the woman hadn't texted back.

Robin looked at her phone. *Mandie is really upset about Charlie. I guess she thinks he broke up with her, even though he didn't say those words? Do you know what's going on?*

When Alice didn't respond, it was because she didn't want to. It usually meant that yes, she knew what was going on, and that only made Robin's teeth itch to talk to her best friend.

"I knew the two of them dating would be a problem," she muttered to herself. And not just a problem for Mandie, but one for Robin and Alice too. She didn't need anything else to come between her and her friends, as her family and her job already did a fine job of that.

She schooled her thoughts, because her family came before everyone and everything. Mandie and Robin's relationship with her came before everything, and she'd sacrifice her Wednesday lunches with her friends for her daughter.

It would be hard—it would be a sacrifice—but Robin would do it.

She did not want her relationship with her daughters to be even an echo of the one she had with her mother. Empty. Hollow. Constant striving to be good enough, when such a thing didn't even exist.

She had asked her mom a few more questions about Jill Bunton, and she'd even gotten the woman's phone number, because she apparently still owned her cleaning company.

Her mother told her that Jill herself didn't go out and clean anymore, but that she had a crew of over two dozen people who serviced the families on all five islands.

Robin had called as if she was looking for someone to come clean her house, and Jill still did all the appraisals and quotes. She was coming tomorrow morning to look at Robin's house, get an idea of what she wanted done and how often, and then she'd get a quote from her.

Robin felt a bit bad wasting the woman's time. She couldn't afford a housekeeper, and not just monetarily. She wasn't sure she could give up the control.

Robin liked things done a certain way, and she didn't see herself paying someone else to scrub the toilets in a way that wasn't what she would do.

She sighed, realizing how much time had passed since she'd texted Alice. Twenty minutes. The woman never went very far without her phone, as she used it so often for business.

The doorbell rang, startling Robin away from her thoughts and her silent phone. She let out a gasp and then got to her feet as quickly as possible. "Focus," she told herself as she smoothed down the front of her blouse.

She had a meeting with a potential new bride and her mother, and this was a fall wedding, so Robin wouldn't be so frantic about it. The fifty-percent deposit would help her right now, and Robin could worry about the work later.

She pulled open the door, her professional smile in place, only to find Alice standing there. She wore a terrified look on her face, and she glanced past Robin to where the movie played behind her in the living room.

Robin swallowed, met Alice's eye, had a silent conversation, and stepped out onto the front porch, bringing the door closed behind her.

"I have a meeting with a potential bride," Robin said, folding her arms as if she could keep her body warmth inside by that action alone. The wind blew between the houses on this side of the island, and sometimes Robin couldn't stand the breeze. It wore at her until she was just too tired to deal with much of anything.

"I'll be fast," Alice said. Reaching up to tuck her hair behind her ear. "What did Charlie say?"

"It was a little murky, honestly," Robin said with a sigh. "Mandie was upset and crying, but the gist of it was that Charlie pulled away from her at lunch today, and when she asked him why, he suggested maybe he wanted to see other people."

Alice's mouth dropped open. She blinked her false eyelashes several times. "He used those words? See other people?"

"Or something like, maybe we shouldn't be so serious." Robin shook her head. "The message was that he obviously wanted to go out with other girls. To Mandie. That's what she thought."

Alice shook her head. "He joined the Academic Olympiad. Today's their first practice after school."

"Okay," Robin said, not quite connecting all the dots.

"The captain of the team is a really cute blonde girl," Alice said. "He had her and a couple of other people from the team over to the house, and I met her. I could tell Charlie liked her." Alice sighed and rolled her neck. "I'm sorry, Robin. I told him he couldn't be flirting with Sariah if he had a girlfriend, and that if he wanted to go out with her, he should have a conversation with Mandie."

"Well, it sounds like he did."

"I'll talk to him. See what he's thinking on his end."

Robin shook her head. "Mandie would be livid. Just leave it. See what he says to you. If it's something I should know, let me know."

"Really?" Alice asked.

Robin nodded as a blue minivan pulled up to the curb in front of her house. "Really. We've always said that, Alice. They're dating. They might break-up. We only get involved if there's a real reason to."

"So..."

"Any other boy? I'd do what I've already done. Soothe my daughter with ice cream and pray to know what else to do. I wouldn't text his mother. I only did you, because we're so close."

Alice reached for her and hugged her, and Robin melted into the embrace. She'd been holding everything so tight for so long, and it sure was nice to know she had someone strong and powerful like Alice Kelton in her corner.

"I love you, Robin," Alice said. "Please let me know if I can help you or Mandie. I'll see what Charlie says." She pulled back and nodded, and Robin gave her a trembling smile.

"Okay," she said, drawing in a deep breath. "My client is here."

Alice looked over her shoulder. 'Thanks so much, Robin," she said in a louder voice, and Alice had always been quite talented at acting. "You're a lifesaver." She practically flounced down the front steps like Robin had just done the greatest of favors for her, and Robin's gaze switched to the two women walking toward her.

She put the professional smile back on her face and said, "Valerie, Jess, welcome."

ROBIN QUICKLY TOSSED THE DUSTER UNDER THE KITCHEN sink as the first tones of the doorbell filled the house. She really didn't need to clean before the maid service showed up, but that was just her ugly, controlling nature rearing its head.

She hurried down the hall toward the small foyer and opened the door. The woman standing there had gray hair with some dark strands still flowing through it. She was beautiful and elegant in more ways than one, and her dark brown eyes had seen so much in her days. They held wisdom Robin didn't know, and she stepped back as she said, "Come in. You must be Jill."

She smiled and came inside, looking at the ground to watch her step. "That I am. You look just like your mother, but not with so many years."

Robin kept her smile in place. She weighed about half as much as her mother too, but she said nothing. She closed the door and said, "I'm glad she reminded me that you ran this cleaning business. I've been so swamped this spring already."

"Yes, wedding season here in Five Island Cove is picking up." Jill flashed a smile over her shoulder. "Tell me what you were thinking."

"My friend, Kelli Thompson, started at a school this year." Robin rounded Jill so she could see her face. She carried a mini-clipboard with her and a pen.

"Oh, you probably know her as Kelli Watkins." Robin waited, expecting something to happen to Jill's face. She did look up from the checklist on her clipboard, her eyes a bit rounder. Maybe.

"I knew the Watkins', yes," she said, but Robin couldn't be sure if her voice was cooler or not.

"It seems everyone did," Robin said. "Guy was like a local celebrity, what with doing all those pieces in Washington." She increased her smile if that was even possible.

"Kelli was one of my best friends. She was so proud of him."

"I cleaned the Glassworks for a few years," Jill said, practically feeding Robin the opening she needed.

"Oh, you did? That must've been fascinating."

"Seeing all the pieces in various stages of completion was interesting," Jill said, giving Robin a closed-mouth smile afterward. "What were you thinking for your house?"

"I honestly don't know," Robin said. "Tell me what you can do."

Jill started to detail that her ladies could come every week or every other week. They could do a variety of household tasks, including laundry and appliance cleaning. Robin said she just wanted the floors done, the office, the kitchen, all the bathrooms cleaned, and the bedrooms vacuumed.

"Let me work up a quote," Jill said. "How many square feet is the house?"

"Twenty-two hundred," Robin said. "No one really uses the bedrooms upstairs. I don't think we need those done."

"Stairs? Swept and mopped?"

"No," Robin said. "If we go up there, I can do that."

Jill nodded, and Robin's phone chimed. The stars felt like they were aligning, because Kelli's name sat on the screen. "Oh, it's Kelli. Speak of the devil."

She'd asked if everyone would be at the Wednesday

luncheon tomorrow, and others had already started to confirm.

Yes, Robin said, though she had several time-sensitive phone calls to make before then.

"Did you know Guy and Paula well?" Robin asked.

"Not well," Jill said. "Guy more than Paula. He hired me, and he paid me." She glanced up and unclipped a card from her board. "Here you go."

"Did you like him?" Robin took the card. "I'll admit, as a teenager, he was scary."

"He had...moments," Jill said, and Robin could tell she was trying to be kind.

"Why'd you stop cleaning for him?" Robin asked.

Jill's expression darkened, and she nodded to the card. "Call me if you'd like to get on the schedule. I listed the available days." She turned toward the front door, and Robin's desperation rose.

"Kelli just found her father's will," she blurted out as Jill walked away from her. "She found a list with your name on it."

Jill stopped and spun back to her. "My name?"

Robin nodded, swallowing at the dangerous look in Jill's dark eyes. "We're just trying to figure out who you all are."

"Who we are?" Jill stepped back toward her. "How many of us are on the list?"

"Eleven," Robin said, pressing her palms together.

"Did he hit on you? Did you...?" Robin couldn't ask her if she'd slept with him. She just couldn't.

"Hit on me?" Jill asked. "No, he didn't hit on me. Guy barely looked at anything besides his art. The man was incredibly arrogant, but he wasn't a sleaze."

Robin didn't want to argue with her on that point. "Can you think of any reason you might be on a list Guy Watkins kept?"

"Yes," Jill said. "The man demanded money from me so he wouldn't destroy my business."

Robin opened her mouth, but quickly closed it, trying to wrap her mind around what Jill had said.

"What?" she finally asked.

"He blackmailed me," Jill said. "And God help me, I paid him." Her face crumbled and she dropped her chin to her chest as she began to cry. "I paid him to keep his mouth shut."

CHAPTER TWENTY-NINE

L aurel sat back down on her bed, tucking one leg underneath her. She took a bite of her caramel cashew ice cream and looked at the papers she'd spread out.

She'd been studying them for hours now, and she'd even slept at Paul's last night just so she didn't have to clean this up and spread it out again.

She really liked staying at Paul's too, so there was that little fact as well. Even now, she smiled as she thought about him. He'd come in late that afternoon, and he was working until eleven tonight so the Chief could have a night at home with his family.

The late hours gave Laurel a chance to study the papers the mysterious Betsy Dinerstein had delivered to the Chief. Laurel had done some digging—something she was very good at—and learned that Betsy was almost sixty years old.

If she fit the woman in with Robin and Alice's age group and timeline of when Guy had likely made the list, she'd have been almost thirty years old at the time of her interactions with him.

A range, really, of twenty-five to thirty-five. Cops didn't assign hard and fast rules to the age of anyone they didn't know everything about.

She hadn't had any gray hair in the police station, and Laurel would not have pegged her for a woman of almost sixty. She'd looked for offspring of Betsy, and she'd learned the woman had two sons. No daughters. No sisters. A couple of sisters-in-law, but they were older than her.

The paperwork in the white envelope she'd swiped from the Chief's desk consisted of six sheets of paper, each a bank statement.

Laurel had sorted them by date, which had taken her a moment to locate among the tiny print. They each showed the same bank account from thirty-two years ago, and during the six-month period from July to December of that year, a deposit of fifty-five hundred dollars had landed in this account.

There was no name on the account, and no number. Anyone could've typed up this list of items in a spreadsheet, though Laurel had analyzed bank statements before and they looked like this.

The other items in the account were what had Laurel eating ice cream and peering down at the pages. She could learn a lot about a person based on what they chose to spend their money on. She was sure Alice's bank account showed withdrawals for pizza and other fast food or dining out, as the woman didn't cook very much.

Someone like Robin would have a higher grocery bill, and she'd have transactions from the home goods store or the florist, as Laurel had literally never been to her house and seen the same pillows twice. Robin always had fresh flowers on the table next to the front door, and Laurel knew whoever's bank account she'd been looking at for the past two days wasn't anything like Robin.

Utilities got paid from this account. Groceries, though surely not as many as Robin bought. Very little in the way of restaurants or specialty shops.

This person bought from the hardware store often, and Laurel had marked those buys with green highlighter. She couldn't tell what they'd bought at the hardware store, but she'd put out a call to Cole's and learned that the code at the end of the transaction belonged to the branch of the hardware store on Bell Island.

This person wrote quite a few checks, which was very normal for the late eighties and early nineties. A lot of people didn't have debit cards, as they hadn't been as widespread then as they were now. Unfortunately, Laurel couldn't tell who or what the checks were for. All she could see was the number and the amount.

Every time the fifty-five hundred dollars had been deposited, within three days, a check for the same amount had gone out of the account. Sometimes the very next day. Sometimes two days, but never more than three.

She believed this was Guy Watkins's account, but she had no way to prove it.

Leaning back, she finished her ice cream with her eyes trained on the ceiling. She needed time to think, and there was nothing that spurred her brain cells more than caramel.

She wasn't sure what these documents proved, other than that someone had been paying Guy Watkins, if he was indeed the owner of this bank account, fifty-five hundred dollars for six straight months.

Thirty years ago, that was a lot of money. Heck, it was a lot of money now—more than Laurel made in a month of patrolling the streets of Sanctuary Island.

That money could account for half of what Kelli had found in the lockbox beneath the floorboards.

"He could've been writing the checks to cash," Laurel said. In her opinion, that was the most likely scenario. It would be the easiest way to get the money out of the bank, and it fit the statements.

Sighing, she reached for her phone. Aaron's line rang, and Laurel knew he'd answer. So she wasn't surprised when he said, "Laurel, what's up?" after only a couple of rings.

"I have a confession," she said. "I was in your office on

Sunday night with Paul..." She told the whole story and that she'd taken the envelope with the bank statements in it, because she recognized the name Betsy Dinerstein.

"Okay," Chief Sherman said with a sigh. "El asked me to dig, and I'd already started. I guess Betsy was faster than I anticipated."

"I'm sorry," Laurel said. "I was just trying to help my friends too."

"Hang on a sec, Laurel." He didn't bother to cover the speaker as he said, "El, it's Laurel, and she's got a piece of the puzzle. How long until dinner?"

Eloise said something, but Laurel couldn't hear it.

"Yep," Aaron said, his voice back in Laurel's ear. "Can you come to my place for dinner? We can go over all of it together."

"You have more?" Laurel asked.

"Yep. Like I said, Eloise asked me to dig into it." He started to chuckle. "I should've known you would too."

"Well, I mean..." Laurel didn't know how to explain. "I'm sorry."

"El says twenty minutes," the Chief said. "See you soon."

Laurel extended the white envelope toward Aaron the moment he opened the door. "They're bank statements."

He took them and said, "From Betsy Dinerstein?"

"Yep." She waited for him to back up, and then she entered the house.

"Laurel," little Grace said, running toward her. "Look at this tiger I drew." She waved a piece of paper in the air, and Laurel would never be able to see it.

She chuckled as she crouched in front of the little girl. Aaron's youngest daughter was an amazing artist, and once Laurel got the tiger to stop waving, she could see the talent.

"Wow," she said, taking in the beautiful lines. "You're getting really good with the colored pencils."

"Eloise signed me up for some private art lessons." Grace grinned at Laurel. "Like those self-defense classes you took."

Laurel smiled back and her and pressed a kiss to her cheek. "Is your daddy gonna put that on the fridge?"

"Nope," Grace said, taking it back from Laurel. "Eloise made a case in the hallway, and we're going to put my best pieces in there."

"Laurel, you're here," Eloise said, and Laurel almost toppled over to straighten faster.

"Hey."

Eloise gave her a smile and hugged her, saying, "You saved us with that phone call. Aaron was getting so frustrated," in a low voice.

"About what?" Laurel asked, noting that Aaron had

bustled on out of the living room the moment he'd closed the door behind her.

"He's trying to make all kinds of pieces fit together, but we're not even sure they're to the same puzzle."

"He must have found a lot more information than I did."

"He's put out a few calls," Eloise said. "Being Chief of Police allows him...certain luxuries."

"I'll bet it does." Laurel grinned at Eloise. "What have you guys learned?"

"The total is up to over ten grand," Aaron called from the other room, and Laurel turned that way.

"He's in the office just around the corner," Eloise said, leading the way. She went in that direction, and Laurel followed her. They hadn't had their massage day yet, and Laurel still felt a little bit out of sorts around Eloise Hall.

She told herself she didn't need to feel that way, but some things couldn't be overcome just because she told herself to stop feeling a specific way.

"Ten thousand?" Eloise asked.

"With these statements," Aaron said, pinning something to a board. "He's up to thirteen thousand per month."

Laurel stopped farther back than Eloise, who went over to his desk and looked at the papers he'd spread out much the same way Laurel had.

He'd organized the board into months, each one

labeled for a fifteen-month period, ending with a yellow sticky note that listed the date Guy Watkins had died.

"These only go for six months," he said. "He's smart to not let them carry on for too long, but this is the biggest amount we've seen yet." Aaron scrawled something on a blue sticky note and stuck it to the statement that Laurel had highlighted in green.

Laurel tilted her head, counting the other papers he'd already tacked up. Four. The ones she'd provided made five.

"Talk to me, Chief," she said. "He was blackmailing people?"

"I think so," Aaron said. "The women I've spoken with —you know, that will allow me to ask them questions— have all admitted to paying off Guy for some reason."

"What reasons?" Laurel asked.

"Ellen Holt paid him eighteen hundred dollars a month because he caught her cheating on her husband."

"She was Kelli's next-door neighbor for a long time," Eloise explained. "The payments stopped when her husband filed for divorce."

"Did Guy tell him about the cheating?" Laurel asked.

"Ellen didn't know. She doesn't think so, because he still wanted money, but Ellen refused to keep paying him to keep a secret she didn't need kept anymore." Aaron kept labeling the blue sticky notes and putting them up near the top of the months.

"Are you coming to lunch tomorrow?" Eloise asked,

looking up at Laurel. "Kelli asked, and I told her we had a lot to show her. We're actually meeting here."

She looked at Aaron, and he shrugged. "I have a shift," she said, feeling her heart stall and then fall to her feet.

Eloise looked from her fiancée to Laurel. "Well, I don't really want you to come if you're sick, but you'll have to make your own decisions." She grinned at Laurel, who heard the slight sarcasm and burst out laughing.

Aaron gaped at his bride-to-be, and then rolled his eyes at Laurel. "Call Dwayne right now. Don't just call in sick."

"Yes, sir," Laurel said, still giggling.

CHAPTER THIRTY

K elli slid a plate of chocolate muffins on the table onto the patio just as Shad came out his front door. "Great minds think alike," he said, putting a platter of banana bread next to her plate. "Is she here?"

"Supposed to be," Kelli said, glancing toward the street. Their twinhome sat at the top of a flight of stairs overlooking the street below, and Kelli loved the view that afforded her.

She could see over the tops of some trees and houses and all the way to the water on the west side of the island, where her front windows faced.

"She'll come," Shad said.

"She sounded afraid, and she had to come all the way from the mainland." Kelli couldn't believe Sidney Tyler had agreed to come at all. Kelli had looked up her number and called her out of the blue, and she hadn't breathed a word about Zach, her supposed son.

Sidney had told her she'd already talked to Aaron Sherman and told him the truthful answers to all of his questions.

Kelli said she'd really just wanted to talk to her for a few minutes. Sidney had said she wanted to visit her sister, who lived on Pearl Island, and she could stop by and see Kelli.

Then Kelli needed to get on the ferry and go pick up Kristen before their luncheon at Aaron Sherman's house.

It was a deviation from their normal Wednesday luncheon at one of the better restaurants in Five Island Cove, but everyone had committed to being there. Every one of them had some information to add to the pot, and Kelli really wanted to stir it all up and see what came out.

A car eased up next to the curb, and Kelli took a couple of steps to the edge of the patio. "She's here."

"I'll get the juice," Shad said. "Give you a minute."

Kelli didn't even have the wherewithal to respond. She watched the tall, redhead unfold herself from the car and look up the steps. Kelli recognized Sidney Tyler, because the woman had been her father's secretary for over a decade. She'd quit suddenly and disappeared essentially overnight, and Kelli hadn't seen her since.

Their eyes met, and Sidney adjusted her purse over her shoulder before she started up the steps.

Kelli watched her approach, a smile coming to her

face as Sidney arrived on the patio. "Thank you for coming," she said, taking Sidney into a light hug she released quickly. "Please, come sit. My boyfriend is bringing out some juice."

Sidney sat at the table, and Kelli did too, perching right on the edge of the hard chair. "I suppose you have all the same questions as the police officer."

"I don't know what he's asked you," Kelli said. When Eloise had called on Sunday night and said she'd told Aaron everything, Kelli had first been horrified and then relieved. The Chief of Police had so much more pull than a petite woman living in a twinhome on Pearl Island.

He'd been accumulating information, and they were meeting later that day to go over all of it. *Everyone* was meeting later that day.

"I just want to know what really happened."

Sidney took a deep breath and then blew it out. "What really happened was your dad combusted. He lost the Glassworks, and things fell apart steadily and swiftly from there."

She reached into her bag and pulled out a folder. "I stayed for another few months, and I did all the receipts and books." She put the folder on the table, and Kelli swallowed just looking at it. She didn't want to open it.

"I kept copies when I left, because it was the only way I could get away without him coming after me for more money."

"*More* money?" Kelli asked.

"Guy had secrets and information on several people," Sidney said. "Men and women around the cove that he knew. Things and situations he'd stumbled into. He started cashing in on those things, because he was desperate to get the Glassworks back."

Kelli didn't look away from the folder. "What did he have on you?"

"I..." She cleared her throat. "I'd gotten pregnant, and I didn't want anyone to know. The man was married, and he was a prominent figure in the cove. I paid your dad for three or four months, but I couldn't hide the pregnancy, and I wasn't willing to terminate it."

"So you left."

"I left," she confirmed. "But not before I made all the copies of everything I had at that point. I told your father about the duplicates and said I'd made my last payment to him. I was done. Out. I never wanted to see him or talk to him again. And I left."

Kelli nodded, meeting Sidney's eyes again. "Was my father a cheater?"

Her eyes widened. "What? No." Sidney shook her head. "Not at all. Your dad just got...lost. Involved in his art so much that creating the next piece became his mistress. His success went to his head, as it often does for creative types who hit it big."

She picked up a piece of banana bread and looked past Kelli to Shad as he came out onto the patio. "This must be your boyfriend." Her smile grew, and she stood to greet Shad.

"Yes," Kelli said. "Shad Webb, this is Sidney Tyler. Sidney, my boyfriend Shad."

"So nice to meet you." He cut a glance at Kelli as he shook her hand. "Should I stay?"

They both looked at Sidney, who nodded as she sat down. "I don't mind." She took a bite of her bread and looked at the folder. "That's what I took when I left. It has all of the information in it. Account numbers. Deposits, which I notated. Some I took right over the counter in the Glassworks' lobby."

"I don't know if I want it," Kelli admitted, reaching for a muffin so she'd have something for her hands to do. She unwrapped the paper from the stump and pinched off a bite of the top.

"You want it, sweetheart." Shad swept the folder off the table and onto his lap. "I'll just hold it for you until you're ready for it." He nodded to her and then Sidney. "Thanks for bringing it. So many things have been in the dark for so long. Kelli's just trying to find the truth so she can move forward."

"I understand completely," Sidney said. "We all have some form of darkness to pass through at some point in our lives."

Kelli nodded, struck by how kind this woman was being to her.

"The truth is, Kelli, that your father was incredibly

gifted in his creative endeavors. He saw things no one else could. He could make hot glass obey him, and he could charm anyone with his jokes. He'd bring them gifts made of colored glass that were meaningful and endearing."

She smiled, and Kelli could feel the friendship and love she had for Kelli's father. She'd seen that side of him too. He'd brought her a horse made of pink glass when she'd wanted a pony for her birthday. The glass in her bedroom windows had come from her dad when she'd said she wanted the colored light in her room. He'd made her mother a ring made of glass that looked like an engagement ring, all faceted and completely composed of a single piece.

"He didn't cheat on your mother, and even after he'd lost everything, I don't think he changed his will. He kept her and you girls in it."

"He didn't have anything," Kelli said, thinking of the wail that had come from her mother's mouth when she'd realized how empty the bank account truly was.

"He had the world," Sidney said, frowning. "It's all there." She nodded the folder in Shad's lap, which held a lot more than five sheets of paper. Probably ten times that.

Exhaustion flowed through Kelli just thinking about looking at it.

Sidney picked up a muffin, having finished her banana bread. She took a few bites, and Kelli poured her a glass of juice, trying to process everything she'd said.

Perhaps, she thought. *Your father wasn't as bad as you thought he was.*

Sadness hit her, because she'd spent so many years thinking the worst of him. What if she'd made a mistake? What if he'd deserved more credit than she'd given him?

She thought of the signed and nearly executed contract between her, Sabrina, and Heather to distribute the money.

If her mom knew the truth, perhaps she'd be more willing to accept her ex-husband's money.

Kelli felt like she was contained inside a mist of darkness, with a dim light down the road. It shone like a pinprick of light, but with every step she took, and every truth she learned, it got bright and bigger.

"My sister is almost here," Sidney said, getting to her feet. "Call me if you need more clarification." She smiled at Kelli and then Shad, turned, and held the railing as she went down the steps.

A car pulled up the moment her foot touched the sidewalk, and she got into the front passenger seat.

"She was nice," Shad said, opening the folder. He flipped a few pages while Kelli watched the dark red sedan drive away. "Thorough."

She looked at him, and he snapped the folder closed. "Good thing you took today off," she said. "Will you help me go through this before I have to head to Diamond?"

A smile grew on his face. "Sweetheart, I'm the financial director for the cove. I can help you go through this in an hour."

He opened the folder, and the first page looked so familiar to Kelli. Handwriting she assumed was Sidney's sat on the light blue, lined paper, with thin columns on the far right.

"Okay," Shad said. "Let's see what we've got."

KELLI FINISHED HER COFFEE AND LOOKED UP AS KRISTEN returned from her bedroom. "Ready?" she asked.

"Yes," Kristen said.

Kelli stood up and put her coffee mug in Kristen's sink. "I hope I don't lose my job. I've taken so much time off in the past couple of weeks."

"You'll be okay," Kristen said. "You call in and get a sub."

Kelli nodded, her nerves like beating drums in her ears. They pulsed through her veins, and they hadn't stopped since she'd found the lockbox days ago.

"I'm going to owe Jean so much more than a gift basket from the bakery," she said, her eyes suddenly filled with tears.

"Jean loves you and Parker," Kristen said. "She's so happy to help."

Kelli nodded and took a deep breath. "Okay. How's the house hunting coming?"

"I actually talked to a a realtor on Monday afternoon," Kristen said. "She came yesterday to look at my house, but I can't sell it. It comes with the lighthouse, and Rueben's not leaving."

"I see," Kelli said, watching the older woman's face. "Can you afford...never mind. That's rude to ask."

"I have some money from Joel's...life...insurance." Her voice trailed off through the whole sentence, and Kelli met her eye.

"You can talk about Joel in front of me."

"Can I?" A blazing fire entered her eyes. "That man took so much from all of us. He's *still* doing it, Kelli. Your dad did all of this—whatever this is—to get his Glass-works back. Because *my husband* stole it from him."

Kelli searched her face, because Kristen never got angry. The only time she'd ever come close had been during a Seafaring Girls meeting when Alice and Robin had been arguing about something at school that day and had refused to speak to each other at their meeting that night.

You can't just stay silent, Kristen had said. *We all need each other on the boat. You don't get to just shut each other out.*

She'd shouted the words right in Alice and Robin's faces, all while the sailboat they'd been on continued to drift closer and closer to the rocks.

With Alice and Robin on the same team, the five of them managed to avoid a painful, craggly death, and Kelli hadn't seen Kristen that upset until this moment.

"We all need money sometimes," Kelli said calmly. "That doesn't mean we turn to blackmail and extortion."

Kristen sighed and turned away. "I just feel so guilty sometimes," she said.

"So do I," Kelli said. "But my father made his own decisions, Kristen. Decisions none of us even knew he was making."

"I don't want you to think badly of him," Kristen said. "The Guy Watkins I knew was a good man."

"And the Joel Shields I knew as a child was too."

Kristen and Kelli watched one another for a moment, the power of what they'd said playing in the air between them.

"I suppose things change, even after someone dies," Kristen said.

"Yes," Kelli said. "They do." She linked her arm through Kristen's. "I wanted my dad to be my hero, and he was. He was a brilliant artist, and he made gorgeous, blown-glass pieces. He has his work in the White House and other prominent places in the US. He suffered some terrible losses that broke him. They would've broken anyone, and I don't blame him anymore."

"You were so...lost after the divorce and after he lost the Glassworks."

"Yes," Kelli said. "I was. But I'm not anymore. I have a great son, and a good job. I live next-door to an amazing man who is kind to me and good for me, and who I like kissing."

Kristen grinned, and Kelli did too. "Good for you, Kelli," she said. After opening the door, Kristen gestured for Kelli to leave first, and then she stepped out and pulled the door closed behind her.

"I guess we can't put off going any longer," Kelli said.

"Not if we want to hear what Chief Sherman has found," Kristen said. "And Kelli, we want to know what he's found."

"Yeah," Kelli said. "I have something to add to it too." She thought of the conversation she'd had that morning, and the thick folder in her bag. She still couldn't believe it, and only she and Shad knew the information she needed to tell her friends in just a short thirty minutes.

CHAPTER THIRTY-ONE

Eloise sat on the front steps at Aaron's house, her fingers flying across her phone screen. Her friends should be here for lunch soon, but it was so much more than just a meal together.

Aaron had really put together a lot of information in a very short amount of time. Each time Eloise walked into his office—a place she rarely went normally—the board behind his desk overwhelmed her.

The way his mind worked astounded her, and she'd fallen deeper in love with him as she'd watched him assemble the board, tack information and evidence to it, and conduct interviews, most of which had been done over the phone.

The man's stamina knew no bounds, and Eloise loved that about him. At the same time, he could sit down with her in the evening and just be, and she liked that too.

She looked up at the first sounds of a car's engine, and stood as Robin pulled into the driveway with Alice and AJ in the minivan with her. The three of them got out, each of them talking over the other.

"Fine, *fine*," Alice said. "We'll ask Eloise."

"Ask me what?" she asked, glancing from Alice to Robin, who had her blonde hair curled and perfectly styled today. She wore a pair of skin-tight skinny jeans and a flowing white blouse with big splashy starfish on it in blue and purple.

Eloise instantly felt underdressed in her black slacks and simple tunic top. She didn't need to be fancy for her work at The Cliffside Inn, but she felt professional enough in the wide-leg slacks.

Alice always looked straight out of the pages of a fashion magazine, even with her reduced income. Today she wore a T-shirt dress that barely skimmed mid-thigh, with a pair of black leggings underneath. She'd pulled on knee-high boots over those, and she too wore more makeup than Eloise went through in a month.

AJ alone looked like she'd rolled out of bed and brushed her hair. She wore a gray pair of sweatpants and a maternity shirt that had a bullseye on the front of it. She still had four months left in her pregnancy, but since she was normally so slim, the baby poked straight out from her body.

"Alice wants to know who came up with the idea of the Free For All," Robin said as she approached at quite the stride for her. Almost like if she reached Eloise first, she'd win.

"Free For All," Eloise mused, taking Robin into a quick air-hug and kissing her cheek. "I think that was you, wasn't it?"

"It was not," Alice said. "It was AJ, because she told everything all the time anyway."

"It sounds like something I would do," Robin said. "I always wanted to know the juiciest gossip back in high school."

Alice's eyebrows went up in challenge, but to her credit, she said nothing. Eloise was thinking the exact same thing though, and she couldn't meet Alice's eyes for fear that she might burst out laughing.

Robin wanted to know the juiciest gossip, even now. She loved being in everyone's business, and she was good a problem-solving and helping Eloise come to different solutions. She listened to others too, so having Robin's mind hard at work on something wasn't necessarily a bad thing.

"I brought the sushi roll," AJ said, bypassing the other two women and pressing her cheek to Eloise. "Thank you so much for putting this all together for Kelli."

"Yes," Robin said, jumping in. "Did she seem upset that you'd told Aaron?"

"No," Eloise said, finally stepping over to hug Alice hello.

"Back in high school," Alice whispered, and Eloise grinned as they parted.

"Aaron didn't keep anything a secret this time. He said last time caused too many problems. So we called Kelli and talked to her on Sunday night before he even really got started."

"Good idea," Alice said. "We got everything sorted with the money and her sisters."

They went up the steps last, catching up to AJ, who panted like she'd never seen stairs before, and into the house.

"We're eating in the office," Eloise said. "Turn left at the corner and then another hard left." Aaron had opened both French doors that led into his office off the dining room and kitchen area, and he'd set up a six-foot table and seven chairs for Eloise before he'd left for the station that morning.

Eloise had seen the girls off to school, and they were coming back here afterward, as she wasn't going to Sanctuary that day. She'd then dressed the table with a sea foam green cloth, a long, low centerpiece of moss and pretty pink flowers that grew along the cliffs here in Five Island Cove, and all the cutlery and dishes for lunch.

She'd catered from one of their favorite places in the cove—The Shrimp Shack—and the food had arrived three minutes before the minivan of women.

"Pick a spot," Eloise said, arriving last. "Aaron's going to be here at noon."

That gave them a half an hour to eat. Then Aaron was going to go over the board that Eloise's eyes went straight to.

Alice noticed it, and she paused inside the doorway, her eyes glued to the back wall. "My word," she said. "The Chief of Police doesn't waste any time, does he?"

"What?" AJ asked, and Alice pointed to the board.

"Goodness," Robin said, dropping her purse onto the back of a chair and facing the wall too. She moved toward it, and Eloise didn't say anything. She'd seen the board as Aaron had built it. She'd listened to him detail the amounts of money, when they'd started, who'd they'd come from, and how long they'd continued.

He had statements from some of the women, and he had pictures of them too. He had color-coded each one, and he'd put up new sticky notes with new amounts of money every time he learned something new.

"Thirteen thousand dollars," Robin said. "September 1985 was a very good month for Guy." The level of sarcasm in her voice could've filled a stadium, and Eloise frowned.

"You shouldn't talk like that when Kelli gets here," she said.

Robin turned, her eyes wide. "Of course. I won't."

"Hello?"

"She's here," Eloise said, spinning to leave the office and go greet Kelli. She and Kristen were coming together, and sure enough, Eloise found the pair of them cresting the top of the steps.

"Come in," Eloise said, glad she'd left the front door open. "We're having lunch in the office. Aaron's got all of his stuff in there." She met Kelli in the doorway and gripped her tightly.

Kelli held onto her too, and the bond between them solidified and strengthened. "Thank you, El. I don't know what I'd do without you and Aaron."

"You'd be fine," Eloise said. "Things just might be slower." She smiled at Kelli as she stepped back, noting the anxiety in Kelli's green eyes. "Kristen, how did the meeting with the realtor go?"

She let Kelli walk by, and then she embraced Kristen. "Well enough," Kristen said into Eloise's shoulder. "She's going to be looking for some places for me to look at."

"Condos? A single house?" Eloise held her at arm's length and looked at her. "There are some nice fifty-five-plus apartments going up on the south beach on Sanctuary."

"Right by the ferry station," Kristen said. "Thalia mentioned those. She's going to be putting together a list, and we'll start searching when she's ready."

"I'm glad you're doing this," Eloise said.

"It's time," Kristen agreed, smiling as they turned and walked through the foyer to the back of the house.

"Okay," Eloise said. "Let's eat. All the food is in here."

"Laurel's not here," Alice said.

"She texted to say she missed the eleven-ten ferry,"

Eloise said. "Something about a difficulty with someone they pulled over this morning."

"I thought she was taking the whole day off," Robin said, joining everyone in the kitchen.

Hugs and greetings went around as Eloise said, "She couldn't get a sub to take her morning slot. She'll be here, and she was here last night. She said not to wait for her." She picked up a plate and handed it to Kristen.

The older woman went first through the line, and Kelli fell into step behind her. The chatter continued, and Eloise contributed by saying, "Laurel and I are going to do massages on Sunday morning. I think she thinks I don't like her much."

"She does," Alice said. "Because of something I didn't really get. Something about you thinking she was cheating with Aaron?"

"What?" AJ asked. "Why would Laurel be cheating with Aaron?"

"She's not," Robin said, shooting a glance at Eloise. Eloise had told Robin all about the whole fiasco a couple of weeks ago, and it sounded like Laurel had said something to Alice about it too.

"You thought she was?" Kelli asked.

"Yes," Eloise said. "I did." She quickly explained the situation while they loaded their plates with crab cakes and put together shrimp tacos with the cabbage, cilantro, and toppings they each wanted.

"I didn't realize she felt so left out," Eloise said.

"There's always been a distance between us that I could feel. I'm trying to bridge that."

"Why does it matter to you?" Kelli asked.

"She works for Aaron," Eloise said. "I don't want things to be awkward for either of them."

They moved into the office and took spots at the table. Eloise looked down to the end, to the only remaining spot. It did feel strange not to have Laurel there with them. She did fit with them, despite the age difference and that she hadn't grown up with them.

Eloise thought if she could put up with them, more power to her. She smiled at that thought and lifted her first shrimp taco to her lips.

"Mm, I love the tartar sauce at this place," Alice said around a mouthful of food. "It's so much better than anywhere else."

"I think we should have a Free For All," AJ said. "Remember when we did that one time?"

"No way," Kelli said. "I'm already in a Free For All. I have nothing else to add to my drama."

The room fell silent for a moment, and Eloise watched Alice and Robin zero in on Kelli. "I think she does," Robin said.

"Yes," Alice said. "I'm sure it has something to do with Shad." She dropped her eyes to her plate. "I veto the Free For All. It's too much right now."

Eloise silently agreed, and she would've vetoed on

Kelli's behalf too. She didn't want to have to spill all of her secrets either. In her opinion, Free For All was a game teen girls played when they slept over at one another's houses.

The six of them were way past that.

"Fine," AJ said. "I just think there's things that need to be said."

"If you have something to say," Robin said. "Say it."

Eloise kept her eyes on her plate, because she knew what was coming in only a few minutes. She'd gone over Aaron's presentation with him, and she knew how it ended.

Her chest felt so tight that she couldn't swallow, and she reached for a bottle of sweet tea lemonade. As she swallowed, a door opened somewhere, and Aaron called, "Baby, I'm here."

"In the office," Eloise said, and he appeared a few seconds later. He carried a backpack over his shoulder, and as he took in the women eating in his house, he smiled.

"Hey, everyone."

Various greetings came from the others, and Eloise stood to kiss him. "There's lots of food."

"Laurel just pulled up behind me," he said, going with her into the kitchen. "She didn't look happy."

"A bad pull-over," Eloise said. "Something like that."

"El?" Laurel's voice came from the garage entrance too, and Prince barked on his way to greet her. The cop dropped into a crouch and scrubbed his jowls, a smile finally covering the tiredness on her face.

She straightened after only a moment and met Eloise's eye and then Aaron's.

"Give me two minutes to get food," she said, approaching them. "Then we can start."

"You sure?" Aaron asked. "I don't have to be back until two-thirty."

"I'm sure," Eloise said, feeling the tension in the room increase with every breath she took. "Let's get this show on the road."

CHAPTER THIRTY-TWO

Alice turned her chair around, as she faced the kitchen and not the back wall where Aaron had carefully outlined every detail of this case.

"I've never had this many women in my house before," the Chief of Police said, smiling out at all of them. "Welcome." He ground his voice through his throat. "Eloise said she just wants to get going. I won't talk long."

Alice glanced over to Kelli, who sat immediately beside her. She shifted her chair closer and took her hand. Kelli tried to put on a brave smile, but Alice could see right through it.

She'd worn smiles like that before. She'd actually thought they'd worked too, but she knew differently now. A smile without joy was only a front. A smile with a ragged edge let everything out. A smile that trembled spoke volumes.

"All right," Aaron said. "I've interviewed almost everyone on the list of names Eloise gave me." His eyes skated around the room, never really landing on anyone.

"From what I could tell, Guy Watkins had a group of people who paid him to keep quiet about certain things." He turned to the board. "He was getting anywhere from two hundred and fifty dollars a month to fifty-five hundred dollars a month from multiple sources. Some of that money came in cash, some in wire transfers, some in the form of a check."

He pointed to the papers. "Some of the women provided me with bank statements. Some were really willing to talk, and some less so. Overall, from what I can tell, he was bringing in over thirteen thousand dollars per month for a few months in 1985. Some payments only lasted a few months. The longest one I discovered was fourteen months, but the time span of when this happened, all-told, was about eighteen months."

He cleared his throat again, causing Alice to shift in her seat. She glanced at Kristen on the other side of Kelly, who gaped up at the board.

Alice knew the feeling. This was so overwhelming, and the things Aaron said so incomprehensible.

Why couldn't this just have been an easy will to settle and an extra eighty thousand in cash? she wondered.

Kelli didn't need more turmoil in her life. At the same time, the ups and downs of the past year had certainly returned the Kelli Thompson Alice had known as a teenager. The Kelli she'd been before her dad had lost everything, the scandal printed on the front page of the paper, and the rumors started getting whispered through the halls.

Kelli had retreated then, and she hadn't really come back until Christmastime, when she'd left her husband for good.

Only a few short months had passed since then, and Alice knew how quickly relationships could develop.

"It's an estimation that he collected over one hundred and fifty thousand dollars from these women during that time. I don't know if the lawyers could get an extortion or blackmail charge to stick. None of the women said they were in relationships with him. His neighbor paid him to keep quiet about an affair she was having. An employee paid him to stay silent about a theft she'd committed at a previous job."

"So you're saying he found out these bad or embarrassing things about others and then asked for money to keep them to himself." Robin looked dubious, but Alice believed it.

In the mid-eighties? Absolutely she believed that Guy could use his considerable charm and influence as a local celebrity to get money from women to buy his silence.

No one wanted their friends and neighbors to know they were unhappy in their marriage. No one wanted to face the wrath of the law for a previous crime, no matter how petty and small it might be.

Alice crossed her legs. She'd kept plenty of secrets in her big house in the Hamptons, and she didn't doubt these women and their desperation to keep their indiscretions in the dark.

"Those are the reports I'm getting," Aaron said. He looked down at his desk, which looked like a paper supply store had exploded nearby. "Things range from adultery, to theft, to having an illegitimate child, to cheating on tests."

"A couple of those names were just teenagers," AJ said. "How did they pay him?"

"One said her mother paid him for a few months, just until she got into the college she wanted. Another said she stole money from her dad's safe to pay Guy." Aaron looked up then, his eyes catching on AJ's.

They sharpened, and Alice pulled in a breath, sensing a storm.

"The only person I haven't spoken with," he said. "Is in this room. The connection between the names on the list is pretty clear—they had a secret Guy Watkins knew about, and they paid him to keep it quiet."

Kelli stood up in one fluid motion. "You said there was nothing, AJ."

"There is nothing," AJ said. "I didn't pay your father anything." Her chest rose and fell, rose and fell, but she didn't stand up.

"Sit down, dear," Kristen said, tugging n Kelli's hand.

Alice didn't know what to do. The crackle of lightning

filled the room, and she felt sure someone was about to split wide open.

"There's something, AJ," Kelli said, her voice nearly silent and oh-so-deadly. "Otherwise, your name wouldn't be on this list."

"I agree," Aaron said calmly. He rounded the desk, leaving the board behind. He perched on the edge of the desk, still several feet away from where the table had been set up for lunch. "You wouldn't return my calls, either, AvaJane, or I wouldn't have called you out in front of everyone."

"I was napping," she said, her voice full of defensiveness.

"You're not napping now," Kelli said.

"Maybe it's time you start telling the truth," Robin added, and Alice gasped as she spun to look at Robin across the table.

"What?" she asked, her eyes narrowed in Alice's direction and then AJ's. "It's obvious she hasn't told us everything."

"Maybe we do need a Free For All," Eloise murmured, and Alice thought she might agree if it meant clearing the air between AJ and everyone else.

CHAPTER THIRTY-THREE

Kelli could not believe her best friend had the audacity to stand there and lie to her. Or rather, sit there.

She couldn't believe she'd believed AJ when she'd said nothing had happened between her and Guy.

She was so done believing everything everyone told her. She was done feeling like the fool.

"Start talking," she said to AJ, the words almost a yell. She thought of all the things she wanted to rage at Julian. Things she'd never said.

Her heart pounded in her chest, and the edges of her vision vibrated as a buzzing started in her ears and brain.

"I don't know," AJ said. "Okay? I have nothing to say. I have nothing to add. Pull my bank statements. I did not give your father any money. Nothing I did as a teenager was a secret from anyone. Even my dad knew I'd sleep with anyone."

She got to her feet. "Is that what you want to know, Kelli? That I literally slept with a hundred boys? Or that my teachers passed me just so I could keep playing sports? Everyone already knows that. Everyone already knows what I loser I am. I didn't need to pay your pathetic father to keep it a secret."

Tears streamed down her face, and she started for the door. "I don't have to sit here and be accused of anything. I didn't do anything wrong!"

"AJ," Eloise said, and Kristen got to her feet and started to follow her.

Pathetic father.

The words bounced through Kelli's brain. Her father had been pretty pathetic. He'd never really gotten along with her mother, and they'd argued plenty long before the divorce. Kelli closed her eyes, feeling abandoned by Kristen, though she knew the woman couldn't really take sides.

She heard the arguing behind the closed bedroom door in the house on Seabreeze Shore, and she needed to get back there. She needed to chase all the ghosts out of that place and make it somewhere she could breathe and raise her son.

At the same time, wasn't the twinhome enough? Parker was perfectly happy there, and perhaps Kelli was trying to reach for a crinkled, burnt-out star not worth touching.

Kelli's eyes flew open as a door somewhere slammed, and she flinched. "I'm sorry," she said. "I shouldn't have shouted." She wanted to sit back down and let someone else step into the spotlight.

Instead, she bent to reach into her purse. "I talked to Sidney Tyler this morning," she said, withdrawing the folder. "She gave me this." She took the few steps to Aaron and handed it to him.

His eyes locked onto hers, and her chest quaked. "I'm sorry, Kelli. I did try to call her on three separate occasions. I left her messages and asked her to call me back."

"I know you did." Kelli grabbed onto him, because she needed someone to hold, and he'd done so much to help her already.

The next thing she knew, Alice had grabbed onto her, and then Laurel. Robin joined them, and finally Eloise.

Kelli didn't hold back her tears, and she sobbed into Aaron's chest. She heard others sniffling too, and Kelli really wished it was a happy moment that included AJ in the circle.

"All right," she said, shifting. That got everyone else to back up and separate. "Let me go over this with you. Shad helped me with it this morning, and I think I got the gist of it."

She took the folder back and set it on the desk. "Sidney

kept records of everything. When she left the cove, she took them with her." She surveyed the group. "She'd gotten pregnant with a married man's baby, and she didn't want him or anyone else to know. Apparently, he was some big wig in the government. So she left the cove."

"Is that Zach's father?" Alice asked.

"Yes," Kelli said. "She still didn't tell me who it was. I guess my dad knew, and she paid him for a few months. Then she made copies of everything that had come through the Glassworks, left the cove, and told my dad that if he kept bothering her for money, she'd take her evidence to the police. She never paid him another dime."

"What did she pay him?" Aaron asked. "I didn't talk to her, because I knew you were going to."

Kelli flipped open the folder, exhaling as she did. "Okay, she paid Guy twelve hundred dollars a month for four months." She looked up at the board. "Right during the height of his blackmailing, it looks like."

She gave Aaron the information and the statements, and he put the sticky notes up and tacked the pages to the wall.

"She took payments at the front desk at the Glass-works," Kelli said. "That's what these are." She took out a clipped portion of the papers. "I bet we can get them to match up with the statements and whatnot you have there."

"Okay," he said, taking the pages. "We can sort through those in a minute."

Kelli looked back at the remaining pages in the folder. "These are my dad's bank statements for two years," she said. "Sidney printed them out and highlighting the transactions she thought were extortion payments."

Aaron took the whole folder and rounded the desk. He flipped some pages and held others up to some pinned on the board. "These are definitely Guy's statements," he said. "They match some others we got from another woman."

"Who?" Robin asked, joining Aaron on his side of the desk.

"Betsy Dinerstein," Aaron said at the same time Laurel did.

Kelli watched the female cop, but she didn't give anything away. Instead, she flew into motion, saying, "Okay, guys, let's start matching up the stuff Sidney took at the front desk with the actual statements and evidence from the witnesses."

She spearheaded that charge, and Kelli acted as a runner from desk to board, pinning things where they belonged until they'd almost all been assigned.

"We've got five here," Laurel said, gazing at the wall. "That don't seem belong to anyone."

Kelli took them, and they were for a smaller amount— only four hundred dollars each. Could these payments have come from AJ?

"They came in on the fifth of each month," she said,

noting the dates. "They gave the cash to Sidney. Maybe I should just call her again and ask her."

"It has to be AJ," Robin said. "No matter what she says."

"We don't know that," Eloise said, shooting Robin a glare.

Kristen had not returned; neither had AJ, and Kelli found herself looking toward the double-wide French doors, wishing they'd walk back through them, arm-in-arm.

They didn't, and Aaron said, "Ladies, this has been some great work we've done, but I have to get back to the station." He surveyed his board too and then turned to Kelli. "I don't know what to do about AJ. I thought she'd open up here. Should I call her into the station?"

Kelli shook her head. "No, let me think about it for a minute."

He nodded and left the office after kissing Eloise quickly. Kelli didn't want to stay for another minute. She loved her friends, but she needed some space.

"I'm going to take a walk," she said.

"Kelli," Alice said.

"Wait," Laurel said.

"I'm fine," she said. "Parker is at the lighthouse with Jean, and there's a little path that goes down the cliff to the beach."

"The one with all the sea lions," Robin said.

"Yes," Kelli said. "I'm going to go there and think for a bit."

"I'll come with you," Laurel said. "I have the rest of the day off."

"I don't want to talk," Kelli said.

"No problem." Laurel smiled, and Kelli wasn't sure if she should let her come or not.

"I have to get back to work too," Robin said. "But I'd come with you if you wanted me to, Kel."

"So would I," Alice said.

"We all would," Eloise said, returning to the table and picking up her plate.

"I just want to be alone," Kelli said. "Sorry, Laurel."

She held up one hand in a half-hearted wave. "I get it."

Kelli nodded, looked down at the copies of the ledgers Sidney had gathered, and put them back in the folder. That went in her purse again, and Kelli started toward the front door.

"Thanks for lunch," she said to Eloise, hugging her quickly. She just wanted to be done, and the first breath of outdoor air went down smoothly and crisply.

She called a ride, and twenty minutes later, her tennis shoes gripped the rock and path as she made her way down to Sea Lion Beach.

Jean often brought Parker down here, but Kelli had a good couple of hours before that would happen.

The wind quieted as she became more protected in

the inlet. Her mind focused only on one thing—walking without falling.

Once she reached the beach, her concentration opened further, and she gazed out at the water, wondering what she'd missed in all the documents, the interview, and her talk with AJ.

She thought about the leggy blonde from high school. AJ had gotten any boy she wanted, because she was tall, tan, and talented at sports. Her mother had abandoned her, causing her to try to find love anywhere she could. More often than not, she sought it in the arms of some boy, and while Kelli had never quite understood how that made AJ feel loved and accepted, she'd accepted it.

She'd loved AJ with her whole heart. She'd been there when AJ had explained what had happened between Joel Shields and her sister.

She simply couldn't believe that AJ would do anything to jeopardize her friendship with Kelli. She'd been right; she had no secrets.

"So what did my dad know about her that caused someone to pay him four hundred dollars a month?"

The sky didn't know, or at least if it did, the vast blueness of it wasn't telling her. The clouds moved ashore lazily, and in the distance a bird called.

Kelli was missing something, but she didn't know what.

Her phone rang, and a smile appeared instantly when

she saw Shad's name on the screen. She swiped on the call and said, "Hey, handsome," in her best flirtatious voice.

He chuckled and said, "Hey, yourself. How was lunch?"

"Good," she said with a sigh. The food had been, at least.

"Did you learn anything new?" he asked.

"AJ wouldn't admit anything," she said, picking out a rock and sitting on it. "She's still insisting Guy didn't have anything to blackmail her about, and she never paid him a dime."

Shad sighed too. "What did everyone else say?"

"I don't think any of us believe her," Kelli said, pure misery accompanying the words. She'd so been looking forward to meeting AJ's baby and being the maid of honor at her wedding. AJ had waited longer than any of them for such major life milestones, and Kelli had always seen herself front and center at them.

But now?

Now, everything had changed.

"I don't know why she can't just admit it," Kelli said. "The fact that she won't only makes things worse."

Shad hummed, then said, "Maybe she didn't pay him anything."

"She had to have," Kelli said. "That's how all the names on the list are tied together. Every single one."

"Yeah," Shad said, and they sighed together. "Where are you?" he added. "Sounds like you're outside."

"Sea Lion Beach," she said.

"It's pretty there," he said.

"Do you want to come hang out with me? Just hold my hand while we listen to the melody of the wind along the cliffs?"

"I'll be there in fifteen minutes."

The call ended, and Kelli took a deep breath and blew it out. "Help me figure out what happened," she prayed, something she hadn't done in a long time. "I don't want to lose AJ."

CHAPTER THIRTY-FOUR

"There you go," Kristen said, handing AJ the cup of calming orange blossom tea. She watched the woman's bony hands wrap around the cup, her chest hitching with a hiccup.

She wished she could erase the pain and disappointment from AJ's world—from all of her girls' lives. She couldn't, and she'd been learning to deal with her own dips in the roller coaster of life.

"Do you want me to stay?" she asked, easing herself into the armchair that faced the couch and loveseat where AJ spent her time if she wasn't in bed.

"You don't need to," AJ said. "Go back to the luncheon. I know you like them." She sipped her tea, her eyes red-rimmed and still glassy. Matt wasn't in the house today; he'd gone to the golf course before AJ had gotten out of bed.

Kristen had gotten several texts from Alice about how the woman had still been in bed when she and Robin had stopped by to get her.

Good, Kristen had said. *AJ's supposed to be in bed.*

She wanted someone to put her to bed with a hot cup of tea and a concerned eye. As it was, Kristen got back to her feet. "Okay, then I'll go. Please call me if you need me."

"I will," AJ said, her eyes migrating out the window to the spring blooming beyond the walls.

Kristen had serious doubts about leaving her, but her maternal senses fired at her, telling her to go. "I love you, AJ," she said, and the woman looked at her as if she'd spoken Japanese.

She didn't repeat the sentiment, and Kristen wondered how many people had told her that they loved her in her lifetime. Her mother had left when she was so young, and she'd immediately stepped into the role of caregiver for her younger sister. AJ's dad had done the best he could, but his solace had been in the bottom of a bottle and not in making sure his children knew they were loved.

Kristen nodded and left the house. She got a ride back to the lighthouse, and instead of going up the rock path to the cottage where she'd lived for years, she opened the blue door and started a slow climb toward the balcony that looked out over the ocean.

When she arrived, she let her breathing be what it needed to be, without shame that it winded her so much to climb the six flights of stairs.

The wind never stopped blowing at the lighthouse, and Kristen had spent almost her whole life with the breeze as a companion. It could be brutal, whipping past houses and uprooting the trees that managed to grow in the cove. It could be soft, whispering secrets from the sea in her ear. It could refresh; it could remind; it could ruin everything.

Right now, the wind was just wind, and Kristen was as used to it as she was the beating of her own heart.

She took a deep breath of the salty air and hugged herself, silently begging someone to tell her what to do. Move into a new house? Call Kelli to make sure she was okay? Send a text on the group chat so they'd all know where she stood?

Where did she stand?

She wasn't sure, but she didn't like how Aaron and the others had basically lined up on one side of the line and left AJ on the other.

She caught movement in her peripheral vision, and she caught sight of two people moving up the path from Sea Lion Beach. Surprise filled her, because no one went down there but Jean and Parker, but this was two adults.

As they drew closer, Kristen recognized Kelli and Shad Webb. She pulled in a breath and spun toward the stairs leading down. She moved as quickly as she could, and she burst from the lighthouse several seconds later.

She heard a male voice, and she turned right to catch them coming toward her.

"Kelli," she said, her breath coming in pants. "What are you doing here?"

"I just needed to think," Kelli said. "I called Shad, and he came to keep me company." She smiled at Kristen as she approached. "Is that okay? I thought it would be okay."

"It's fine," Kristen said. "You're always welcome here." She switched her gaze to Shad. "Hello, Shad."

"Oh, this is Kristen Shields," Kelli said. "I was just telling him about the time you made me sail the catamaran and I cried and cried. Remember that?" She wore a beautiful smile, and Kristen could see the girl she'd once been.

"Yes," Kristen said with a chuckle. "Kelli was afraid of the water."

"So she says," Shad said, his voice soft and rich.

"My boyfriend," Kelli said, tucking her arm through Shad's. "Shad Webb."

"So nice to meet you," Shad said, reaching out to shake her hand.

"And you." Kristen smiled at the sight of them, because they looked amazing together, and Kelli seemed to glow with this man at her side.

"Can I show you something?" Kelli asked, her smile slipping.

"Sure," Kristen said.

"How's AJ?" Kelli asked as they started walking toward the parking lot.

"She's... I honestly don't know," Kristen said. "I didn't stay for long, but she didn't look good."

Kelli nodded but didn't say anything. She retrieved her bag from where she'd dropped it near the fork in the path that led up to Kristen's cottage, and she removed a folder.

"Sidney Tyler brought these to me. There's a lot here, but some of these papers... They're ledgers from the Glassworks. I'm not sure what they mean, but then I noticed that they looked like something else I'd seen before."

She flipped open the folder, and Kristen's heart did a somersault too. She recognized the light blue paper instantly, and she drew in a sharp breath.

"You made us do our calculations for wind speed and nautical mileage on paper like this," Kelli said, lifting a single sheet from the folder.

"Those came from one of Joel's notebooks," Kristen said, the words scratching in her throat. She picked up the top paper, the light blue color assaulting her eyes. "Guy had these?"

"Not Guy," Kelli said slowly. "His secretary, Sidney. She kept track of money people were dropping off for things for a few months." Kelli's fingers ruffled the papers. "Five months."

"This paper came from Joel's notebook," Kristen said. "I don't know how Guy got it. Or Sidney."

"Maybe it was a common notebook being sold at the time," Shad said.

Kristen hummed in agreement, because she really didn't know. She didn't want to look at another piece of paper and try to make sense of it, she knew that.

This wasn't that hard to make sense of. Sidney had highlighted a four hundred dollar transaction that had happened on the fifth of March.

Kristen looked down the lines on the paper, and each month, the payment arrived on the fifth. "In cash?" she asked Kelli.

"These were the cash transactions, yes," Kelli said.

Kristen looked at the year at the top. 1985. March, April, May, June, July. She closed her eyes, her memories flying backward to that time.

She heard the conversations she'd had with her husband. She'd gone over the checking account with him. They'd puzzled through things together.

"I know what this is," she whispered, her throat raw.

"What?" Kelli asked, and Kristen opened her eyes as she leaned closer. "What did you say?"

"I think I know who paid these," she said, though there was nothing notated beyond the words "cash fund" next to the dollar amount. "Sidney didn't say?"

Kelli and Shad exchanged a glance, and Kristen's stomach clenched. "I didn't ask her this morning," Kelli said. "But I called her just now."

"It was Joel, wasn't it?" Kristen asked, her voice barely audible above the wind. She remembered a brief stint of time where their pay for keeping the lighthouse was suddenly less, and she'd asked him about it. He'd claimed there'd been a mix-up at the nautical office, and he'd take care of it.

Of course he would. Joel took care of everything.

He had too.

A few months later, they'd gotten all of the money they hadn't been getting, plus a "bonus."

She knew now that her husband had bought the Glassworks out from underneath Guy, and that extra money had come from the rent Joel had charged him once he'd lost his building.

That hadn't lasted long, as the bankruptcy had come soon after that. The dissolution of Guy's marriage and Kelli's family. The complete break-down of Guy's livelihood.

Kelli didn't answer, but the look on her face said everything.

Kristen calmly stacked the papers back in Kelli's folder, and the younger woman closed it. "I know what this is for," Kristen said. "I'll take care of this."

CHAPTER THIRTY-FIVE

AJ's chest felt like a sinkhole. It filled with water the way a cenote did in Central America, and she struggled to breathe against the pressure and lack of oxygen that came with the sensation of drowning.

Her phone buzzed, and AJ turned it over to look at it. *Almost there*, Amy had said, and AJ's eyes filled with tears.

Her sister had been nothing but kind to her since they'd come back together over the holidays. AJ loved going out to Pearl now, because her nieces ran to her, always exclaiming something about school or their friends. She took Matt, and they had family meals with Amy and AJ's father, and the rifts that had seemed so big and so cracked between them had started to heal over.

AJ had texted her sister the moment she'd sat in the RideShare car she and Kristen had taken back to Matt's, and Amy had said she'd be there as fast as she could.

AJ wasn't sure if she closed her eyes and fell asleep or not. The next thing she knew, Amy walked in, calling, "It's just me, Ava."

"In the living room," AJ called, trying to sit up more. She didn't mind the bedrest so much, as long as she had something to occupy her mind. Having someone to talk to had been wonderful, as was simply watching a movie or playing a game on her phone.

AJ loved being busy too, but she'd taken the opportunity to slow down. Really slow down.

"There you are," Amy said, rounding the corner and appearing in the living room. She hurried toward AJ and hugged her. The kind gesture and strength of her sister made AJ tear up and cry, and she didn't care that she clung to Amy while she did.

"Okay," her sister soothed. "It's okay. Tell me what's happening."

AJ couldn't even give the situation a voice. She honestly had no idea how all of them could sit there and accuse her of the things they had. She shook her head as Amy sat on the loveseat, concern riding in her eyes.

"My friends." AJ's throat closed, and she shook her head, unable to continue.

"You and your friends always had some drama," Amy said with a smile. "You've always worked things out."

"Not this time." AJ returned her gaze out the window and wiped at her eyes. "They think I've done something really horrible, and they don't believe that I didn't. I have no proof."

She'd told them to get her bank accounts, but she didn't even know how someone would do that. Did banks keep records of closed accounts from thirty years ago? Didn't seem likely.

Amy sat silently for a few seconds. "Lucky for you, I picked up groceries on my way over, and I'm going to make the most amazing lobster mac and cheese." Amy grinned at her and got to her feet. "You can keep talking while I get things started."

AJ didn't have anything more to say. She let Amy chatter about the kids and her husband, and she asked AJ when Matt's kids would be in town, if they were coming to the wedding, and more.

Amy had really grown into a confident woman, with plenty of ability to make small talk, and AJ loved her for coming all the way from Pearl to simply be with her.

Eventually, the lobster mac and cheese was done, and Amy handed her a bowl. "You've barely said ten words."

"I know," AJ said. "I'm sorry. It's just nice to listen to you talk about normal things."

"What happened with your friends?" Amy perched on the loveseat again and dug into her own comfort food. She glanced up at AJ, who was trying to find the perfect bite of seafood with macaroni.

Their eyes met, and AJ felt the story surging up her throat and out of her mouth. She told it as quickly as she could, and then she took a bite of her now-cold mac and cheese.

Once again, Amy took precious time to think before she spoke. AJ needed more skills in that arena, and she admired her sister so much. "Maybe the payment wasn't because of something you did," she said. "Maybe he'd listed your name, because of something...you'd seen?"

"Then wouldn't he be paying me to keep quiet?" AJ frowned, more confused than ever. "I never paid him a dime."

"But you did have a secret," Amy said.

"No," AJ said. "I didn't have any secrets when I was a teenager. Everyone knew everything about me."

Amy nodded and got up and took AJ's cold food from her. "Let me heat this up." She went back into the kitchen, and a few minutes later, she returned with a fresh bowl of mac and cheese for AJ.

"When were these supposed payments?" she asked.

"Over quite a few months in 1984 and 1985."

"Do you know when you were supposedly paying him?"

"That spring and summer," she said, lifting her eyes from the bowl of mac and cheese to meet her younger sister's.

"That was when..." She cleared her throat. "When Joel assaulted me. That happened that spring, remember?"

AJ's eyes widened, as the same conclusion had just reached her mind. "I did have a secret."

"Maybe someone else knew that secret," Amy said.

"I never told anyone, Amy," AJ said. "Not Robin, not Alice. Not Kristen. No one."

"I didn't either," she said. "So who else knew?"

"Guy, obviously."

"But he wasn't there." AJ shook her head. "Someone would've had to tell him so he could then blackmail them."

Amy's eyes so much anxiety, and she looked at AJ so earnestly. "There were exactly three people who knew what happened at the field that day."

AJ sucked in a breath, her heart pounding so loud and so quick now.

"Joel," she said together with her sister. She instantly fumbled through her blankets, trying to find her phone. Her hands shook, but she finally located it and started tapping to get to Kelli's name.

She just had to believe her. AJ couldn't stand the though of Kelli thinking she'd done something nefarious, and she could still hear her best friend yelling at her.

Tell the truth, AJ.

She *was* telling the truth, and she hoped Kelli would at least pick up and listen to what she had to say.

CHAPTER THIRTY-SIX

K elli stood in Kristen's cottage, Shad right behind her as the older woman dug through a filing cabinet. Kelli shuddered, and Shad's arm came up to her waist, his eyes searched her face.

She didn't look at him though. She couldn't shake the memories from less than a year ago of the mess this cottage had been. The pictures Alice and Robin had sent of the huge stacks of papers to be shredded. The damaging documents that had turned every one of their lives upside down.

Eloise had left her position at Boston University very soon after that. Alice had filed for divorce. AJ had left her long-time boyfriend and moved back to the cove. Robin had accepted that she couldn't control everything, and she'd softened considerably. Kelli herself had walked away from her marriage instead of giving in to her husband's every demand, and she'd allowed someone else to help with her son.

She'd been rebuilding her relationship with her mother, and Robin was working on that too. Kelli spoke with her often about it, and the two had definitely grown closer.

So much had been launched into motion with Joel Shields's death.

"I don't know where it is," Kristen said. "I probably shredded it." She sighed as she straightened. "I didn't think I'd need to keep bank statements from thirty years ago."

"Thirty-five," Kelli murmured, but she didn't need to correct Kristen. She drew in a deep breath. "It doesn't matter."

She met Kristen's eye. "You said you remember having less money those months. Sidney says Joel brought in the payments. My father...probably just wrote down AJ's name, because she was the one they were really keeping quiet."

Kristen sank into the office chair. "Do you think Joel offered any money to AJ?"

"I don't know." Kelli wasn't going to ask her either. She'd seen the look on AJ's face, and she needed some time to herself. She wouldn't be surprised if AJ had called Matt or her sister, and she wouldn't be alone right now. Kelli had accused her of something terrible, and guilt cut through her stomach, making her flinch as if in physical pain.

"Let's call her," Kristen said. She stood and gave Kelli a kind smile. "Let's call them all. They have today off."

"I don't want to go back to Aaron's," Kelli said. "I appreciate everything he did, because he put everything together in literally three days. He worked on this for me non-stop. But I don't want to face that board again."

The scope of what her father had done baffled Kelli, and she wasn't sure she'd made the right decision by pursuing the trail. AJ had asked her if it mattered if she knew, and Kelli had wanted to know.

"I think we should give her a few minutes," Kelli said. "I'd like to go to Bell to the house." She looked at Shad. "Will you come with me?"

"Of course," he said.

"You don't have to go back to work?"

"Not today." He offered her a kind smile, and Kelli turned to Kristen.

"Would Jean take Parker?"

"I can if she can't," Kristen said, her dark eyes so compassionate. "What do you need from that house, Kelli?"

The question dove into her mind and started swimming around. Kelli honestly didn't know. She said as much, turning to leave the cottage.

She'd not come here after the Seafaring Girls meetings ended and she left the cove. Kristen and Joel were still living in the lighthouse then, and Kelli had heard when they'd retired, but she hadn't known they'd only moved fifty yards from the iconic symbol in Five Island Cove that they'd maintained for almost five decades.

Kelli glanced at the lighthouse, which had always been such a safe place for her. The house on Seabreeze Shore had possessed a similar feeling and sanctuary for her growing up.

Losing that normalcy and stability in her family life had been devastating for her. Sometimes, she still feel like she was reeling through space, unable to find an anchor as the cosmos spun past her.

The house anchored her.

She hugged Kristen, saying nothing. They had nothing to say anyway. The love between them seeped into the air around them, and Kelli found Shad smiling at the pair of them when they parted.

"Ready?" He reached for her hand, and Kelli slipped hers into his.

"Ready."

The ride to the ferry station and across the water to Bell Island happened mostly in silence, and Kelli basked in it. She enjoyed the lapping of the water against the boat, and the chatter of those around her—students going home from school and moms with their kids.

She missed this time of the afternoon, when the sky held golden possibilities. When she'd once headed home, a place where her own mother would be waiting for her with a smile and a question about how her geometry test had gone.

Her mother had always known what was going on in Kelli's life—at least until her father had lost the Glassworks and they'd then lost everything. After that, her mother might not be home in the afternoons, and she might not check in with Kelli about her homework or grades for weeks at a time.

She now knew the turmoil that could happen in an adult's life, and another round of guilt ran through her when she remembered her mom's face and mini-tantrum when she'd been forced to take refuge in the house on Seabreeze Shore.

She took a deep breath, trying to inhale that gold and shine into her lungs, into her life.

As the ferry docked, she faced Shad. "I think I might need to sell the house on Seabreeze Shore."

His eyebrows flew up, and he asked, "Really?" A smile appeared on his rugged, handsome face. "What's going on inside that head of yours?" He guided her off the ferry, and they started the short walk to the house.

"I thought it would be a fresh start for me," she said. "That's what I've been trying to do, right? But it just seems to bring heartache."

"It also yielded twenty-five thousand dollars," he said.

"True." Kelli let her thoughts tangle a little bit, then she started sorting through them. "I think it would be an amazing space for a yoga studio, but I'm not sure I want to live there."

"So convert it to a yoga studio," he said. "You could use the entire bottom floor for that. The kitchen could be used as a juice bar. You know, all those cleansing juices every spa in the cove tries to sell as healthy."

He grinned at her, and Kelli edged closer to him. She liked being near him, and she was glad she had someone safe to bounce her ideas off of.

"And upstairs, you can keep an office," he said. "Or massage rooms. Or just storage."

Kelli nodded, the idea starting to take shape inside her mind. "I'd need a loan."

"Or just use the money you were going to buy furniture with," he said. "Stay in the twinhome with me." He leaned over and pressed a sloppy kiss to her forehead.

She giggled while he chuckled, and then they rounded the corner. The road started up, and this last quarter mile could be a beast in bad weather. Kelli had made the climb several times, and the prize—the view from the house in every direction—was worth it.

She and Shad arrived at the house a few minutes later, and Kelli went into the carport and unlocked the garage entrance. The house didn't smell as unused and abandoned as it had previously, but it definitely had a new scent she couldn't place right away.

Nothing seemed out of place, and Kelli strode through the kitchen, seeing juicers and blenders where they'd mix up strawberry smoothies and celery and cucumber juice blends.

Past the tiny room where she'd sheltered during the storm, where she normally kept the bean bag for the next time she and AJ needed to escape from the real world.

The front of the house opened up, and the grand staircase went up on her left. She paused, taking in the colored glass above the window. She closed her eyes as the dazzling light danced through her vision, and she saw fitness classes on both sides of the entrance. She heard women laughing and talking. She saw friendships forming and strengthening.

"I don't need couches," she said. "I need yoga mats and a speaker system for music."

"I know a guy who can help with the speaker system," Shad said, his touch on her waist light and welcome.

Kelli's phone rang, and Eloise's name sat on the screen. She swiped on the call and said, "Hey, El."

"I hate to bother you," Eloise said, and she sounded worried and regretful at the same time. Urgent too. "Are you okay to talk for a minute?"

"Yes," Kelli said.

"I know today has been hard enough," she said. "But there's something else you need to know. Something Aaron just found."

Kelli looked at Shad, and it was clear he'd been able to hear Eloise though Kelli hadn't put the call on speaker.

She did now, and said, "You're on speaker with me and Shad. Do I need to sit down?"

"I would," Alice said, and Kelli instantly moved over to the stairs.

"Okay," she said. "Is everyone there?"

"Me, Robin, Alice, Laurel, and Aaron," Eloise said. "Kristen left with AJ, and I haven't spoken to them."

"I left Kristen at the lighthouse," Kelli said. "She's okay."

"We'll go get AJ right after we get off the phone," Robin said.

"Must be good news then," Kelli said, her heartbeat spinning through her veins. She hated feeling her pulse, as it was something that should just exist without being detected. Hers pounded at her, telling her to hang up and flee.

"Go on," she said. "I'm ready."

"I found a number on some of the documents," Aaron said. "I didn't notice it at first, because there are lots of numbers to look at. But Sidney had highlighted this one on a couple of the statements she had."

"Okay," Kelli said.

"I noticed it matched up to some documents we got from Betsy Dinerstein and then I found the same number on Minerva Thacker's statements. They both provided the complete copies as evidence."

"What kind of number?" Shad asked.

"It's a bank account number," Aaron said.

Kelli closed her eyes, the world going soft around her. The humming of the furnace couldn't be heard, and the breeze wasn't strong enough to rattle the windows today.

Her breathing filled her ears, as did her pulse.

"It's the bank account number that received the payments," Aaron said. "I called the bank, Kelli, and they confirmed that the account still exists."

Her eyes flew open. "What?"

"It's an open, active account," Aaron said. "Well, I don't know about active. It's open."

"But my father died years ago."

"He had listed people as beneficiaries upon his death."

"Who?" she demanded. "How much is in the account?"

"They wouldn't tell me the amount," Aaron said. "I have the number, but I'm not Guy Watkins. I do know the manager there, and she told me the beneficiary. That person would have to go in to get everything transferred over and gain access."

"Who is it?" Shad asked.

"It's you, Kelli," Aaron said.

"Just me?" Kelli asked. "What about Sabrina or Heather?"

"Just you," Aaron confirmed.

Kelli looked at Shad, her eyes wide. "Cove First National?"

"Yes."

"There's a branch in the grocery store where my mom works," Kelli whispered.

"I'm calling a RideShare right now," Shad said, tapping on his phone.

"We'll go figure it out," Kelli said.

"Okay," Aaron said. "Listen, Kelli, I want to apologize again. I really thought today would go better than it did."

"It's not your fault," Kelli said. "Really, Aaron, I appreciate everything you've done. I don't know what you had to give up to help me so quickly, but I appreciate it."

Her phone buzzed again, indicating another call coming in.

"AJ's calling," she said. "I have to go."

She didn't wait for Aaron's confirmation, and though some of the women with him—Robin, Alice, Laurel—started talking, Kelli swiped their call away and tapped to answer AJ's.

CHAPTER THIRTY-SEVEN

"I'm going," Robin said, shouldering her purse and facing the group in Aaron Sherman's office. "Who's coming with me?"

"I am," Alice said, joining her.

"Me too." Laurel stepped out from behind the desk.

"Of course I am." Eloise kissed Aaron quickly, and the four women left his office.

"Can your boyfriend give us a police escort?" Robin asked Laurel.

"No," she said, jangling some keys. "But I can." She grinned at Robin, and they practically ran out the front doors of the station to get to the cruiser. Robin's need to get to AJ overwhelmed her, and she'd really like a transport system like the kind she saw in science fiction movies.

"Those back doors only open from the outside," Laurel said. "But I'll get you guys out when we get there."

Robin claimed the front passenger seat, while Alice and Eloise got in the back.

"I've never ridden in a cop car," Alice said. "It's kind of exciting."

"I went out with Aaron once," Eloise said, buckling her belt. "He never turned on the siren."

"It's usually pretty boring," Laurel said. "Every once in a while, we get a domestic disturbance outside the Chinese restaurant."

Robin met her eyes, recognizing the moment Laurel had become an important part of their group. She reached over and squeezed Laurel's hand, and Laurel started the car.

"Here we go." She flipped on the siren and the lights, which went round and round and flashed against the building as Laurel backed out. "I'm going to go fast. Hold on."

Robin barely had time to lift her hand up to the handle above the door before Laurel floored the accelerator, and the huge engine in the police vehicle responded instantly.

"My word," Alice said from the backseat, and Eloise shrieked, the sound dissolving into a giggle a moment later.

"We need to get there fast, right?" Laurel asked, and

Robin braced herself as Laurel practically put the car on two wheels around a corner.

They got to AJ's fast, and Laurel turned off the siren but not the lights before she jumped out of the vehicle. She yanked open Alice's door, and Robin got Eloise out on her side.

Together, the four of them seemed to breathe together as they faced the house. They took their first steps together, and Robin had never felt more powerful.

She'd always loved being part of a group. A squad. A family.

Her heart squeezed that she couldn't be home today when Mandie and Jamie would arrive. Things had not been settled between Charlie and Mandie, but she hadn't come home crying yesterday, so that had been an improvement. Robin would still like to be there, and she'd already set an alarm for when she should text her daughter.

"AJ," she called as Laurel opened the door. "We're coming in."

Laurel led the way, but Robin was right behind her. They found AJ in the living room, her sister standing to greet them from the loveseat.

"She's on the phone with Kelli," Amy said, her eyes wide. "What's going on?"

"We love you," Robin said, catching AJ's eyes. "It doesn't matter if you did something or didn't do something."

"She didn't," Amy said forcefully, glaring at Robin. "She's telling Kelli right now."

"What's she telling her?" Alice asked.

Amy glared at her too and folded her arms. "AvaJane didn't pay anyone anything. She did have a secret at the end of her high school career, but she kept it for Joel Shields, not herself."

Confusion ran through Robin for half a second. "Joel Shields," she said.

"Of course," Eloise said, pure relief in her voice. "Joel Shields and what he did to you."

Amy clenched her arms around herself even tighter. "She told you about it."

"Just last year," Alice assured her. "We didn't know until after Joel died."

Amy's teeth clenched and then released. She nodded, and then she vocalized the thoughts in Robin's head. "We think Joel paid Guy, who somehow found out what he'd done. We think he'd noted it as AvaJane Proctor, because it was really her secret to keep."

"Makes sense," Laurel murmured. "Did anyone pay AJ any money to keep quiet?"

"Not that I'm aware," Amy said, doing a double-take when she looked at Laurel in the police uniform. "Officer Baker."

Laurel smiled at her. "Good to see you again, Amy. How's Darcy?"

"Good, great," Amy said, nodding. "I can't believe you remember her name. She got lost years ago."

"I remember the good ones," Laurel said, her smile so perfect and so kind. Amy relaxed, and Robin was so grateful Laurel was with them. She also wanted to hear more about Laurel's "boring" job, as she hadn't detailed many instances from it.

"Can we get on speaker?" Alice asked, moving further into the living room.

AJ pulled the phone from her ear and tapped. Kelli's voice came through the line with, "...so I don't need to know more, AJ. I really don't. I know you didn't do anything, and I'm so, so sorry that I thought you did."

"Thank you," AJ said.

"I didn't mean for this to take over everything," Kelli said, obviously tearful.

Robin perched on the edge of the coffee table and leaned toward the phone. "We're all here, Kelli. AJ's okay, and she knows we love her."

AJ met Robin's eyes, and Robin nodded. AJ began to sniffle and weep, and Alice stepped right over to her and hugged her. Alice could be so supportive, and Robin loved that the most about her.

"Are you going to the bank?" Robin asked.

"The RideShare just arrived," Kelli said. "I'll call you when I have more information."

"We'll be here," Eloise said, and the call ended.

The silence in AJ's living room could've filled drums

for days, and Robin knew it was her job to break it down and chase it out of the house.

"I'm sorry for how things went today," she said. "You didn't deserve to be attacked like that."

"It's frustrating to have zero proof," AJ said. "I won't run my articles without proof, but I literally only have my word."

"And it's good enough," Robin said at the same time Alice said, "That's all we need."

Eloise wrung her hands, and Robin nudged her with her elbow. That got Eloise to move, and she exploded toward AJ as she burst into tears.

"I'm so sorry, AJ. I asked Aaron to help, and he's so good at finding things. I didn't know it would incriminate you."

"It didn't," Robin said. "We know that now."

"Do you?" AJ asked, hugging Eloise so her voice was muffled.

Eloise pulled back. "What do you mean?"

"Why do you believe me now?" AJ looked around at everyone. "When you didn't before?" The sharpness in her eyes suggested all would not be forgiven in an instant.

Robin cleared her throat and looked around the room. "Because we've had a moment to think. I hadn't even seen that board before this morning," she said.

"And Amy just told us that Joel made the payments," Alice added.

"But you didn't come over here knowing that," AJ said. "We still don't *know* that. It's just a guess Amy and I have."

"Kelli confirmed it," Amy said, her voice entering the conversation. "She said she and Kristen looked at the ledgers the secretary kept, and she said she and Joel had less money for those few months, and it was right after... AJ saw me with him."

"So how did Guy Watkins find out?" Laurel asked, her mind ever working on the case.

"I don't know," AJ said. "I never told anyone. Amy didn't either."

"Joel wouldn't tell him," Robin said. "That wouldn't be smart."

"Maybe it came out accidentally," Alice said. "After they'd been drinking, or if they were arguing... When did he buy the Glassworks from Guy?"

"August, 1985," Laurel said, drawing every eye to her. She shrugged and added, "I've looked at the case Aaron had. He *is* very thorough."

"The payments stopped in August," AJ said. "They lasted five months, from March to July. Then Joel bought the Glassworks, and that was enough to turn the tables on Guy."

"Maybe Guy saw Joel too," Amy said. "That day at the field. He used to walk along there for inspiration."

Robin looked at her, and she realized that life was often seen by more than just the people living it. "Anything's possible," she said. "Except AJ paying Guy Watkins to hold one of her teenage secrets." She reached out and took AJ's hands in hers, leaning further forward. "I'm so sorry, AJ."

"Thank you," AJ said again. "You really don't need to apologize forever."

"We're all sorry," Alice said.

"Yes." Eloise wiped her eyes and took a seat on the loveseat.

"Okay," AJ said. "I accept the apologies. Now, someone tell me about this bank account Kelli is going to check."

HOURS LATER, ROBIN FINALLY ENTERED HER HOUSE. HER safe haven from the storms of life. The one place she didn't have to have perfectly styled hair and gobs of makeup on her face.

"I'm home," she called, and a general cry of excitement filled the house from down the hall. She smiled as the other three members of her family appeared at the end of the house, and she dropped her heavy purse just inside her office as she passed.

"Mom, you'll never believe what happened today," Jamie said, rushing forward to talk to her first.

"Mm, what?" Robin stroked her youngest daughter's hair back from her face.

"Damien Robinson asked me to go to the movies with him."

Surprise darted through Robin. Jamie was far too young to start hanging out with boys. Wasn't she?

In that moment, Robin realized her daughter wasn't eight years old anymore. She was thirteen, and yes, she was definitely old enough to spend time with boys.

"Alone?" she asked.

"Not alone," Jamie said. "He's going with a few other people, and he asked me to come."

"Do you know these people?"

"Yes," Jamie said. "But I don't normally hang out with them. They're in my theater class."

"That's great," Robin said, glancing down the hall to Mandie. "And we like this Damien Robinson fellow?"

Mandie nodded slightly, and Robin looked back at Jamie. She *clearly* liked this Damien Robinson. "All right," she said. "When is the movie? It's not rated R, is it?"

Jamie continued to tell her about the PG-13 movie they were going to go see on Friday night while Robin hugged Mandie and kissed Duke.

The man had dinner on the counter, and Robin didn't care that it came from a box. He opened her salad and handed her the little tub of ranch dressing to go with it. She smiled fondly at him, and when Jamie stopped talking, she looked at Mandie.

"Charlie?"

Mandie shook her head, her sadness draping over her like a wet blanket. Robin wouldn't be able to lift it off, even if she tried. She couldn't protect her daughter from everything, no matter how hard she tried.

"So it's official?" she asked.

"I talked to him after school for a couple of minutes today," Mandie said. "He's still gorgeous, of course. He makes me smile, and I like him *so* much."

Robin glanced at Duke, who was frowning.

"He said he really liked me, but that he thought he might like to try dating other girls." She shrugged. "What am I supposed to do? Go nuts on him?" Mandie shook her head and looked down at her pizza. "I said okay, if that's what you want. He said that was what he wanted, but that he was really sorry. He did seem sorry." She shrugged. "Maybe he'll go out with a few girls and realize how awesome I am and come back."

"Do you want him to come back?" Duke asked.

"I don't know, Dad." Mandie reached up and wiped her eyes. "We've spent a lot of time together. I feel like I have no one now."

Robin reached over and covered her daughter's hand with hers. "I'm so sorry, sweetie."

"Then he went into Academic Olympiad, and I know *exactly* who he's going to ask to prom."

"Who?" Robin asked, though she knew too.

"Sariah Page," Mandie said with a hint of disgust. "She's so pretty, and she always gets the boys. She won't date them exclusively, though, so it'll be interesting to see what Charlie does then. He's not good alone either."

"You should've seen his mother," Robin said. "She's just like that."

Their eyes met, and Mandie smiled. Robin did too, and when she looked at Duke, he grinned back at her.

"I'm so glad you're home," he said. "I don't like being here alone either."

"Hey, you're the one going to Alaska in only a few weeks," Robin said, and she missed her husband already.

"Yes," he said. "And then you won't have to work seventy hours a week. We'll be back on top of the bills, and life will go back to normal."

"Ah, normal." Robin lifted her slice of pizza and took a bite. After swallowing, she added, "I wonder what that's like."

They all laughed, and Robin felt peaceful and calm among these people where she belonged.

Her friend drama would calm, and her Wednesday lunches would sustain her through the summer.

She glanced at her phone, hoping to see a text from Kelli.

Nothing yet.

CHAPTER THIRTY-EIGHT

Laurel always felt one step behind and ten minutes late. Such was the case as she arrived at Kelli's twinhome to find all six of the other women already seated on the patio at the top of the steps.

"Thanks," she said to the driver, scanning her police card to pay for the ride. She got a half-price discount that way, not that she was hurting for money.

She'd taken another personal day in order to be here, and she told herself it was worth it. She *wanted* to be here with these women. They were important to her, and she'd never belonged to a group like them before.

"There she is," Alice said, rising to her feet. "How'd you get a Friday off?"

"One of my friends called in a favor with the Chief," Laurel said, cresting the stairs and grinning at Eloise, then

Alice. She hugged Alice and then Robin, who'd saved her a seat between the two of them.

Laurel had realized she was one of the only women who could fill that spot, and she glanced toward Kelli, who also wore a warm smile.

"Thanks for coming, Laurel," she said. "I know it's a long way."

"Only if you leave late," Laurel said, smiling. "And only if your partner doesn't call to tell you seriously the lamest joke ever."

"How is Connor?" Robin asked, picking up a basket of rolls and handing it to Laurel. "You have to jump in. AJ's been eyeing that rye roll for twenty minutes."

"I've only been here for five," AJ said. "So that's not entirely true." She lifted another buttered and jammed rye roll to her mouth and smiled at Laurel.

"Connor's good," Laurel said as Eloise then indicated she wanted the bread basket. "Is it warmer out here on Pearl?"

"We are the furthest south," Kelli said, picking up the pitcher of lemonade. "This is sugarless, by the way." She poured herself a glass and lifted it as if asking if Laurel wanted some.

"Please," she said.

"You're not getting off that easy with Connor," Robin said.

Laurel stretched out to start piling ham on her roll. "Why?

He's good." She wasn't seeing him. If anything, Robin should be asking how things were with Paul. They had a romantic dinner planned for that evening, after Paul finished with his afternoon meeting with Aaron and the administrative team.

"She got a new assistant." Alice nodded to the cheese platter. "I saved you that brie. The grapes are amazing too."

"Where'd you get all of this?" Laurel asked. "It looks so much better than anything I've seen at the supermarket on Diamond."

"Shad took me to this whole foods place," Kelli said, practically glowing as she spoke. "They had the most amazing produce. The bakery was phenomenal. I got the cheese there too, off their olive bar."

"Ooh, olive bar," Robin said. "I love a good olive bar."

"You've never even been to an olive bar," Alice said.

"I have too."

Eloise started to chuckle, and Laurel grinned at everyone. These were the women she knew. Unstressed, bickering at each other, talking about grapes and rye rolls and olive bars.

She took the cheese and fruit and added it to her plate. "Who's your new assistant?"

"Millicent Fulsom," Robin said, actually straightening her shoulders. "She's wonderful, and she's looking for someone. She's in her twenties, and I think Connor is too." She looked at Laurel with questions in her eyes.

"He just turned thirty," Laurel said. "A couple of months ago."

"That's still not too old," Robin said.

"She fancies herself a matchmaker," Eloise said.

"Hey, I got you that first date with Aaron, if you'll remember right."

"Oh-ho," Alice chortled at the same time Eloise said, "You did not."

"I did too," Robin said indignantly. "You're not taking that from me."

"You didn't earn that," Alice said.

"He asked her out in front of me," Robin said. "And she didn't even realize it. I had to tell her."

Laurel sat back and watched them argue the point back and forth, thoroughly enjoying herself. The food really tasted fantastic, and she met Eloise's eyes several times as the story of how she'd met the Chief and their romance had started came out.

"All right, all right," Kelli finally said. "Who's ready for me to talk about the bank account?"

The mood at the table shifted instantly, and Laurel herself sat up straighter. She wasn't sure why; she had no vested interest in how much money Kelli had found in her father's thirty-plus-year-old bank account.

Her curiosity was piqued, and she wanted to know simply so she could support Kelli should she need it.

Laurel had the feeling that she'd need it, if the anxiety

pouring from her eyes was any indication. Could others see it too? Could they feel it?

Laurel had the moment she'd laid eyes on Kelli, despite the fun meal they'd shared before this conversation started.

"It's a lot," Kelli said, bending to retrieve a folder.

"My word," Alice said. "I've had quite enough of all the notebooks and folders and scraps of paper."

"Haven't we?" Kristen asked, grinning around at everyone.

It seemed hard to believe that only two days had passed since the Wednesday lunch that had caused a rift in the friend group.

Laurel had seen them weather a couple of storms now —literally and figuratively—and she admired them all for different reasons.

"I'm not going to live in the house on Seabreeze Shore," Kelli said, opening the folder. "I'm going to keep it, but I'm going to open a yoga studio—a wellness studio, Shad calls it."

She wore sunshine in her expression, and Laurel couldn't straighten her own mouth watching her.

"A wellness studio?" Alice said, craning her neck to see the papers in the folder. Laurel stayed back, out of the way, because it was very important to both Alice and Robin to be in the know. She could wait, and she noticed AJ looking, and Eloise rising up to stand so she could see better too.

Kristen stayed back, and Kelli perched on the edge of her seat, her back very straight as she took out pages and arranged them.

"I've been working on an idea," she said. "Using some city planning software Shad gave me access to."

"This is amazing," Robin said. "Yoga and fitness classes are perfect for those large rooms downstairs."

"A juice bar and snack bar in the kitchen area," Eloise said.

"Would you help me with some of the booking software?" Kelli asked, pure hope in her eyes. "Since you just went through all of this with Cliffside."

"Absolutely," Eloise said. "The support desk is so amazing as well. Any time I have a problem at all, they're right there, available on chat or by phone."

"Sounds perfect," Kelli said. "I'm thinking about doing massages in the bedrooms upstairs. Maybe just one. One for an office for myself. I'd like to run the place, as well as offer classes. I really liked teaching in Jersey."

"Kel," AJ said in an awed voice. "I've heard you talk about this, but it's so different seeing it in full color."

"It's going to take some money and time to get it set up," Kelli said, energy practically buzzing from her very pores. "But I have the money now, even after Heather and Sabrina take their part, and I put in my two weeks' notice yesterday."

"Wow," Robin said, lifting her eyes from the four-sheet spread of the wellness center. "You've been so busy."

"I've hardly slept," Kelli admitted. "But I feel like I need to seize this opportunity. If I don't, I'll just keep working at the school and wondering if I'm doing the right thing. I'm not going to wait to find out. I'm going to do it, and if I fail, well, then, I fail."

"You're not going to fail," Laurel said, and that drew a few eyes in her direction. "You've obviously thought about it for a long time, and I've seen the way you organize your purse." She surveyed the group of them, finding love in Kristen's dark eyes. She soaked in that, because while she had a mother of her own, she lived on Nantucket and Laurel didn't get to see her that often.

"You can tell a lot about a woman from the contents and state of her purse," Laurel said with all the soberness in the world.

Alice burst out laughing first, followed closely by Eloise and Robin. Even Kristen laughed, and Laurel sure did love these women. She was so glad she'd met them, and that they'd been so welcoming and accepting to her.

"Do you ladies want coffee?" Shad asked, and Laurel's eyes switched from Kelli to the man who'd come out of the twinhome beside hers.

"Yes, please," Alice said, as did a couple of others. Shad went back inside to get brewing, and Laurel watched Kelli sigh.

Laurel knew exactly what she was feeling, because Laurel caught herself sighing like that after her dates and interactions with Paul.

"All right," Robin said. "We've got Eloise getting married in only fifteen days. AJ at the end of May." She looked between Alice, Laurel, and Kelli. "Who's going to be next?"

"Are you kidding me right now?" Alice asked, folding her arms. "Not me."

"I don't know," Kelli said.

Laurel cleared her throat as Robin's eyes landed on her. "I'm hoping Paul will ask me to marry him soon."

A moment of silence marked the calm before the storm, and Laurel grinned and laughed as the other six women all launched into various forms of congratulations —which weren't warranted yet—and demands for more information.

"HERE YOU ARE, MA'AM," THE HOSTESS SAID, PULLING OUT Laurel's chair for her. She took it, her excitement climbing. She took the menu from the hostess and half-listened as she said who their waiter would be.

Laurel didn't care, because she couldn't look away from Paul in that light blue shirt and brightly colored tie.

"This place is amazing," she said once the hostess had left them to study the menu.

"I called for these reservations three weeks ago," he said, his eyes as equally as shiny as she felt. "Have you really never been here?"

"Nope." Laurel grinned at him. "Believe it or not, I didn't date a lot of rich men before you."

He chuckled and shook his head, the laugh lines around his eyes sexy to her. She loved the gray in his hair, and the way he seemed to know exactly what she needed and when.

"Paul," she said, replacing her menu on the table and reaching across it to him.

He looked up, saw she was serious about something, and lowered his menu too. "Yeah?"

"We don't normally dress up and go out," she said, taking both of his hands in hers. "What's going on?"

"Nothing's going on," he said easily, though he looked a little nervous to her. "By the way, I'm not rich. We're cops, Laurel. You know I'm never going to be rich, right?"

"I know." She grinned at him. "I don't care."

"I was thinking..." He lifted one of her hands to his lips and kissed her wrist. "What you're thinking about where we might live. Did you want to keep your place? I know you worked hard to get it."

Laurel's heart started to pound harder against her ribcage. "Are we talking about moving in together?"

The waiter appeared, and he carried a bottle of wine. "Champagne tonight?" he asked.

"Yes, please," Paul said, releasing her hands.

Laurel hadn't known him to drink much, but they'd not really gone to many restaurants where a waiter dressed in a tuxedo offered them a drink that probably cost over a hundred dollars.

Paul settled away from the table and took his hands with him. Laurel definitely thought there was something going on, because she could read people, and she knew Paul really well by now.

She put her hands in her lap too, glad she'd been able to fit into the slinky black dress she'd pulled from the back of her closet. The last time she'd worn it had been for her sister's wedding almost eight years ago, and Laurel's body shape had definitely changed as she entered her thirties and then her mid-thirties.

The waiter poured the champagne and left, and Paul lifted his glass to her.

Laurel picked up hers and lifted it slightly. "What are we toasting?"

"Us," he said simply, and he took a sip.

Laurel did too, and she could admit she liked the fruity, bubbly champagne. She took a bigger drink and set her glass down, determined not to drink too much tonight.

"I don't want to talk about moving in together," Paul said, leaning forward. "I want to talk about marriage."

Laurel's eyebrows went up at the same time her heart grew wings. "Really?" she asked.

"Too soon?" he asked.

Laurel considered him and then said, "No," slowly. "I'm in love with you, Paul. I trust you."

"I'm not sure which of those makes me happier," he said, his grin blinding with such straight, white teeth. "I love you, too, Laurel."

She grinned at him, wishing they'd had this conversation in a place where she could feel his hands on her waist and kiss him after such a statement.

He got up and came around the table, sliding into the booth on her side quicker than she could move over.

He put his arm around her. "I'm not great at planning these romantic things," he said quietly, and Laurel tucked herself right into his side. "Plus, you're about as cop as they come, and you can see right through me."

"I ruined it," she murmured.

"Not at all." His lips touched her ear and sent shivers through her. He cracked the lid on a black box and rested it on her knee. "I'm in love with you. I love it when you stay the night with me, and I love sleeping at your place. I love waking up next to you, and I love making coffee for you and trying to gauge how much cream to put in it."

"It's the caramel that's always too much," she said, turning her head to look at him. It was mighty hard to tear her eyes from the diamond ring on her lap, that was for sure.

"Ah, yes," Paul said, chuckling. "Not too sweet."

"No," she murmured, touching her lips to his.

"Will you marry me, Laurel?" he asked, the breath from his mouth drifting down her neck as he moved to kiss her there.

"Yes," she whispered, and Paul lifted his head.

Pure joy spilled from him, and Laurel laughed with him as he took the ring from the box and slid it on the appropriate finger.

Laurel gazed at it, happier than she'd ever been.

"What kind of wedding do you want?" he asked, nuzzling the hollow behind her ear.

"Something simple," she said. "With our family and friends."

"Lacy and frilly?"

"Not too much," she said, thinking of Robin. "Can I ask Robin to put something together for us?"

"When are you thinking?" he asked. "It'll be a whole police affair, don't you think?"

"Kind of like the Chief getting married," Laurel said. "We have a lot of the same friends."

"We better look at the events calendar for the station and the cove. Then we can pick a time when there's nothing major going on."

"In the summer?" Laurel asked, shaking her head. "There's always something major going on."

"Things are fairly quiet once September hits," he said.

"That's four months," she said, counting quickly. "Actually five."

"Too soon, or not soon enough?"

Laurel looked at him, their eyes locking. Love like Laurel had never known moved through her and she said, "Not soon enough."

He chuckled as she kissed him, quickly sobering enough to make it a meaningful, lasting kiss that turned Laurel's blood to lava.

When they separated, she said, "I'll talk to Robin. Let's send them a picture."

Paul posed with her, first with a joyous, smiling selfie, and then he twined his fingers through hers as she took a picture of her left hand, where the glinting diamond would tell her friends everything they needed to know.

She sent both pictures to the group message string, did the same for her mother, promising to call her later, then silenced her phone and looked at her fiancé. "I want dessert first."

Paul chuckled and moved back to his side of the booth. "Dessert first you shall have," he said, and Laurel grinned at him.

CHAPTER THIRTY-NINE

K elli looked at the house where her mother lived now, noting that Devon had already arrived. "Go see Grandma," she said to Parker as the car came to a stop. Her son jumped from the car, his new toy in his hand.

Kelli thought nine was young for her son to have a cellphone, but he'd be ten in a few more months, and she wouldn't be going to Diamond Island with him anymore. She'd decided to put in her two weeks' notice, and she'd be done at the junior high before May first.

She inhaled deeply as she got out of the car, clutching the folder she'd brought to show her mom the designs and ideas she had for the house on Seabreeze Shore.

Kelli felt herself retreating from the hard conversation, the way she had so often in the past. She pushed against that desire, because it was time to stop running from hard things. She'd been facing them head-on for several months now, and she liked how strong she felt. She liked that she'd taken control of her life and that she was making her dreams into realities.

She heard Parker and her mom talking and laughing, and that gave her an added measure of strength to get up the steps and inside the house. She closed the door behind her, bringing her mother's attention to her.

"Hello, darling," her mom said, moving past Parker to hug Kelli. "I thought you might not come."

"We just missed the first ferry," Kelli said. "I had a slow start to this morning." She'd had quite a few restless nights, that was for certain. She hugged her mother while Parker showed Devon the cellphone.

"I can't believe you got him one of those," her mom said, pulling back and moving to stand next to Kelli, facing the house. It was a comfortable house, with plush couches in a dark brown fabric and cheery curtains over the windows.

"Well, I quit my job at the school," Kelli said.

Her mom gasped. "You did? Why?" The little yorkie her mom had adopted ran over to them, and she bent to scoop her into her arms.

Kelli grinned at the little dog and reached over to pat her head. "I'm going to open a yoga studio and wellness center in the house on Seabreeze Shore." Her smile only grew every time she spoke those words. "So I'm not going to be going to Diamond with him. It only texts and calls; no data."

Her mom simply searched her face, and Kelli lifted the folder. "Let me show you." She went into the kitchen at the back of the house, where Devon asked her if she wanted coffee. "Yes, please," she said, taking a seat at the table.

She spread the folder open and pulled out the four sheets that formed a square—the footprint of the house. "Down on the main level, we'll do fitness classes—one on each side of the stairs. I'm putting in a sliding barn door across what used to be the office. That will be the more tranquil space. I'm going to teach yoga there."

She glanced up at her mother, who peered at the papers as if they held calligraphy she didn't understand.

"I'll do aerobics on the other side," Kelli said. "I've got plans to hire more instructors. I know what it looks like, because I worked at that gym in Jersey for years." She felt so much confidence in her ability to do this and do it well. Shad said that enthusiasm and confidence poured off her, and Kelli hoped that was true.

"In the back, I'm going to have a juice bar," she said, pointing to the rendition. "There won't be any tables or anything. More like a counter, where people can order what they want, and the chef will make it for them."

"A wellness center," her mom read, reaching out to trace her fingers along the top of the plans where those words sat.

"Upstairs," Kelli said, shifting the papers to reveal the footprint of the house on Seabreeze Shore on the second floor. "I'm going to have two massage rooms. The master bedroom is going to be for couples. Heather's bedroom is going to be for singles. My old bedroom is going to be the admin office."

That was her whole pitch, though Kelli could go on and on about how she'd already ordered the tables, the linens for the bathrooms throughout the house, the yoga mats, and that she and Eloise were going to meet the moment she returned from her honeymoon to go over the scheduling software.

"I can do this, Mom," she said.

Her mom looked up from the papers, her expression bright with hope. "Of course you can, Kelli." She reached out and cradled her face in her palm. "Of course you can. I don't doubt that for a second."

"That house is important to me," Kelli said. "I know it's not to you, and I totally understand that. I think this way, the house will be used and enjoyed, and I think it's going to be really great."

Her mom smiled, the corners of her mouth wobbling just a little bit. "I can't wait to come."

Kelli's eyebrows shot up. "Really? You'll come?"

Her mom nodded and swiped at her eyes. "Yes. I need to put that chapter of my life to bed, and I can't wait to see that house used in an appropriate way. It's a lovely house."

"It is," Kelli said, her own eyes filling with tears. "Thank you, Mom."

They hugged, and Devon set a mug of coffee on the

table. "This looks fantastic," he said. "Are you taking men and women?"

"Yes." Kelli's voice sounded somewhat strangled, but she swallowed the lump of emotion in her throat. "Everyone is welcome. I might get a male instructor just for a men's class. We'll see how everything is received."

"It's going to be great," her mom said. "Everything like this is on Diamond, and this will be great for people on Bell and Pearl."

"I hope so," Kelli said, her mother identifying the one thing she was worried about—location. The house on the cliffs above the shore had amazing views for a family. But for a wellness center? Would people come?

She cleared her throat again and gathered up the papers. "Will you sit down for a second, Devon? I have one more thing to talk to you two about." She glanced from her mother to Devon, the man she'd been dating for quite a while now. He took a seat, his brown eyes warm and inviting.

Kelli wasn't sure how to start. *The paper*, she thought, and she pulled out the remaining papers in the folder. "Dad had a lot of money in the bank, Mom. He had a private account no one knew about until very recently."

She set the paper on top of the folder and looked at it. The numbers there still sent a staggering shock through her body. She turned the folder and pushed it in front of her mother. "He didn't cheat on you. That much I've learned and been able to verify. Sidney Tyler said she never slept with him—she was having an affair with someone else that drove her to leave the cove."

She glanced at Devon, because this impacted him too, most likely. He didn't seem to be going anywhere, and Kelli wouldn't be shocked if her mother married him sooner rather than later.

"He blackmailed people, though, so it's not like Guy Watkins was a stand-up guy in the community. That's what this money is. It's been in this account for years, with only one beneficiary on it, and that person didn't know she was the beneficiary, because she didn't know about the account."

Her mom looked up from the paper, her eyes wide and filled with astonishment.

"This can change our lives," Kelli said quietly. "I've already told Heather and Sabrina about it. I just need to know if we should split it three ways or four."

Her mom started shaking her head. "No. I don't need money."

"Honey," Devon said, and he slipped the folder away from her to look at it.

"I know you don't need it, Mom," Kelli said gently, though she thought her mom could definitely use the money. "But you should take it. You and Devon should go to Mexico or Hawaii and get married." She grinned at the two of them. "I'm using a lot of mine to get the wellness center off the ground. Heather said she's going to pay off all of their debt and then she and Garrison are going to take that trip to Iceland they've always wanted to take. Sabrina is going to buy a sailboat."

Kelli reached over and covered her mom's hand. It shook beneath her touch. "He's gone, Mom. The money is here. We might as well use it."

"This is life-changing money," Devon said, his voice half-stuck in his throat.

"Yes," Kelli said, taking the folder with the statement back from him. She tucked it away. "I have all the legal papers already drawn up. It's just a matter of filling in the amount and putting on your name, Mom. I think you should take it."

"You girls won't be upset?"

"Absolutely not," Kelli said firmly. "It's one call to Alice, and everything is done within a few days."

"Alice is such a good friend," her mom murmured.

That was beyond true, and Kelli loved Alice even more for her steadiness and knowledge with what to do with this bank account. The amount hovered near a million dollars, and even split four ways, that was enough money to do exactly what Devon had said—change a life.

More than one, Kelli thought. Her father had probably not planned to have her life—or anyone's but his— impacted by the money, but he wasn't here to do anything about it.

"It's just money, Mom," she said softly. "You can't take it with you. Enjoy it while you can, and then we'll split it anyway."

Her mom finally relaxed and looked at her. "I see what you're doing. Already planning on me dying." She grinned and then started to laugh. Kelli hadn't heard her mother laugh in so long, and it sounded like beautiful music to her ears.

She grabbed onto Kelli again, her laugh quickly changing to a sob. "Okay," she said through the tears. "Okay, I'll split it with you girls."

Kelli wept too, not even trying to stop herself. "I meant what I said about Mexico," she whispered. "You and Devon clearly love each other."

Her mom only nodded, and when she pulled away, she ducked her head to wipe her eyes. "I think Devon and I will get married on a beach right here. We'll get you three girls back here with your families, and then it doesn't matter what the location is."

Kelli pressed her lips together and nodded. "We definitely need a family reunion here in the cove." That way, Heather and Sabrina might be able to see that things changed, and people changed, and they didn't need to stay away to save their sanity.

"Mom, those big pelicans are back," Parker said, bursting though the back door. "Come see."

"Yes," Kelli said, stepping out of the awkward mood as she rose to her feet. "Let's go see the pelicans." She grinned at her mother, left the folder with her entire future in it, and stepped toward the back door to go look at some birds with her son.

"When are you and Shad going to get married?" her mom asked in a near-whisper as they stood on the back deck that faced the shoreline.

Kelli warmed from head to toe but merely shrugged. "It's too soon to know things like that," she said. Parker ran through the backyard, flapping his arms like he was the pelicans they could see flying over the water.

"But you like him, right?"

"Yes," Kelli said, thinking *adore* was a better word for how she felt about Shad. Her phone rang, and Alice's name sat there. "Oh, Mom, it's Alice. I need to answer this." She stepped away from her mom and answered with, "You literally just saved me from an awkward conversation with my mom and her boyfriend about Shad. Thank you."

Alice laughed, and Kelli felt freer and lighter than she had in a long, long time. "I'm glad. Did you already talk to her about the money?"

"Yep," Kelli said. "She's in, Alice. Make it a four-way split and add her name to the paperwork." Joy sang through her, and Kelli answered Alice's questions and spelled her mother's name for her, just to make sure she got it right.

"Thanks so much, Alice. I mean it."

"It's no problem," Alice said. "The things we've been through the past year, I swear." She sighed, and Kelli felt it way down deep in her core.

"Life is interesting, isn't it?" Kelli said. "I mean, who

would've thought I'd come back to the cove and live here?"

Alice laughed lightly. "Ditto."

"I'm glad we're all here, though," Kelli said, thinking of her road back to Five Island Cove.

"Me too," Alice said. "Especially you, Kel. I can't wait to see what you do with the wellness center."

"Should be an interesting summer," Kelli said, thinking of Eloise's wedding coming up in only a couple of weeks. AJ was getting married too, and her baby would be here come August. Most of all, though, Kelli thought of her own relationship with Shad and how it could grow this summer.

"Yep," Alice said. "We'll need to keep an eye on Robin after Duke goes. She's not good when they're not together."

"Definitely," Kelli said. "And we need to make Laurel set a date. I'm afraid she won't if we don't pin her down."

"Leave her to me," Alice said. "She's coming for lunch tomorrow. I'll see what I can do."

Kelli smiled and said, "We need to get Kristen into a new place too."

"Yes," Alice said slowly. "Let's put that on our agenda for when Eloise gets home from her honeymoon."

"I'll be done working at the school by then," Kelli said. "I'm excited to come to the Wednesday lunches." The sound of the doorbell came through the line, and Alice said she had to go.

Kelli hung up and took a deep breath, her thoughts running through all she needed to do for the wellness center and to take care of the people she loved.

"It should definitely be an interesting summer."

———

Read on for the first couple chapters of Four Weddings and a Baby, the next book in the Five Island Cove series, for more secrets, more romance, and more great friendship and sisterhood fiction that brings women together and celebrates the female relationship.

FOUR WEDDINGS AND A BABY
CHAPTER ONE:

E loise Hall woke when her fiancé's alarm went off. Thankfully, the first light of day had started to seep through the curtains, and Eloise knew she wouldn't go back to sleep.

She'd had a terrible time falling asleep too, because today marked only three days until her wedding, and her dress was completely tailored and ready to be picked up.

Robin would be by at nine-thirty to take Eloise to the dress shop, and then they were finalizing the fruit platter with the caterer as well.

She'd selected a seasonal fruit buffet, and the caterer now knew what they could offer.

"Getting up, sweetheart?" Aaron asked from his side of the bed.

"Yes," she said. "I promised Billie I'd help her with her

hair today, and I've got a call with Marge before Robin's coming."

"I can't wait to see the dress," he said, coming around to her side of the bed. He leaned over and kissed her.

"Three days," Eloise said, feeling soft and warm inside this house, this bed, the arms of this man.

"Not a day sooner, I'm sure," Aaron said, smiling.

"Not a day sooner," Eloise said. "Can you imagine the scandal that would hit the Cove Chronicles if it got out that the Chief of Police had seen his bride's dress before the wedding day?"

"If that's the huge scandal that get attaches to my name, I'll take it," he said, sighing as he sat on the bed near her knees.

"Are they going to print the article about your dad?"

"He says this kind of stuff happens every election year."

"I don't understand what would possess someone to want to run for office."

"It takes a special breed of human being," Aaron agreed, his hand moving down Eloise's leg. "You and the girls will be back in time for dinner with my parents?"

"Of course," Eloise said, enjoying Aaron's touch against her skin. "We'll be on the five-twenty ferry, and we'll be here by six."

"Great," he said. "The food will be delivered at six-thirty, and we'll eat soon after that."

"I'll make sure the girls are at nearly their best before we leave the inn," Eloise said.

"They're my parents," Aaron said. "They know what Billie and Grace are like. Right after their mother left, my mom came over. We were all a horrible mess, and I don't think I'd brushed poor Grace's hair for a week."

Eloise lay in bed and listened to him talk for a few more minutes, and the he stood. "I'm going to go shower, love."

"Okay." Eloise rolled over and closed her eyes, letting the soothing sound of the rainfall shower head lull her back to sleep. When Aaron came back into the bedroom to put on his shoes, she woke again.

"I love you, El," he said on his way out the door, and Eloise repeated the sentiment back to him.

A few minutes later, she got out of bed and padded down the hall in her nightgown, where she found Aaron making coffee and Billie shoving books in her backpack.

The silence in the kitchen meant they'd started this Thursday with an argument, and the way Billie looked at Eloise with such earnestness confirmed it.

"Make sure you have your math homework," Aaron said, turning and sipping from his mug.

"I've got it, Dad," Billie snapped.

Eloise wasn't sure what they'd argued about, and she swept into the kitchen to get a cup of coffee, her eyes on Aaron. "What's going on?"

"Billie wants to bring a date to our wedding," he said.

Eloise had not yet picked up a cup, a fact she was very glad of, for she'd probably have dropped it. Her eyes flew back to Billie, who cocked her hip and put one hand on it.

She'd matured a lot this year, and Eloise loved her fiercely. The protective streak she possessed for Billie didn't make sense to her, and she knew it was only stronger for Aaron.

"It's not a date, Dad."

"When you bring a boy to a wedding, it's a date," Aaron said.

"He's my friend."

"Who is it?" Eloise asked, placing both palms against the countertop. She stood next to Aaron, and she hoped they were a united front. She'd taken Billie's side several times in the past, and she didn't want to undermine Aaron with his daughter.

"It's Chris Knight."

"Chris Knight?" Eloise and Aaron asked together. "Oh, no," Aaron added, shaking his head. "I know those Knight boys. They're always in trouble, and I've heard enough of their name to last a lifetime."

"First," Billie said. "They're his half-brothers, and much older than him, Dad. He gets his own chance, doesn't he?"

"He should—"

"That's what you're *always* saying," Billie said. "Don't judge, Bills. Everyone gets their own chance."

"Billie," Aaron said, his voice soft but powerful. Eloise

glanced at him, hating that he and his daughter argued so much.

They didn't really, usually only when it came to Billie and the fact that she was growing up.

"He's just my friend," Billie said.

"I thought we liked a boy named Alex," Eloise said.

"I do," Billie said. "That's why it's not a date if Chris comes with me to the wedding. You said there'd be dancing, and we're in the same dance class. I told my teacher about the dancing at the wedding, and she said anyone who dances outside of class gets extra-credit."

She shoved another notebook in her bag and zipped it closed. "He asked if he could come, because he's not a great dancer, and he needs the extra-credit."

"So you didn't invite him," Eloise said.

"No." Billie stepped into the kitchen. "Will you braid my hair now?"

"Yes, dear, get the stuff."

Billie went to get the comb and hair ties, and Eloise got out her coffee mug. She said nothing, because Aaron needed to make this decision himself.

"I suppose the boy can come to the wedding."

"He'll probably step on her feet and cause a scene," Eloise said dryly. "They'll trip into the cake or something."

Such a thing would be a disaster, what with all the press that would be at the wedding. Eloise reminded herself that Aaron was only Five Island Cove royalty, and that literally no one outside of these five tiny islands in the middle of the sea would know about their wedding, whether someone tripped into a cake or not.

She braided Billie's hair and kissed Aaron good-bye, hurried Grace through eating and getting her shoes on, and sent the girls out the door to school.

She retrieved her phone from the bedroom, where she kept it plugged in overnight, and checked it on her way to the shower.

She had three missed calls from Robin. Shock and fear struck her as one giant lightning bolt.

No matter what, three calls from Robin before eight o'clock in the morning was not good. Eloise's fingers fumbled as she dialed her friend and wedding planner.

"Eloise, I don't want you to freak out," Robin said when she answered the phone.

"I'm already freaking out," Eloise said. "You called three times."

"There's been an accident at the dress shop," Robin said, and she sounded breathless, as if she'd run from her house to Beachfront Avenue, where the dress shop sat.

"What kind of accident?"

"Emma called," Robin said. "I haven't seen the dress yet, but El..." She blew out her breath. "I'm on the way right now, and I'll let you know. I just wanted you to be prepared."

"What happened?" Eloise asked again. "Just tell me, Robin. Then I can be prepared for what I might find."

The dress had taken the longest for her to find and

tailor. She had a love-hate relationship with it as it was, but in the end, she truly did love the dress, and she felt strong and sexy in it at the same time. She knew Aaron would love it, and Eloise felt the first hot tears enter her eyes as she waited for Robin to explain further.

"A pipe burst," Robin said, sighing again. "Overnight. It apparently gushed for hours, and some of their dresses got wet."

"No," Eloise gasped.

"I don't even know if one of them was yours," Robin said. "And things dry out, El."

"I'll change and meet you there," Eloise said. She could reschedule her call, as she understood the nature of emergencies better than most.

"Okay," Robin agreed readily. "I'm leaving now."

ELOISE CLUTCHED HER PURSE, AS IF THE TIGHTNESS IN HER knuckles would keep all of her emotions in check. Before she'd returned to the cove only a short nine months ago, Eloise lived a fairly mundane life. She taught college students about biology, and she'd enjoyed it. Her life had been predictable, and she'd never gotten calls like the kind she'd had with Robin a half-hour ago.

She hadn't dared to call Aaron, because she couldn't stand the thought of postponing the wedding. They'd been waiting long enough as it was. Absolutely everything was in place, and Eloise just wanted to walk down the aisle and pledge herself to Aaron.

She'd packed everything in her tiny house on Sanctuary. All she needed to do was move it, something she and Aaron were planning to do after their honeymoon. He'd taken time off work, a feat not easily achieved for the Chief of Police.

"Looks like the street is closed, ma'am," the RideShare driver said.

Eloise pulled her attention from the side window where she'd been looking toward his voice. He peered through the windshield. "I think this is as far as I can get you."

"Here is great," Eloise said, her voice steady and strong. She was not going to break down over this. It was a dress, not her health. Aaron hadn't abandoned her at the altar. Everything else would still be flawless. "Thank you." She swiped her payment card and got out of the car.

In front of her, the street had been closed, and a pair of police officers worked the scene, along with five or six people dressed in dark blue polo shirts with the Five Island Cove utility logo on them.

"Ma'am," someone said as she took her first step down the sidewalk. "You can't come this way. It's closed."

"My dress," she said, glancing around for Robin. If she couldn't get down the street, maybe Robin couldn't either. "I got a call from Judy's Bridal about my dress."

"They're down on the other end of the street," he said.

"Okay," Eloise said. "I can go around?" She could walk a block over and then down.

"Eloise?"

She turned toward the sound of a familiar voice. "Paul," she said. "The dress shop called about my dress."

He wore a sympathetic look as he approached. "I'll take you." He nodded to the utility worker. "She's okay. I'll get her down there." He reached for her, and Eloise let him put his arm around her.

"How bad is it?" she asked as they navigated past the yellow caution tape. The left side of the street had been dug into, and Eloise wished the smell didn't remind her of the sewer. An image of her dirty and stained dress flashed through her mind, but she quickly pushed it away.

"They've called the mainland for new pipes," Paul said. "This street is going to be shut down for at least two days."

"Mm." Eloise didn't own any of the shops here, but going into a weekend, she wouldn't be happy to be shut down.

"Watch your step here," Paul said, taking her onto a board that went over the hollowed-out street.

She followed him carefully, watching where she put her feet until she stepped back onto cement. Paul delivered her to the end of the street, past another barrier keeping people out. Eloise spotted the white tent where a few women had crowded, and in the next moment, she saw Robin.

"Thank you, Paul," she said, pausing to look up at him. She put her hand on his arm. "Please...don't tell Aaron anything. I'll talk to him as soon as I know what's going on."

Paul looked from the tent where dresses hung on portable racks to her. "Good luck, Eloise." He bent down and hugged her, and Eloise clung to him a little bit.

She cleared her throat as she stepped away, and Robin took the last two steps to her. She grabbed her in a hug and said, "Come see. It's not so bad."

"Really?" Eloise asked as she started walking with Robin. They arrived at the tent, where Eloise picked out her dress instantly. "Not so bad?" She took in the once-white lace that now held a shade of gray no one wanted on their wedding dress.

There was no way that would come clean. The strongest bleach couldn't take out sludge.

The bottom of the dress looked like someone had dipped it into a vat of dye the color of mud, and it seeped up the skirt until it finally petered out. Only the middle of the dress—from about the knees to the wide sash around her waist and into a few inches of the lace that covered the bodice—remained clean.

She reached out and touched the wide straps that went over her shoulders. They too had the look like someone had dropped gray ashes on them and then rubbed them into the fabric.

"This is terrible. There's no way I can get this cleaned."

"Yes," Robin said, hooking her arm through Eloise's. "We can. I've already called Mike, and he's waiting for us." She tightened her hold on Eloise's arm. "It's just mud. He can clean it."

"This isn't mud," Eloise said, drawing back her fingers from the sooty substance. "What *is* that?"

"It's debris from the ceiling," Robin said in a miserable voice. "Mike is a miracle worker, El. Let's get this over to him." She released Eloise's arm and picked up the dress. "I've got my van."

She seemed so positive and so sure, and Eloise grabbed onto her optimism as she went with Robin. That was all she could do. Oh, and pray. She could do that too, and Eloise kept up a stream of pleading as Robin put the ruined wedding dress in the back of her van.

"Do we have a back-up plan?" Eloise asked as she got in the passenger seat.

Robin looked at Eloise, pure nerves in her expression. "Let's go shopping as soon as the stores open," she said. "Just in case."

FOUR WEDDINGS AND A BABY
CHAPTER TWO:

A lice Kelton bent to take the pizza out of the oven just as the front door opened. It would be Laurel, the female cop that had joined their friend group last summer. Alice had really taken a liking to her, and she found herself fiercely protective of the other woman. She thought her former abusive relationship had something to do with that, as Alice had come to view her marriage with Frank as abusive too.

In some ways, Alice was so much better off without Frank. She'd regained her confidence and control over her life, and she liked that. In other ways, though, she had quiet moments of loneliness, despite being surrounded by people she loved and who loved her.

"It's just me," Laurel called, the door closing a moment after she finished speaking. "Smells good in here." The dark-haired woman appeared from the hallway, dressed in her police officer uniform and wearing a smile.

"It's just boxed pizza," Alice said, returning her smile.

"It's better than a protein shake." Laurel sat at the bar, a long sigh coming from her mouth.

Alice watched her, her mind moving through several scenarios.

"I know that look," Laurel said, reaching for a can of soda. "Just spit it out, Alice."

"When are you going to set a date?" she said.

The *pop-hiss!* sound of Laurel's can filled the air, and then her eyes widened. "You didn't check your phone." She looked around as if Alice's phone would be right there, blinking that she had a message.

Alice had left it in the bedroom, because she'd used it as an alarm for when Arthur had to leave. Her face filled with heat though she tried to keep it cool. "Not for a while," she admitted. "Did you set a date?"

"September eighth," Laurel said, her face falling slightly. "It's later than I'd like, but we'll basically be taking the whole force for the wedding. And if we wait until after Labor Day, things will be quiet here in the cove, and Aaron said we could each have two weeks off."

"Wow," Alice said. "Two weeks."

"Yeah," Laurel said. "It's almost five months away, but it's okay."

Alice nodded in agreement. "Are you going to move in with him before the wedding?" She turned to get out the pizza cutter. If she could keep Laurel talking about Paul and their upcoming nuptials, then Alice wouldn't have to talk about Arthur. She couldn't believe she'd kept their relationship as much of a secret as she had.

Robin asked the most questions, of course. Alice had been able to put her off every time with a simple, "Yes, I'm still seeing him."

It had only been three weeks, though she supposed she hadn't dated Will for much longer than that.

"No," Laurel said. "My mother would be mortified." She grinned as she tipped her head back to drink from her soda can. "What about you?" She set the can on the counter. "Things going well with Arthur?"

Alice kept her gaze on the pizza as she cut across it. "Yeah," she said, not able to hide her smile. With Laurel, she didn't have to hide as much. The woman could be very discreet, and Alice liked that. She herself wasn't great with secrets, and she thought maybe she could just tell Laurel about Arthur.

No, she thought. *Keep it to yourself a little longer.*

"Things are going well," she said. "I mean, it's been three weeks, but yeah. Good." She shrugged and finished cutting the pizza. She got out a couple of paper plates and handed one to Laurel.

"What about Charlie?" Laurel asked.

"That boy," Alice said, shaking her head and seizing the safe topic. "He's going to be the death of me."

"Why's that?" Laurel rose up onto her feet to get a

couple pieces of pizza, and Alice sat down next to her at the bar.

"He's already kissing Sariah. I caught them last night on my own front porch."

"He *is* a cute boy."

"Yeah, who broke up with a different girl only two weeks ago. If that." Alice wasn't sure how many days it had been. Maybe only ten or so. No matter what, it felt fast to her. She hadn't breathed a word of it to Robin, as it was her daughter Charlie had broken up with after almost a year of dating.

"He'll figure things out," Laurel said.

"I hope so," Alice said. "I talk to him until I'm blue in the face. I'm not sure it's getting through."

"I think more does than you think." Laurel offered her a supportive smile, and Alice did appreciate that.

"September eighth," Alice said, lifting her pizza to her mouth. "What are you thinking? Beach? Indoors? What kind of dress?"

Laurel started to talk, and Alice simply listened to her talk about her first planning session with Robin and how they'd already started looking for dresses online. "I'm not very feminine," Laurel said. "So I don't know about the dress. I honestly just want to wear a skirt with my police uniform."

"Then do that," Alice said. "Will Paul wear his dress uniform?"

"I think so," she said. "I just mentioned it to him last

night, but we got interrupted before we could talk too much about it."

Alice nodded as if she understood interruptions. In a lot of ways, she did. She could have her whole day planned, only to have everything implode by ten a.m. Nothing on her to-do list would get gone, and the hours slipped through her fingers like smoke.

"So..." Laurel said, and the hair on Alice's arms stood up. "Tell me about Robin and her mother."

Alice looked at Laurel, searching her face. "Why? What happened?" Her protective streak kicked in, because Jennifer Golden had a special way of making Robin feel two feet tall and completely insignificant. Robin had been fighting with her for decades, and Alice knew how hard she'd been trying to build a bridge between them.

Her mom didn't make it easy, that was for sure.

"Her mom arrived during our session a few nights ago, and they got in a little fight."

Alice waited for Laurel to say more, but she remained silent. "What did Robin say?"

"Nothing," Laurel said. "I waved to her and slipped out while they were arguing. I haven't spoken to her since. I mean, a text here or there about the wedding."

If Robin hadn't said anything, Alice didn't want to betray her confidence. "They've never gotten along," Alice said. "They fought like crazy when we were teens, and Robin's been trying to prove she's good enough for her mother for her entire life."

"She's literally one of the best people I know," Laurel said, her eyes wide.

"I know," Alice said. "You won't find someone who cares more."

"She knows everyone on the island, and she knows all the best deals. She's so organized."

"She's pretty, she's thin, she's been married to the same man for almost twenty years." Alice shook her head. "Nothing is ever good enough for her mom. I know Robin tries, but I think she just gets tired."

Laurel nodded and dusted her hands together, her pizza gone. "I was just wondering. She's never said much about her family—her parents and siblings."

Alice wasn't surprised by that at all. She drew in a deep breath. "I can't wait for Eloise's wedding. I think they're finalizing the fruit platter today, and then everything is set."

Laurel's eyes widened again. "Didn't you hear? Eloise might postpone. You really need to look at your phone."

Alice sucked in a breath, her heart positively stopping. "What? Postpone? Why?" She got to her feet and started toward her bedroom, her heartbeat flying through her veins.

"Her dress got ruined," Laurel called after her, and Alice cried out.

"You're kidding." She swiped her phone from the nightstand and saw all the missed messages in the group text. "Eight-four messages. My word." She tapped and started reading, unable to get a proper breath.

Laurel had announced her wedding day. The others had congratulated her and said they'd mark their calendars.

Robin had got on and said they'd had a "slight problem" at the dress shop, but that she and Eloise had taken the dress to a cleaner. AJ and Kristen had asked the most questions, and Robin fielded them all, not Eloise.

The truth was, they didn't know if the dress would come clean. They were shopping for alternatives that day, and Alice didn't have to imagine the anxiety Eloise must be feeling. It ran through her right now.

Eloise had then said, *I might push things back. I need a dress to get married in.*

Everyone had gotten on and expressed support and concern for her. Everyone except Alice, of course.

The string had gone quiet after that, and Alice cursed herself for putting her phone on silent while she made love with Arthur. The truth was, though, the phone distracted her when it went off during the brief time Arthur had in the middle of the day. She'd learned to put it on silent so they could enjoy one another, and she'd never missed much.

Until today.

She typed out a quick message of congrats for Laurel, though the woman sat in the kitchen, and then one of sympathy for Eloise, asking, *What can I do to help? I knew a woman in the Hamptons who could get the most gorgeous dresses. Maybe she could help?*

She stepped back into the kitchen, noting that Arthur had also texted since he'd left her house.

"You got it?" Laurel asked. She drained the last of her soda and met Alice's eyes.

"Yes," she said. "She can't postpone. The press will go crazy."

"Not to mention the Chief has everything set so he can be gone." Laurel wore a look of sympathy. "I don't think she'll actually postpone. She probably just feels like she needs to."

Her phone chimed, and she looked at it. "Oh, it's you."

Alice nodded as she sat back down, Arthur's message shining in her face. *I miss you already. Dinner tonight? My place after that?*

Alice only had two words for that—*yes, and yes*—and she sent them while Laurel said something about Kelli's wellness center.

"Okay," she said a moment later. "I better get going. I can see you've got someone better to talk to."

Alice lifted her head, surprised and embarrassed at what Laurel had said. "No," she said. "You don't have to go."

"Yeah, I can tell it's Arthur," Laurel said, grinning. She clearly wasn't upset. "You're glowing."

Alice's face heated again. "I am not."

"You are," Laurel said, laughing. She stood and leaned

over Alice's shoulder, clearly looking at her phone. "Oh, and making plans for tonight, I see."

A message popped up, and Alice gasped as she read it. Laurel did too.

She practically threw her phone across the kitchen, really only managing to toss it a foot or so, where it slid toward the opposite edge of the counter.

"My goodness," Laurel said, sitting right back down. The barstool moved as she did, creating a terrible noise against the floor. "Alice...?" Her name was full of questions, but Alice didn't know how to answer any of them.

Arthur's message burned her retinas and she'd never get rid of the words. *I know it's fast, but I'm thinking about marriage. Can we talk about that tonight?*

Seconds ticked by, each painfully loud in Alice's ears.

"What are you going to say?" Laurel asked, her voice finally breaking the silence.

Her phone chimed, and Alice's eyes flew to it.

Slowly, as if encased in quicksand, Laurel reached for it. Alice wanted to shout at her not to read the texts—especially not the ones Arthur had sent before he'd come over that morning. She deleted his texts several times each day, because her children picked up her phone at will, and she didn't need them to see anything that would indicate her physical relationship with their school counselor.

"Oh, my," Laurel said, breathing out heavily. She put

the phone in front of Alice, who couldn't help looking at the text.

We can eat that seafood scampi from The Bridge and just talk about it. Then I'll do that thing you like at the edge of the bed.

Alice pressed her eyes closed, her whole body hot. She definitely liked the things Arthur did in the bedroom. He was an excellent lover, and Alice wasn't embarrassed of a consensual, adult relationship with him. She enjoyed talking to him, and she enjoyed kissing him.

"How long have you been sleeping with him?" Laurel asked.

"I don't think that's the most important question," Alice said, her voice hoarse.

"No?" Laurel asked. "What is then?"

She looked at Laurel, pure shock moving through her. "Who wants to talk about marriage after three weeks of dating?"

Her phone chimed again, and she and Laurel both bent over it.

You've gone silent, which means you don't want to talk about marriage. It's just a conversation, Alice. Nothing too serious.

"Nothing too serious," she repeated. "Isn't marriage serious?"

"Just tell him that," Laurel said. "Maybe you do want to talk about marriage though."

Alice swallowed, because she wasn't sure. "I haven't even been divorced for a year," she said.

"Well, you could be the fourth wedding this summer," Laurel said with a smile. "Might have to fight Kelli for the spot though. She and Shad seem to be getting pretty serious too."

"Is there a limit on the number of weddings we can have this summer?" Alice teased, flipping her phone over so whatever Arthur said next would stay secret for a few extra seconds. "And you can't even breathe a word of this to anyone else."

"I wouldn't dare," Laurel said, smiling. "And I think the limit is four. Four weddings, Alice. So if you want that spot..." She let her words hang there, though she was clearly teasing. She got to her feet and gave Alice a side-hug. "I have to jet. Duty calls."

She started for the front door, calling over her shoulder, "And answer that man. He's dying."

Alice picked up her phone the moment Laurel closed the front door behind her and re-read all of Arthur's messages.

Her fingers hovered over the screen while her mind whirred and whirred. Finally, she typed, *We can talk about marriage...if there's plenty of shrimp scampi AND that carrot cake from Shirley's.*

She grinned at her message, her smile widening at Arthur's response that came in a few seconds later.

Carrot cake ordered.

Alice pressed her phone to her heart, letting the fantasy of her own summer beach wedding run through her mind. Could she really marry Arthur Rice so soon?

Don't be ridiculous, part of her mind told her, while the other half thought, *Why not?*

"Mom?" Charlie called, and Alice hastened to delete the messages from Arthur as her son's footsteps came closer. "There you are," he said, stepping past her and taking a piece of pizza. "Is it okay if I go over to Sariah's after work? You never answered me."

He wore eagerness and hope on his face, and Alice didn't have the heart to tell him no. "You be safe with that girl," she said.

"I am, Mom," he said, grinning at her. He grabbed onto her and hugged her. "I won't be late since it's a school night."

"I'm going out with Arthur tonight," she said. "I won't be late either. Ten for both of us."

"Okay," Charlie said, hurrying back the way he'd come. "Love you, Mom."

"Love you too," she called, and her fantasy warped and disappeared when she thought about how she could possibly tell her twins that she might marry their counselor.

Read *Four Weddings and a Baby* today.

BOOKS IN THE FIVE ISLAND COVE SERIES

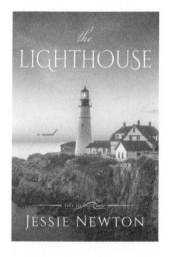

The Lighthouse, Book 1: As these 5 best friends work together to find the truth, they learn to let go of what doesn't matter and cling to what does: faith, family, and most of all, friendship.

Secrets, safety, and sisterhood...it all happens at the lighthouse on Five Island Cove.

The Summer Sand Pact, Book 2: These five best friends made a Summer Sand Pact as teens and have only kept it once or twice—until they reunite decades later and renew their agreement to meet in Five Island Cove every summer.

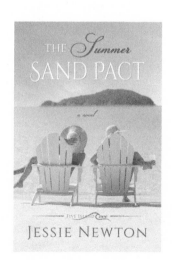

BOOKS IN THE FIVE ISLAND COVE SERIES

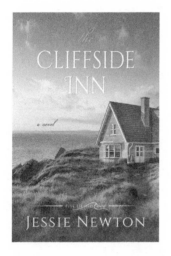

The Cliffside Inn, Book 3: Spend another month in Five Island Cove and experience an amazing adventure between five best friends, the challenges they face, the secrets threatening to come between them, and their undying support of each other.

Christmas at the Cove, Book 4: Secrets are never discovered during the holidays, right? That's what these five best friends are banking on as they gather once again to Five Island Cove for what they hope will be a Christmas to remember.

BOOKS IN THE FIVE ISLAND COVE SERIES

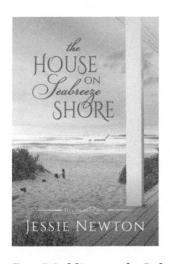

The House on Seabreeze Shore, Book 5: Your next trip to Five Island Cove...this time to face a fresh future and leave all the secrets and fears in the past. Join best friends, old and new, as they learn about themselves, strengthen their bonds of friendship, and learn what it truly means to thrive.

Four Weddings and a Baby, Book 6: When disaster strikes, whose wedding will be postponed? Whose dreams will be underwater?

And there's a baby coming too... Best friends, old and new, must learn to work together to clean up after a natural disaster that leaves bouquets and altars, bassinets and baby blankets, in a soggy heap.

ABOUT JESSIE

Jessie Newton is a saleswoman during the day and escapes into romance and women's fiction in the evening, usually with a cat and a cup of tea nearby. The Lighthouse is her first women's fiction novel, but she writes as Elana Johnson and Liz Isaacson as well, with over 175 books to all of her names. Find out more at www. authorjessienewton.com.

Made in the USA
Coppell, TX
05 January 2022

70969375R00267